RIVEN

ALSO BY MINDEE ARNETT:

Onyx & Ivory
Shadow & Flame
Avalon
Polaris

BY MINDEE ARNETT

BALZER + BRAY

An Imprint of HarperCollins*Publishers*

Balzer + Bray is an imprint of HarperCollins Publishers.

Riven

www.epicreads.com

Library of Congress Cataloging-in-Publication Data
Names: Arnett, Mindee, author.
Title: Riven / by Mindee Arnett.
Description: First edition. | New York : Balzer + Bray, [2023] | Audience:
Ages 14 up. | Audience: Grades 10-12. | Summary: "Mars Darksvane, a magic user,
teams up with Fura Torvald, a noblewoman, to save the oppressive and dangerous
island of Riven"-- Provided by publisher.
Identifiers: LCCN 2022029584 | ISBN 9780063057838 (hardcover)
Subjects: CYAC: Fantasy. | Magic--Fiction. | Nobility--Fiction. | LCGFT:
Fantasy fiction. | Novels.
Classification: LCC PZ7.A7343 Ri 2023 | DDC [Fic]--dc23
LC record available at https://lccn.loc.gov/2022029584

22 23 24 25 26 LBC 5 4 3 2 1

First Edition

For Jordan

This story would never have been without you.

"For the life of every creature—its blood is its life."
—LEVITICUS 17:14

PROLOGUE

THE KNIGHT AND the initiate stood together and watched the world end.

Neither of them had known what was coming when they ascended the stairs of the White Keep's western tower. They arrived separately, Malena, the initiate, furtively glancing over her shoulder every few steps to make sure no one was watching her, while the knight, Finn, had climbed the same path an hour before, walking with the confidence that his position conferred upon him.

Reaching the top, Malena drew a breath to steady herself, torn between her desire to see Finn once more and her fear of discovery. Only they wouldn't be discovered. Not today, when every other soul in the White Keep was focused on the ritual unfolding below.

Finn smiled when Malena's gaze met his. Anticipating her arrival, he'd removed his helm and gauntlets already. The rest of the starsteel armor encasing his body glistened like scales. "You made it."

A blush warmed her cheeks. "It was easy with everyone else so preoccupied."

"Shall we watch?" Finn held out his hand, and Malena took it, their fingers entwining.

The intimacy came naturally to them now, although the illicit nature of the touch remained thrilling. Relationships of any kind, romantic or otherwise, were forbidden between Consortium adepts and the Rivna Knights, who served as both guardians and judges of the adepts. And although Malena was only an initiate, the strength of her kull, the lifeblood that fueled her magic, meant she would achieve the rank of adept soon enough.

That is, if the ritual today succeeded. If it failed . . . then all the magic of Riven would fail with it. For years now it had been weakening, draining away like a river going dry. Today's ritual might not be their last hope, but if it was not successful, their options were few.

Together, Finn and Malena walked to the edge of the tower. A crowd thronged the courtyard below, encircling a vast pool filled with a crystalline liquid—the Rift. Curved white pillars of hollowed bone framed the edge of the Rift pool, creating a canopy over its surface. In the spaces between each pillar stood a gray-robed adept, waiting for the ritual to begin. Rivna Knights flanked the pool, keeping the observers at bay.

"I'm glad you weren't assigned that duty." Malena indicated the knights below, whose names she didn't know but whose faces she recognized as some of Finn's comrades.

"Me as well. We drew straws for the duty. I lost." A smile curved his lips as he squeezed her fingers.

She returned the smile, but it soon crumbled. The tension in the courtyard below reached them even up here, the anticipation of the ritual's fate, the cost of failure. The Rift— the source of all magic in Riven—was dying. Even she, young and inexperienced as she was, could sense it. When she first arrived at the White Tower a year ago to start her training, the pool at the heart of the Rift had glowed and shimmered like sunlight on water, even in darkness. Now the liquid looked dull, like the sky at twilight. Not that the Rift only existed here—this was merely the place where it opened to the surface. Its power ran through all of Riven, like a deep, unseen lake with thousands of rivers and tributaries branching from it. The pool was merely the opening to its heart.

"You're afraid," Finn said, and it wasn't a question.

Malena shifted her gaze to the head of the pool where the Grand Chancellor waited, his hands folded in front of him, face hooded beneath his robe. A shiver caressed her neck. "Some of my teachers believe the ritual is dangerous. That what the Grand Chancellor plans to do is anathema."

Finn arched an eyebrow, his gaze following hers until it came to rest on the Grand Chancellor as well. "I've heard similar rumblings. There are many in the order who don't trust the Chancellor. Most don't, in fact, and yet he never does anything to warrant our intervention. He knows the line and does not cross it."

"He's clever," Malena agreed. "But I don't know if he is devious." What she did know was the way he made her feel whenever she stood in his presence—like she was trapped in a cage with a ravenous lion.

Finn cleared his throat. "They called Luther Jörgensvane

clever as well. Before he became Luther the Terrible." Luther the Terrible, the first and only adept to reject the Consortium's creed of "Service Over Self," who used his magic for ill gain and not in service of Riven and its people. It was Luther's destructive reign that had given birth to the Order of Rivna Knights. Riven could no longer risk an adept following in Luther's path.

"The Grand Chancellor is not another Luther," Malena said, despite her reservations about the man. "He's not seeking ultimate power. His passion might border on obsession, but that obsession is merely to restore the Rift. Something that benefits all of Riven."

Finn grunted. "I don't doubt his purpose. Only his methods."

Malena didn't reply; she merely watched as sixteen prisoners bound in chains appeared in the courtyard below. With their bodies clad in sackcloth and hoods over their heads and faces, it was impossible to tell who exactly they were—or whether they were male or female, young or old. All she knew was that they'd been found guilty of some crime or other, their sentence to be carried out here, in service of Riven and the magic that made this island nation great.

"I doubt them, too." Malena swallowed the lump rising in her throat. As an initiate, she understood that magic required sacrifice. Each time she channeled the Rift, she felt what it cost her, the physical and mental toll it took on her to channel the power the Rift could provide. Often after a working, she felt like a sponge rung dry, empty and brittle around the edges. But the small sacrifices of adepts were no longer enough to obtain the magic Riven required. The Rift needed more, a sacrifice on the level of that which had first created it, when the combined strength of the nine Titans slew Jörn, the World Raven.

A sacrifice of blood. Of life.

But the Titans' defeat of Jörn had been through battle, one that had raged over the entire island of Riven, leveling mountains, gouging rivers and waterfalls, caving hills into cliffs. The two enemies had been equally matched, the brave, cunning raven against the nine giants. Jörn's death had been honorable.

This, though. This was slaughter. No matter if the prisoners deserved it. Malena watched as one by one, each prisoner was placed before an adept standing between the pillars, forced to their knees with their arms secured behind their backs. Then each was given a draught of some dark, nameless liquid, a potion the Grand Chancellor and the most talented adepts of the Consortium had concocted for this purpose. The prisoners gagged at the taste but afterward fell silent, heads bowed, showing no sign of fear for what was to come.

When the first of the adepts drew a knife, the naked blade flashing in the sun, Melena turned away and walked to the far edge of the tower. She had no desire to watch what would happen next. Finn followed a moment later, coming to stand behind her, one hand resting on her shoulder.

"It is necessary," he said, but his words fell flat.

Malena fixed her gaze on the castle in the distance, the city of Hàr Halda, capital of Riven. The valley between brimmed with color, rich pastures dotted with horses and cattle, green fields of corn and beans, and yellow fields of wheat. Homesteads with low, flat roofs resided here and there among the fields, the barns next to them large and painted red. The idyllic sight, the island's beauty built from the power of the Rift, was almost enough for Malena to let herself believe Finn's words were true. She leaned into his touch, her eyes slipping closed.

The first wet cough rent the air, the sound like a knife blade to Malena's ears. She flinched, eyes flashing open as another sound joined the first, the prisoners dying one by one. Others followed, a cacophony of pain and suffering. Malena covered her ears with her hands, but the sound grew louder, unstoppable, until it was as if the earth itself was gasping.

At that moment, a tremble went through the tower. It rocked so violently that Malena stumbled forward, striking the ledge. Only Finn's quick, firm grip of her waist kept her from tumbling over the side.

"What's happening?" said Malena.

They ran back to the Rift, peering over the edge to the courtyard below, each holding the ledge as more tremors racked the tower. They ought to flee to the safety of the ground, only there was nowhere safe anymore. Thick white smoke poured from the Rift pool, filling the courtyard and spreading through the windows and doors of the keep. It moved with purpose, like something alive, something with a will. A malicious one. Wherever the smoke reached a living person, it forced its way into their nose, mouth, and ears. And what it touched, it devoured. Skin blackened, peeled, and flaked away. The bones beneath turned to ash.

Malena choked on a scream, but the sound was drowned out by a series of booms that felt like the sky being ripped asunder. The sunlight turned to shadow, the wind shrieked over the tower, yanking Malena's hair free of its braids. The Rift's ruinous white breath had reached the valley beyond. Finn and Malena crawled on hands and knees to the opposite edge of the tower, drawn there by dread.

The valley was hidden from sight, the space filled with smoke. As it had with the adepts and knights in the courtyard, it consumed every living thing it touched; horses and cattle turned to ash, trees and grass to dust. How far would it go? When would it end? Distant eruptions echoed all around. Flashes of crystalline light in the distance. Whatever was happening, it wouldn't stop here.

Malena and Finn reached for each other, finding what comfort they could as their world ended around them.

And it was an end.

But also a beginning.

The sacrifices that day—both intended and not—sated the Rift's hunger to overflowing, giving birth to a second form of magic. A physical one. One able to be wielded by all, not only the few born with the ability to channel the Rift's energy. This new magic was powerful, plentiful, and deadly. It changed the face of Riven and its people forever.

It was the magic of Ice.

PART ONE

MERCENARY

ONE

THE SUMMONS TO the Fortune's Den arrived the same way it always had: clutched in the talons of a once dead raven. Its eyes glowed with the light of the magic animating its body, white orbs casting halos on the windowpane as it tapped the glass with its beak. Once, twice, thrice. Then a pause, followed by another set of three strikes, as steady as a just wound clock.

Hearing it clearly across the small space of his apartment, Mars grumbled and sat up on the straw-stuffed mat, disturbing the tiger-striped cat snoozing atop his chest. Rooftop hissed before settling down in the divot left by Mars's body. As the raven knocked again, Mars scowled at it. What was the point of having a hideout when Una's messengers could find him regardless? No matter where he went in the city, the little shits could track him down, all thanks to the ampoule filled with his blood that he'd given his mistress ten years before, on the day he'd started working for her. She kept it inside a locked room deep in the bowels of her gambling hall, the headquarters of her business enterprise. Through a potent mix of magic and science, the ravens tracked blood to blood with the efficiency of a shark.

"Tell your lady I don't work for her anymore!" Mars shouted at the creature. The raven stared coolly back at him, its dead, frozen gaze coaxing gooseflesh down his arms. Or perhaps that was just the cold air biting his bared chest, the blanket having slipped off his shoulders.

Rising unsteadily to his feet, his body sore from lying too long on a hard surface, Mars stumbled toward the window, shooing the raven away. "Go on, get out of here, bird."

How he wished he'd succeeded in stealing that ampoule away from Una. He'd tried, the day after he'd completed his last contract, the day before he told her he was done working for her for good. But the blood she kept—one vial from each of her mercenaries—was too well guarded, even for him, the Shadow Fox, the very best agent in Una's employ. In the end, he'd had no choice but to walk away without it, knowing it was just a matter of time before she used it to find him. And yet weeks had passed since then, months. Long enough that he'd started to believe she might have forgotten about him.

Apparently not.

The bird tapped the pane again, and it would keep on tapping until it either delivered its message or the magic that fueled its existence ran out. Mars briefly contemplated the latter option, but knew he lacked the patience to see it through. Una's ravens ran on an entire shard of Ice, enough magic to last a week.

"All right, you little bastard, you win." Mars yanked the window open, letting in a chill, salty breeze and the sound of gulls crying down in the harbor. This high up, he could see ships bobbing in the water like toys in a child's bath, the sea stretching out to a horizon blurred by the reddish streaks of the setting sun. He'd slept an entire day away without meaning to.

The raven held out its right leg mechanically. A card was clutched in its talons, the paper as black as its feathers. This close, the bird's lifelessness was more apparent—the glossy coating of paraffin wax on its feathers, the metal hinges reinforcing its joints, and the brass knob embedded in its chest hiding the Ice compartment. Yet these anomalies paled next to the smoldering stench of its rotting flesh as the Ice slowly burned its way through the vessel housing it. Mars felt the magic at work in there like an itch beneath his skin, quickening the flow of blood in his veins.

Holding his breath, he grasped the card in one hand and with the other pushed the bird backward off the ledge. The raven flapped its wings, slicing him across the knuckles with one of its talons as it fell. A second later it rolled over midair, caught an updraft, then soared away, back to the Fortune's Den.

"Prick," Mars said.

At least Una had sent a raven, rather than a dozen guards to forcibly haul him back to her. For a moment, he considered tossing the card out the window as well, but he couldn't quite convince his fingers to let go. He resisted looking at it, though, his eyes fixed on the harbor as thoughts rolled like waves in his head. More than a hundred docks, most of them with ships lashed to their long sides, cut narrow slashes through the dark water. People bustled about, setting the moorings, storing the nets. He ought to head down to the pier and book passage on a ship. Riven might be a small island nation, but positioned as it was between the great powers of Vest in the east and Osway in the west, it was crucial for trade and safe passage through the Murmurry Sea, which even in high summer was plagued with storms and rough waves. Mars had not yet saved the total amount of money he intended to before leaving the island forever, but he could afford to fall short of his goal if it meant escaping before Una sent even less polite messengers after him.

Yet the idea of walking past the fish markets right now turned his stomach. For the past ten months, he'd spent his days there, up to his armpits in slimy guts and scales as he sweat and bled and stank his way through each day working for any fishmonger or fishwife willing to pay. Even now, after a good scrubbing with lye soap, he could still smell the stench seeping out from beneath his fingernails. No, he could wait until morning.

Are you sure? a voice whispered in his head. It was the same one that had taunted him since he left Una's service. The voice of perpetual doubt, his closest companion these days, ever since his last job with Una had torn his world apart.

A breeze caressed his face, teasing the tips of the dark hair hanging unbound past his shoulders, hiding the shaved sides of his head. He brushed the hair back roughly, some of the strands catching on the frayed edges of the leather cuff fastened to his wrist. He needed to replace the cuff, along with the one on his other wrist, but he'd been putting it off. After all, he would no longer have need for such accoutrements once he left Riven and the Rift of magic that lay beneath it—its presence both the blessing and the bane of his existence.

Slowly, and with a dull thud in his chest, Mars turned the card over and stared at the symbols etched on its black surface. Una never conveyed her messages in words, which could be read by anyone who might intercept one of her messengers. Instead, she used symbols that only the foxes of the Fortune's Den were trained to read. In this case, a serpent coiled around a horned helmet with two wolves flanking either side. The picture was exquisitely rendered by an artist's hand. Una took pleasure in all things beautiful and spared no expense, even for this scrap of cardstock destined for the fire once read. Then again, a lot of the jobs coming into the Fortune's Den required a unique card, and in all his years as a fox there, Mars had never seen one like this. It wasn't the combination of symbols so much—the horned helmet telling him the purpose of the job was intelligence gathering, while the wolves indicated multiple threats and the serpent a target both sly and dangerous. No, it was the coloring. Ice white. All save for the poison green of the serpent's eyes, an indulgence by the artist, no doubt. One meant to catch the gaze and draw it in.

Ice white. Not gold or silver or bronze, but Ice. The color told the foxes the payout of the contract being offered, and while Mars had worked plenty of bronze and silver and even a couple of golds in his time with Una, he'd never once come across a job valued in Ice. The notion stole his breath away.

Una knows you well.

Mars shifted his gaze to the floorboard in the corner of the room, the second one from the end. It looked like all the rest around it, old and dirty, the nails loosened by time and wear. But beneath it lay a locked box, one guarded by the traps that were his specialty. Every herring he'd scrimped and saved and bled for these past ten months was tucked away inside it. Almost enough for passage off the island, and to set him up wherever he landed. A pittance compared to what Una was offering him, but it was honest money for honest work.

Rooftop rammed her head into his arm, distracting Mars from his thoughts. Acquiescing to the cat's demands, he raised a hand to scratch behind her ear. For a second, he let the cat's purr vibrate through his fingers.

No, he decided, Una didn't know him at all. She only believed she did. Mars was leaving this land of magic and mercenaries behind once and for all. He wanted to live in a place so far from the sea, he never had to smell fish again. A place where dead things stayed dead, where no one would condemn him just because of the scars on his wrists, where the memories that haunted his nightmares would finally fade.

Only . . . the night was young, and he wide awake. He examined the image on the card once more, rendered in Ice white, the serpent's green eyes seeming to fix on his with a stare so lifelike, he half expected it to slither off the page. Ignoring the summons might only result in Una sending guards, and there was no harm in hearing her out.

His gaze shifted from the card to the line of blood across his knuckles where the raven had scratched him. It seemed a shame to waste even so small an amount of blood, and with the certainty that no one below would see him, he offered it to the Rift, summoning fire to his fingertips. As the card burned, the blood on his hand dried into dust and was no more.

TWO

MARS WAS ONLY ten years old when he first discovered his ability to channel Rift magic. Younger than most, though he could not have known that.

A hundred years ago, before the Cataclysm when the adepts had nearly destroyed Riven with their machinations, Mars's abilities might have been something celebrated by his parents, should he have even known his parents. But these days, manifestation of the power of an adept meant a life spent in chains.

Even as a homeless orphan, Mars had understood this. Adepts were dangerous, deviant, like rabid wolves. If one was discovered, it would not be long before someone arrived to take them away—whether it was one of Riven's many corrupt government agents or one of its many corrupt crime lords, it was hard to know which was worse. But Mars had contemplated this much since the moment he realized he himself was an adept. It happened one morning while he stood on his favorite corner where Sotunham Road crossed Vesper Street. Although it wasn't yet noon, he'd already scored twice. The first mark was a young woman with a small child, who'd taken in Mars's grubby hands and dirty face with a look of pity and horror. She pressed a herring into his palm before he'd finished stretching out his arm to ask for it. The second was a man stumbling home from a nearby gambling hall, flush from his wins and still half-drunk on cheap wine. He'd given Mars two herrings and a honey-flavored cigar.

"May the Titans share their luck with you as they have with me," the man said, ruffling Mars's long, mangled hair.

"Thank you, sir," Mars stammered, disbelieving his eyes—and his luck.

But he should've known better. No sooner had the man rounded the corner than Gisela's gang had appeared, Gisela herself among them. Mars couldn't remember when he had first learned to avoid gangs like Gisela's—groups of orphaned children who banded together for survival—but he'd learned the lesson well. Only, Gisela's gang rarely ventured this far north. Not that it mattered. They were here now, and in moments they'd beaten Mars senseless, stolen his herrings, and left him lying in the gutter.

The rage that had stolen over Mars as he climbed to his feet, wiping away the blood stinging his eyes, felt like a gale wind. He screamed and threw his hands out toward the retreating children, wanting with all his heart to hurt them as they'd hurt him. No sooner had the thought come than the ropes holding a nearby scaffold had snapped, and the whole mechanism crashed to the ground, catching a few of the gang beneath its terrible weight.

Anything could've caused those ropes to break—too

much strain, damage from gnawing rats, an act of fate—but Mars had known it was him, the same as he recognized his own voice when he heard it or his own face in a mirror. Fortunately, no one else had seen.

Of course they hadn't, but Mars had, as the echoes of the falling scaffold faded. The people of the city always looked through him, as if he didn't exist, same as they did with all the other street urchins, including Gisela and her gang. The poor, without access to Ice and the power it provided, were a reminder of what so many people paid for access to that power. And if people could ignore the costs, they did.

He'd been lucky, very lucky, that first time. Not only had he not been caught, he'd been given the answer to his prayers, the edge he needed to survive on the mean streets he called home, to *thrive*. In time, he'd learned to wield his magic subtly, surreptitiously, and it allowed him to work his way up from beggar to thief to con artist, and eventually to a fox. It enhanced his senses, his reflexes, even his thoughts. All he needed was a little blood—and will. No, there was nothing vile about the magic at all. The only bad thing about it was the risk of getting found out, his ability enthralled to serve the whim of whatever master was rich enough to claim him. But Mars would not be found out. Even at ten, he was clever and careful, and luck had always remained with him.

But now, as he stared at the entrance to the Fortune's Den, he couldn't help but wonder if that luck was running out. It certainly hadn't gone his way on the last job. *Not when Orri—*

He silenced the thought before it could form.

In the months he'd been away, the only thing that had changed about the Den was the faces of the guards at its entrance. The club resided in Jakulvik's Folly District, an area home to gambling halls, taverns, and other establishments of a similar ilk. Not that there were any establishments quite like the Den. Its mistress, Una Almadòttra, called it a pleasure palace. A fitting enough description. Within the safety of its walls, patrons could partake in all manner of vices, everything from drink to dust to games to companionship. Maybe even all of them at once, if you had the herrings to spend.

But for Mars and the other mercenaries in Una's employ, it offered pleasures of a different kind. Ones he'd missed more than he'd allowed himself to admit, he realized. As he approached the entrance, the old anticipation built inside him, the longing for the thrills provided by his previous employment so deeply imbedded in him that no amount of regret could quite kill it for good.

Despite the early hour, a crowd waited outside the door, an even mix of men and women, young and old, commoner and kith. There were even a few politicians, who served the Helm, the governing body of Riven. Some wore the latest fashions and expensive jewels, while others sported little more than rags—whether you were rich or poor, the Fortune's Den could cater to you. A single herring got you through the door and onto the main floor. Four more gave you access to the upper level and its high-stakes gambling tables. But the best rooms—and the rarest pleasures—could be found in the sublevel, where the entry fee of fifty herrings was enough to separate the big spenders from the mere hopefuls. Few other than the kith ventured down there.

Mars folded his arms across his chest as he joined the queue for entry, keenly aware of how dingy his surcoat appeared, the hem frayed and the fox-fur lining the collar and sleeves mashed flat in places from too long spent folded inside a trunk. Where once these formal clothes had been his usual attire, they felt strange after months of wearing little more than plain trousers and the rough-spun tunics best suited for work at the docks. He might've been more at ease naked.

This was a bad idea. He shouldn't have come. He should be in his hideout, waiting for dawn and the chance to book passage before it was too late.

"Eh, you there," someone called over the crowd.

Mars looked up. The guard at the door locked eyes on him, her lips parting in an astonished grin. "I don't believe it. Mars Darksvane." She waved him forward with one hand, the other casually resting on the hilt of the arming sword fastened at her hip. A single-shot pistol adorned the other. "Come up here. Make way."

The crowd gave Mars irritated looks as he jumped the queue. To them, he was just another would-be patron of the Fortune's Den. To this guard, though, and her partner standing on the other side of the entryway, he was the Shadow Fox, a legend among Una's stable of employees.

Mars came to a stop before the guard and flashed a smile, pleased to see the faint blush creep up her neck. Perhaps he hadn't shed as much of his mercenary skin as he'd thought.

She was pretty and looked close to his age, eighteen or nineteen at most. Typical of Una's guards, she was built like a boulder, broad-shouldered and tall, capable of tossing out unruly drunks or wrestling a distraught gambler to the ground.

"What's the likes of you doing coming through the front door, eh?" The girl gave him a once-over, her gaze lingering on the scar on his face, a thin half circle that rimmed his left eye before slashing down over his cheek like a bident held upright.

"Didn't you hear?" the other guard said, sneering. "The Shadow Fox quit."

The girl snorted. "Impossible. Nobody quits." She motioned for Mars to enter.

He almost walked right on in. It would be so easy to pretend he still worked for Una; it would even save him a herring. But he wasn't going to cross that line, not when he was so close to getting out. Every concession he made was one more tether anchoring him to Riven. Reaching into his surcoat, he withdrew a coin and dropped it in the offering plate.

"Your friend is right. I'm just a regular customer these days."

Ignoring the girl's shock, Mars strode through the door. Familiar sights and sounds enveloped him as he entered the vaulted main hall. Voices raised by liquor and loss blended with the lively bounce of fiddles streaming down from the balcony where the house musicians played. Dozens of people lingered at the billiard tables set in rows along the far wall, while more ringed the dice tables. Others drew smoke from ornate hookahs while lounging on sofas set next to burbling fountains.

Thick carpet cushioned Mars's footfalls as he wove his

way toward one of the standing tables to join a game of Thrice. A large space had opened up, and it was only as he slid into it that he realized the reason for such an unlikely gap at a popular table—the player next to him was a dying man. It wouldn't be tonight, maybe not even the next, but soon, near enough that no one wanted to be next to him, as if his sickness might be contagious. But what he had was not anything anyone could catch.

Mars couldn't tell the man's age, but he guessed young, someone fresh from a stint in the Ice mines, a voluntary one, it seemed. Mars's stomach pinched at the thought. Only the most desperate wretch would work the mine by choice, and from the looks of this fellow, he'd volunteered more than once. A scaly red rash, purple and white in places, covered the skin on his face, neck, and arms. His fingers were red, too, and swollen to twice their normal size, the skin around the nails flaking off like chalk. Patches of grizzle, all that remained of his hair, spotted a skull blue-black with veins. His extreme thinness made him look one wind gust away from disintegrating.

Mars peeled his gaze off the man, pity and revulsion roiling in his belly now. Unconsciously, he pressed his fingers against the scar atop his left hand, a brand in the shape of a nine-pointed star. By law, every Rivener was required to serve a time of tithing, working the mines from the age of sixteen to eighteen—two years the maximum length a young, hale person could withstand exposure to the Ice in its raw, poisonous form. The enneagram brand was record of that service.

Of course, Mars had never even seen an Ice mine, let alone set foot in one. And he had Una to thank for the brand, for getting him out of his compulsory service. But not everyone was

so lucky as to have a wealthy benefactor capable of circum-
venting the rules. This poor, desperate fool had surely served
multiple times. Working the mine after your required two
years on behalf of another paid well, but only if you lived long
enough to enjoy it. Which this fellow seemed to be attempting
to do, burning through his coin at the tables while the Ice's poison burned its way through his body.

Ignoring his desire to flee, Mars nodded at the dealer,
who inclined his head, then called for bets from the rest of the
players. Retrieving a few coins from his surcoat, Mars placed
half of them into the pot and picked up the dice, savoring their
weight in his hand and the thrill of risk tingling through him.

His mind flashed to his small purse of herrings stashed
under the floorboard at home, and for the briefest moment, he
considered rigging the throw. It would be so easy. Everyone's
eyes were on the table, awaiting his toss, none on him. With a
single flick of his hand, he could loosen the blade hidden in his
cuff, making a thin slice in his wrist, just enough blood to give
the Rift the necessary sacrifice to ensure the dice landed as he
wished.

Mind your luck, that voice said, and he heeded it. He wasn't
a lowly child beggar anymore, but the Shadow Fox. Someone was surely watching, and the risk of discovery—even
of suspicion—wasn't worth it. He was trying to leave Riven
forever, not end up enthralled because of his ability to wield
Rift magic. He flung the dice across the table, letting them fall
where they would.

"A win," the dealer announced over eager shouts. "Again,
sir? All in this time?"

Mars shuffled the remaining coins, his heartbeat slowing even as it pounded harder in his chest.

That's when a hand landed atop his, the nails painted a vibrant red. "Not right now, I'm afraid."

Flinching at the familiar voice, Mars turned his gaze to Bekka Darksdòttra. She'd managed to get close without him noticing. He was rustier than he'd thought. Plucking her hand from his, he scooped up the rest of the coins and added them to the pot. "Excuse me, kitten, but I'll decide when I'm finished."

Bekka gave a snort. Save for the color of her hair, dyed crimson to match her nails, she looked the same as the last time their paths had crossed ten months ago. "So I've heard, and yet here you are. Running back the moment you're called. Like a good little pup."

"And here you are, so eager for a pet." Mars flashed his teeth in a smile. "But that will have to wait." Turning back to the table, he rolled the dice.

"Win," the dealer announced again. "Shall you try for a third, sir?"

"No thank you, my friend. I know to quit while I'm ahead." Mars collected his winnings, then wandered away from the table, scanning the room for a new game while he waited to see what Bekka would do. Or more specifically, what Una wanted her to do. He needed to know where he stood with the Den's mistress before he faced her. The memory of the card flashed in his mind, a part of him wishing he hadn't burned it.

Only a moment passed before Bekka followed him, her shoulders curved down in a sulk, arms folded at her waist. She wore a fitted black bodice trimmed in red fur over a matching skirt. Herding him was beneath her, or so she believed. Then again, Bekka believed a great many things, including the delusion that she was his rival. Among Una's foxes, Mars had no rival. He'd closed every contract he'd ever accepted, a claim no other fox could make. And by the look on Bekka's face, she knew it, even if she wouldn't admit it aloud.

Mars began to steel himself to follow Bekka to his meeting with Una, but a gathering crowd at one of the nearby card tables caught his eye, and he walked over to see what all the fuss was about, Bekka trailing him. Instead of money, the players were gambling with artifacts, making the stakes unusually high for the main floor. Several of the magical items on the line already lay in the center of the table: a battered compass, a spoon, a bag of marbles. To a foreigner, they might seem mundane objects, save for their peculiar coloring, a metallic cobalt blue. But it was that very coloring that marked them as magical. Unlike Una's ravens, which ran on Ice that must be replenished regularly, these objects were crafted by adepts and imbued with the never-ending power of the Rift. The magic in them would remain, so long as the Rift beneath Riven remained.

One of the players, a dark-skinned man wearing a hooded green cape of plain-spun wool, stood from the table and reached into his trouser pocket, withdrawing a pair of spectacles, which he placed next to the other artifacts.

"What do those do?" another player asked in a skeptical tone. The metal on the spectacles was so thin, it was hard to be certain of the make.

In answer, the man picked up the spectacles and held them before his face. "Observe."

Mars fixed his gaze on the man, but the moment the stranger slid the spectacles on, Mars felt his eyes moving away, as if compelled by an invisible force. He made to return his eyes to the man, but try as he might, he couldn't do it, not directly. Only when he turned his head could he glimpse the man through his peripheral vision, a blurry shape at best.

Gasps filled the air as the crowd came to understand the spectacles' magic. Mars's fingers itched to pluck them off the man's face. Glasses that could repel an onlooker's vision? The man must be some kind of fool to flaunt such an artifact in here. Every fox in the Den would want them, including Mars.

Resisting the temptation, he retreated from the table, his attention turning to the grand staircase descending from the center of the room like a giant maw. The gilded railing glistened in the light of the chandelier overhead. The truly interesting games would be down there, and he contemplated the new weight of herrings in his pocket.

You should leave, warned that familiar voice in his head. Ignoring it, Mars moved toward the stairs, Bekka trailing him once more.

He had only a moment's notice before it happened, a quick buzz of magic jolting through his body. He halted just as the air before him wavered, like a reflection in a pond disturbed by a wake, and a cloaked figure appeared from out of nowhere.

Mars drew a deep breath to steady his voice and dropped into a bow, his braided hair falling over his shoulder. "Good evening, Una."

The mistress of the Fortune's Den pulled back the hood of her cloak, revealing a black mane of hair encased in a silver snood. While the outside of the cloak was a solid, inky blue, the interior was lined throughout with intricate symbols stitched in metallic blue thread, glistening like stars in a night sky. It was an artifact, one of much greater value than those at the gaming table. It allowed its wearer to disappear and reappear somewhere else at will. Mars didn't like to think how much blood the adept who made it must've given.

Una stared at him a moment, dark eyes narrowed over her hooked nose, her cheekbones sharp as blades. Then a smile broke over her thin lips as she stepped forward and pulled him into an embrace. "I've missed your face, boy."

Mars submitted to the hug, despite wanting to squirm away. "Perhaps you should give your ravens eyes that you can look through when you send them to spy on me."

Releasing him, Una waved a dismissive hand, an artifact ring on her finger flashing. "I've no desire to glimpse you using the privy, or something else . . . unsavory." She paused and eyed him up and down, a frown making a wrinkle in her otherwise flawless pale skin. "Though I must say, you're looking a little worse for wear. Dock work disagrees with you."

"It agrees with me more than it does the fish."

Una chortled and held out her arm for him to take. "Come along, little fox. Let's find somewhere more comfortable to catch up."

With Bekka trailing sulkily behind them, they headed downstairs and through halls lined by a honeycomb of rooms, many with their doors closed to give the patrons inside their privacy. Magic burned thicker, headier down here, its presence making Mars's palms itch and his body hum with energy. He was so distracted by it, he collided with a man exiting one of the rooms.

"Watch it." The man shoved Mars with both hands. His soured breath reeked of too much alcohol, enough to turn anyone belligerent.

Mars raised his fists to retaliate but froze at Una's curt gesture. "You must forgive my guest," she said, bowing her head slightly to the stranger. "He's not known for his gracefulness."

Recognizing the irony in Una's tone, Mars held in a snort of laughter. The belligerent man was a high-ranking member of the Belen Kith, judging by the tattoo of three boars' tusks over his right eyebrow, and therefore not to be trifled with. While the Helm governed Riven, everyone knew it was the nine kiths who truly ruled it—and they weren't afraid to show that power to any commoner they came across, mistress of the Fortune's Den included.

The man scowled at Una, baring teeth. "Titans curse you both." He spat on the floor, some of the spittle dotting Una's satin slipper. The woman had ordered men killed for less. But not a kith.

"Please tell the bartender you may have a drink, on the house." She bowed again, then stepped back, motioning for Mars and Bekka to give the man room to pass.

A moment later, the Belen man was gone, and they moved on, soon arriving in the centermost chamber, where Una kept her private office. Curtains as red as fresh blood hung about the room, giving the impression of windows, even though they were underground. An ornate desk occupied the far side of the area, with two sofas set across from each other filling the middle.

To Mars's dismay, they weren't alone; two of Una's guards, in red-and-silver uniforms, stood over a young woman who crouched on the floor near the sofas, hands cradling the sides of her face as trembles racked her body. She wore the flowing, sheer garments favored by Una's sweet girls. Judging by her state of undress, it looked like she'd been dragged away mid-engagement with a client.

"What is this?" Una halted at the sight of the room's occupants, her nostrils flaring in a way that made Mars flinch. The guards sensed the danger as well, both shrinking back a span. All the outrage Una must have felt at the Belen man's insult seemed to rise to the surface now.

The elder of the two guards cleared his throat. "We've found the thief, madam. Caught her in the act just now. Had more than an ounce of dust on her."

Una's expression darkened into cold, tightly bridled fury. Although she was a mistress of spies and secrets, she despised deception above all else, especially from one of her own.

The girl cowering on the floor let out a wail. "It's not true!"

Silently, Una kneeled and took hold of the girl's hand with one of her own, the one bearing the artifact ring. "Have you been stealing from me?" Una asked as she stroked the girl's face with her opposite hand. Her gaze was soft, her voice gentle, a concerned mother tending a wayward child.

The sweet girl drew a breath, the sound wavering with tears. But before the girl could respond, Una's ring gave her the answer she sought, the metallic lines threaded through the silver beginning to glow.

With a disgusted groan, Una stood, releasing the girl's hand as she addressed her guards. "Cut off her nose and put her out. She is done here."

The girl began to shriek as the guards nodded. They grabbed her by the arms and hauled her out into the hallway.

Poor, stupid kid, Mars thought as the girl's cries slowly faded, leaving behind a silence thick with dread. A dust addiction wasn't pretty—Mars was unable to fathom why anyone who'd ever seen a person fresh from the mines would willingly consume a substance made from raw, pulverized Ice—but Una's sentence all but guaranteed the girl would never work again. It was a reminder of exactly who Mars was dealing with—and all the reasons he needed to get out. His fate would be far, far worse if Una ever discovered the truth about him.

She almost did, the voice whispered. Orri's face appeared in his mind's eye, the way he'd looked just before Mars had killed him.

"Sorry about that," Una said, drawing Mars back to the present. "Always unfortunate when a new employee fails to live up to expectations." She smiled, her manner calm and friendly once more. It was hard to believe she was the same person who had just ordered someone mutilated and dumped on the street. She motioned to Bekka. "You're no longer needed here."

Wordlessly, Bekka bowed and headed for the door. Mars watched her go, until the last moment when she cast him a cold, vicious smile over her shoulder. Mars frowned, unsettled. With an effort he turned and sat on the nearest sofa, motioning for Una to get on with it.

After a moment, the Den's mistress took the sofa across from him. "I must admit, I wasn't entirely sure I could draw you back so easily."

Mars arched an eyebrow, feeling the tug of his scar against his cheek at the movement. "You say that like I had a choice."

"Oh, come now, my dear." Una wrinkled her nose, and Mars inwardly rolled his eyes. "Of course I respect your decision to leave, but if anything, I'm doing you a favor. I'm offering a million-herring payout for this job. Enough to place you in the lap of luxury for the rest of your life, no matter whether you want to settle in Osway or Vest or do the sensible thing and remain here in Riven where you belong."

The thought of that much money stole his breath away. But only for a moment.

Mars set his face in a grin, his only option to play along. "You really are a cunning old witch, aren't you?" He'd never told anyone his plans to leave, least of all Una. Far as she knew, he had given up mercenary work in favor of an honest, simple life. Unease spread through his stomach like bellows expanding. She must've been keeping an even closer eye on him than he realized.

Una shrugged. "You're not the first of my foxes to be soured by a bad job. But in my experience, all that's truly needed is a little time away to clear the head. Or in your case, a few months making a boring, smelly living among the fishes.

Yes, time dulls even the worst memories." She paused, and for a moment she truly seemed the concerned mother. "Orri's death wasn't your fault."

Mars looked away, her words a gut punch. *You have no idea.*

No, of course she didn't. That was why he'd had to kill his best friend, after all. *It was him or me. Him or me.* He gritted his teeth until the truth became real once more, the regret retreating like the tide beneath a waning moon.

Swallowing the bile stinging the back of his throat, Mars faced Una once more. "Get on with your pitch."

Una cast him a smug look. "How well do you remember Henrik Torvald?"

Mars gaped at her, wondering if she was toying with him. Why else comfort him about Orri's death one moment, then bring up the cause of it the next? Mars would never forget the man. Kithborn, rich, soft—Henrik Torvald should've been an easy kill. Instead, he'd turned out to be a secret adept, same as Mars. And when Henrik had used magic to defend himself, Mars had had no choice but to answer with his own magic. Kill or be killed. It was the mercenary's creed.

But Orri had seen. He'd realized at once what Mars was, the truth turning them into enemies.

Una knew none of that, and she never would.

Mars sighed, knowing that if he wanted to keep his secrets, he'd better play the game. "I remember him. Husband to Elìn Torvald, dòttra of the Torvald Kith." A very significant man indeed, which was no doubt the reason someone had paid to have him assassinated. Each of the nine kiths of Riven controlled one of the Ice mines, but the powerful families were always at war with one another, hoping they could somehow claim a second mine and establish their dominance over the rest. As the dòttra, Elìn was the matriarchal ruler of the Torvalds, the strongest of the kiths, which meant Henrik's assassination had most likely been an act to wound her.

"Very good." Una nodded. "Well, this new job concerns his daughter, Fura Torvald. She's in need of protection."

Mars drew a breath and let it out slowly, disbelief thudding in his ears. "Let me get this straight. You want me to protect the life of the daughter of the man whose life you paid me to take just a few months ago?"

Una smiled. "As a matter of fact, I think you're the perfect fox for the job."

THREE

MARS LAUGHED. THERE was no humor behind it, only incredulity. He couldn't help it. The idea was so absurd…so stupid… so *offensive*.

When Una's expression didn't change, Mars said, "Are you sure you're not the one pilfering dust around here? We're responsible for her father's death, Una."

Una rolled her eyes. "Don't be a fool for sentiment, Mars. The client is responsible for all actions taken on a contract, not us. We are the weapon, not the will."

It was a familiar maxim around here. A way to avoid those niggling doubts about the ethics of providing such services. And it didn't apply to just the foxes, but to the rest of the Den's employees as well, whatever vice they provided, be it a sniff, a drink, a roll. *It's always their own decision*, Mars thought, reflexively. Freedom of choice—it was the Rivenish way, after all.

He leaned back against the sofa, arms crossed over his chest. "I believe I've given enough to the Torvalds' will."

"We're mercenaries. We never say *enough*."

No, he thought, picturing Orri. *Not until we die.* Mars cleared his throat, forcing thoughts of his friend from his mind. "As I recall, your card didn't include a shield. It indicated intelligence gathering from a difficult source while contending with multiple threats—nothing about protection."

"That would be why this contract is valued in Ice." Una raised a hand to the diamonds encircling her throat, her finger idly tracing the wolf's teeth strung between the glimmering stones. The faded enneagram brand on her hand twisted at the gesture. Not for the first time, Mars wondered if hers was real, or as fake as his. "The card I sent referenced the second of what are in fact two separate contracts. The first is the protection of Miss Torvald, a task which is crucial to the second."

Mars tilted his head, intrigued despite himself. "Which is?"

Una let her hand fall back into her lap. "Extracting information of which Fura Torvald will soon be in possession. Therefore, keeping her safe is crucial. At least for a time."

Mars rose from the sofa and crossed the room to the bar, pouring himself a glass of honey rum. He didn't bother offering Una one. She did not drink. Or use dust. Or gamble. Or partake in any of the vices she supplied. She was a woman rife with contradictions.

He downed the glass, then poured another, contemplating Una's words. Two contracts meant two clients. Quite the tangled web.

"The protection of Fura Torvald will surely be the easier of the two," Una called over her shoulder. "While I was more than willing to accept the contract, from what I gather, the young Miss Torvald can very well take care of herself."

Like her father? If Mars had been any other assassin,

Henrik Torvald would've killed him easily. Was it possible his daughter was also a secret adept? Mars doubted it. Adepts were rare, one in ten thousand, if that, and the ability to wield Rift magic was not an inherited trait. He supposed if it were inherited, the ability would've died out long ago—it wasn't as if enthralled adepts were allowed to lead normal lives and do normal things like having families.

Mars took another sip, then faced Una once more. "Give me the details."

Una smiled, and Mars hated the idea that she thought he was seriously considering the job. Almost as much as he hated himself for being here at all. "Surely you know the Assembly is fast approaching."

An involuntary groan escaped his lips. "How could I forget?" Hardly a day went by when he wasn't solicited for a contribution to the Fifth, who was still raising the necessary funds to attend the Assembly, the Helm's annual legislative meeting. Although the Fifth was the Helm's head of state, it was the poorest funded of the positions. The Helm's other members—four elected leaders from each of the four farthings of Riven—all received patronage from the various kiths, while the Fifth, by law, could only receive patronage from commoners. He was the people's leader.

"Indeed. Praise be to the nine it's almost here." Una shook her head, her expression serious once more. "Young Fura Torvald will be attending by her mother's side. You'll accompany her to Hàr Halda and ensure her safety through the duration of the Assembly. That's three weeks from now, which gives you plenty of time to prepare. You will have until the end of the Assembly to obtain the information from Miss Torvald needed to complete the second contract."

Mars didn't bother asking what information he was supposed to gather. Una wouldn't reveal that level of detail until after he'd signed the contract. Information like that was too easily bought and sold.

Despite his reservations, the notion of completing a job at the Assembly appealed to him. The stakes didn't get any higher than that, and even though he was the best of Una's mercenaries, she'd never had a job during the Assembly that required his particular set of skills.

Which meant something didn't add up for this one. Drink in hand, Mars returned to the sofa and fixed his gaze on Una. "Why me?"

"Many reasons, not the least of which is that a job such as this one demands the talents of the most skilled fox in my den." Una leaned toward him, elbows resting on her knees. "But that's not the only reason. Most of my available foxes are older than thirty; the plan I discussed with the client requires a fox of your age. You're also handsome and charming and capable of throwing around a fair amount of ego, which will work in your favor."

Mars blinked. "Why would a bodyguard need to be my age? Or . . . any of the other things you just mentioned?"

"Ah," Una said, the sound of a schoolmistress pleased with her favorite pupil. "You won't be posing as a bodyguard. There's a new rule in place for the Assembly this year—no kith is permitted to bring any hired guards, nor will any weaponry be allowed within Hàr Halda's walls. With so many high-profile assassinations of late—Henrik Torvald's being one—not to mention the uptick in border skirmishes, one can understand the decision." She grinned as she said this, knowing full well that she herself had had a hand in a large portion of this mayhem.

"If no guards are allowed, then what role will I be assuming? Mars asked. Half a dozen ruses occurred to him—cook, driver, valet—yet none of them necessitated someone his age.

Una pressed her lips together as if stifling a laugh. "You'll be attending the Assembly as Fura Torvald's new beau."

"Beau?" The word came out breathy, his mind flailing in its attempt to make sense of it.

"Yes. There are some people in the world who enter into romantic relationships with others of comparable age and similar interests." Una smirked. "All you must do is play the part of the foppish young rich boy blindly infatuated with her."

Finally grasping her point, Mars felt his mouth fall open. He quickly shut it again. Henrik Torvald had nearly killed him, and his assassination had destroyed Mars's life. For a moment, Mars tried to envision what that would be like, all that time spent with Fura Torvald hanging on his arm as he feigned tender feelings for her. Only nothing came. His mind couldn't fathom it. Even if he could, the job would surely require his magic—how else was he to keep her safe without weapons? He hadn't become the Shadow Fox by his physical prowess alone, after all.

But he couldn't risk getting caught again. This was the reason he'd decided to leave Riven, after all. It didn't matter what the payout was—he wouldn't be able to spend it if he were discovered and enthralled. Even Orri, his best friend, the person he'd trusted most in his life, had been willing to betray him the moment he discovered the truth. The pain of it, the shock of seeing the look that had come over Orri's face in that moment—hatred mingled with greed—haunted Mars still. No, he couldn't afford to lose anything more.

Setting down his glass, Mars rose to his feet. "It's been nice seeing you again, Una, but I'm going to pass."

Una stared up at him, her steady gaze full of unspoken promises. "Sure you are."

"I mean it, Una."

"I'm certain you do. But when you change your mind and come back to see me, would you be a dear and use the side entrance? Best not to attract so much attention again."

Hiding his irritation at her smug certainty, Mars headed for the door, closing it behind him to punctuate his intention never to return. But once he was alone in the hallway, doubt immediately crept in. What made Una so certain? It wasn't as if she'd threatened him—as he knew she could. She still possessed the vial of his blood, and with it she could end his life in a moment. And she hadn't offered to barter, either, offering him additional incentives to agree. No, she had simply stated his return as a given, a guarantee.

The memory of Bekka's parting smile came back to him now. The too-knowing, too-gleeful look in her eyes. Like the cat off to lick the cream. Like she knew something he didn't.

Because she did.

Blood rushed in Mars's ears as the purpose of the evening's events suddenly became clear. He'd been played from the beginning. Bekka, the ego stroke, it'd all been a ruse. A classic misdirection.

The doubt inside him shifted, turning to desperation. Surely he was mistaken. Una couldn't have taken his money. She wouldn't stoop so low. Only, he needed to be sure.

Still alone in the hallway, Mars quickened his steps, but only by a degree. Una was right. He didn't want to attract attention now. Just the opposite; he needed to be sure he wasn't seen.

Minutes later, and with a new pair of spectacles on his face, he exited the Den. The moment he rounded the corner, out of sight of Una's guards, Mars disappeared into the shadows of the nearest alley.

Then he broke into a run.

From the rooftops, Jakulvik appeared a different city altogether, a shadowbox cut from sharp angles and planes, rounded domes, and pointed arches. The bright, ringed moon overhead provided enough light to see by, but it made the dark spaces between each building appear fathomless. In a previous life, Mars would've reveled in the thrill of leaping from one rooftop to the next, that split moment of hanging just above the jaws of certain death before landing safely just beyond their reach.

But now all he felt was terror. He'd chosen the rooftops not for the excitement, but for the speed, to avoid the congested streets below. Bekka was fast, and she had a head start. He couldn't afford to lose a single moment.

His breath came hard, his arms and legs aching from exertion. He was still in decent shape from his work at the docks, but not like he had been when he was a fox, constantly in training. Fatigue made such dangerous acrobatics more dangerous still.

At last, he reached the final jump, a spot on the edge of a tenement building next to the dilapidated warehouse of his attic hideout. Sucking in a deep breath, Mars prepared to make the leap from the building's edge to a corner spout across the way that once had been carved into a likeness of the World Raven, but was now little more than wind-worn stone. It was an impossible distance for a human to cross without the aid of rope or a grappling hook.

Or magic.

Flicking both wrists, Mars winced at the sudden flare of pain as the blades cut into him, releasing the needed sacrifice of blood. A second later, the Rift's power began to flow through him, power enough to give him the wings he needed. He launched off the roof, stretching out his body to his full length as he called upon the magic to propel him forward. His legs struck the edge of the spout, and he nearly ricocheted off it. Righting himself, he scooted down the ledge, jimmied the attic window open, and tumbled inside.

Rooftop hissed at him before vanishing through a hole in a wall. Mars went at once to the second floorboard from the end, dropping to his knees like a supplicant in prayer. His hands shook and sweat dripped from his chin as he pulled the board aside, preparing to release the first of the trip wires below. But even as he did, he realized there was no need. All the traps had been disarmed by an expert hand. One trained at the Fortune's Den.

No. No. No, Mars silently screamed as he pulled out the lockbox, feeling the unbearable lightness of it, the promise of its emptiness.

Wrenching the lid free, he peered inside. It was all gone. Every coin he'd collected these past few months, down to the last herring. In their place lay a card, folded in half, with his name printed on the front. Mars opened it, recognizing the familiar scrawl.

You'll get it back when the job is done. I give you my bond.

—U.

With a strangled cry, Mars crumpled the card. He wanted to hit something. He wanted to return to the Den, grab Una by the throat, and strangle her until she relented and gave him back what was his. But most of all, he wanted to kick himself for ever going down there in the first place.

Would it have even mattered? Whispered the voice in his head.

The answer resounded in his mind, loud as clanging cymbals. *Impossible. Nobody quits,* the guard at the Den had said. It was true. Mars had always known it. That was the purpose behind the blood ampoules—to ensure Una's foxes remained obedient. Disobedience meant death. All she had to do was destroy the ampoule, releasing the magic in it, which would soon destroy the fox who had given the blood. Mars had known the risk from the moment he allowed them to take the blood from him. But he hadn't understood what he was giving up—what Una was taking. Not then.

She will never let you go.

An invisible weight seemed to drag him down, his legs giving way so that he collapsed onto his side. All those months of working. For nothing. It had all been in vain.

Feeling sorry for yourself now? The voice taunted. *At least you're still alive. Unlike Orri.*

The truth stung, but Mars welcomed it, some of the weight sloughing off. He sat up and uncrumpled the card, reading it once again.

I give you my bond.

Mars examined the lockbox's interior once more, and this time saw a small red bead lying in one corner. He pulled it out, pinched between his fingers, and examined the golden fox painted on its side. *Una's bond.* This wasn't a mere platitude or some false promise. Una adhered to the old ways. She was a follower of Rivna, the ancient code of honor, which claimed that once a bond was given, it could not be broken, lest the oathmaker sacrifice their entry into Asvaldur, the eternal feasting hall of the Titans and the honorable dead of Riven. It might all be nonsense—probably was—but Una was a believer nonetheless.

It was cold comfort, but he knew, at least, that if he fulfilled the contract, she would indeed give him back his money. Not to mention the payment for the job. *Enough to place you in the lap of luxury for the rest of your life,* she had said.

Luxury wasn't what he wanted. Freedom was what mattered. Freedom from her.

He swallowed, desperation making him dizzy. He could just start over. Return to the docks, find more work, toil away the hours for months on end . . . but then what? Una would never let him go, not unless he found some way to convince her to release him. Or maybe force her to. He didn't know how, but there must be a way. She was not invincible or impervious to pressure. With the right motivation, she might give in, might make a deal. He just needed to find the best leverage point, something she couldn't refuse.

He thought about the job. The information he was tasked to extract from Fura Torvald. Una had gone to great lengths to draw him back. There was an opportunity here, he knew it.

Besides, it wasn't as if he had any other choice.

With a heavy sigh, Mars raised his hands to his hair and carefully threaded Una's bond onto a few strands he'd worked free of the braid, tying it to himself. There it would remain until he finished the job—keeping Fura Torvald safe through the Assembly and retrieving whatever information she possessed. He was the Shadow Fox, after all, and the Shadow Fox did not fail.

FOUR

HIS FIRST WEEK back at the Den's training compound was a perpetual lesson in humility—and regret.

The humility came as Mars quickly realized his skills were far rustier than he'd thought they'd be. In the first three days alone, he died six times in the simulations. As the name suggested, these were practice runs of the many jobs a fox might be expected to perform—thieving, assassination, kidnapping, and so on. Only, the victims and other parties involved, such as guards and family members, were played by other foxes, some of them initiates, some active foxes between missions, and some retired foxes turned teachers. That meant all of them were far more capable and aware than any ordinary mark would be. Which was the point. If a fox could complete the simulated job even against such formidable obstacles, they could surely accomplish it in real life. The dying was simulated as well, of course, using wooden weapons and kill zones designated by red circles drawn on clothing. One hit to a kill zone by an opponent's weapon meant instant defeat. To Mars's shame, Bekka had managed to slay him twice—an accomplishment she would never let him live down.

The regret, though, was far worse. Everywhere he looked, every room he entered or familiar face he encountered, reminded him of Orri. The past few months he'd spent in isolation, he'd been able to keep the memories of his friend at bay. But here, in the place the two of them had spent years of their lives together, they waited around every corner, like thieves lying in ambush. He and Orri had been initiates together, both orphans recruited off the streets of Jakulvik—Mars from the west end and Orri from the east—and both gifted pickpockets. Their friendship had seemed inevitable, although for Mars, it had taken a long time to get comfortable with the idea of being friends with anyone. It wasn't just growing up alone on the streets, sleeping in alleyways or on rooftops with a makeshift shiv of rusted iron or splintered wood clutched in his fingers, hiding from groups like Gisela's gang, and avoiding anyone eager to turn him over to the city watch. No—it was his ability to do magic that made him truly wary of getting close to anyone. The things he could do were easier to hide if he remained alone. He couldn't be identified if no one knew his name or where he lived, and he couldn't let down his guard if there was no one around to let it down to. But slowly, Orri's relentlessly cheerful nature, not to mention the way he'd latched onto Mars like a little lost puppy the day they'd met, had worn Mars down enough that he'd let Orri into his life. But never close. Mars knew better than that. No one could be trusted with his secret. Because people in Riven were all the same—only caring about themselves, their own survival, or their own coin. Never what it all might cost someone else.

Not like you're any different, the voice reminded him. Mars didn't argue. He *was* just the same. The moment he'd seen the realization dawn in Orri's eyes, and how he'd raised his pistol at Mars, his aim as true as that of any other fox, Mars hadn't hesitated. He hadn't waited to doubt, wondering if he could change his friend's mind, convince him that he was still his friend, even if he was also an adept. Convince him to keep Mars's secret, not to kill him, or worse, to capture him and tell Una. Mars had done what he'd needed to in order to save his own skin. With his Rift magic, he'd yanked the pistol from Orri's hand, then drew it into his own and fired. Point-blank. Kill zone.

Shuddering at the memory, Mars rolled over on the bed in his dormitory room, then stood and crossed to the window, throwing the curtains open to let in the light and banish his dark thoughts. Sunshine streamed across the room, falling across a glinting object lying on the floor just in front of the door. A crow's feather. The sight provoked a weary sigh in Mars. The feather meant someone intended to challenge him to a duel. Although not part of a fox's formal training, duels were a common practice, one encouraged by Una. The art of dueling went back hundreds of years, to the time of the Rivna Knights and the Consortium. It was said that the knights used dueling to settle disputes and establish their ranks, ensuring only the best and strongest would lead. And although so much about how Una conducted business stood in exact opposition to the code of Rivna, it didn't stop her and her foxes from honoring what practices they could. Besides, it made for great entertainment.

If you weren't the one dueling.

Picking up the feather, Mars contemplated going back to bed, but there was no avoiding it. Once the challenge was made, it would be met. It could only be Bekka behind it, and he reveled in the idea of putting her in her place.

Finding his rival in the hall waiting for him a few minutes later seemed to confirm his assumption. That is, until she flashed a grin at him so large, it appeared to swallow half her face. "I hope you've spent the morning petitioning the Titans for their favor."

Mars rolled his eyes. "When it comes to ego, there's no matching yours, pray as I might."

Bekka laughed, unfazed by the insult. "You think I gave you the crow's feather? Why would I, when I've already proven myself better than you?"

Her words stopped him cold. "If not you, then who?"

"The Reaper."

Mars held his breath, dread squeezing his throat. What sort of fresh hell was this? Although Mars had been in the Den a week, he'd thus far managed to avoid crossing paths with Rafnar Magnùsvane. He'd been so successful that he'd come to assume the Reaper was away on an assignment. Although Mars might be the most successful of Una's foxes, Rafnar was the most ruthless, his reputation as Una's executioner spreading far beyond the foxes of the Fortune's Den to all its patrons. Failure to pay a debt to Una, no matter how small, resulted in a visit from the Reaper. Any debt incurred in the Den always came due.

"How do you know it was him?"

Bekka folded her arms over her chest, her grin turning

smug. "The whole Den knows it by now. When Rafnar says anything at all, people listen, and he hasn't been quiet about this challenge. The odds are five to one against you."

Mars gritted his teeth, guessing they should've made it ten to one. Although he'd come a long way since resuming his training, he was still far from sharp enough to best Rafnar Magnùsvane in hand-to-hand combat. Not without relying on his magic, that was. Which he didn't dare. Not here, and with so many foxes sure to come to watch.

As he made his way to the training grounds a short while later, Bekka trailing him, he could hear the crowd's anxious rumblings. She hadn't been exaggerating. There was blood in the water and all of them were sharks.

With a sigh, Mars ran a hand over his head and down the length of his braid, his finger rubbing against Una's bond tied in his hair. Its presence steeled his resolve. He would survive this beating and the bruises to both body and pride that would come with it.

Silence spread like a wave through the assembled crowd at his arrival. Comprised mostly of initiates and foxes, along with a couple of guards, mingled groups stood here and there around the edges of the sparring ring. Mars scanned the faces for Rafnar but didn't see the man anywhere. Perhaps Bekka had been toying with him.

No. As his gaze traveled to the training grounds' central area, he spotted the man sitting in the Shrine, a place marked by a ring of standing stones, each twice the height of a tall man, set around a statue of Ragna, the hidden Titan, mistress of shadows and patron of mercenaries. Dozens of objects hung from pegs drilled into the sides of the stones, each one a tribute to the dead. Somewhere among those items was Orri's arm ring. Mars had placed it there himself the day he'd fled this place.

At Mars's arrival, Rafnar roused himself, coming slowly to his feet and raising his arms over his head in a languorous stretch. He'd already removed his tunic in preparation for the match, his bare chest covered in thick dark hair spread over bulging muscle. Despite his age, rumored to be upward of fifty, he remained fit and hale, the only hint of his advancing years the gray threading his beard, which hung past his collarbone. His head was shaved bald, the sides of his skull adorned with intricate tattoos.

Lowering his arms to his sides, the Reaper stepped out from the Shrine and approached the edge of the sparring ring where Mars waited. The man jangled as he walked, the dozens of tokens strung through his beard knocking against one another. Each of the iron coins was a symbol of a life taken in service to the Den. Mars had more than a dozen such tokens himself, as did most of the foxes here, but the Reaper was the only one who wore them. Their meaning was well-known in Riven, and no assassin was so bold—or foolhardy, depending on who you were asking—to advertise themselves in such a way.

No assassin, except the Reaper.

Rafnar held out a crow's feather to Mars as he entered the ring. Seeing it, Mars swallowed, wondering how deep the man's anger at him ran. The source of that anger was obvious—Rafnar did not approve of Mars's attempt to quit.

Although there was no true fondness between them, Rafnar was as close to a father figure as Mars had ever known. He had given Mars his introduction to the Den, the day after he'd caught Mars trying to pick his pocket. For years afterward, Rafnar would check up on Mars, following his progress through initiation to full member. The Reaper had always been a man of few words, his presence in Mars's life less like that of a mentor and more like a vision of Mars's future self, haunting him from the shadows.

This duel spoke loudly enough, though, about his feelings on Mars's leaving.

"Prepare," the ringmaster said, motioning toward them with outstretched hands.

In response, Mars removed his tunic and tossed it aside. Then he bent to remove his boots and stockings before stepping onto the soft padding of the ring. He left his arm cuffs in place, hiding his scars and the blades tucked inside them. No one commented on the cuffs. They were his tribute, same as Orri's arm ring had been—the very things that would hang from the standing stones if he ever died in service to the Den.

Around them the crowd murmured, making their final bets, anticipating the violence.

"Begin," the ringmaster said, sounding as eager as the rest. Mars hoped that was his imagination; it was the master's responsibly to call the duel before it got too violent, or someone was killed.

Rafnar rushed Mars immediately, and although Mars was able to duck and weave and avoid the bigger, slower man at first, it was inevitable that Rafnar would land a punch sooner or later. The punches Mars managed to land—several body shots, a jab to the jaw, and a solid left hook to Rafnar's temple— only hurt his hand, as if Rafnar's body were chiseled from marble instead of meat. By contrast, Mars's first mistake made him seem as if he were made of glass. He let his left hand drop as he threw a right cross, the punch coming in hard but slow enough that Rafnar dodged it easily, jerking back out of reach and at the same time countering with a right cross of his own. The man's hammerlike fist collided with Mars's temple, send- ing stars shooting across his vision in the split second before black curtains fell over his gaze.

Mars woke a few moments later, lying on the sparring floor with blood pooling into his left eye, leaving his vision red-hazed and blurry.

Una stood over him, glaring down. "That didn't go well. I was hoping you'd be performing better by now."

He groaned, realizing he'd been knocked out cold in one punch. The only punch. He sat up and pressed his palm to his temple. "The man outweighs me by seven stones at least. What do you expect?" He glanced at Una, dismayed that she'd been there to see the beating.

"I expect better." Una threw a towel at him. "Get yourself cleaned up and meet me in the Lair in an hour. The timetable for your contract has changed. You leave tomorrow."

Mars exhaled in relief as he picked up the towel and pressed it to the split skin on his temple. Una might not be thrilled with how rusty he was, but he was happy to learn his stay at the Den was ending sooner than expected. With renewed vigor, he clambered to his feet, only to take a step back as he realized Rafnar was hovering next to him.

"You deserve worse," the big man said, then turned and strode away, jingling with each step.

Mars stared after him, disquieted by the notion that the man had been holding back.

Bekka, who'd been idly observing the exchange from nearby, snorted in amusement. "Don't take it personally, Mars. Rafnar hates a quitter."

Mars shook his head, aware of the slight weight of Una's bond in his hair. If only quitting were truly an option.

The Lair was what Una called her war room, the place where all the jobs contracted to the Den were planned. It was a chamber of secrets, a hall of shadows, and easily the most disturbing place in the compound. The space had previously been a crypt, one whose former occupants had been unceremoniously evicted by Una decades ago when she first discovered the entrance. Jakulvik was one of the oldest cities in Riven, witness to the births and deaths of thousands through the years, but with rocky landscape surrounding the city on three sides and the ocean abutting it on the last, it had never offered much in the way of space for burying the dead.

Mars shivered as he descended the long, narrow steps to the vault door. The walls on either side were lined with bone, which left faint white dust on his sleeves as he passed by, a flimsy testimony to names forgotten. The constant reminder that he could someday share the same legacy as these abandoned skeletons only contributed to his discomfort.

Coming to a halt outside the door, he raised the iron knocker and struck it three times, two quick knocks and a short pause before the third. It opened a moment later. Una stepped aside to allow him through before sealing the door behind him.

Damp, cool air filled the vaulted chamber, the murky light of the torches set about the circular room doing little to dispel the darkness. As they did the walls outside, skulls and bones formed the walls here, too, hundreds of empty eye sockets staring back at him.

But they weren't the only ones. Mars felt the eyes watching him before seeing who they belonged to. The first was a small, balding man with a belly like a tabby cat's hanging loose and long below his belt. Gellir Persvane, Una's resident scientist and one of her most important employees—not to mention one of the creepiest and most unsettling. Catching Mars looking at him, Gellir returned his attention to whatever he'd been tinkering with on the worktable he stood behind—some new device born of his devious imagination, no doubt.

With a conscious effort, Mars pulled his attention away from Gellir, but he dared not give more than a glance at the other person in the room—a man sitting motionless in a chair positioned in a dark corner. If he tried hard enough, Mars could pretend this person didn't exist at all. It was best that way.

"So," Mars said, joining Una at the main table in the center of the room, "the schedule has changed?"

Una's expression was blank, her gaze fixed on the detailed map of Riven painted across the table's surface. It depicted every city and geographical point of note, including Jakulvik in the south and the empty expanse of the Mistgrave filling the island's center, sight of the Cataclysm long ago. "The client has demanded more time with you to prepare for the Assembly."

Mars arched an eyebrow. "By *the client*, do you mean Elìn Torvald?"

"Who else?" Una glanced at him.

Who else indeed. In the time he'd been here, Mars had done all he could to discover the identity of both his clients—the one behind Fura Torvald's protection contract and the one seeking whatever information the girl was supposed to possess. The first was not hard to guess—Fura's mother was the likely client, particularly in the wake of her husband's assassination—but the latter was much more difficult to surmise, and Una had been tight-lipped about it. The secrecy wasn't unusual. Mars rarely knew the names of his clients. It minimized risk in the event things went sideways on a delicate job like an assassination or a kidnapping.

We are the weapon, not the will. A weapon couldn't disclose names if captured.

Mars touched a hand to his bruised face. "Well, I suppose the preparation the dòttra has in mind will be less painful, at least."

"I wouldn't count on it," Una replied, a little too casually for Mars's comfort. "But it's too late to worry about whether or not you're up to snuff. We need to discuss your second assignment."

Finally. Whatever object he was seeking, Mars knew it was far more important—and valuable—than keeping the young heir to the Torvald Kith alive. Mars held still and waited for her to go on.

Wordlessly, Una bent toward the table and placed a small wooden box on its surface.

"What's this?" Mars asked.

"The only information I have to give you." Una clucked her tongue. "Open it, but gently. It's fragile."

Mars picked up the box, which fit easily into the palm of his hand, and lifted the hinged lid. Inside lay a torn piece of onionskin paper, so thin that a single exhaled breath might be enough to destroy it. Still, there was writing on it: the ink scribbled across its surface shone in what was some sort of equation. Or part of one, at least. There was a series of letters and numbers, but what caught Mars's attention was a symbol he didn't recognize. A spider's web, or perhaps a wheel. . . .

"As you can see," Una said, "you'll be looking for a formula."

"A formula? Like math?"

"More like chemistry." Una pointed at the strange weblike symbol. "That right there is something called the Primer. And the missing piece is the rest of the formula for creating it."

Mars tilted his head, hoping that a different perspective would make the symbols make sense, but it didn't help. He raised his eyes to Una's. "What's this Primer do?"

Una took the box from his hand and closed the lid. "That is not our concern. The complete formula for creating it is what we are after. Finding it is your task."

"Easier said than done," Mar replied, unable to hide his

dismay. "How can you be sure the rest of it still exists? Onion-skin paper isn't known for its durability."

"Oh, it exists." Una let out a small, strange laugh. "What you are looking at is a copy, or part of one. But there is an original. Henrik Torvald created this formula, and he left the only exist-ing copy of it for his daughter. That is what you are meant to discover."

Mars cocked an eyebrow. "Any suggestions how?" With-out some clue where to begin, it would be like groping for a keyhole in a pitch-black room.

"I'd wager your best bet is to win young Miss Fura's trust." Una replied. "Do that, and sooner or later she's likely to let something slip."

"Are you saying I'm going to have to find a way to extract the information from Fura herself?" Mars asked.

"Potentially."

"Sounds like this job would have been much easier be-fore my previous one," Mars said. His tone was light, masking his frustration and anxiety. If he hadn't been sent to kill Hen-rik, they could have gotten this information from him directly. But a formula on a piece of paper? Something so small could be hidden anywhere. If Fura Torvald had it, she might even have destroyed the written evidence, knowingly or unknowingly. If so, her memory might be the only place the formula still ex-isted. He gritted his teeth. "One of your other foxes might be better for this sort of job."

"Not an option," Una said, the barest hint of a smile on her lips. "With the dòttra's husband having been recently murdered, her daughter is going to be under constant watch, even with you there to protect her. This is not a job for an enforcer. It's a job for a spy."

Mars sighed and held out his hand for the box. "How do you know Fura will have the formula with her when she leaves for the Assembly? She could just leave it hidden somewhere at home."

Una didn't relinquish the box to him. "My sources assure me there's no chance of that. It's far too valuable, and there are rumors she might have intentions for it at the Assembly, selling it, perhaps."

Great. Mars inwardly cursed. Things would be even more complicated. He held out his hand for the box once more.

Una shook her head. "You'll be given a copy to take with you, transposed on something far less fragile. Or so I hope." She turned and snapped her fingers at Gellir. "Is the artifact ready?"

Gellir didn't answer at first, his attention on his work. He wore a monocular fixed over his right eye by a headband, the other eye squeezed shut in concentration.

Una cleared her throat at his continued silence. "Gellir."

Letting out a sigh that set his droopy belly wiggling, Gellir straightened from his hunched position and raised the monocular to his forehead. "It's ready."

"Good." Una turned back to Mars and motioned him deeper into the room, where a reclined medical chair stood, not far from the hidden entrance to the compartment where Una kept the blood ampoules. For a moment, Mars fantasized about using his magic to subdue Una and the others, forcing the compartment open to steal his blood ampoule, then disappearing forever. But it would only ever be a fantasy. There were dozens of ampoules in there, all identical. Only Una knew which one belonged to Mars, and there was no way he could steal them all, not without possibly damaging a few and killing the foxes bound to the blood—or maybe killing himself.

"Have a seat, dear boy," Una said, clapping her hands to get his attention. "Let's get this over with."

Mars obeyed, trying to hide his dread at what would be coming next. It wasn't the first time he'd endured the chair, but he hoped it would be the last.

Gellir scurried over to him as soon as he sat, carrying a glass slide in his hand. He tilted the glass toward Mars, allowing him to see the artifact lying inert on its surface. It was a small strip of human skin bearing a tattoo: a talon. The symbol of the Torvald Kith, one only its members were permitted to wear. Kith insignia were sacred; the intricate designs were impossible to accurately reproduce by anyone besides a kith's artist, and anyone trying to pass off a fake would be executed upon discovery.

That was how Mars knew: this was no fake. If Elìn Torvald was his client, then she had commissioned the tattoo for this purpose. Mars could've kicked himself for not realizing this was coming sooner. Of course he would need a kith tattoo if he were to accompany a Torvald to the Assembly; Fura would never be allowed to date someone outside the kith. And Gellir working on the insignia meant it had been imbued with some sort of magic. *At least it can be removed when I'm done,* Mars told himself, but found little comfort in the thought.

Especially as he saw the figure in the chair facing the wall slowly rise.

Dùnn, Una's enthralled adept.

Gellir hurried over to the man to help him navigate his way. The adept was tall and thin with skin the color of old parchment. He walked with a pronounced limp, one leg dragging behind the other. Mars didn't know what all had been done to him before Una picked him at a black market auction, but it must've been the worst sort of torture. The adept's left hand was missing, as were his eyes and tongue, all forcibly removed by whatever kith had first owned him. The maiming of adepts was the most effective way of controlling them, weakening them physically to weaken them magically. Most adepts cowed to the maiming quickly to avoid further pain, but not Dùnn, it seemed. Which was probably why he'd ended up for sale. There were few adepts outside the kiths' control, and those that were tended to be treated like he had been.

On his remaining hand, Dùnn wore a glove that looked as if it had been fashioned from crystal, but Mars knew it was a rare metal known as starsteel. It was the only substance capable of rendering Rift magic inert. Known as a hobble, the glove's sole purpose was to contain an adept's ability.

Revulsion and pity mingled in Mars like a caustic agent, eating away at him from the inside. This would've been his fate, if he'd been discovered. If he'd let Orri live. *Una would've paid him a fortune for me.*

Mars leaned back in the chair without being told, but didn't close his eyes as Gellir first pressed the piece of tattooed skin above his eyebrow, then stepped aside to guide Dùnn toward him. Gellir was the architect of the artifact, but Dùnn would be its maker. Only his sacrifice of blood could imbue the thing with Rift magic.

Gellir did most of the physical work for the adept. He raised the man's hand in its hobble and opened the lock on the compartment over the palm with a key he wore around his neck. Then he withdrew a tool from his belt that resembled a small ice pick and positioned the tip over Dùnn's exposed palm. Gellir jabbed downward with one quick, sharp motion. The adept didn't react even as the blood bubbled up from his palm. He merely stood there, allowing Gellir to guide his bleeding palm toward Mars's forehead and press the flow against the piece of skin lying there. Heat spread through Mars's face, followed by a tingling sensation that soon turned to fire. The magic burned through him, and he felt his blood burning back in response—an eagerness inside him to make his own sacrifice.

He resisted, teeth gritted, and a moment later it was done. Mars sat up and raised a hand to his forehead, the magic still tingling through his skull.

"You want to be mindful about touching it," Una said, but the warning came too late.

A haze spread over Mars's left eye, and for a second he thought he had lost his vision, but then an image appeared before him—the same one he'd seen on the onionskin. The piece of Henrik's formula.

"How do I get rid of it?" Mars swiped at the air in front of his left eye.

"Just press the artifact again," Gellir said, smirking.

Mars did so, and the image faded as quickly as it had come. He blinked at Una, making sure it was gone. "Well, that's handy. I'm not likely to forget what it looks like, at least."

"Yes," Una said, fixing him with a withering glare. "And it's better than keeping a copy of it on your person for someone else to discover. Above all, no one else must know what you're truly after."

Mars understood. The Primer, whatever it was, was a secret—but Una and her employer wouldn't be the only ones after it.

FIVE

THE NEXT MORNING, Una herself escorted Mars to the train station, where she introduced him to his guide into the Torvalds' world, a man by the name of Askalon Enoksvane. He was Elìn Torvald's truss, the title given to the high counselor of the dòttra or vane of a kith. It was a position of utmost authority, one regarded with an almost holy reverence. Which meant the person bearing such a title usually took themselves far too seriously. One look at Askalon's rigid posture and stern expression was all Mars needed to know that he was no exception.

Accompanying Askalon was Fura's lady's maid, a young woman named Katrìn Darksdòttra. She was pretty in an unconventional way, her nose slightly squared and her front teeth prominent. An old burn scar ran the length of her face on the left side, the flesh pink and permanently puckered, and she wore her dark hair bound in a single braid that fell nearly to her waist.

"This is Halfur Karlsvane," Una said, introducing Mars by the name he'd be using on the job.

"Yes, I'm aware," Askalon said. "I chose that name."

Mars didn't flinch. It wasn't unusual for a client to supply his identity for a job like this, but they usually went along with the ruse in public. As Mars would now. "Please, call me Hal." He extended his hand.

Ignoring it, Askalon turned a sour look on Una. "This the best you have to offer?"

The disdain in the man's voice slid through Mars like ice water down his veins. Despite the fine clothes he wore, the black surcoat trimmed in gray fox fur and tailored to fit his frame, he suddenly felt like that orphan standing on the street once more, begging for a coin.

"The very best," Una said, with a smile on her face but a chill in her tone.

"We shall see." Askalon motioned to Mars. "Come along, then. The train departs soon."

Mars gritted his teeth, hating the man already. That was a kith for you. Mars could be adorned in gold and diamonds, but all this man would ever see was a commoner.

It was going to be a long journey.

Not long after, Mars and his new companions had found an empty table in the dining car. They sat down, Askalon and Katrìn side by side and Mars across from them. Immediately the truss unfolded a newspaper and disappeared behind it, while Katrìn pulled out a knitting wheel from her handbag and set to work.

With little else to do, and knowing attempts at conversation would be a waste, Mars turned his attention to the window, where the outskirts of Jakulvik now passed by. It felt as if he were watching his life slipping away, the buildings and cobbled streets soon giving way to barren countryside. It was too open, too exposed, nothing but craggy ground spotted with rough tufts of yellowish grass, awash in afternoon sunlight. Not a shadow to be seen, except the one cast by the train itself as it rolled along, carrying him farther and farther.

Doubt crept over him as the silence stretched on. Thoughts of his last job crowded his mind, and before long he imagined half a dozen ways this one could go wrong as well. Perhaps all the kith would be like Askalon—able to take one look at him and know the truth. He was a commoner. No, not just that—he was a secret adept. The lowest of the low. Just one mistake, and he would be found out. He clenched his fists, fighting back the urge to flee.

"Sugar with your tea, sir?"

Flinching slightly, Mars pulled his gaze from the window and forced a smile to his lips as he looked up at the waiter standing by the dining-car table. "Three, please." He would've preferred coffee, and would've taken it black, but such a request would've raised eyebrows, especially from the train's servants. Wealthy highborn gentleman did not drink coffee. At least not in public.

"Very good, sir." The waiter pulled the lid from the sugar bowl, plucked out a cube with the tongs, and deposited it into the teacup with punctuated efficiency. The second and third quickly followed. "Will that be all?"

"Yes," Askalon said, not bothering to look up from the paper. Next to him, Katrìn's fingers slowed in their knitting.

The waiter gave a polite nod, then retreated from the table as quietly as a shadow. In another life, he would've made a great merc, Mars considered. Then again, he could be one, the waiter bit just a cover. Remembering there would be other parties interested in the formula, who would no doubt find him a threat, Mars considered forgoing the tea. Just in case. He had a myriad of antidotes packed in his trunks, but there were some poisons that couldn't be counteracted. He had a few of those with him, too, including hoar, the deadliest of all. With conventional weapons banned at the Assembly, he'd packed as many unconventional ones as he could.

Then again, he was probably being paranoid. He picked up the teacup and blew a breath over the steaming surface.

"You've quite a sweet tooth, Halfur," Askalon said. He'd lowered the paper enough to cast Mars another of his derisive looks—the thirteenth, by Mars's count.

Putting the teacup to his lips, Mars made a point of slurping it down, hiding a wince as the liquid scalded his tongue. He should've taken a splash of cream, too.

Askalon rolled his eyes and returned his attention to the paper.

"The way I see it," Mars said, assuming his most refined voice, each syllable precise as a drumbeat, "in this short life, one should savor every sweet thing one can." He paused for effect, taking a careful sip. "And I hear Miss Torvald is very sweet indeed."

The taunt had the desired effect, as Askalon folded the paper with a snap and set it on the table, his dark eyes narrowing. Like Mars, he wore his hair pulled back in a braid, the sides shaved, but his shoulders were broader than Mars's, his muscles harder beneath his thin silk shirt. "A word of advice,

Mr. Karlsvane. Don't get so carried away in your role that you lose your head."

"And I wouldn't risk calling Fura 'sweet' to her face, either," Katrìn added. She flashed a capricious grin at him, her dark eyes glinting. "Not unless you desire to *literally* lose your head."

Mars smirked back at her. "I'll keep that in mind."

"See that you do. Neither of us care for messes."

Mars grinned, some of his earlier gloom fading away at the banter. "If you don't mind me saying, I've never known a lady's maid to speak so frankly about her mistress."

To his surprise, Katrìn laughed, her hands pausing in their rhythmic movement with the knitting needles. "And how many lady's maids have you known before me?"

"Oh, I've known enough." Mars took another sip of tea, amused by her blush.

"He's not wrong, Katrìn," Askalon said, casting her a sidelong look. "It is unseemly behavior for someone in your position." He inclined his head toward Mars. "You'll have to excuse Katrìn. She and Fura share a unique bond. They were children together. Henrik Torvald adopted her as a baby, and she and Fura have been inseparable ever since."

Sisters, Mars thought. Katrìn was an orphan like him, as her surname, Darksdòttra, made evident. She was a daughter of the dark just as Mars was a son of the dark, a euphemistic way to say that neither of them had a father or mother whose name they could claim. *Orri would've liked her*, Mars thought. He guessed Katrìn to be eighteen or thereabouts, roughly the same age as Fura and himself.

Mars waved Askalon off. "There's no harm done." He

made a note to befriend the girl, knowing her closeness to Fura could be a weakness for the young kithswoman—and an advantage for him.

They fell into silence again, but at least Mars had fresh thoughts to occupy his time. Outside the window, the flat barrenness had given way to jagged hills as they headed farther inland, following the vein of the Iselgà River. The train no longer chugged ahead in a straight line but began to wind along the path the river cut through the landscape, slithering back and forth like a giant snake. It felt like a different planet, so far from the coast, with no sign of civilization anywhere, but Mars had to admit that the scenery was lovely. Swaths of deep green grass ran in strips between the hills' rocky cliffs and alongside the numerous waterfalls.

Soon, however, the train made another long bend around a hill only to straighten out once more as it entered a wide valley—and there was the city of Valdri. It sprawled around a towering, rock-sided hill, atop which was the Torvald estate, looking down on the town like a watchful lord.

Mars breathed a sigh of relief, his legs buzzing to be up and moving. All of him buzzed, in fact, and it took him a moment to realize it wasn't nerves. He knew this feeling—the hum of magic. Craning his neck, he glimpsed the walls of a fortress in the distance, the pale bricks tinged with blue.

An *Ice mine*, Mars realized, the heart of the Torvalds' power.

"Have you never seen an Ice mine before, Mr. Karlsvane?" Katrìn asked, following his gaze.

"Not since my tithing," Mars said, the lie slipping from his lips easily. He held up his right hand, which bore the enneagram brand that Una's adept had burned there not a few years ago. "But I've never lived near one. It's easy to forget they exist sometimes." In some ways, this was even more of a lie than the first. There wasn't a day he didn't think about Ice. Its existence was the main reason he had to live in fear, hiding his magic at all cost. The adepts had brought Ice into this world through the Cataclysm. Just because the people of Riven relied on Ice for the magical lifestyle and luxuries it provided didn't mean they could forget the cost of it—or the cause.

"You're lucky," Katrìn said. "We never forget it here." She took a deep breath, then let it out slowly. "Although, if the government has its way, we might all be getting a lot more familiar with the mines."

Mars frowned. "What do you mean?"

"The Helm is considering adding another term of tithing for all citizens."

"What?" Mars made no effort to hide his shock at this.

"Katrìn." Askalon glared at her, a warning.

She glared back at him, lips pressed tight, silencing herself.

Interesting. Mars leaned back in his seat. "Why even propose such a thing?" he asked.

"Because the Ice is—"

"That is enough, Miss Darksdòttra." Askalon pressed a hand against the table, and something about the gesture drove the fight out of Katrìn's eyes. Mars's questions would have to wait.

The train began to slow. Askalon folded his paper and

rose from his seat, turning to Mars. "Go gather your personal effects. We'll meet you at the carriage."

The entirety of Mars Darksvane's personal effects fit on his person. Halfur Karlsvane, though, dandy and playboy that he was, possessed several trunks, including a birdcage with his very own falcon inside. Fortunately, the servants took care of those, leaving Mars relatively unburdened as he stepped off the platform and headed toward the waiting carriage.

Before he reached it, a messenger approached on horse-back, calling for Askalon. "You're needed at the Archive, sir," the boy said, waving a letter at him.

Askalon took the letter and read it at once. Then, with a deepening scowl, he exited the carriage and motioned for Mars to take his seat. "Katrìn will see you to the estate."

Katrìn waved at him, and a moment later she and Mars had boarded the carriage and were off, jostling down the streets of Valdri. The switchback path up the hill to the Torvald estate took a long time to traverse at their slow pace, but at last the black-and-gold filigreed gates of the estate came into view.

Turning her head to the window, Katrìn shouted to the driver, "We're to stop at the temple first."

Mars cocked an eyebrow. A temple of Rivna? Not a place he wished to go. Ever. "I thought we were heading to the estate."

Katrìn shot him an impish look. "We'll get there. Eventually."

Mars frowned. He disliked unexplained detours—and the potential reasons behind them. Perhaps this was the dòttra's idea, and Katrìn was merely following her wishes.

The carriage pulled to a stop. As Katrìn made to exit, Mars asked, "What is our purpose in coming here?"

She stepped out of the carriage, casting him a smug look over her shoulder. "Your education."

With an annoyed sigh, Mars followed her. Ahead, a paved walkway led toward the Rivna temple, a squat, white-walled building capped with black and gold roof tiles. A white stone statue of the Torvald eagle perched above the entrance. Mars felt his steps grow heavy. As a rule, he avoided Rivna temples. His life as a mercenary meant standing against everything Rivna represented. Rivna said killing was only honorable in matched combat, enemies fighting as equals. To kill a man in the dark, unseen, unprovoked, was shameful, sinful. Rivna said to always tell the truth in both word and spirit, but a mercenary donned disguises and lived their life surrounded by lies. And worst of all, Rivna said that to live and die with honor was all that mattered, but Mars knew money was what really counted.

The hypocrisy of the kith was something he'd lived with his whole life. It was what fueled the only existence he'd ever known—the kith refusing to act dishonorably with one hand, while hiring mercenaries and crime bosses to carry out their dirty work with the other. All with some misguided belief that so long as they themselves weren't wielding the knife, it meant they'd be accepted in Asvaldur when they died. Hardly different from Una, who rested easy with the belief that the work she performed wasn't her or her foxes' responsibility, but that of the kith who'd hired them. *We are the weapon, not the will.* It was a system built on one believing the costs of their actions were not theirs to bear.

And to think there were some who would wonder why Mars thought it was all nonsense.

Inside the temple, the foyer felt like a tomb, with no sign of the clerics who were supposed to attend to it. Statues of nine of the Titans flanked the sanctuary entrance, each standing with head bowed and arms set forth in supplication.

Katrìn approached the statue of Vigny and pulled out a dagger concealed in the folds of her skirt, then placed it on the stone woman's outstretched arms like an offering. "Only holy weapons are allowed inside. Leave yours here."

Mars drew a deep breath. Not only did he not belong here, the last thing he wanted to do was surrender his weapons. But he saw no way to gainsay Katrìn; and besides, he wasn't going to be able to bring his weapons to the Assembly. Surrendering his sword, daggers, and pistol, he chose the statue of Svölnir, lord of the Titans, to hold them. Ragna, the Titan he would've chosen, wasn't an option, not here in a temple of Rivna.

"What now?" Mars asked, straightening his cuffs. At least with his magic he was always armed.

Katrìn turned and headed through the main door into the sanctuary. The room was open and devoid of furniture, the floor a muted gray and the stark white walls unadorned, save for the banner bearing the Torvald coat of arms hanging at the front of the hall. The rising eagle etched upon it clutched a wreath in its talons that read *Honor Above All.*

Mars barely glanced at it, though, his attention drawn to the lone figure kneeling in the center of the sanctuary floor, head bowed and knees slightly spread. He was not surprised by the tableau; from what he knew, most worshippers at a Rivna temple spent their time in meditation. What was unexpected was that this person was clad in ancient armor of a kind Mars had only ever heard described in stories. Made from hundreds of pieces of starsteel sown together like the scales of a fish, the armor covered from head to toe, leaving the person beneath entirely featureless—and utterly protected.

This was a Rivna Knight.

Mars was momentarily frozen. He hadn't known the ancient order still existed. Long ago, before the Cataclysm, the Rivna Knights were the peacekeepers and guardians of justice in Riven. Their primary purpose had been to serve the Consortium, and to ensure no adept ever used their power for self-gain, as Luther the Terrible had when he had appointed himself king of Riven for a time, slaughtering thousands in his conquest. The knights had defeated him, only to fail once and for all when the Cataclysm struck. The knights hunted down adepts in the years that followed; later, when the kiths rose to power, they began to claim adepts as their own, and the order lost its purpose. Now, the memory of the Rivna Knights had faded into story and little else.

Yet here one was, myth made flesh. Or starsteel, rather. The sight of the knight stirred an odd, nameless feeling in Mars's chest, making the skin there feel tight, the muscles contracting.

He drew a breath against the sensation and pulled his gaze from the knight. "What's the meaning of this?"

"A test." Katrìn turned to the wall next to the door they'd entered through and approached a weapons rack that Mars had failed to notice. She selected a practice arming sword and dagger from the rack, both made of polished wood, and held them out to him.

Mars stared at the weapons, dumbfounded. *A test?* This was ridiculous, absurd. He was a fox of the Fortune's Den. "And what if I refuse?" he said.

"You will be beheaded," Katrìn deadpanned.

When Mars didn't move, she gave a light laugh. "I'm kidding. But in all seriousness, you've been hired to keep my mistress safe. We would like to see a demonstration of those skills." She raised an eyebrow at him, a challenge in her voice.

Mars sighed, and let his gaze travel to the silent, kneeling knight. This wasn't a test, but a duel, no different from the one Rafnar had called for. This knight, whoever he was, needed to prove himself Mars's better. *So be it.* Mars had nothing to prove but everything to gain by completing the job.

"Very well." He removed his surcoat and hung it from the weapons rack. Then he rolled up his sleeves, ensured his arm cuffs were tight around his wrists, and returned to Katrìn, accepting the arming sword and dagger at last. "What are the rules?"

"You fight to the yield."

He nodded, a part of him wanting to point out the unfairness of the match, with him in just his shirt and his opponent in full armor. Armor made of starsteel, no less, which would render any magical attack inert—the reason it was used by the order.

Katrìn stepped back, motioning Mars forward. "Prepare."

At her word, the Rivna Knight rose, turning to face him. Like Mars, the knight wielded a wooden arming sword and dagger, both clutched in gauntleted hands.

"Begin," Katrìn called, and the knight charged forward at once.

The sudden movement took Mars by surprise, and he stumbled backward, raising the sword just in time to deflect the blow. "Whoa, friend," Mars said through gritted teeth. "Easy now. It's my first time."

The knight responded to the taunt with another strike, this one a vicious swipe from the left. Mars parried with the dagger, then countered with the sword. The knight deflected with an easy sidestep.

Mars's heart started to race as he and the knight began to spar in earnest, trading blow for blow, counter for counter. The knight was maddeningly fast, despite the weight of the armor, often spinning out of reach with stunning, graceful ease. Yet Mars was taller and his blows more powerful, giving him a chance at keeping up.

As the seconds stretched into minutes without any reprieve, Mars's frustration grew. Sooner or later fatigue would undo him if he didn't find a way to end this. Yet the knight fought with such precise skill that Mars struggled to find any advantage. Until at last, the knight made a mistake, parrying Mars's strike too high and with too little force, allowing Mars to bind the other blade. He slid his sword down the length of the knight's and then, with a vicious twist of his wrist, wrenched the sword free of his opponent's hand.

The knight grunted in shock—or outrage—and in the

next second kicked out at Mars, catching him in the hand with a steel-encased foot. The blow smashed Mars's fingers, breaking his grip on the sword, which clattered to the floor. Hissing, Mars countered with his dagger, but the knight caught it in kind. They began to spar dagger to dagger, but the smaller, weaker weapons weren't designed to withstand such a beating. Mars saw the splintering starting in the shaft of his dagger just as he heard the crack in his opponent's. In seconds, they were weaponless. As before, the knight held the advantage here, thanks to the armor.

The pain in Mars's side grew, expanding outward until it radiated up into his shoulder and down past his hip. He couldn't draw the breath he needed, the stitch preventing him. But neither could he yield. Not here. Not while his client was surely watching. He needed a way to end this. Soon, before the knight managed to land a blow. With the force of that armor, it would be nearly as bad as taking one of Rafnar's punches.

Magic. The thought came to Mars in his desperation. He knew he shouldn't use his abilities; the risk was high, but as his pain intensified to the breaking point, he at last flicked his wrists, drawing a small amount of blood. As always, the Rift answered his call, power flowing into him, but the moment he tried to channel it outward, strengthening his punch with it, he felt the magic press back. He'd forgotten . . .

The knight struck him hard in the chest, and as the starsteel met his magic, it ricocheted, making the punch all the stronger. Mars fell backward from the combined force, his head slamming against the floor. The knight, no doubt thrilled at delivering such a blow, charged forward and placed a boot against his throat. The metal edge pressed heavy against his skin, shutting off the flow of air through his windpipe. Mars raised his hand to the boot, trying to force it away. For a second, he nearly succeeded, but the knight leaned forward, putting more weight into the hold. If he could only use his magic, throwing the knight off would be easy, but Mars knew better than to try again.

"Do you yield?" the knight said, speaking at last. The sound of the voice was not at all what Mars was expecting. It was female. "Do you yield?" the woman said again, and Mars slowly nodded, realization of who this must be dawning in his mind like a cold sunrise.

As the knight retreated, Mars leaped to his feet, grabbing his throat against the first painful breath. Katrìn appeared next to him, but Mars kept his gaze on his opponent, watching with mingled fascination and dread as she removed her helmet at last and long blond hair, pale as spider silk, spilled down.

Her resemblance to her father struck him like a fist to the sternum.

Mars turned to Katrìn, who stood watching him with a hooded gaze, all the impishness she'd shown him earlier gone. "I take it this is Fura Torvald?"

Katrìn nodded. "Indeed."

Mars sighed, understanding at last why he'd been brought here. This wasn't a test at all, and he was damn certain Elìn Torvald had no idea it was happening, either. He wondered briefly if Katrìn and her mistress had been behind Askalon's convenient departure as well. "You expect me, a fox of the Fortune's Den, to quit? Just because Miss Torvald knows how to defend herself?"

Fura spoke, raising her voice to be heard over the distance she'd placed between them. "I wasn't aware that dishonor was a concern for mercenaries."

The disdain in her voice made Mars's skin prickle, although he realized it shouldn't have come as a surprise. Not here, inside a temple of Rivna. Like Una, Fura was clearly a believer in the old ways—the conviction that an oath once made could not be broken, that there was an eternal feasting hall waiting for the dead who kept their vows, all those who fought for what they believed in, who lived and died with honor. The opposite of him.

Shrugging off the sting, Mars gestured about the room. "Was this little demonstration of your skill your idea, then?"

Fura didn't answer. Neither did Katrìn.

Fools, both of you, Mars thought. That was the problem with the old ways, all that honor nonsense. It was a game that only worked if everyone played by the same rules. But in the real world, people made their own rules. The enemies threatening Fura wouldn't come at her head on, shouting their intent in a fair fight. No, they would attack from behind, moving like shadows she would never see coming. Shadows like him.

Even this pathetic attempt to dissuade him from taking the job drove home the truth of her naivete. It would've been more effective to just slit his throat while he slept or slip poison into his cup. But no, someone who fancied themselves a Rivna Knight would never sink to such depravity.

"What shall it be, merc?" Fura said. "I can have you on the next train in an hour."

Mars turned and held the woman's gaze, trying to ignore how striking she was, with features like porcelain and eyes green as poison. A small tattoo of the Torvald feather perched over her left brow, marking her as the kith heir. "And what of my fee? It is considerable, you know."

A muscle ticked in Fura's jaw. "I'll pay you half of what my mother promised your employer."

"And what would your mother think if the person she hired simply left without completing his task?"

"That's no concern of yours," she said, defiantly.

Mars nearly rolled his eyes. Half the fee would be a good purse, but this spoiled rich girl would never have offered it if she understood how contracts like the one between Una and her mother worked. Besides, his reasons for being here had little to do with the money Una was getting for Fura's protection. *It's the formula I'm after,* he reminded himself. Her father's formula. And the only way he was getting that was by following through with the job.

Mars flashed Fura a cold smile as he ran a hand down his braid, rubbing a finger against Una's bond. "Thank you, but no. A merc never agrees to half of what he could potentially be making. That is the measure of my honor."

Fura's cheeks reddened, but she said no more. Mars guessed her precious code of Rivna wouldn't allow it.

SIX

A SHORT WHILE later, they arrived at the estate, and Mars was escorted immediately to his room. He took a slow turn about the place he'd be staying until they set out for the Assembly, marveling at the luxury. The bedroom was many times larger than his entire hideout back in the city. The four-poster bed, big enough to fit six of him, loomed atop a stone dais set in the center of the room. A columned fireplace lined one wall, while on the opposite wall, the balcony doors stood open, letting in a teasing breeze of cool, fragrant air.

So many ways to kill him in here, he realized, wishing for a smaller, more secure room. *Then again*, he thought, as he eyed the palatial private bathing chamber through the open door across the way, *what a way to go.*

"Is the room to your liking, Mr. Karlsvane?" asked the valet who'd escorted him here.

Mars suppressed a laugh and returned to character. "It could use a fountain and a pair of songbirds to go with it."

The valet gave a puzzled frown, his mouth opening to voice a question.

Mars waved him off. "I'm kidding. The room is fine."

"Very good, sir." The man gestured toward the door with a hand clad in a blindingly white glove. "Shall I see to your trunks?"

"No," Mars answered with a reluctant sigh. "I'll take care of them." He wasn't sure whether any of the servants, aside from Katrìn, were aware of who he really was, and he didn't want to explain a case full of small vials of liquid that contained his poisons and antidotes.

"As you wish, sir." The valet arched an eyebrow as a clacking sound issued from the shuttered birdcage set among the trunks. "Pardon me, but wouldn't your falcon be better situated in the mews?"

Mars grimaced. He'd forgotten about the damn thing. "No, I prefer it with me."

The valet's eyebrow lowered. "Very well, then. You're to have dinner with the dòttra in an hour. Please see that you are appropriately dressed." He eyed Mars's clothing, rumpled from his sparring match with Fura.

"I will." Mars waved the man out the door.

Alone at last, he made quick work of emptying his trunks, wincing at the ache in his bruised fingers as he locked the more questionable items inside the wardrobe and stowed the key beneath the mattress. The whole time, the thing in the cage kept making noises that sounded convincingly like a bird. Eager to escape the annoyance of it, Mars tossed off his clothes and headed to the bathing chamber.

When he emerged some time later, draped in a towel and with water still beading his hair, the thing in the cage had grown louder, more insistent. With his agitation rising, Mars proceeded with getting dressed, but in moments had reached his limit. Marching over to the cage, he ripped off the cover and glared down at the thing inside.

"What do you want?"

The magic falcon peered up at him with eyes the color of beeswax. It craned its head to the side, falling silent. Mars waited, unsure what to expect, gooseflesh rippling down his arms. The bird was once dead, but it wasn't like one of Una's ravens. On the surface it looked entirely real and alive, no knobs or metal hinges, and best of all, no stench of rot. It was an artifact, fueled by Rift magic instead of Ice, which meant it wouldn't run out of energy.

Which had its benefits and its drawbacks.

Kack-kack-kack, came the rasping sound once more.

"I said be quiet." Mars snapped his fingers at the bird.

The falcon kacked again.

"Please tell me there's an off switch." Mars leaned closer, silently cursing Una for saddling him with such a burden. The falcon was to be his way to send her updates on his progress. Falconry was a regular pastime among the wealthy elite, making it a convenient disguise. But a damn noisy one at the moment. The bird nipped in his direction, and Mars pulled away.

"What if I order you to be silent? What then?" He brandished a finger at it, racking his brain for the instructions Una had given him concerning the bird. According to her, it could be commanded by its name. Worth a try. "Feykir, I command you to be silent."

The falcon kacked again.

"I mean it, you stupid bird. I'll send you to the mews and leave you there forever." Somebody might notice that his pet falcon didn't eat or shit or do anything remotely normal except make noise, but he was near feeling like it would be worth the risk.

Kack.

A knock sounded on the door, and Mars swore under his breath. He took his time answering it, trying to regain his sense of calm.

Askalon stood in the hallway, his heavy brow furrowed. "Just who are you talking to in there?"

"My bird."

"Your what?"

Mars enjoyed the confused look on the man's face as he motioned to the cage behind him. "My bird."

Askalon stepped into the room, uninvited, and examined the creature with a critical gaze. "It's a fine-looking falcon," he said after a moment. "But why not keep it in the mews?"

Mars shrugged. "Emotional support."

"Right." Askalon gave a derisive snort. "Are you ready to go? Best not to keep the dòttra waiting."

Mars donned his surcoat, then, leaving the foul bird uncovered, followed Askalon out into the hallway. As they walked in silence, Mars focused on the path, committing all he could to memory. He would need to learn his way around here if he hoped to search for the Primer formula. If he could uncover any clues before they even departed for the Assembly, it would only make his job easier. But the estate was enormous, full of long corridors and numerous rooms. His was on the third floor, and as they descended to the second, Mars saw that many of the doors they passed stood open. Beyond each were rooms even more lavishly furnished than the one he'd been given.

Reaching the main floor, they crossed through a vast living hall full of sofas, writing desks, bookcases, and lounge chairs—enough distractions for a dozen people or more—yet it was entirely devoid of inhabitants. There was something dreary about a house filled with all that unused furniture, like a once proud ship left to rot in a harbor.

"Is this place always so quiet?" Mars said.

"It didn't used to be." Askalon slowed and turned back to face a portrait they'd just passed, which hung askew. He quickly straightened it before moving on. "But access to the estate has been restricted ever since the dòttra's husband died."

Since he was assassinated, Mars thought, struck by sudden dizziness, as if the floor had tilted sideways between one step and the next. He should not be here. Una was insane to force him into this situation. He would be found out. He would—

With an effort, Mars halted the train of his thoughts before they derailed him. That was the past, a job completed and nothing more. All that mattered now was this one.

"That reminds me." Askalon halted once again, facing Mars this time. "There are several rules here at the estate, all of which you're to abide by for the duration of your stay." He pointed downward. "You're free to go where you wish on the ground floor and the second. On the third floor, you should stick to your quarters only, and you're to stay off the fourth floor entirely."

Mars glanced at the ceiling. "How many floors are there?"

"Five, if you count the underground floor."

"I see." From what Mars knew of estates, the top floor was reserved for the servants' quarters, not the sort of place guests were likely to go anyway. He didn't know if the rule about the top floor made it more or less suspicious.

"Tell me," Mars said, following Askalon, "how was your visit to the Archive?"

"A waste of time."

Mars started to press him for more but lost his chance as Askalon stopped before a set of double doors and pushed them open, ushering Mars inside.

Mars halted a few steps in, surveying the room and its occupants. His eyes traveled at once to Fura Torvald, standing next to the fireplace on the right-hand wall. No trace of the Rivna Knight armor remained; she was clad in a blue silk bodice with a low-cut neckline and a matching skirt that opened in the front to reveal lacy petticoats of white and sage green billowing out from beneath. Her eyes lit on his, scorn thinly veiled behind her neutral expression.

Ignoring the look, Mars turned his gaze to the person already seated at the head of the long dining table. Elín Torvald looked like an older, grayer version of her daughter. Like Fura, she wore a fitted bodice and open-front skirt, but hers was black silk trimmed in gold fur. She watched him with a cold gaze that reminded him a little too much of the once dead falcon in his room. Above her left eyebrow was a small tattoo of the Torvald eagle, a symbol of her position as head of the kith.

Its faded lines emphasized to Mars just how long this woman had held the rank.

"Madame Torvald," Askalon said, bowing. "May I introduce Halfur Karlsvane."

Elìn rose slowly from her chair, as regal as a queen from her throne. "Welcome, Halfur. My daughter and I are pleased to meet you at last."

Mars pursed his lips, amused at this confirmation of Fura's deception. For half a moment, he considered exposing the little "test" she'd given him, but he resisted. Fura's trust could be an asset in his assignment—as Una had suggested—or, at any rate, there was no advantage to being on her bad side. He strode forward and accepted Elìn's outstretched hand, bowing to kiss it.

"Well met, madame." He stood, releasing her hand, then turned to Fura. "And you as well, Miss Torvald." He bowed, the precision of the gesture that of a proper kithsman.

"Good evening, Mr. Karlsvane," Fura replied. She was a consummate liar as well, it seemed.

Holding back a grin at the irony that a practitioner of Rivna could be so good at deception, Mars placed a hand on his chest. "Please, call me Hal."

She narrowed her gaze at him. "I would prefer to have your real name, sir."

Elìn's voice cut through the room like a knife through tissue paper. "As far as you're concerned, that is his real name, daughter." Elìn sank back into her chair and motioned to Mars. "Please have a seat, Halfur. Dinner is ready to be served."

Mars did as the dòttra bid him. Askalon took the opposite chair while Fura sat down next to him, keeping her distance from Mars. The moment they were settled, the door at the back of the room opened and a line of servants walked in, carrying trays laden with various delicacies of Riven. There was smoked lamb and brined salmon, aged cheeses nested in crowberries, sweet rye bread so dense and dark it was almost black, and rare yrsawine, made from southern vines that only blossomed once every seven years.

Elìn made polite conversation as they selected their choices from the servants' offerings. "How did you find your trip here from the city, Mr. Karlsvane?"

"The train ride was nearly as pleasant as the greeting I received upon arriving," Mars said. He gave Fura a sly glance, hoping their shared secret would create a sense of camaraderie, but her expression remained neutral.

"I'm glad to hear it." Elìn made an odd gesture with her hand, motioning toward the back of the room. The servants reacted at once, the entire lot retreating. "Now," the dòttra said, the cordial facade she'd been wearing falling away, "let's discuss the business at hand."

Mars felt the shift in her tone. Here was a woman in full control of the world she inhabited. She reminded him of Una, but with a sharper edge, one that undoubtedly came from her privileged position as head of a kith.

"I believe you've been given a basic understanding of the purpose behind the contract you've been hired to fulfill," Elìn continued, "but I need you to be aware of the full extent of the danger. Ten months ago, my husband was assassinated."

The taste in his mouth turned sour. Mars picked up his wineglass and took a quick sip. "My employer informed me. I'm sorry for your loss."

The dòttra ignored his perfunctory condolence. "I'm sure she did, but I doubt she was aware of the reason he was targeted."

Mars held his breath, a strange weightless feeling coming over him, as if he were floating outside his body. He cleared his throat, hoping the subject would turn soon. "And what was it?"

"Retribution." The dòttra's fingers clenched and unclenched in an unconscious gesture. "The Skorris were behind it. They believed that we—that is, the Torvalds—were responsible for a tragedy that struck their Ice mine a year ago. They believe *I* am responsible."

Are you? Mars wanted to ask, but didn't. He knew better. Besides, it didn't matter. She was kith and a dòttra, and there was nothing innocent about either. Still, news about a tragedy at an Ice mine, one harmful enough to invoke a need for retribution, alarmed him. Mining Ice wasn't like mining coal or precious gems, where the danger lay in the solidity of the mine shafts. Ice was a thing unto itself, like an ocean. One did not need shafts or any other man-made structures to mine it. Just the opposite. Ice came to you. It grew and kept on growing, no matter how much was taken, which was part of both its value and its insidious nature.

"What sort of tragedy was it?" Mars asked.

"I don't wish to discuss it." Emotion darkened Elìn's voice as she went on. "What matters is that the Skorris will stop at nothing until they have satisfaction. Until they have taken everything that matters most to me."

The sound of her emotion made his stomach clench, the feeling made worse by the raw pain he glimpsed on Fura's face as her mother talked about her father's death. All at once he saw Henrik again—the way his eyes had narrowed when he first spotted Mars, there to kill him, while Orri stalked from another direction. Two assassins sent to ensure the kill. Then Mars remembered the way the man had died, screaming in agony as the Rift magic ripped through him, snapping his bones, contorting his body into a hideous, unnatural state.

"Una assures me you are the best," Elìn said, and the sound of his employer's name pulled Mars out of the grip of his memories. "I'm risking much in trusting that it's true."

Mars nodded, drawing a relieved breath at being back in the present once more. "I am the best."

Fura made a derisive snort at this, and Elìn snapped her head toward her daughter, her gaze cold enough to freeze air. "Don't you dare make light of this, Fura."

"I don't need his help, Mother," Fura said through gritted teeth. "I can take care of myself, as you well—"

"Enough." Elìn slammed her hand against the table hard enough to rock the dishes.

Fura closed her mouth, her teeth clacking as they came together. Mars winced, uncomfortable with the thick tension, made worse by his fear. If they ever found out he was responsible . . .

Elìn returned her attention to Mars. "As I was saying, Fura

is surely a target, and I am relying on you to see that she remains safe through the entire Assembly."

Dozens of questions popped into his mind, none of which he had any business asking, and yet he couldn't help myself. "If you don't mind my asking, wouldn't it be safer for Miss Torvald to simply not attend?"

"Absolutely not," said Fura, eyes darting at him.

"It most certainly would." Elìn sighed, the sound of her exasperation clear. "But Fura is right. It's not really an option. She is of age this year and must be formally acknowledged as my heir, an event which can only occur during the Assembly when all the kith come together. We could delay until next year, but there's significant risk to the process of succession if anything were to happen to me before then."

Mars cocked his head, uncertain about the full extent of kith law. Then again, he didn't spend much time thinking about common laws, either. He only needed to know enough not to break them unless he intended to. "Could someone else be named your heir if that were to happen?"

"There are those who would try. I would prefer not to give them the opportunity."

"I understand, madam." Mars tucked his chin in a faint bow. "I will not fail."

Elìn regarded him coolly. "Success, unfortunately, is not wholly dependent on you. Everyone at the Assembly must believe you are kithborn, or the consequences will be dire. Impersonating a kith is punishable by death, and the Skorris would use just such a discovery to openly attack you—and those with you."

"They would kill your daughter outright?" Mars found this hard to believe. From what he knew of it, kith law wasn't much different from Rivna, honor and justice and all that. Last he checked, murdering a bystander was far from honorable.

"No, not outright." Elìn drummed her fingers on the table, their tips painted gold to match her dress. "But provoked by the outrage of discovering such a deception, there's no telling what might happen or what excuse they might use to harm her."

"This is exactly why we shouldn't bring him." Fura cut a hand toward Mars.

Elìn shook her head. "You cannot have it both ways, Fura. That was the agreement. You either submit to the deception required to ensure your safety, or you do not go."

The latter was clearly not an option. Mars saw the truth clear as glass in Fura's expression. At last, and against her will, it seemed, she gave a nod of consent.

"Very good." Elìn tented her hands in front of her. "This is the reason I summoned you here early, Halfur. I believe it best that you get to know my daughter and our way of life before we leave for the Assembly. I must be absolutely sure you can pull this off." She paused, her eyes on her daughter once more. "Both of you."

Fura nodded again, lips pursed.

"To help facilitate your learning, I have arranged a series of daily activities designed to make you more comfortable posing as a member of our kith, and to allow the two of you the chance to get acquainted with one another." Elìn gestured toward Askalon, who reached into his surcoat and withdrew two pieces of folded paper. He handed one to Mars, the other to Fura.

Mars glanced at the schedule, unsurprised to see the list of activities, all of them common pursuits for the kith. There was dancing, fencing, horse riding, archery, falconry, and so on. All things he could do in his sleep—the ones that really mattered, that is.

Fura's eyes darted down the page. "Is all this really necessary, Mother?"

"Quite." Elìn took a long, satisfied drink of her wine. "Askalon will oversee your progress. You should know, Halfur, that as my truss, there are no secrets I keep from him. When he speaks to you, he speaks for me."

To his credit, Askalon didn't gloat at this. "The name you've been given," he said, "comes from my family. Karl was my older brother, though few remember him. He vanished at sea years ago after a trip abroad. We've spread the rumor that you are his long-lost son, finally returned to Riven."

Karlsvane. Son of Karl. Nephew of the truss? That made Mars practically royalty among the kith. "I'm honored," Mars said, with only a hint of irony.

Askalon bristled, but didn't comment.

Elìn rose from the table, then leaned her hands against it. "Festivale starts in eight days. The celebration will be your proving ground. If the two of you successfully convince our people—both the commoners and the kith who've known you all your life, Fura—that your relationship is real, then we will leave for the Assembly as planned." She paused, fixing Mars and Fura both with a stern look. "Don't disappointment me."

"As you wish, madam." Mars nodded, trying to hide his pleasure at the turn of the events. Surely after so much time with Fura, he would be able to win her confidence and discover the formula.

Then again, the scowl on Fura's face as they parted company a few moments later warned him that a thousand hours spent in her presence might not be enough to get close to her.

Despite the early morning before him, Mars remained awake late into the night. He could've slept—the falcon having finally quieted—but he couldn't make himself lie down. His mind spun with all that had happened; witnessing the emotional aftermath of one of his assassinations had been an uncomfortable experience, one that lingered even now, as Henrik's death played over and over in his mind. What had he gotten himself into? Forget the kith wanting to kill him for being an imposter—the Torvalds would kill him first if they knew the truth.

Don't be foolish, said that voice in his head. *How would they ever know?*

It was true. They couldn't know. Not unless he revealed the truth himself—which he never would.

His mind and body keyed up from the situation, and aware of the short time frame he had, Mars decided to make the most of it with a midnight tour of the estate. While he didn't expect to find anything related to the Primer sitting out in the open, he suspected that a working knowledge of the layout of the massive home could only help him complete his task. He just needed to wait until everyone else was asleep.

Donning his darkest clothing, he headed for the door,

hesitating to make sure all was silent beyond before stepping out. Once satisfied, he left, stepping into a hallway bathed in shadow and strips of moonlight. He flicked his wrists against his cuffs, offering a sacrifice to the Rift. With the magic flowing, he drew the shadows toward him, wrapping them around himself like a cloak. Then he moved down the hallway, confident in his disguise.

But as he rounded the corner to the next hallway, he froze at the sound of footsteps. They were faint, but close. He stared down the corridor, his vision enhanced by the magic still flowing through him. He saw no one, but the footsteps were retreating now, as if the person had just passed him by. Mars followed, determined to find their source, keeping one hand gripped on his sword hilt. Worries of an assassin coming after Fura slid through his mind, her mother's warnings still fresh in his thoughts.

The footsteps led him to the staircase, and to his surprise, the hidden figure began to ascend, up to the forbidden fourth floor. For a second as he followed, Mars spotted something pale and slender on the steps ahead—a slippered foot. Whoever this was, they hadn't come from outside. No assassin would be wearing a bed slipper. And no assassin would be so careless, either. The person made no attempt to soften their footsteps as they hurried their pace.

Mars followed, but at a distance, slowing down as they reached the staircase to the fourth floor. Here the moonlight was twice as bright. He drew the shadows tighter around him, offering the Rift a fresh sacrifice. The moonlight worked in his favor though, its presence doing odd things to the air around the disguised person. It seemed to shimmer and distort, like a reflection on water, and Mars guessed the person was wearing an artifact cloth, not unlike the one Una possessed.

Mars followed as the figure ascended the stairs, which opened into a wide room. As they came to a stop before a set of ornate doors, Mars halted, hand tighter on his sword. The sound of keys jingling echoed down the corridor, and the person let out a soft curse, struggling to see the keyhole in the dark. Then they threw back the hood of the artifact cloak, revealing long, pale hair and a familiar profile.

Mars drew a breath and held it. *Fura Torvald, what are you up to?*

The young woman cast a furtive look over her shoulder, but didn't see him. A moment later, she slipped through the door, locking it behind her.

Mars stepped closer to the door, his mind racing. *And who are you hiding from?*

SEVEN

EVEN THOUGH MARS was eager to learn what was behind that door on the fourth floor, he knew better than to rush in after Fura. No, he needed to get the lay of the land first, have a better understanding of the rhythm of life in the house. Who went where, when, and how often. It would take time and careful observation not to get caught. Fortunately, years of working as a fox had taught him that most vital of skills for a mercenary to possess: patience.

He woke the next morning having slept little, but the intrigue of Fura's midnight escapade brought him fully awake at once. He dressed quickly, then headed down to the dining hall, assuming he would find her breaking her fast, but only Askalon was present.

The truss looked up from his newspaper, the headline on the front page proclaiming in big black letters that the Fifth was on his way to the Assembly. Apparently, he'd been able to raise the funds needed to attend what was ostensibly the most important political event of the year. "Fura is taking her meal in the library. I suggest you join her there. Do you know the way?"

"I think I can manage." Mars remembered spotting it on

the way to dinner the night before. Plucking a pastry off the tray set next to Askalon, he gave a polite bow goodbye, then hurried from the room.

He did indeed find Fura in the library, sitting at a table behind a barricade of books.

"Did you sleep well?" he asked, pulling out the chair next to hers.

By the way she jumped at his voice, he guessed she hadn't heard him come in. She cast him an annoyed look. "Fine, thank you." Then she immediately fixed her attention on the book opened before her once more.

Mars sat down, taking a moment to examine Fura's features more closely. As before he saw hints of her father in her face, especially the green in her eyes. Clearing his throat, he leaned nearer to her. "What are you studying?"

She turned the page, ignoring him at first. "I doubt you would find it interesting."

"Oh, I don't know. I've a curious mind. Besides, we're supposed to be getting to know each other."

A debate waged in her eyes, whether to play along as her mother wished or be true to her Rivna convictions. Finally, she exhaled. "This is a detailed analysis of the growth and decomposition rates of Ice."

"Interesting choice." Mars scratched his chin, then, in a playful voice, added, "I thought kith heirs were supposed to spend their time shopping and going to parties."

Fura rolled her eyes. "Someone spends far too much time reading the scandal sheets."

Mars winced at his failed attempt at teasing. He had completed many a job surrounding the kith, enough to know that such heavy reading wasn't typical of anyone her age, let alone a highborn lady. "So tell me, then. What has drawn your attention to such a lofty topic this lovely morning?"

Sighing, Fura closed the book. "Is this how it's going to be between us?"

Frowning, Mars cocked his head. "How do you mean?"

"You, pretending to care about what interests me, all the while wasting my time with your pestering?"

Mars clenched his fingers, annoyance prickling down his skin. He opened his mouth to try again, determined not to be dissuaded, but Katrìn chose that moment to appear.

"What pestering?" she said, a mischievous grin on her face.

"Alas, it seems I am the pest," Mars replied, making light of the situation. "Simply for asking about her enticing reading choices."

Katrìn set down the tray of tea and cinnamon rolls she'd brought with her. She glanced at the book, then rolled her eyes in much the same manner as her mistress had. "You might as well tell him, Fura. He'll hear about the bill soon enough."

Fura looked ready to argue, but then gave in with another sigh. "Very well. I'm reading up on the growth rate of Ice so I can be fully informed on the subject in order to address my concerns on bill fifty-one to my helmsmen before they vote on it."

She was hoping to influence a vote? Mars supposed it made sense. Once she was formally acknowledged as Elin's heir, the helmsmen representing her farthing would be wise to consider her opinions on proposed laws if they wished to enjoy her patronage in the future. Mars didn't envy any of the Helm. How hard it must be to live as a real-life puppet, with all the dòt-tras and vanes pulling their strings.

"And what is bill fifty-one?" Mars asked.

"Do you remember what I said on the train?" Katrìn asked, helping herself to a roll. "About how we could all be required to start serving additional tours working the mines?"

"I do." This time, he managed not to reflexively touch his fake enneagram brand. He saw that Fura bore one as well, and although hers was undoubtedly legitimate, he knew for certain that she hadn't served her time of tithing. She was in too good of health, for one thing, and given her age, she would've just finished her time in the past few months, if not weeks. For another, she was a highborn kith, which meant she'd surely had a proxy—someone paid to complete the tithe on her behalf.

"It's a bill designed to address the growing rate of Ice," Katrìn went on, as seemly well-informed on the subject as Fura. "The growth is exponential, and there's no way the kith can keep up with mining it based on the current laws."

This time Mars did touch his brand, comforted by the knowledge that his employer knew how to bilk the system, no matter what laws were passed. "That's disturbing news." It was an understatement. As much as he personally never wanted to work the mines, he understood full well the need for it. If the Ice were left to grow and expand at will, unharvested, the result would be another Cataclysm-level event. It must be harvested, or all of Riven would perish.

Mars started to ask how the kith proposed to handle it, but he held back as Askalon appeared.

"Good morning," the truss said, casting Fura a warm smile. "It's time for your dance lesson."

Pursing her lips, Fura nodded, then rose from her chair, leaving the books where they lay. "I'll need a moment to change my shoes. I'll meet you there."

Amused to see she was wearing the same slippers as the night before, Mars bowed, then followed Askalon from the library to the ballroom. The dòttra had spared no expense in their training—a string quintet was already present to provide them music to dance to.

As soon as Fura arrived, Askalon requested a waltz from the ensemble, then urged Fura and Mars to get on with it. Aware of the man's scrutiny, Mars put on his best performance, every movement crisp and precise, with a bit of flair here and there, which he knew would impress an onlooker.

"I'm glad to see you can dance, at least," Askalon said, halfway through the first song.

Mars smiled, choosing to accept the compliment at face value and ignore the implied insult. Yes, he could dance, all right, but he doubted how believable the affection between him and Fura was going to be if they performed this way at Festivale. Fura was so rigid, she felt more like a combatant in a sparring match than his dance partner.

"I will not bite, Miss Torvald," Mars said, growing weary of the tension as the waltz gave way to a slower volta. "Your mother expects us to look like we're enjoying each other's company." He paused as he bent toward her and gripped her waist, then hoisted her into a lift, shifted her body to the side, and gently let her down once more. "Surely, you can't find me so intolerable."

"Do not fret, Mr. Karlsvane," she said, as stiff as ever. "When it comes time to assure my mother, I will play my part."

Mars arched an eyebrow at her, catching her gaze for once. "Please don't be offended by my doubt. It's only that you wear your feelings for me like a signpost hung about your neck."

She started to glare at him, caught herself, then forced a cold smile to her generous lips. "And what do they tell you, Mr. Karlsvane?"

"That you'd rather be doused in honey and chained naked to a hungry bear than dance with the likes of me."

She surprised him by laughing, the sound far warmer than her smile. "You've a way with an image, sir." All at once, she seemed to transform in his arms, her body softening, allowing his body to ease closer to hers as the dance steps demanded. His pulse quickened in response, the scent of her lavender perfume reaching him. Drawing a husky breath, Fura tilted her head close to his, whispering in his ear, "And although it is true that I despise what you are to the very core of my being, I can and will convince my mother otherwise when the time comes."

Her breath warmed his cheek, even as her words sent a spike of ice through his chest. She did indeed despise him, and yet she'd proven her point well—that she was in full control of her considerable charms.

Anger prickled inside him, both at her insult and the surprise she'd given him at her ability to play the seductress. Before he could think better of it, he rose to the challenge, edging even closer to her, daring her to draw away. Let her learn that his charms were considerable, too. "Be careful, little princess. I'm a far more experienced player in this game than you."

With crimson rising in her cheeks, Fura pulled back from him, freeing herself from his arms. "Don't call me princess. Ever." She spun toward Askalon, her skirts whirling about her. "I believe that's enough dancing for the day, truss."

Askalon quickly nodded his consent, despite the half hour remaining in the lesson. Perhaps he feared Fura might stab him in the eye with a hairpin if he dared refuse. She certainly looked ready to stab Mars as she launched another glare at him before stalking off. Mars watched her go, wanting to kick himself for antagonizing her. That was the exact opposite of what he should be doing. Only she made it so difficult. He might have better luck trying to pet a porcupine than winning her trust.

I despise what you are to the very core of my being. Yes, winning her trust would take a damn miracle.

His lack of progress continued as he failed to investigate the fourth floor the next two nights. The first night, he had discovered Fura heading up there once again, and the second night she had brought Katrìn with her, both hidden beneath the artifact cloak. He could disguise himself in shadow to pursue them, yes, but he couldn't walk through doors unseen. He pondered how Fura had even come to possess such an artifact. Although he guessed it had been made by one of Elìn's enthralled adepts, of whom he'd only heard mention and hadn't yet seen, he questioned whether Elìn had knowingly allowed her daughter to have it. If he ever had a child, he certainly wouldn't hand over a tool that made secrecy so easy.

The third night, when he sensed Fura and Katrìn passing by once again, he attempted to wait until they returned—surely they wouldn't spend the whole night up there—but exhaustion claimed him first.

He woke the next morning filled with despair at the prospect of another riding lesson, for the third day in a row, scheduled right after breakfast. The dòttra had scheduled additional lessons when it was discovered that this was one element of feigning highborn status at which Mars didn't excel.

How he hated horses.

It was a hatred he hadn't known he possessed, having had little experience with the beasts, his entire life spent living in the city. The horses in Jakulvik all came harnessed to a carriage or cart, their wild, expressive eyes hidden behind blinders and their wild, unpredictable movements inhibited by long wooden shafts and leather harnesses. They were well-broken, uncomplicated things that seemed hardly different from a train, save for the occasional whicker or random expulsion of steamy, smelly shit.

But the horses here on the Torvald estate were living things, with personalities and opinions of their own. And the only instrument to curtail those often contrary opinions was a pathetic piece of metal in their mouths attached to two thin bits of leather. To say nothing of the tiny little saddle, a mere strip of wood padded by an equally inadequate amount of leather. Everything about riding was backward, too. The only thing to truly hold on to were the stirrups, but last he checked, his feet couldn't grip nearly as well as his hands.

Of course, both Askalon and Fura excelled at riding, and they found Mars's ineptitude endlessly amusing.

"Do try and stay in the saddle," Askalon said as he handed over the reins of Mars's mount, a short, rawboned creature called Pudge. "That is primarily the point of riding, after all."

"Thank you." Mars returned Askalon's smugness with a look of mild relief. "Now, if only Pudge here would see it that same way."

Fura tsked. "Nonsense, Mr. Karlsvane. Pudge was my very first pony when I was a small child. There's no safer or easier mount to be had."

Mars cursed his hasty comment, embarrassed by this fact, although he refused to let it show. He patted the horse's furry neck, feigning affection. "Well, that explains it, then. No doubt he misses you and feels obliged to take it out on his usurper."

Fura snorted in amusement, then turned and climbed onto her mount with effortless ease. Today she wore a red surcoat trimmed in fox fur over a gray bodice, the skirt opened in the front and back to allow her to ride astride. Beneath it, her matching gray riding breeches fit like a well-tailored glove down her long legs. Catching himself staring, Mars glanced away. He and Askalon mounted as well, the latter with the same ease as Fura, while Mars's attempt looked more like someone falling up the stairs.

They headed through the gardens on their way to the open countryside. Mars sat rigid in the saddle, doing his best to protect his tender bits from the horse's jostling movements.

He was fine at the walk and could even handle the canter when it came to it, but the trot was a lesson in torture.

Fura seemed to know it, too, constantly setting a pace that was too fast for old Pudge to match without breaking into a trot every couple of strides. She rode up front, while Askalon rode beside Mars, calling out corrections to his position every other moment.

"Give it a rest, Askalon," Fura said after a while. "It's a beautiful day, and no amount of nagging is going to make a difference. Our guest just needs more time in the saddle."

"I suppose you're right." Closing his eyes, Askalon turned his face up to the bright morning sunshine. "Shall we gallop some, then?"

"Oh, let's," Mars said, making no effort to disguise his sarcasm. Then again, he could handle a gallop, at least until his legs tired from standing in the stirrups while the horse moved beneath him.

Ignoring him, Fura tilted her chin toward Askalon. "First to cross the pond wins?"

"Agreed. Whenever you're ready, lìtja."

Mars noted the man's use of the pet name for Fura—*little love*. In many ways, their relationship struck him as something like a father with his daughter. It was strange witnessing it, as Mars couldn't help thinking about her real father and how Henrik and Fura might've been together.

With a devilish laugh, Fura heeled her mount forward, the sleek bay leaping into a run. There was no need for Mars to do the same, Pudge already having made up his mind to not get left behind by the herd. Mars had learned it was best just to let the horse have his head and do what he may, allowing Mars to focus on keeping his body in a neutral position in relation to the saddle.

The wind beat against his face as he leaned forward, legs and back muscles straining as he fought to stay standing in the stirrups. A thrill rushed through him at the speed, and for a moment he could see why some people found this enjoyable. If only horses could be ridden this fast all the time. But as Fura turned them toward the woods in the distance, Mars knew the fun would soon come to an end. The trail was uneven, full of ditches, fallen logs, and every other manner of pain-causing shifts in the horse's movement. Mars considered slowing down until he caught Fura glancing back at him, a challenge in her gaze. He knew he had no chance of beating her in a race, their mounts far from equal, but he could prove himself capable of keeping up.

Charging through the first line of trees, Mars ducked beneath a canopy of leaves, rough branches scraping through his hair. He was glad Pudge wasn't any taller. The shift in light from the open grounds to the woods left him straining to see while his eyes adjusted. Fura and Askalon were already well ahead, and he could sense Pudge's panic at being last starting to build. Mars braced, focused entirely on keeping the stirrups in place at his feet.

The trail wound to the left, and the other two horses disappeared behind the trees. From what he could remember of the path, they weren't far from the pond, but the trail was short and bendy, a perfect recipe for a fall. Yet somehow, he managed to stay in place this time, the speed perhaps working to his advantage by not allowing him time to overthink things. Pudge blundered through a ditch, which the other two mounts had jumped a moment before. Mars held fast, his fingers wrapped in the horse's mane, the reins all but useless at this point.

The path curved once more, then straightened toward the pond ahead, its glistening water mirror-bright in the sunshine. On the far side of the pond, two dogwood trees stood, bent toward one another strangely, one dotted with budding white flowers, their boughs creating a natural trellis over the trail. Fura was a blur of light as she raced toward the trellis, bent low over her horse's neck, her long hair, golden in the sunshine, fanning out behind her.

Mars felt the trap a moment before Fura passed beneath the trellis, magic itching over his skin. "Stop!" he tried to shout, but his voice was drowned out by an explosion.

White light burst over the pond and through the clearing, blinding him. Pudge let out a shrill scream as he slammed to a halt, then spun on his haunches, flinging Mars from the saddle as easily as a stone from a catapult. Mars landed hard, his head and neck ramming the ground, the blow knocking him senseless for a moment.

When he came to, the white light was already fading, leaving behind thick smoke that clouded the air. It burned his eyes and throat and made his skin crawl. More magic, but not the wild, flowing power of the Rift. No, this was Ice. And in a vaporous state like this, it could very well be poisonous. He needed to get away from it, but he had no idea where Fura and Askalon were.

Clambering to his feet, Mars drew his sword and pistol

both, flicking his wrists against the blades in his cuffs, the sacrifice ready. Through the smoke he heard Askalon shouting for Fura. The stupid fool. Shouting would only have him caught all the quicker by their unknown assailants. Mars scanned the smoke for them, to no avail.

Frustration surged inside him. *I need to see.*

At once, magic burned through his hands and up his arms in answer. He hadn't called for it on purpose, but with the blood already given, the magic proved eager. Returning his pistol to its holster, Mars held out his left hand before him, magic flowing through his palm and fingertips. Wherever he pointed, he could see the outlines of shapes through the smoke. A tree here, some bushes, the edge of the pond.

There, ahead, he spotted Askalon, rushing blindly through the smoke. The truss didn't see the figure lying in wait for him, a club at the ready. The figure swung before Mars could call a warning, the blow landing across Askalon's neck and shoulders. He fell with a heavy thud and did not rise.

He wasn't dead, though. The assailant hadn't struck to kill, only to incapacitate. Mars crept forward, guessing there were at least two assailants, possibly more. The figure that had struck Askalon had been wearing goggles, no doubt infused with Ice to allow him to see through the smoke.

Mars moved to the side of the trail, taking cover behind the trees as he searched for Fura. He moved as quickly as he dared. She was surely the target, and the thought of her being assassinated right here, within his reach, made his heart race. He had to stop it. Now. Fura was a fierce fighter, but that wouldn't matter if she'd been knocked out by the initial blast, or by the effects of the Ice vapor. If they were here to kill her, the job would be a simple one.

Mars soon spotted the two assailants through the smoke. They were gathered around Fura, binding her hands and feet. *A kidnapping?* He couldn't make sense of it, but it didn't matter. They couldn't get away with it.

"Hurry, there's no telling how long her companion will be down," one of the assailants said.

Good, Mars thought. They didn't know he was here. It had paid to be on the slow, old horse.

With the smoke already starting to dissipate, he drew his pistol and stepped into view. "Let her go."

Both men jumped in surprise, one of them stumbling backward so hard he almost fell. Righting himself, he raised his hands in surrender. His companion, less fazed, raised his hands more slowly, then threw something at Mars, a small, glowing object. Mars shielded his face on instinct and the object struck the back of his hands, exploding in another release of blinding white light and smoke. Startled, Mars's finger tightened on the trigger of his pistol, discharging the single shot in the gun up into the trees.

Tossing the useless weapon aside, Mars spun, slashing through the air with his sword in case either of the men had dared to get close. The blade met flesh, and someone screamed. Mars raised his left hand, calling on the magic to let him see once more. One of the men had fallen, a gash to his neck, blood spurting like a geyser from the artery. A lucky swing, one that had possibly saved Mars's life.

Moving his left hand about him, Mars searched for the

other assailant—the one who'd thrown the Ice-fueled smoke bomb—knowing the man was still there.

"Give up now," Mars said, "and I'll see you're treated fairly." It was a lie. All he intended to do was interrogate the man for every bit of information he could squeeze out of him—none of this made sense. Kidnapping Fura had nothing to do with retribution.

But it might have everything to do with the formula.

There was no response, and no sign of the assailant, either. Behind him, he heard Fura groan, coming around.

"Your friend is already dead." Mars turned a slow circle, searching for the man through the smoke.

A branch snapped somewhere to his right, and he pivoted, just making out the shape of the assailant hunched among the bushes.

"Surrender now, and you will be spared the same fate," Mars said, peering straight toward him.

The man slowly backed away, his steps careful but uncertain. He couldn't know Mars was using Rift magic to see through the lingering smoke.

Mars took a step toward the man, determined to find his answers, but he had other ideas. He retreated at once, but called out a warning before he fled. "Tell Miss Torvald that the Wake is watching. She must hand over her father's secret to us—or die."

And with that, the man vanished into the trees.

EIGHT

ONE UNEXPECTED BOON of surviving an assault and near kidnapping was getting the afternoon off from lessons. Mars made the most of it, starting with a long soak in the boat-size tub in his bathing chamber, followed by a long nap, lying naked on the bed with the balcony doors thrown open to the ever-present breeze. He'd earned the respite. Not only had he saved Fura from abduction, he'd also endured the lengthy interrogation by her mother that had followed.

He'd given Elìn a simplified version of the story: there had been two attackers, one now dead and one escaped—and nothing else. He did not mention that the escaped assailant was part of the Wake, nor the man's threat. Mars had learned long ago that information was currency, and he chose never to spend any he didn't have to. For all Elìn knew, the men were there to kill Fura, not kidnap her. If Elìn knew about the Primer, whatever it was, surely Henrik would've sent the formula to her, not Fura. Which raised another question—why *had* he given it to his daughter and not his wife?

And why was the Wake after it? There'd been nothing on the dead man to identify where he came from or who had sent him. No kith marks, no mercenary tattoos, and nothing to indicate the Wake, either. Not that Mars knew how to identify a member of the Wake, exactly, as the underground group no doubt intended to protect themselves from the law and the kith. The Wake was a secret society nearly as old as the Ice mines themselves. They sought a single objective—to end the kith's power over Riven. Yet the most they ever managed to do was wreak havoc on the daily lives of Riven's citizens through their random acts of protest and occasional destruction of property. In recent memory, they'd claimed responsibility for derailing a freight train full of cargo owned by the Krog Kith, destined to be sold in Jakulvik. The act had no doubt irritated the Krogs and possibly put a small dent in their fortune, but the real losers were the people of Jakulvik who'd needed the furs, salted meats, and lumber the train carried to get through a long winter. The Wake rarely, if ever, hurt the kiths where it counted.

Their interest in Henrik's formula, though, was telling. Mars had already suspected that the Primer had something to do with the kith's delicate balance of power—this much was obvious from the value of the contract—and the Wake's desire for it seemed to indicate they were onto something bigger this time. But what? If only Una had told him what the Primer was for, he might have been able to anticipate these enemies a little better. He knew not to bother asking. Even if she did know what it was, she wouldn't disclose anything more than she already had.

Not about the formula, at least. But she might let something else slip.

Rising from his nap, he sat down at the writing desk to

begin the arduous task of composing a message to Una, one that wouldn't give him away if it were intercepted. That part was easy enough. The foxes had a shorthand language to convey such messages in few words and with certainty that they wouldn't be understood by anyone else. No, the hard part was the wretched falcon. The bird had been mostly quiet, as far as Mars knew, at least in the few hours he was allowed in his room, but he didn't savor the idea of handling it. Approaching the cage, he kept waiting for the once dead falcon to make a fuss. But it only watched him with its glassy eyes, as still and silent as a corpse.

"Do you have to be so creepy?" Gritting his teeth, Mars opened the cage door. The falcon raised its foot, the quick motion making Mars flinch. With a muttered curse, he slid the tube with the rolled-up message inside the harness, trying his best not to touch the bird itself. Once done, he said in a firm voice, "Feykir, I command you to deliver this to Una and no one else." Then he flung the cage door wide open and stepped out of the way.

For a moment, the bird only stared, lifeless. Then, with a loud shriek, it launched itself from the cage, flew across the room, and disappeared through the open balcony door.

Relieved to have that over with and half hopeful the awful thing would get snatched up by an eagle, Mars turned to the next order of business: getting into the room on the fourth floor. Tonight would surely be the best opportunity. Although Fura would recover just fine from her injuries, the dòttra had reacted like her daughter was a porcelain doll on the verge of shattering—she had ordered servants to watch over her at all times and had posted half a dozen guards outside her room. He imagined Askalon would be patrolling the hallway as well. Fura wouldn't be partaking in any midnight excursions this night.

Even so, Mars waited until well past midnight before leaving his room. Fortunately, after his long nap, staying awake proved easy. Cloaking himself in shadow once more, magic pulsing in his veins, he moved slowly down the corridor toward the stairway.

Luck remained with him, and he climbed the stairs and reached the room without encountering anyone. Raising his hand, he channeled a trickle of magic through the door—just enough to unlock it. The lock gave way at once, and he slipped inside, closing the door silently behind him.

Moonlight filled the vast chamber beyond, streaming down through the domed glass ceiling. A canopy of stars stretched overhead, the sky that cradled them a deep, liquid blue. The far wall was sheer glass as well, giving full view of the grounds and even farther, to the valley below, where the city lights were like a reflection of the night sky. Mars drew a breath in wonder at the sight. He hadn't known there was an observatory on the estate. Then, looking closer, he noticed the slight metallic-blue glow of the windowpanes and realized he hadn't missed anything in his initial appraisal of the estate's exterior: the entire room was a giant artifact, the magic disguising its existence from the outside.

True to the room's purpose, a massive telescope occupied the center of the floor. A long, spiraling staircase wrapped around its base led up to the observation platform, the steps wide and inviting. Mars had half a mind to trot up there and check out the view, but good sense held him back. The information he needed wouldn't be found among the stars.

Turning slowly, he took in the rest of the room. To the right was a workshop area that reminded him of the one in Una's Lair where Gellir worked. Beyond that were a reading chair and a writing desk cluttered with opened books. More books lined most of the back wall, in row upon rows of shelves, unbroken except for the occasional space made for a painting to hang. The nearest portrait drew his eye, and Mars moved closer for a better look. It depicted a young girl in pigtails, the braids tied with green ribbon, the same shade as the girl's eyes. The sight of Fura as a child took him off guard. Guileless eyes watched him from a warm, round-cheeked face, no hint of the enigma she would become—a kith princess evidently more interested in politics than parties, who spent her spare time training as a Rivna Knight and wandering dark corridors in secret.

Mars walked down the row of books to the next painting, another portrait of Fura, slightly older than in the first. In moments, he realized that all the paintings were of her, a veritable timeline of her life stretching between the bookshelves. A sinking suspicion of just who this observatory belonged to rose in Mars, the suspicion confirmed when he reached the last portrait in the line. It was of Fura again, but this time, she hadn't been painted on her own. A man with steel-threaded hair and hooded green eyes stood next to her. Neither of them was smiling, exactly, yet the man's joy shone as clearly as the moon above, bright and ephemeral. It was painful to see, especially as another image superimposed itself over the one before Mars: the man a few years older and with all the joy, all the life, gone from his face as he lay dying from the wounds Mars had inflicted upon him.

We are the weapon, not the will.

Mars turned his back on the portrait as well as the memory. So this was Henrik Torvald's office, or laboratory. He wondered if the man had built the observatory himself, or if he'd allowed one of the Torvalds' enthralled adepts to do it for him. It was troubling to think that Henrik had been powerful and clever enough to hide his magic from the dòttra—for surely she would never have tolerated letting an adept run loose in her household, let alone married one.

Mars had met Elìn's adepts the day before, when the dòttra had summoned him to their workshop so he could be measured for a special outfit Elìn planned for him to wear during Fura's proclamation-as-heir ceremony. The adepts were close enough in appearance that they could've been siblings, although they weren't. One was female and one male, but both were so thin and shapeless, they appeared androgynous. To Mars's surprise, neither was outwardly maimed or scarred. If it weren't for the starsteel hobbles encasing their hands, he wouldn't have known they were adepts. Yet one glance at their empty eyes and faraway expressions told him something horrible had been done to them.

"Surprising, aren't they?" Elìn had said, a smug smile perched on her lips. "I prefer my adepts docile and willing."

Mars had nodded. They were surprising. Unsettling in their lifelessness.

"Would you like to know how I do it?"

Mars didn't answer, but Elìn hadn't needed one. She reached into a pocket and withdrew a small glass vial full of a glistening powdery gray substance that he recognized at once.

"Dust?" It wasn't a question, but shock.

Elìn nodded as she approached the female adept, uncorking the vial. "I've found that honey is more effective than vinegar."

With the promise of dust at hand, the female adept suddenly came to life, her eyes widening and a strange, mewling sound gurgling up in her throat. She tilted her head back at once, mouth opened and pale, her pink tongue eagerly sliding over her cracked lips.

Mars's stomach clenched in horror as Elìn tilted the vial over the adept's mouth and tapped it once, just enough to send a small measure of the powder tumbling out. The girl's jaws snapped shut greedily, entrapping the dust.

"Don't you worry that it's killing them?" Mars asked, his voice breathy with disgust.

"All things die," Elìn said, shrugging. "All that matters is how much of a purpose they serve while still alive."

The coldness of the dòttra's reply chilled Mars even now, and he shoved the memory away, wishing he could purge it from his mind forever.

He forced his thoughts onto the task at hand, trying to figure out why Fura was spending her nights here, and if it might have something to do with the Primer.

He headed to the desk. Of all the areas, it looked the most recently used, covered in books and papers and various scientific instruments. He could easily picture Henrik once having sat there. Even in the brief time Mars had observed the man before that final confrontation, there'd been something studious about him.

Sitting behind the desk, Mars pulled the first open book toward him. It wasn't printed, but handwritten, full of Henrik Torvald's messy scribbling. A journal of some sort? The writing continued on the next page, only this section included scientific formulas, advanced mathematics, and sketches of odd objects. Touching his finger to the artifact tattoo over his brow, Mars studied the formula and its strange weblike image for a few moments, then searched for a matching image in the journal. He found nothing, not a single trace of it anywhere.

He pulled the chain on the lamp on the desk, the Ice inside it activating and providing the light he needed to study the writing more carefully, trying to decipher what it was describing. Even if the formula he was after wasn't here, the pages could hold some clue about the Primer. Only, he couldn't make sense of any of it. He could read the words well enough, most of them, anyhow, but he couldn't begin to grasp their meaning. The writing went on at length with peculiar topic headings such as "The Transference of Energy," "Blended Inheritance," and "Selective Emergence." Might as well have been a foreign language.

Annoyed, Mars pushed the tome aside and reached for the next one. It proved equally baffling. He wondered if its contents made sense to Fura. Not that it would do him any good, given her feelings for him. Besides, she was already enough of a challenge, even without considering that she might have been a scientific genius like her father apparently had been.

Sighing in defeat, Mars leaned back in the chair, his gaze drifting once again to the wall of books and the portraits between them. Those pictures revealed far more to Mars about the man than the journals did. For one thing, there were no depictions of Elìn. In fact, nothing in the room bore the dòttra's touch. It was clear that the dead man was fonder of his daughter than of anyone else in his life. He supposed that explained why Henrik had left the formula for Fura.

Even stranger was the notion that perhaps Fura knew her father had been a secret adept. Mars didn't see how they could've been so close without her knowing. He wondered if Henrik's ability had anything to do with the Primer. Rift magic was powerful, limited only by how much blood the adept was willing to shed.

He turned his gaze to the most recent portrait. It couldn't have been painted all that long ago, and yet Fura seemed much, much younger in it. No, that wasn't right, exactly. She looked nearly the same as she did now, only the painted Fura was warm and open. *Innocent.* It wasn't hard to guess the reason for the change in her, if she had felt as strongly for her father as he had for her. His death had affected her, changed her, *hurt her.*

And you did it, that ever-present voice spoke in his mind. *You killed him. Just as you killed Orri.*

Around Mars, the once lovely room became a haunted place, the tomb of a dead man. A sudden urge to flee came over him, and he reached for the lamp—

Only to freeze at the sound of the door unlocking. *Shit.*

He extinguished the Ice lamp too late, the flash giving

him away as the door opened and a cloaked figure slid quickly inside.

"Who is in here?" an icy voice demanded from the doorway.

Mars silently cursed. There was nowhere to hide in the wide expanse of the room, the moonlight stretching to every corner except where he stood next to the desk. He could summon shadows, but his movement might be noticeable if he tried passing through the moonlight. Shadows weren't supposed to move by themselves, after all.

"Show yourself." A hiss of metal cut through the air, the sound of a blade being drawn.

Bracing himself, Mars flipped on the lamp once more, making Fura jump in the sudden brightness. She'd removed the hood of her cloak. "Rather brave of you, Miss Torvald, confronting an intruder on your own in the dead of night."

Fura had startled at the sight of Mars, but she recovered quickly. "I don't need anyone to protect me from you. Or don't you remember our confrontation the day of your arrival?"

Mars arched an eyebrow, then lowered it. "Like you didn't need anyone to help you today?"

The question had the desired effect, her defensive posture easing slightly. Like it or not, he had saved her. Not that he was looking for gratitude. He simply wanted her to know that he knew the truth: of course she was on her own, because she wasn't supposed to be here, either.

"Yes, well, thank you for that." Fura touched a hand to the back of her neck where the assailants had struck her. Such a blow would've kept most people in bed for days afterward.

Lucky for Fura, her mother's docile, well-heeled adepts had tended her. Healing was just one of many tasks adepts performed for their masters; Rift magic was as versatile as it was powerful. Mars had never tried healing anyone himself, though. He was in the business of inflicting harm, not undoing it.

Fura drew aside her cloak to sheath the knife she'd drawn, and Mars glimpsed the pale, shimmery nightgown she wore beneath. Pulling the cloak closed once more, she faced him, her cold eyes boring into his. "What do you think you're doing here?"

"What I've been hired to do—keep you safe." He stepped around the desk and moved to its front. Fura drew closer as well, ensuring they could talk without shouting. "Your mother wished me to keep a watchful eye on the house and grounds for any further attacks." It was a thin lie, but he believed he could stretch it enough to cover himself.

Fura made a disgusted face. "She's overreacting. I'm daughter of the Torvald dòttra. There's been a threat on my life since the day I was born. The first time someone tried to kidnap me, I was six years old. The man made it all the way to the border between our territory and the Jens's before he was stopped."

Mars frowned. "I thought kith law says no heir not yet of age can be harmed by another kith. To do so would be a great dishonor."

A smug expression rose on Fura's face as she pursed her lips. "The men who did were not kith or followers of Rivna. Kith law doesn't protect us against those who don't respect it."

Mars caught her insinuation easily. He folded his arms over his chest. "Mercenaries, you mean." He returned her smug look with one of his own. "The thing about mercenaries, Miss Torvald, is that someone hires them. You do realize that this whole charade, *Rivna*, is the very thing that keeps people like me in business."

"Charade?" She arched an eyebrow, and a small, incredulous laugh escaped her throat.

"We are the weapon, not the will," Mars said through gritted teeth.

"Excuse me?"

He sighed, drumming his fingers against his arm. "We might be the ones doing the dirty work, but it's your people we're doing it for. I believe that's the definition of hypocrisy."

Fura bristled, her hands stretching down to her sides as if she wanted to draw her weapon again. "Dirty work, you call it? I was held captive by a stranger for three days at six years old. That's not dirty. It's inexcusable."

Glancing at the man in the portrait with Fura, Mars wondered how Henrik had reacted to that situation. He must've been beside himself.

Mars pushed the unhelpful speculation from his mind. Kidnapping contracts were routine in the Den, and often included a lucrative payout and little mess. He'd never turned one down. Then again, none of his targets had ever been children.

But would that have stopped him?

He shrugged. "And yet one of your fellow kiths decided to circumvent the sticky honor code of Rivna by hiring a merc to do the dishonorable action for them."

Fura swallowed, the cords in her slender neck flexing visibly. "Why do you do it?" The question came out breathless.

Because it's who I am. A mix of anger and shame stole over Mars at the voice in his head, a flush burning up his throat. "For the money, what else," was what he said, his words sharp as a lightning crack. "Not all of us are born into fortune. Some of us spent our childhood sleeping on the streets, not inside a gilded cradle."

Fura shook her head, oblivious to the scorn in his words—as well as the truth of them. "But how can you do such things? Even for money? To steal babies, prey on the innocent, kill someone when their back is turned, when they are defenseless? I'm not going to pretend that I love everything my mother and her rivals do, how things work in Riven—" She paused for a moment, like she was going to say more but reconsidered. She shook her head. "But it sounds to me like they're not the only ones lying to themselves about their responsibility for the terrible things that happen here."

Mars swallowed, bile burning the back of his throat. He did not reply, knowing that any explanation would be lost on her. Such a girl, coddled all her life, couldn't begin to understand the desperation of want. Of need.

Fura shook her head again, the moment of honesty vanishing. Her expression hardened. "None of this matters. I ask you again, Mr. Karlsvane, what are you really doing in here? No matter what my mother asked of you, I know she wouldn't send you snooping about our house on your own in the middle of the night."

Mars straightened from his slouched position on the

desk. "I've been hired to protect you, regardless of whether or not you believe you need it. To do that I need to know all I can about those who would do you harm."

"And you thought to find it here?"

"This room belonged to your father, did it not?"

Fura drew a sharp breath, her nostrils flaring. "I hardly see how that matters."

Mars glanced away from her toward the man in the portrait. "I was looking for confirmation that he was killed for the reasons your mother believes." Mars hesitated, uncertain of his voice. He never used to have a problem lying. He took a breath and forced his gaze back to Fura. "If he were killed for any other reason, that might play a part in how I keep you safe in the coming weeks." Not entirely a lie, but he wanted to raise doubt in her mind, give her reason to trust him.

Tears stood out in Fura's eyes as she raised her hand to the compass rose pendant she wore around her neck. He'd never seen her without it. She drew a deep breath, keeping her voice free of the emotion so clear on her face. "You are mistaken. There are no secrets to be found here."

Mars debated asking about the Wake, but couldn't without revealing what he'd learned during the assault. He wasn't sure he was ready to take that gamble yet, not when she was so suspicious of him, so distrusting.

"Now, please, get out before I tell my mother what you've been up to," Fura said, her disdain for him like a shield over her grief. "I doubt she would be pleased by your deceptions."

Mars bowed his head. "As you wish." He moved to the door, and Fura stepped far to the side, allowing him plenty of room to pass, as if he were a leper she feared would spread his sickness to her.

Out in the darkened corridor, Mars drew a deep breath, trying to banish the volatile feelings churning in his chest. He felt tipped over and spun about. He wanted to call it quits, to board the nearest train and never return. But that wasn't an option. He needed to complete this contract. He needed to find the formula for the Primer, and with it, a way to buy his freedom from Una.

There are no secrets to be found here, Fura had said. Only, she was lying. She possessed the secret he needed—and he would find it. For Fura was right about him. He was a mercenary, paid to do these things, and he refused to let guilt stand in the way of completing the job and collecting what was due him. And like all good spies, whenever he encountered a stone wall like Fura, he would simply find another way round.

NINE

━┼┼━

OVER THE NEXT few days, the tension between Mars and Fura grew and festered. Although Fura remained civil toward him—especially whenever Askalon was watching, or on those rare occasions when they dined with Elìn—her animosity lingered beneath the surface, hiding behind every too-polite word.

For his part, Mars was lying low, giving her space in the hopes that the tension would dissipate. He'd given up trying to win her confidence, at least for the time being. At present he would settle for he and Fura proving themselves to Elìn's satisfaction during Festivale. Then he'd have the rest of the Assembly to either get Fura to reveal her secrets to him—or to uncover them himself.

To that end, he spent as much time as he could turning over every rock around the estate. He returned to the observatory twice more—avoiding detection by Fura both times—to examine the remaining books, but he didn't find the Primer symbol anywhere. Next, he searched Fura's rooms—and Katrìn's, which were connected to Fura's—but again found nothing. From the beginning, he'd hoped to lay claim to the formula before traveling to Hàr Halda, as trying to find out what Fura knew about the formula or had in her possession while also trying to protect her during the Assembly would only make both jobs that much more difficult.

With only three days left before they departed, Mars woke to the unpleasant sound of a bird tapping on his window.

"For the love of the nine, you've got to be kidding me." He rolled over, glaring at the window across from the bed and cursing his luck. A storm had moved in during the night, the force of it strong enough that he'd shut the balcony door. It figured that Una's foul falcon would return this morning. And early, too, dawn not yet a promise on the horizon.

Muttering a curse, Mars crawled from the bed and shuffled toward the balcony. Feykir flew through the door the moment he opened it, kacking loud enough to make Mars's head rattle. It didn't help that he'd only gone to bed a few short hours before, after another fruitless search of the estate. And what little sleep he had gotten hadn't been restful, his mind plagued with worries about Festivale, which started today.

Sighing, Mars left the balcony door open and walked over to Feykir's cage. The falcon held out its leg with the tube fastened to it. Mars made quick work of removing the tube and locking the bird inside the cage.

The scroll stuffed into the tube was short and to the point. Una started off her encoded message by relaying that the Wake's interest in the formula didn't surprise her. She was intrigued that they had been able to work their way through the Torvalds' border patrols, but she felt they were ultimately of no consequence. The Wake could sometimes be dangerous, but were too underfunded and disorganized to be much of a threat, particularly once the Torvalds reached the Assembly, which the Wake had little hope of infiltrating.

Mars hoped she was right, but he doubted it. The assailant who had threatened Fura hadn't seemed like a man easily dissuaded.

Una ended the letter by telling him it was best to focus his energy on finding the formula—the sooner he did that, the less he had to be concerned about the threats against Fura Torvald's life.

"So predictable," Mars said as he crumpled the scroll. Una's reputation would take a hit if word got out that one of her foxes had failed to protect his charge, but it would be a small price when weighed against what she apparently expected to get paid for the Primer. That said, the message hadn't been entirely useless. If the Wake's interest in the Primer came as no surprise to Una, that meant it likely posed a threat to the kith in some way. It wasn't much of a clue to finding the formula, but it confirmed his suspicions at least.

He debated going back to sleep, but soon thought better of it. Today was a busy day—he would be accompanying Fura as she visited the nearby city, the first time Mars would be leaving the estate since arriving. He was looking forward to it, despite the contingent of guards who would surely shadow their every step. At least being out in public meant he probably wouldn't have to worry about another attempt to kidnap Fura—he doubted the Wake would be foolish enough to waste resources on something so sure to fail. Instead, he could focus all his efforts on trying to get Fura to stop acting like she was walking through a nest of vipers every time she was near him. She had as much reason to accept his presence as he did hers—as far as she knew, anyway—but that wasn't enough to count on to keep himself close to her long enough to find the formula.

"The real job is never what you expect when it begins," he muttered, and stumbled into the bathing chamber to start getting ready. Distantly, Feykir kacked as if in agreement.

Later that morning, Mars, Fura, and Katrìn climbed into the carriage to take them down the big hill into the city of Valdri. Mars sat across from the women, the three of them passing the journey in mutual silence. They'd spent enough time together these past few days to have worn out all the usual small talk, and neither Fura nor Katrìn were interested in discussing anything more substantial than the weather—warm and getting warmer, at least for Riven. As a result, both women had donned dresses with short, puffed sleeves that left most of their arms bare. Mars could hardly keep himself from sneaking glances at Fura's arms, long and curved with muscle.

During the long ride down the hill, Mars gazed out the window, admiring the view of the city. With Festivale starting, the streets seemed to writhe with people, like a giant, colorful snake threaded through the city. He couldn't wait to be down in the throng, brushing shoulders, wending past stragglers, and waving off hawkers crying out from behind their booths. He knew better than to expect that he'd be able to enjoy himself in the city, but it was a blessing nonetheless to be spending a few hours here. Country life didn't suit him.

"So tell me, what events are on the schedule for today?" Mars slid his gaze between his two companions.

Fura turned her head toward the window, still not interested in talking to him, but Katrìn reached into the side pocket of her skirt and withdrew a small card. She frowned down at it a moment, the gesture causing the burn scar on her face to pucker. "We're due at the orphanage first, then a quick stop at the Ice mine. After that, we have a few hours free before the tournament finals. We finish the night on the lawn for the Felling." Katrìn looked up, a pert smile on her face and a wink in her gaze. "Fura will be Light Maiden this year."

Mars arched an eyebrow in Fura's direction, but she kept her gaze trained on the window. "That's quite the honor." In the Fellings Mars had attended, the duty of first lighting was always given to the fairest maiden at Festivale. Superstition held that once the Light Maiden lit the fire, she was fated to meet her true love before the next year had passed. He imagined Fura wasn't keen on the notion.

Katrìn cleared her throat, tucking her amusement back where it had come from. "Askalon will be competing in the tournament. He made it into the dueling finals."

"Great for him." Mars smiled, pleased at the prospect of being out of Askalon's smug, watchful gaze for the day. That might even make things easier. "I neglected to mention it earlier, Miss Torvald, but you look lovely today." The compliment came out less smoothly than he intended, probably because he really meant it.

Fura pulled her gaze from the window and offered him a quick smile, though one that was impossible for him to read. "Thank you."

It was a small thing, but he counted it a win.

The orphanage was a long, squat building on the north side of Valdri. Surrounded by taller buildings on all sides, it seemed as dull and dreary as Mars had always imagined such a place would be. Despite being an orphan himself, he'd never been near an orphanage before. His first few years on the streets, he'd lived in perpetual fear of being picked up by the city watch and thrown into the orphanage, rumored to be little more than a prison for children where they served rats for dinner and doled out lashes liberally. Once he was older, Mars chalked these tales up to exaggeration, but gazing at the Valdri orphanage now, he had his doubts.

The headmistress, a bony old woman with gray hair like steel wool, was waiting on the front steps for them, flanked by who Mars guessed were two of the older girls from the orphanage. Both were wan and as bony as their mistress. The smiles they offered in welcome to the dòttra's daughter looked ragged around the edges and thin in the middle.

Fura, for her part, smiled warmly back at them. During the time he had known her, she had been cold and distant, a woman resigned to her duty as a kith's heir. But now she grew animated as she carefully listened to the headmistress describe the workings of the orphanage, pointing out to Fura updates to the dormitories, the playground, and the infirmary with something like pride in her voice.

Mars trailed toward the back of the group, watching Fura from afar and wondering at the change in her. This was not a place for happiness. But by the time they had settled down in one of the classrooms, she had become a different person altogether, each word light and every gesture unplanned.

A gaggle of little children, ranging in age from three to eleven, were ushered in by the orphanage attendants and seated around Fura to listen to her read from a book of Rivna myths. Again, Mars kept his distance, listening, amused despite himself, as Fura entertained the children. And entertain them she did, her face forming expressions he'd never seen before, each word she spoke filled with wonder or anger or fear or curiosity—whatever the story called for. The children were enraptured.

With each passing moment, though, Mars grew less enchanted, as he recalled the opulent wealth he'd been surrounded by these past few weeks and how this place paled in comparison. He couldn't help but pity the children, with their large, eager eyes and hopeful faces, completely unaware of the life they'd be living in a few short years. They were orphans; soon, they'd be out on the streets, making money any way they could, with no hope of living in the sort of comfort and safety enjoyed by the people who watched over them from up on the distant hill miles away. Mars knew the hard, cold life they had to look forward to; he'd lived it. He shook his head, a mix of sadness and frustration roiling inside him.

Toward the end of the story, the attention of one of the younger children began to wander, and the little girl, probably no older than three, padded over to Mars and demanded to be picked up. He smiled awkwardly down at the girl, trying in vain to dissuade her. Seated next to him, Katrìn stifled a giggle, but she made no move to help as the girl balled her little fists in his shirt and hauled herself up into his lap. Fortunately, one of the attendants rescued him after a moment. Mars thanked the woman and tried to brush the incident off, but it was easier said than done when he realized the little girl had left some sticky residue on his shirt.

"My goodness, Mr. Karlsvane," Fura said to him afterward. "You looked close to fainting when that small child accosted you."

He nodded, not bothering to deny it. "I know of no creature more intimidating."

Fura gave him an odd look at this, but she said no more.

They ended their visit in the headmistress's office, where Fura, on her mother's behalf, made a generous donation to the continued care of the orphans.

Then they departed for the short ride to the city's outskirts—and the Ice mine.

Mars's discomfort in visiting the orphanage paled next to his dread of this place. His skin was crawling with the foul magic leaking from the fortress long before the carriage dropped them off at the thick iron gates barring the entrance. At least he wasn't alone in his unease. Fura and Katrìn both looked tense. They squeezed hands as they followed their escort through the gate and up the stairs to the observation tower, where the warden waited to greet them.

Mars held his breath as he caught sight of the mine through the large, paneled window lining the front of the room. He couldn't deny it was beautiful. A sea of glistening white spread out before him, like an ocean of crystal. An ocean of Ice. It was enormous. It even seemed to exist in waves, some portions higher than others, places where the miners hadn't plied their trade more recently. *The growth is exponential*, Mars heard Katrìn saying once again. He saw people moving about down there, harvesting the Ice. They might as well have been trying to hold back the tide. They walked like the elderly, backs stooped and heads down. Only, most of them would be younger than him, teenagers serving their tithe or young adults serving as proxies for the kith.

Resisting the urge to rub his false enneagram brand, Mars pulled his gaze off the pit and forced his attention to the conversation unfolding between Fura and the warden.

"Cryin' your pardon, miss, but the dòttra's letter said nothing about you going down into the mines. It's quite irregular and, to be frank, downright dangerous."

"I'm aware of the risks," Fura said in a tone Mars knew meant she wouldn't be taking no for an answer. "But I have brought these gifts to distribute among the volunteers." She gestured to the basket Katrìn had carried in, its contents hidden beneath a linen cloth. "As you surely must realize, we would never be able to mine all the Ice without their sacrifice. This small token is the least we can do."

Mars cringed. If he'd known their purpose in coming here, he would've taken a nip of hemshade with his breakfast—just enough to make him puke his guts out for an hour or two and earn him a pass on this excursion. Coming to the mines was bad enough, but visiting the miners was downright horrific. He remembered the ageless boy in the Fortune's Den, desperately spending his coin while the life seeped out of him. Mars had no desire to witness more of that.

The warden sighed, his bulging belly trembling at the gesture. "Well, it is your mine, miss. Or it will be, one day. Since you insist, I will take you down there myself." He sounded less than happy about it. Mars didn't blame him. The toxins in Ice didn't discriminate between miners and guests. "But I insist you wear all the required safety equipment for the duration."

"Of course. Thank you, sir." Fura inclined her head.

The warden sighed again as he led the way out of the observatory and down the stairway to the guardhouse on the ground floor. There they stopped inside a large stone chamber housing the safety equipment—thick leather gloves that reached all the way to the armpits and triple-folded fabric masks that covered the nose and mouth. Donning the latter, Mars felt as if he'd become a caricature of himself—a masked criminal, like the roadside bandit in a salacious romance novel. Fura, meanwhile, looked like the heroine, a beautiful highwaywoman with only her poison-green eyes flashing like gems above the mask.

Following the warden, they stepped out from the guardhouse onto the floor of the mine itself. Mars felt the raw Ice more keenly here, its reeking magic like stepping through a wall of steam. Nausea roiled in his belly, sweat breaking out on his skin. Next to him he sensed Katrin shudder. At least he wasn't the only one visibly sickened by this place.

It seemed they'd arrived in time to catch one of the later lunch breaks, and the mess hall was full of miners taking a rest. Or at least as much of one as these workers were capable of, living here. Most were as thin as the orphans, the constant nausea from exposure to the Ice robbing them of appetite.

Still, the appearance of the dòttra's daughter stirred them. Taking the basket from Katrìn, Fura moved among the tables. As at the orphanage, she seemed to come to life, her manner engaging, her smiles easy, although brittle underneath. Now it was hard to smile in the face of such misery. Even Mars, who made it a habit not to notice any suffering that didn't belong to him, sensed it. He couldn't help but think of Una's ravens as he looked among the workers. Some bore lesions on their arms and necks or cheeks, weeping and open sores. Others had yellowed eyes or patches of missing hair. The skin of those with fair complexions shone an angry red.

Mars and Katrìn trailed behind Fura as she handed out bottles of healing salve—their contents wouldn't last long, but they were still eagerly received. Fura spent a moment talking to each miner, asking their name or where they hailed from. It was little more than meaningless small talk, and yet the way she did it made it sound intimate somehow, like a reunion between long-lost friends.

But then, as they rounded one of the long rows of tables, Fura stumbled to a halt, her breath catching in her throat. "Natasja?" She stared down at a woman with lank brown hair and a coltish face. "What are you doing here?"

The woman looked petrified, her sore-encrusted mouth opening and closing like a fish's. Then she pressed her lips together and dropped her head in a bow. "Good day, mistress. It's nice to see you again."

Fura's eyes widened above the face mask, her shock a tangible force.

Mars leaned toward Katrìn, who also bore a shocked expression, and whispered, "Who is she?"

Katrìn blinked before stammering, "Natasja was Fura's proxy."

The revelation didn't surprise Mars at first—not until he did the math. Fura's tithe would've ended a year ago. This woman should not still be here, unless . . . she'd taken payment to be a proxy again. *Six years in the mines? Her own tithe, plus two as proxy tithes?* It was surely a death sentence.

Fura seemed to have come to the same conclusion, a look of horror shadowing her face now. "But what about your mother and sisters?"

Natasja's gaze dropped to the floor. "They will be well taken care of."

Fura started to speak, but a moment later she closed her mouth with an audible click. Around them, the entire mess hall had gone as quiet as the sea after a storm. Fura slowly nodded. "I am glad to hear it. I wish them the fortune of the nine, and you as well."

It was a hollow blessing, and everyone knew it. Natasja was the walking dead, sacrificing her life to feed her family.

"Why would she serve again?" Katrìn whispered to Mars. "It doesn't make sense."

Mars nodded, even though it did make sense to him. It made *perfect* sense. Although he would never commit himself to a cold and painful death in the Ice mines—not for anything, not like this—he understood what could drive a person to make

such a choice. *Desperation and want.* It was a universal motivation, one that manifested itself in different ways. He could understand it because he had been there before. In the moment
he had killed Orri, sacrificing his friend to save himself.

But thinking about Katrìn, growing up in the opulence of
the Torvald estate, same as Fura, it didn't surprise him that she
couldn't fathom it.

And yet from the tears brimming in Fura's eyes as they
left the mess hall, Mars wondered if maybe she was beginning
to understand. Or if she thought she did. Only, he didn't see how
anyone who'd lived their whole life as Fura had could ever truly
understand.

The sooner Mars finished this job and was away from this
damn country, the better.

When they departed the mine a short while later, Mars wanted
nothing more than to return to his rooms at the Torvald estate and spend a few hours scrubbing his skin with lye soap.
Not just because of the toxins from the Ice, but because of the
smothering feeling of despair Natasja's situation had left on
him. An irrational part of him was angry with the girl for vol-
unteering in the first place. There were other ways to make
money, ones that didn't require killing yourself. He nearly said
something to Fura, but one look at her smoldering expression
had been enough for him not to wade into it. He preferred to
keep his head attached to his body.

Fura ordered the driver to take them to Geldur Court, a
nearby district. Mars had learned enough about Valdri in the
past week to know this area of the city was a slum. Then again,

its proximity to the Ice mine would've told him the same, re-gardless. No one would live so close to that poisonous place if they could afford to live anywhere else.

The carriage came to a halt and Fura rushed out. Mars gave Katrìn a puzzled look, but she just shrugged, and they followed, finding themselves in a small but busy marketplace at the hub of several cross streets, all of them narrow and lined with decrepit buildings that looked one strong gust of wind away from tumbling down. The booths spread through-out the center of the square were hardly better, although sur-prisingly well stocked. Everywhere Mars looked there were Festivale trinkets for sale—dolls of all nine Titans, wooden figurines of Jörn the World Raven, and toy tridents and spears for the children.

And oh, how many children there were—dozens of them, running around in packs like wild dogs. At the sight of them, Mars's unease from the Ice mine melted away. This felt like home. Or at least it would've, if not for Fura marching them through the square with half a dozen guards trailing behind. Mars hurried after her, trying to keep pace, until Katrìn put a hand on his arm.

"She will want to be alone for this."

Mars frowned at her, then glanced back to see Fura come to a stop in front of a small cart full of cheap, random objects for sale—knit socks, garlands woven of wildflowers, canvas dolls with crudely painted faces, even a basket of small green apples. The woman tending the cart paled at Fura's sudden ap-pearance and fell into a clumsy bow.

"Who is she?" Mars asked, coming to stand next to Katrìn.

"Natasja's mother."

"Oh." Mars regarded the woman, and the solid patch of scaly gray scars covering her face. Ice burns, the disfigurement was called. Natasja's mother had served her time in the mines as well—and then some. Mars turned away. This was no concern of his. All he wanted was to forget about the woman in the mine and her sad family.

Ignoring the uncomfortable twinge in his chest, he strolled over to a nearby booth and feigned interest in a pair of wire earrings shaped like turtles. The merchant, a short balding man with bad teeth, approached him, eager to negotiate a price. Mars waved him off with a practiced hand. He knew how to speak the language here.

Finding nothing of interest at the first booth, Mars moved to the next. He was just bending to examine a copperwire pendant twisted into the shape of a fishhook when he felt something brush his side. Instinct kicked in, and without even standing up, he reached back and snagged the arm of the person behind him.

At a petrified squeal, he turned and stared down at what he'd caught. A young girl, no older than eight or nine, was glaring up at him as she thrashed about, trying to free herself from his grip.

"Let go of me!"

"Hush, now," Mars said, looking her hard in the eye, "unless you want the watch on you."

The girl stilled at once. She stared up at him, tears coming to her eyes. "Please, sir. Let me go. I didn't mean no harm. I just bumped into you, is all."

Mars grinned down at her. Now here was a child he could relate to—he didn't believe those tears for a moment. "You were trying to lift my purse."

"That's not true, sir. I—"

"Enough of that 'sir' nonsense." He loosened his grip on her arm but didn't relinquish it. Crouching, he put himself at eye level with the girl. "I'm not going to turn you in. But if you don't listen to what I tell you, the next mark will."

Now he had the girl's full attention. The cunning on her face made her seem older than he'd originally thought, and he guessed that like a lot of street kids, she was small for her age. Or maybe it had something to do with growing up near the mines. There was something waxy about her skin and misshapen about her features. Two of the fingers on her left hand were fused together by extra skin.

"You made a novice mistake trying to pick my pocket just then." Mars leveled a hard look at the girl. "When your mark's attention is fixed on something, that's the time you approach, slow and easy, like trying to pet a stray cat, see? That grab-and-run you tried only works when the mark is already getting jostled 'round. Like out there." He motioned to where the crowd was thickest. "You got it?"

The girl narrowed her eyes at him. "Who are you, anyway?"

Mars smirked. She must be confused, him dressed in these kith clothes but speaking to her like a street urchin himself. "That's none of your concern. Now, something for your trouble and so you don't forget." He reached into his pocket and withdrew two herrings, which he pressed into the girl's thin, dirty hand, her clawlike fingers closing reflexively over them.

She didn't thank him as he released her. She didn't even smile; she simply pocketed the coins, then spun and darted into the crowd.

Mars stood to find Katrìn staring at him as if he'd grown a second head. "Did you just teach that girl a lesson in thievery?"

He shrugged, refusing to be embarrassed. "Every kid needs a mentor."

To his surprise, Katrìn laughed. The sound was closer to incredulity than mirth, but at least it wasn't judgment. "I suppose you're right, although wouldn't it be better to show her how to make an honest living?"

"Not hardly," Mars scoffed. "The wages for honest work around here aren't enough for living."

Katrìn seemed to consider this a moment, her gaze taking in the decrepit buildings and poverty of the area. She shook her head. "Did you have such a mentor?"

Mars thought about it a moment, Rafnar's and Una's faces coming to mind. Only, they didn't exactly count. "The streets are full of teachable moments. I've been on the receiving end of all of them."

"You were once like that girl?"

"More or less." He folded his arms over his chest, uncomfortable with the way Katrìn was looking at him now, as if seeing him in a new light—a sinister one, no doubt. Or worse, a pitiable one.

"Did you ever know your parents?" Katrìn said.

The question surprised him. The last person to ask him that had been Orri. Mars shook his head. "Not that I can remember." He supposed he'd been too young. His earliest memories of any adult acknowledging his existence were of Rafnar and Una.

Katrìn nodded. "Me neither. I was fortunate to have Henrik treat me like his daughter. Still, it makes me sad sometimes."

Mars frowned. There hadn't been much room for sadness in the way he'd grown up; he'd barely ever thought about his parents. "It's a shame Elìn doesn't seem to share that affection," Mars said, wanting to keep the conversation focused on Katrìn. He'd observed on more than one occasion that Elìn merely tolerated her daughter's adopted sister like she might a houseguest she hoped would soon depart.

"The dòttra has always resented me, I'm afraid."

At that, Mars looked to where Fura was still talking with Natasja's mother. "I think I know what that feels like."

Katrìn followed his gaze. "Fura? Oh, you have no idea, my friend. The dòttra can be trusted to act in her own best interests; Fura would cut off her own arm if she didn't agree with its principles." At the look on Mars's face, she laughed, more warmly this time. "Don't worry, merc. She'll thaw out a bit when we get to Hàr Halda."

"*If* we get to Hàr Halda," Mars said, unable to keep the doubt out of his voice. For some reason, he didn't feel the same need to keep Katrìn at arm's length the way he did everyone else in the Torvald Kith. It might've been her kind, easy nature, or perhaps something deeper like their shared history—she a darksdòttra and he a darksvane.

She eyed him, head tilted. "You really care about this job, don't you?"

Mars looked around the district again: the poverty, the

hunger, the ruins of the Ice industry. "I need this job," he said, honestly. "I'm just not sure Fura's going to come around."

"Oh, she will," Katrìn said, matter-of-fact. "Nothing's going to keep her from going to the Assembly." She paused, then dropped her voice. "Look, maybe she just needs to see that you're not as ruthless as you try to pretend you are. Like you were with that girl just now."

"The kid's a fool." Mars gestured in the direction the girl had run off. "I was just trying to keep her from getting arrested."

Katrìn nodded, a knowing grin on her face. "If you say so. . . ."

Mars started to protest, but stopped as Fura rejoined them, her cheeks flushed from whatever words she'd exchanged with Natasja's mother.

"We should depart," she said. "We're due in Helholm Square."

TEN

THEY MADE THEIR way back to the carriage, and a short while later arrived in Helholm, the economic hub of Valdri. The ride had been spent in silence, Fura making it clear she had no interest in speaking.

Fortunately, the tension from their experiences at the mine and Geldur Court slowly dissipated as they traveled from the outskirts of Valdri to its vibrant central square. There was simply too much distraction for a sober mood to endure. Everywhere they looked, street performers were plying their trade—dancers twirling about with streamers of colorful ribbon, musicians strumming bright, raucous songs, jugglers tossing flaming batons, and drunken revelers loudly enjoying every bit of it. On one street corner, they stopped to watch a satirical reenactment of the Battle of Follies, which consisted of two actors dressed up as the titans Grìrmir and Dròtt shouting poetic obscenities at each other between thrusts of their flimsy toy swords. It was humorous enough that even Fura cracked a smile.

Afterward, Mars stepped into a bakery to purchase three strawberry tarts drizzled with chocolate and caramel. Katrìn accepted hers eagerly, but he had to coax Fura into trying hers. At the first bite though, Fura's reluctance gave way to a look of bliss so profound, Mars returned to the bakery for another.

The time passed all too quickly, and long before Mars wished to, they departed the square and headed to the lawn at edge of the city where the tournament finals were to be held and the Felling afterward. As they climbed the stairs to their seats in the spectators' box, Mars spotted the dòttra, sitting on the highest seat in the center of the box with an elected helmsman of the farthing seated next to her. Elìn cast Mars a significant look as he sat beside Fura. He smiled back, feigning a confidence he didn't truly feel.

"Look, there's Askalon." Katrìn pointed to a group of competitors loitering at the left side of the field. The truss's somber gray suit of padded armor stood out among the more colorful uniforms of his competitors.

"By the nine, does he never do anything fun?" Mars said, mostly to himself. "He looks like an undertaker."

To his surprise, Fura let out a small snort of amusement. "Askalon takes himself very seriously."

Mars arched an eyebrow at her. "One could argue you have that in common."

She twisted her lips into a determined line. "You're not wrong about that."

Her admission took Mars by surprise, until the bitterness in her tone registered. Remembering how upset she'd been earlier, he considered making no reply, leaving her alone with her guilt—or whatever this was. But then he remembered Katrìn's advice that he ought to show her he wasn't as ruthless as she thought him to be, even if it wasn't true. "Natasja's situation is not your responsibility, you know," he said gently.

Fura sucked in a strangled breath, and Mars braced, expecting her to lash out, but then she exhaled, expelling her anger with it. "Maybe you're right, it's not my responsibility. There's nothing I could have done to convince my mother not to hire a proxy. But it is still my guilt."

"How did you even know it was her?" From what he understood of the law, proxies' identities weren't disclosed, to prevent the sort of conflicts that could arise from such knowledge—blackmail, smear campaigns, blood debts . . . All the things that Una's foxes were hired for.

"I happened upon the payment in my mother's ledger and followed the money to its source."

"You 'happened upon it'?" Mars made no effort to hide his skepticism.

Fura shot him a scathing look. "All right, yes, I went looking for it." She hesitated, her reluctance at sharing anything personal with him evident, but this time she plunged ahead. "I had to know who it was. I had to do something to . . . to make amends. I wanted to serve the tithe myself, but my mother forbade it."

Mars returned her look with one that questioned her sanity. No one in their right mind would choose to mine Ice if they didn't have to. But he knew better than to say such a thing aloud. "Well," he said after a moment, "you can hardly blame your mother for wanting to keep you safe and healthy."

"Perhaps." Fura's nostrils flared at the admission. "But the difference is, not every mother can afford to."

"True enough." Mars nodded, troubled by the injustice, and yet he wasn't sure the alternative would be better. "But it's not as if there's a choice. If there was no one to work the mines, then—"

"Another Cataclysm, I know." Fura exhaled, her eyes squeezed shut in frustration. Then she opened them and eyed his false brand. "You know what it's like in there. Can't you see that something has to change?"

He didn't break his gaze; he was too experienced a liar for that. He just rubbed the brand and softened his expression. "That would be great, if it were possible. But the Ice is here to stay, and getting worse, apparently, considering all that bill fifty-one stuff."

Fura turned back to the raucous games and revelry before them. "Not if I have anything to say about it. I will change the world."

Mars couldn't help it. He laughed, amused by the sudden reminder of her naivete, as if she were still the little girl in Henrik's portraits. It was the kind of surety that could only be born of a life spent in privilege, one that had led her to believe she could make the world into what she wanted it to be. "Oh, Fura, what could you possibly do about it?"

Too late he realized his mistake. She whirled on him, her scowl transforming into a snarl. She stood abruptly and whispered something to Katrìn, and the two of them switched seats. Katrìn gave Mars a pitying look before she fell into whispered conversation with Fura.

Mars inwardly cursed himself for his stupidity. Why hadn't he kept his mouth shut? He was supposed to be smoothing her feathers, not ruffling them. Anxiously, he glanced at the center box to see Elìn watching them. *Dammit.*

The rest of the tournament was an agony of waiting. Perhaps the dòttra would believe that Fura being livid with him was, in fact, the perfect way to convince people they were two teenagers in love?

In the meantime, Askalon was named champion. The dòttra herself crowned him victor and presented him with a trophy—an evertorch cast in bronze. Mars eyed the valuable artifact enviously. A never-ending source of light would come in handy. If he were ever to make an artifact for himself, it might be one of those, except he would craft it to shine its light only for him and no one else, a useful tool for someone who had to move about in darkness. Too bad he didn't have the first clue how to make one. Artifact knowledge, the kith guarded as carefully as their adepts. Una had spent a fortune purchasing the book Gellir used to build the artifacts Dùnn imbued with magic.

With the tournament over and night descending, the crowd dispersed. Fura and Katrìn disappeared into the throng making its way to the nearby lawn to await the Felling, the last event of Festivale set to take place at midnight. The time in between would be spent feasting and drinking. Dozens of bonfires made merry points spread across the vast stretch of neatly mowed grass, all of them framed by iron gallows from which wreaths dangled, high above the flames. Several people were already playing games of Tempt, making giant leaps over the fire as they tried to snag the wreath and claim its fate for the coming year.

Mars trailed after Fura and Katrìn, worry pounding in his head. Katrìn had said nothing would keep Fura from attending the Assembly, but maybe she was wrong. Or perhaps she'd been toying with him, setting him up. But no, he couldn't see her being so duplicitous. Why, then, was Fura behaving this way, sabotaging everything? Surely her mother would call the whole thing off—unless he found a way to change the tide.

He hurried to catch up to them, only to come to a halt as a familiar voice said, "Do you believe the legends, Mr. Karlsvane?"

Mars turned toward the voice, his heart in his throat as his gaze fell on Elìn, standing a few feet away from the massive wicker statue of Jörn that had been built in the center of the lawn, ready for the Felling. The World Raven had been rendered in his traditional pose—wings fanned upward and sleek, feathered head craned to the right, beak open. The smell of the oil coating the wicker permeated the air around the statue.

Forcing air into his lungs, Mars offered the dòttra a polite bow. "Which legend do you mean, madam? If it's the one that says it took the combined strength of all nine Titans to kill Jörn, I surely do. It's an awfully large beast, after all." He craned his head back in emphasis. "Then again, true or not doesn't really matter."

Elìn cocked her head. "How do you mean?"

He shrugged. "It's the stories themselves that matter, the meaning they bring to an otherwise meaningless world."

"That's a cynical point of view for such a young man," Elìn tsked. "But that's not the legend I meant." She turned her gaze up to the World Raven's head, then drew her eyes downward to the ground upon which the beast perched. "I was speaking of the most important one, which claims it was Jörn's blood that created the Rift."

A prickle of unease slid down Mars's back, one that had nothing to do with his job hanging in the balance. The source of adept magic was not his favorite topic of conversation. Especially not with a woman who by law could slap a pair of hobbles on him and claim him as her possession if she ever discovered what he could do. "I suppose it had to come from somewhere. Might as well be a mythical raven the size of the island."

Elìn nodded, either unaware of his sarcasm or ignoring it. "I like to believe it's true. There's something ennobling about the idea. The clerics say there's a little Rift magic in all of us born to the island. Kull, they name it."

"Lifeblood," Mars said. The blood of the raven.

"Yes, that's right. It's kull that binds us all together. It's what makes us Rivenish."

Mars made no reply, silently gritting his teeth. He didn't feel a part of Riven any more than he felt a part of the Torvald Kith, no matter the mark on his forehead. He belonged to himself only.

Not true, the voice in his head argued. *You belong to Una.*

The thought stung, and he clenched his teeth. *Not for long.* That is, if he could get close to Fura somehow.

The dòttra faced him, her wistful attitude of a moment ago fading away to reveal the steel beneath. "I will tell you, Mr. Karlsvane, I'm wondering if our engagement is at an end." She gestured to her right, where off in the distance, a small crowd of young people had gathered round Fura and Katrìn, a fair number of them young men. "My bold daughter seems on the fence about whether she will accept my terms for attending the Assembly."

Mars smiled broadly at her and gave another bow. "I wouldn't concern yourself with that, madam," he said, rising with his palm pressed to his chest. It was a bluff, and he could tell Elìn guessed the same, but she didn't call him on it. It wasn't about him at all, but Fura.

"I certainly hope you're right. It would break my heart to deny her the chance to claim her birthright, despite my reservations. It's difficult being a mother, you know. Every day is spent balancing what is best for your child with what they want."

As Elìn glided away, Mars worked his jaw back and forth to loosen it from all the gritting, then went in search of a drink—something to bolster his spirits for the battle before him. Once accomplished, and with the Felling drawing ever closer, his worried thoughts finally retreated enough for his innate confidence as the Shadow Fox to take over. He wended his way through the boisterous crowd toward Fura and her gaggle of would-be suitors. They were ringed around one of the bonfires, a game of Tempt in full swing.

With relative ease, Mars slid up next to Fura, mostly thanks to Katrìn, who had beckoned him closer. After a gentle prod from her friend, Fura introduced him to the others.

"Is it true your father was lost in a shipwreck and you grew up on a tiny island ruled by heathens?" one of them asked, with the insufferable voice of one born entitled. He eyed Mars's kith tattoo suspiciously.

Mars grinned back at the boy, ignoring the implied insult that he didn't truly belong among them. "Yes! Fortunately, they were cannibals. Otherwise, we would've starved."

For a second, everyone stared at him in shock. Then someone laughed, and a few others joined in, the tension breaking. Mars kept his grin in place, teeth bared suggestively. With the alcohol heating his blood, he felt ready to put these contentious snobs in their place. If he was going back to Una empty-handed, he at least would enjoy himself first.

The perfect opportunity came a few moments later, when another of the young men took his turn at Tempt and failed. "I don't know why you keep trying, Kort," Fura teased. "You were nowhere near to snagging that wreath."

The tall, broad young man snarled a laugh, then raced toward the fire again, taking a huge leap but not getting any closer to the prize. Mars examined the symbol engraved on the iron gallows from which the wreath hung, identifying which of the nine fates they were playing for—luck. Not a bad a prize. According to legend, whoever claimed the wreath would be fated to be lucky in every endeavor for the next year. Total nonsense, Mars thought. There was no actual magic in the wreaths, or the fire, or the gallows. Only in people's belief in them.

Still, it was a game worth winning. But Fura was right, nobody could jump that high. Not without help. The wreath would be lowered as the night wore on, until someone did manage to claim it, but Mars didn't see the point in waiting.

"I can get that wreath," he said, loud enough for all to hear.

Fura openly scoffed. "Kort has six inches on you, and even he hasn't come close."

Mars shrugged. "I'm willing to make a wager on it."

Now he had everyone's attention. Highborns loved nothing so much as a chance to squander their money. The betting quickly ensued, Mars having to do little besides nod.

"Wait a moment." Fura silenced the chatter with a raised hand. "Before we do this, we should specify exactly what Mr. Karlsvane has to do in order to win."

Mars smirked, amused at how well she knew him.

"It's Tempt, Fura," said Kort. "All he need do is get the wreath from the gallows, and he's won."

"Not good enough." Fura folded her arms and thrust out her chin. "He must jump over the fire while getting the wreath. No climbing the gallows or any nonsense like that."

Mars pressed a palm to his heart. "You wound me, dear lady, to imply I would take such liberties with the rules."

Katrìn let out a laugh, and Fura elbowed her in the side.

"Nevertheless," she said, openly scowling now, "those are the rules."

"Yes, jump over the fire and claim the wreath. Got it." Mars nodded as the rest agreed to the terms.

Hiding a smirk, he took a few steps back from the bonfire and motioned for the others to clear a path. Then, ever so gently, he flicked his wrists against the blades in his cuffs, sighing as the magic flowed into him. He couldn't use his magic to jump to the wreath—that would certainly give him away—but jumping that high wasn't his plan. What he planned wouldn't need much magic, just a little steadiness and clarity.

With the crowd waiting expectantly, Mars held his ground, his gaze taking in the width of the fire, the height of the wreath, as well as its size and likely weight. Then, drawing once more on the magic, willing it to sharpen his senses, he plunged forward. At the same time, he reached across his body for the knife sheathed at his belt. Fingers on hilt, he raised the knife, took aim, and released it. The blade struck true, severing the twine holding the wreath to the gallows. As it started to fall, Mars made his leap over the fire, one arm raised to catch the wreath well before it fell into the flames. He landed on the other side free and clear.

All the spectators cheered. They didn't mind that he'd technically not jumped to it, given how impressive his knife throw was. All except Fura, that was.

"You cheated," she said as Mars came around the fire to rejoin her and Katrìn.

"I beg to differ." Mars bowed. "I believe the terms were that I was to jump the fire and claim the wreath. I did both. There was nothing said about not utilizing my throwing skills." Mars turned toward the boy who'd made the comment about the heathen island and added, "Thank goodness for my uncivilized upbringing."

Standing nearby, Kort laughed. "And what skills they are, Mr. Karlsvane. I'm more than a little envious."

"Call me Hal." Mars glanced at Fura, encouraged to see the look of amusement that was starting to break through her icy expression. Maybe he had a chance to convince her after all. He stepped toward her, raising the wreath. "Please, my lady, will you wear my wreath and accept my luck?"

Some of the women in the crowd cooed at this, delighted by such a romantic gesture. Mars wished he could thank them all, knowing that their reaction gave Fura little choice but to accept.

With a tight-lipped smile, she inclined her head and allowed him to set the wreath upon her brow. The dark green ivy that formed the wreath's frame looked like a black crown against her pale hair, the dramatic color offset by the white asphodel and pale purple hedge nettle woven through the ivy.

"Kiss!" some of the people surrounding them began to chant, and a blush rose up Fura's throat. Mars waited, breath held. But before he could act on the opportunity, a horn blew, calling for the start of the Felling. The same people calling for the kiss now started herding Fura toward the World Raven so she could perform her duties as Light Maiden.

Mars kept stride with her, growing desperate with the end of Festivale so near. They reached the statue of Jörn in short order. Several clerics, garbed in red robes, led Fura before the statue when she arrived, bestowing her with a necklace made of nine individual chains, each bearing the icon of one of the Titans—Svölnir's trident, Vigny's cauldron, Alanta's net, and so on. Predictably, Ragna's icon was nowhere in sight, the hidden Titan remaining just that.

Meanwhile, other clerics were handing out torches to the crowd, flimsy things little more than pieces of straw bound with string. Mars accepted his distractedly as he fought to keep his place on the edge of the circle forming around Fura. These people were relentless, though, stepping on toes, shoving elbows. Mars finally let them by—he couldn't care less about the superstition that claimed that the sooner one threw their torch on the World Raven, the greater their fortune. Even if he could use some of that luck now. Because he truly had no idea what Fura would decide about the Assembly. She continued to ignore him as she'd done most of the night, her focus on the ceremony as the clerics struck the flint to light her torch, a real one that would burn for hours. As Light Maiden, Fura would be expected to navigate the crowds, lighting torches and wreaths, anything meant to be burned in honor of the celebration.

The crowd grew silent as Fura's torch began to burn, sputtering at first, then blossoming into full flame. Solemnly, Fura stepped toward the World Raven, her skirts fanning out behind her in the slight breeze. Reaching the statue, she held out the torch to the raven's chest, the oil-drenched wicker catching fire at once.

The crowd cheered and pressed in closer, eager for their own lighting. Helpless to stop it, Mars ambled forward. Fura turned to perform her duties but stilled at the sight of him, her eyes fixing on his. The crowd, so eager a moment before, suddenly grew quiet, all their attention on the Light Maiden and the prophecy of true love.

Fura took a step toward Mars, holding her torch aloft. He raised his own and waited. Reaching him, Fura lifted her other hand. Mars did the same, shocked as Fura twined her fingers through his. Then she pulled him forward—into a kiss.

For a second, Mars almost botched it, his shock making his body tense. Then he settled and leaned into the kiss, his insides thrilling at the sound of the crowd's cheers. Their reaction to the kiss was even louder than to the Felling.

"That was . . . unexpected," Mars said when Fura released him a moment later and the crowd returned to its revelry. "I suppose this means you're agreeing to your mother's terms about the Assembly?"

She smiled back at him, her green eyes flashing. "You're not the only one who knows how to manipulate, Halfur. Or whatever your name is. My business at the Assembly is too important to sacrifice on account of someone of your character. And, just maybe, I've decided that you might be more of an asset than a liability. We'll see how long that holds true." She raised her torch to his, the straw bursting into flame so quickly it singed his fingers.

Mars tossed it toward the wicker raven, aware that Fura had singed him in more than one way this night.

Not that it mattered. All that meant was that he was one step closer to the Primer formula—and being free of Una at last.

PART TWO

KITH

ELEVEN

MARS PACED THE floor of the sitting room, grateful for the thick carpet softening his footfalls. He'd been waiting for Fura to emerge from her apartment suite for less than five minutes, but it felt like half a lifetime. Since arriving at Hàr Halda the day before, he'd been on edge, every nerve in his body primed like gunpowder ready to ignite. He couldn't explain it. It had nothing to do with the job—he was no more worried about keeping Fura safe and finding the formula now than he had been in Valdri. No, the trouble seemed to be the high city itself.

The moment Mars had stepped through the city gates, passing beneath the shadow of a statue of Svölnir with his customary trident in one hand and the severed tentacle of a sea monster held aloft in the other, his blood had rushed through his veins as if from a sudden fright. The feeling had been brief but intense, over in a second, yet the sensation lingered, a low, steady hum vibrating through his body, until he felt like a stringed instrument being plucked over and over again. Even now, despite at least a couple of hours asleep, he felt it still. Not as intensely as yesterday, but enough to make him irritable, like having an itch that couldn't be reached for scratching.

At the sound of the door opening at last, Mars halted mid-stride and did his best to look casual, arms crossed in front of him, one leg resting on a toe, but Fura's piercing look and quick frown told him he wasn't fooling anyone.

"Are you quite all right?" She stepped into the room with Katrìn following close behind.

With a quick glance at the clock on the mantel, he gave a curt nod. "I don't wish to be late."

Fura made a face as she smoothed the front of her skirt. She wore Torvald colors today, a golden-colored bodice and matching outer skirt over shimmering black petticoats. "Nothing starts on time during the Assembly."

Mars grunted his lack of surprise. "No matter. There're a few things we need to discuss on the way." He held out his arm, but Fura hesitated. Sighing, he shook his sleeve at her. "I promise I washed it first."

A small smile cracked her frosty surface, and she stepped toward him, sliding her arm through his like they were any normal couple. For a second, her touch turned his thoughts away from the pressing matter at hand and back to the night of the Felling and the kiss they'd shared—or the one she'd shared with him, rather. With an effort, he pushed the memory away.

"Do you know the way to the March?" Fura asked as Mars guided her toward the door, holding it open for her and Katrìn both.

"I suspect I can find it." In truth, he'd committed to memory every inch of the city map before he'd left the Den, including which apartments normally housed which kith. With the Torvald talon tattooed on his brow, the last thing he wanted was to wander into the wrong corridor and cause some unforgivable offense. Although the Assembly was neutral ground, all fighting forbidden by kith law, what happened here wouldn't be forgotten when the kiths returned home. Mars preferred to get paid for any feuds he started, inadvertently or not.

After a short walk, they exited the Torvald apartments and stepped out onto the lawn of the Red Court, so named for the red-hued sandstone used to construct most of the buildings in the area. Hàr Halda was divided into three such courts, all of them connected to one another yet geographically isolated enough to keep the more volatile kiths apart. The Red Court formed the eastern half of the city, currently home to the Jens, Belens, Erlings, Krogs, and Torvalds. The remaining kiths—Hadder, Lux, Aster, and Skorri—occupied the White Court in the west. Mid Court, set between the two, housed the politicians, including every member of the Helm as well as the Fifth and his cabinet members.

"What do you wish to discuss?" Fura raised her free arm to brush back a strand of hair that had been teased loose from the multitude of braids she wore by the sudden breeze blowing across the lawn. Since their ascent of the sheer cliffs that marked the edge of the Crown, as this central area of Riven was known, the wind had become a steady companion. Mars guessed they were some several thousand feet above sea level on this part of the island.

Peering around, he resisted a shudder, that plucked feeling strong inside him for a moment. It didn't help that he felt utterly naked without his weapons. Although there must have been hundreds of people, if not thousands, in this ancient city, the place felt tomblike in its stillness. The unwavering streets and the worn buildings lining them felt like the bones of a corpse, all the flesh and life stripped away by time and abandonment. For years after the Cataclysm, Hàr Halda had been uninhabitable, the air itself poisoned by corrupted magic.

Shaking off the feeling, Mars focused his attention on Fura, although when he spoke he made sure to be loud enough for Katrìn to hear as she walked behind them. "Now that we're no longer at your estate, there are several rules I must insist you follow to ensure your safety. The first being that you go nowhere in the city without me."

As expected, Fura bristled at this, her arm tensing around his. "That will be quite impossible. There are many social activities for females only during the Assembly."

"Like what? Knitting class? Somehow I don't see that appealing to you."

Katrìn let out a snort from behind them while Fura glared. "Maybe so, but I think you're overestimating your importance. I am not foolish enough to wander around alone, and I am fully capable of defending myself, armed or not."

Mars shook his head. "No offense, but your ability to fight matters little. A mercenary isn't just going to attack you like some overeager soldier in his first battle."

Fura's nostrils flared. "If you're trying to frighten me into compliance, it won't work."

"I would never try. But surely you must realize there are some things I know that you don't, given my profession. Such as how easy it is to slip poison into an untended glass, or to run a razor blade over an exposed artery so fast you don't even know it's happened until you're dead."

"Really, Halfur," Katrìn said with a gasp. "There's no reason to be so vulgar."

Mars glanced over his shoulder at her. "The truth is rarely pretty." He turned back to Fura, aware of the horror beneath her gaze, the certainty she must be feeling that to be able to speak of those acts with such authority, the man holding her arm right now had surely committed them. *I despise what you are to the very core of my being,* he heard her saying once more.

"Very well." Fura rolled her eyes. "I will bring you along wherever I go. It's certain to be delightful."

Katrìn laughed out loud at this. "He'll be the life of the party."

Mars's frayed nerves snapped at the mocking, and he came to an abrupt halt, letting go of Fura's arm. She continued a step, then turned to face him, wearing a falsely guileless expression that bordered on saccharine.

"Something the matter?"

"The danger is nothing to laugh at." He raked Fura with a glare, then turned it on Katrìn for good measure. "Even those two amateurs from the Wake managed to harm you that day. But here you will face professionals."

Fura and Katrìn exchanged a look, some secret communication passing between them, and too late Mars realized his mistake in mentioning the Wake. *Damn.* He needed to get a grip before he blew it.

"I'm sorry, Halfur," Katrìn said, sounding sincere. "You're right. We shouldn't take it lightly."

He drew a deep breath, reining in his temper. "Thank you."

Fura cleared her throat, her stilted manner leaving little guess that she was merely placating him now. "What are the rest of your rules?"

Guessing that anything he said would go unheeded, it took all his will to continue. "The most important, aside from not going off alone, is to avoid routine. Vary the paths you take to the dining hall or library or stables, whatever it may be. Habit is the assassin's friend. Also be suspicious of unexpected packages or letters, anything you have to open when you can't be sure what's inside." He paused, again having to force himself to go on. "And lastly, trust no one."

"Even you?" A hint of a mocking smile hid behind Fura's lips as she asked the question. Sunlight breaking over the nearest building caught her eyes, the green in them flashing. All at once, he found himself thinking of the kiss again.

Steeling himself, Mars forced his gaze to remain on hers. "I'm being paid to keep you alive. In that you can trust without doubt."

He held out his arm, and after a moment, Fura took it again. They walked on, this time in silence.

Mars distracted himself from his tumultuous mood by focusing on his surroundings. Hàr Halda resembled no city he had ever seen. With its various towers and crenellated battlements atop the fortress-like outer walls, it looked more like a castle in a child's fairy story, the picturesque home of the hero prince, perhaps, or the sinister abode of the wicked queen.

Or maybe just a den of liars and thieves, Mars thought as they arrived at the base of the March, the northern portion of the city wall, where a crowd had gathered. All the Helm was present, along with the heads of the kiths, their heirs, and their advisors. Mars searched the faces, making note of Elìn with Askalon standing at her right. The Torvald dòttra was deep in conversation with Stefàn Jarlsvane, one of the helmsmen of the South Farthing. Even from a distance, Mars could guess the topic of their conversation—bill fifty-one. The question of what to do about the expanding Ice was all anyone was talking about, it seemed.

On the other side of the crowd stood Ulrik Skorri, vane of the Skorri Kith, a tall man with steel-gray hairs threaded through the black of his braid. His son and heir, Gregor Skorri, sulked next to him, a bored look on his face, one eyebrow slightly cocked, scorpion tail tattoo prominent on his brow. Mars had met the Skorris yesterday, upon their arrival in the high city, and their hatred for the Torvalds had been a palpable thing, enough that Mars vowed to track every scorpion tail that came within ten feet of Fura.

They joined the crowd, Fura selecting a space near to Elìn but far enough away that she would not have to converse with her mother and the truss. Mars plastered a pleasant look onto his face as he took his place beside her, cursing that strange restless feeling. He needed to ingratiate himself to these people if he wished to maintain the ruse that he was Fura's beau. Besides, some of them might prove useful in helping him discover the importance of the Primer formula and why possessing it was worth threatening Fura's life.

One of the nearby dandies called out a greeting to Fura and she returned it, making the introductions. Mars made note of name and face.

From somewhere atop the wall, trumpets sounded, putting an end to all the mindless chatter below.

"That's our cue," Fura said when the noise ended, and they moved together along with the rest of the crowd toward the waiting lift.

"Is this to be your first Bounding, Mr. Karlsvane?" some young lady asked him as the crowd bottlenecked before the lift entrance. He nodded, but could think of nothing interesting to add.

"If we're lucky," the girl went on with a coquettish giggle, "we'll spot a riftworm in the mists. My brother says one appeared last year, but I was too young to attend."

Fura flashed a patient smile at the girl. "I'm afraid there's no chance today." She turned her head toward the sky, blocking the sun with an upraised hand. "It's far too fair a morning." There was a note of dismissal in her tone, and the girl was wise enough to take the hint, disappearing into the crush pressing toward the lift.

"Where's Katrìn?" Mars asked, realizing she was no longer with them as they stepped into the cagelike contraption.

"Servants take the stairs."

Mars started to reply but broke off as the lift began to move with a creak of metal gears. "How old is this contraption?" He noted the rusty single chain, as thick around as a man's waist, that connected the platform to a massive crane affixed to an overhang on the guard tower above.

"As old as Hàr Halda itself, I would wager," said Fura.

Mars frowned. He hadn't realized such technology had existed so long ago, but then his gaze caught on the faint metallic blue twining the metal like veins.

Glancing up, he asked Fura, "The lift is an artifact?"

Fura shrugged. "It might've been once, before the Cataclysm, but it runs on Ice now." She joined him in glancing at the ceiling. "No one can say how it worked before, though. Hàr Halda is full of such relics."

The notion unsettled him. To his knowledge, once the sacrifice was made, an artifact never lost its power from the Rift, yet these had. He wondered if that had something to do with the Cataclysm itself—Hàr Halda was not far from ground zero, as it were. He made a note to keep an eye out for more of these artifacts, if only to satisfy his curiosity. It was strange to think he was in a city built by adepts—by their own free will.

As the crowd exited the lift onto the top of the March, the trumpets sounded again, this time joined with other instruments common to a procession, various drums and woodwinds. Soldiers in padded white uniforms—members of the Fifth's guard and the official police force of the Assembly—helped organize the group into the correct order. Fura and Mars joined Elìn and Askalon. Each kith would perform a portion of the Bounding at set intervals along the wall. Mars had glossed over most of the details of this particular ritual in his preparations, but now that he was up here, he regretted the decision. Not that anything in any book could've prepared him for the sight that waited on the other side of the March.

The Mistgrave.

Mars moved to the edge of the wall, drawn by a terrible mix of awe and dread at this visceral marker of the Cataclysm. The mist rose nearly as high as the March, covering all the land beyond in a colorless gray as far as the eye could see. It was so thick, it seemed more like a veil, one that could be cut and divided by even the dullest knife. The only thing visible beyond the March was a single table-topped mountain, far in the distance, with a ruinous white tower perched atop it. Skarfell, the long-ago home of the Consortium, where the adepts of old had wrought their terrible destruction.

For a second, Mars felt a powerful urge to reach out and touch the mist, see if he could capture it with his hands, push it back. He resisted. If even half of the legends about the Mistgrave were true, then it was more dangerous than the worst of the Ice mines.

"This way, Halfur," Fura said, squeezing his arm.

Blinking to clear his vision from the glimmer of the sun, Mars fell into step next to her as the procession started, Elìn and Askalon ahead of them. It should've been Henrik attending the dòttra instead of the truss, Mars realized, but he pushed the uncomfortable thought away before it could find purchase in his mind.

They walked toward the left side of the March, away from the edge by the Mistgrave. Ahead, Mars saw a figure, a servant wearing the colors of the Erling Kith, standing at the right, apart from the procession. The elderly man stood at attention next to an elaborately carved staff set in a cradle upon the edge of the wall and jutting out from it at a sharp angle. The procession halted as it drew alongside the servant, the music ceased as the Erling heir stepped out from the line. At his appearance, the servant pulled the staff free of the cradle, then faced the heir, bowing his head as he held up the staff like an offering, balanced atop his palms. The young heir accepted it, turning it upright.

Stepping past the servant, the heir moved farther down the wall where the first of the boundary markers waited, the slate-gray stone painted with the Erling sigil of the rampant bear. A faint glow of Ice emanated around the edge of the marker. These were no relics, but new additions added for the Assembly. Wielding the staff like a hammer now, the heir struck the marker. A loud gong, unnatural in its intensity, rang out, making the ground tremble. From somewhere out in the Mistgrave, something seemed to move in response, a dark shape shifting in the formless gray.

The band started playing again and the procession moved on, but the Erling heir stayed on the right side, beating the staff against more markers set at intervals. Each time that awful, skull-shaking gong rang out, the Mistgrave seemed to roil in response.

"Did you really see a riftworm last year?" Mars asked, leaning close to Fura to avoid shouting.

She shrugged, speaking in and around the gongs. "Some claimed so, but I did not." She turned her gaze toward the mist. "It's easy for the imagination to conjure shapes out of that."

He could see her point. "You don't believe they're real, then?"

Elìn turned back to look at him, her lips pinched. "Oh yes, they're real, Mr. Karlsvane. If you listen carefully, you can hear their answer even now."

Mars frowned as Elìn looked away again. He concentrated on the sounds, trying to distinguish anything amid the racket made by the Bounding. After a while, he heard a faint rumbling noise like the earth itself growling. A shriek followed it, only to be drowned out as the music started once more. Vaguely, Mars recalled the purpose behind the Bounding—to remind the creatures that inhabited the Mistgrave that the boundary to their world lay here, at the March. Stories claimed that those creatures had been ordinary humans and beasts once, but were corrupted in the Cataclysm, transformed by its magic into deadly monsters. Mars had dismissed the Bounding ritual as some silly display of unity against a troubling past, but after hearing those sounds in the mists, he realized it was downright foolishness instead. Riftworms, the largest of the Mistgrave's inhabitants, were said to be blind but keen of hearing. No doubt the music and Ice-fueled drumming did little more than draw them near to the wall and stir them into a frenzy.

The procession carried on. After he'd struck the last boundary marker belonging to his kith, the Erling heir tossed the staff over the side of the March into the Mistgrave. For a second, Mars heard a scraping sound below, and it coaxed a shiver down his spine.

The Aster Kith continued the ritual next, followed by Lux, then Hadder, as the procession made its way along the March, passing out of the Red Court into the Mid. At last, it was Fura's turn. Katrìn waited at the ready next to a new staff and the first of the Torvald markers. Fura stepped out of the procession, and Katrìn, just like the four servants before her, grasped the staff with both hands and pulled it free from the cradle.

Mars heard a distinctive snapping sound, the noise registering in his brain too slowly for him to react. Not that he could've done anything to stop what happened next. No one could move that fast.

There was half a second of silence, of stillness—and then the staff exploded in a flash of green fire.

TWELVE

THE SMALL INCENDIARY device was known as a salvo to those in the business. They were easy to come by and surprisingly useful. They could be crafted to inflict a range of damage, everything from minor burns to the complete dismemberment of whichever poor bastard had the misfortune of setting it off. It all depended on the chosen ammunition. Not that such salvos were usually set at random—they were purposely planted and used on a designated target. That was perhaps their greatest appeal: the ability to direct the attack exactly where you wanted it with little collateral damage.

Not that any of this occurred to Mars in the seconds after the explosion. His only thought was of Katrìn, her screams ringing in his ears, louder than the gongs had been. He raced toward her, knocking Fura aside in his hurry to assess the damage. The green fire was already out, its purpose more to instill fear than to inflict harm.

And yet Katrìn was still burning from an unseen fire.

"Get it off!" She flailed about, rubbing her blistering hands.

"Shit." Teeth gritted, Mars ripped off his surcoat. The salvo must have been loaded with weep, a caustic substance activated by the oils on human skin. "Hold still." He fell to his knees beside Katrìn, throwing the fabric over her hands as he pinned her arms to prevent the weep from spreading. Even so, a few droplets landed on his cheek and started to burn. He resisted the impulse to swipe at it. Doing so would only spread the weep further.

"Katrìn!" Fura reached for her friend, but Mars pushed her back with his shoulder.

"Fura, get away from there," Elìn shouted.

Mars ripped his gaze to Fura. "Get me a drink."

"Have you lost your mind?"

"Alcohol will stop the burning."

By now, members of the Fifth's Guard had surrounded them, the captain shouting orders.

Mars ignored him as he tightened his hold on Katrìn. "Don't struggle. You'll just make it worse." He hauled her to her feet, half carrying her as she sobbed into his chest. Fura moved into position next to him, ignoring her mother's continued shrieks, and in moments she'd taken charge, ordering the guards to run ahead and give warning to the infirmary.

"You do it, Braga," the captain called out. "You're the fastest."

"Yes sir," the guard called Braga answered back. Something about the woman's voice tickled Mars's memory, but he was too focused on Katrìn to give it much thought.

They made quick time to the lift and off the March, yet every second dragged at Mars, seeming to slow him down. His face was aflame, the pain making his head throb, but it was nothing compared to what Katrìn was feeling. Her cries had quieted, but her silent tears were somehow more concerning.

To his relief, help arrived not long after they reached ground level. Nurses in gray uniforms swarmed around them. In moments Katrìn was carried off to the infirmary with Mars and Fura ushered along after her. When they arrived, an attendant immediately took command of Mars, dragging him into one of the curtained rooms. In moments, the tiny woman was pressing an alcohol-soaked rag to his blistered cheek. He hissed at the sharp sting and counted to ten until it finally settled into a dull ache.

With the worst of the pain gone, Mars could think clearly again. Thoughts raced in his mind, questions of who had set the salvo and why. Was it a warning? For whom? Fura? Elìn? He waited as patiently as he could while the nurse applied a salve, but the moment she finished, he rose to his feet.

"Where have they taken her?"

The woman led him to another area of the infirmary, where Katrìn was lying in a bed with several nurses attending her. Fura hovered nearby, one hand pressed to her mouth. She shot Mars a look as he entered, her expression caught between anger and fear. The fear he understood; it wasn't easy to watch your best friend nearly be incinerated. As for the anger, it was surely at whoever had set the salvo in the first place. And maybe a little at him for being right about the danger.

When the head nurse finished applying bandages to Katrìn's hands and arms, she rose from the bedside and addressed Fura. "The scalding is not deep. She will recover in a few days and will be able to serve in her full capacity soon."

"Is there not more you can do?" Fura pursed her lips—Katrìn's usefulness as a servant was the least of her concerns,

but this nurse couldn't guess that. Even if the woman suspected their friendship, she wouldn't dare comment on it. Mars
guessed Fura hoped an adept would tend to Katrìn, but such
magic was rarely used on servants.

"We have given her something to make her sleep. That will
speed the recovery."

There was a note of dismissal in the woman's voice, but
Fura ignored it. Pointedly, she strode around to the other side
of the bed and sat down on an empty stool. "I will wait with her
until I'm certain the threat has passed."

Mars sighed. That meant he would be staying, too, although he doubted Katrìn was the one in true danger, despite
her injuries. He wanted to get on the trail of whoever had set
the salvo.

The nurse looked ready to protest, but she didn't get the
chance as Askalon appeared in the doorway. After a nervous
glance at his truss's rank, she quickly excused herself.

Once they were alone, Askalon addressed Mars. "The
dòttra wishes for you to join her right away. She's still on the
March with the Fifth, discussing what happened. She's hopeful
you'll notice something useful." It was clear from Askalon's tone
that he believed it unlikely, but he continued all the same, ever
the obedient servant to his dòttra. "You're to pretend you're
bringing her word about Fura. I'll stay here and keep an eye on
these two."

Hiding his relief behind a nod, Mars faced Fura. "Katrìn
will be all right, as the nurse said. The weep's harm is in its
spread, but we kept it contained."

The anger in Fura's face faltered, giving way to a softer

expression as her eyes drifted to the burns along his cheek. "Thank you for your quick thinking."

He nodded, feeling no satisfaction at being proved right.

He hurried back to the March, taking the stairs instead of waiting for the lift. As Askalon had said, Elìn was there, speaking alone with a tall, richly dressed man while soldiers stood guard on either side of them at a distance great enough to respect their privacy. Not just any man, but the Fifth himself, Patrek Arnasvane, the head of state. The man who governed Riven. Well, as far as he was able to, with the Helm blocking him at every turn.

"Shit," Mars whispered, smoothing down his shirt and regretting the loss of his surcoat.

After a brief argument with the head soldier—settled only when Elìn motioned to him—Mars approached.

"How is my daughter?" Elìn asked before he had a chance to speak.

"She is fine, madam." Mars bowed twice. First to Elìn, then to Patrek. "Her servant was the only one harmed in the attack."

"I'm relieved to hear it." Patrek said, offering him a grim smile. Mars couldn't place the man's age. The white in his beard and careworn lines on his face suggested age, but beneath his fine clothes, his body looked trim and muscular, like that of a young man in his prime. "Please, tell us everything that happened."

Mars did so, although he didn't mention that the explosive was a salvo. Halfur Karlsvane would have no reason to possess such knowledge.

"You did well, acting so fast to get help." Patrek clapped Mars on the back with a strong grip. "I give you my bond in thanks." Dropping his hand away, the Fifth reached into his coat pocket and withdrew a small white bead with some tiny image painted on it, too small for Mars to make out clearly.

He accepted it with a bow and quickly threaded it into his hair, not far from where Una's bond hung.

"We're fortunate to have you with us this year," said Patrek.

"Indeed," Elìn replied, her tone dismissive. "Although the question remains, Fifth, as to who is responsible and what's to be done. There can be no doubt my daughter was the intended target here. How do you plan to ensure our safety for the rest of the Assembly?"

At once, Elìn had Patrek's full attention, and Mars seized the opportunity to sidle over to the wall and examine the remains of the salvo. As he'd guessed, the anchor had been placed on the cradle for the staff, carefully hidden from view. The chamber would've been affixed to the staff itself, connected by a thin piece of string. The staff had taken the worst of the damage, shattering into a dozen pieces that were strewn about like confetti.

Mars kneeled and gently rifled through the splintered remains. He wasn't sure what he was looking for. It wasn't as if there would be anything special about the salvo that would link it to the mercenary who set it. The explosives were simple in design and available from a dozen different sources. Una had the Den's salvos crafted in house, but freelance mercenaries could pick them up on the streets from private crafters or at the black markets. Not even magic could trace a salvo to its source.

Although magic would enhance his senses. Mars hoped it might even calm his nerves, for already that awful plucked feeling, banished for a short while by all the excitement, was creeping back over him.

Carefully, Mars rotated his wrist, drawing a faint line of blood. The magic surged inside him in response, hard enough that he gasped and nearly stumbled backward.

"Are you all right, young man?" Patrek said, his voice suddenly booming inside Mars's head as if the man were shouting into his ear. "What are you doing over there? It might not be safe." The sound of footsteps approaching made his brain rattle inside his skull.

Mars squeezed his eyes closed, struggling to ease the magic back to a manageable level. Several seconds passed before he was able to open them again. "Sorry, sir," he said, raising a hand to his temple. "I got dizzy there a moment."

"Not surprising. Those burns look unpleasant. Perhaps you should return to the infirmary." Patrek offered Mars a hand, helping him to stand.

For a second, with their hands clasped, Mars felt the other man's heart beating through his palm, clear as a hammer striking an anvil. *What in the nine?* Mars let go at once, his hand tingling and the magic a vibrant energy inside him.

He cleared his throat and inclined his head to the Fifth. "Thank you, sir. I shall do that." With a quick glance at the dòttra, who waved her dismissal, Mars turned and headed slowly back to the line of soldiers.

At least the awful plucked feeling inside him was gone, driven off by the heady feel of magic. He felt like he could fly, as if he could simply run and leap off the edge of the March and soar above the entirety of the Mistgrave, all the way to Skarfell.

Instead, he focused his thoughts on the attack, summoning to mind the memory of everything that had happened. With the magic enhancing his senses, he recalled every detail so sharply, it was as if it were happening all over again inside his brain. But there were no new details to help him.

That is, until he reached the line of soldiers and a later memory slid into his thoughts. That voice that had been so familiar. *Braga*, the captain had called the guard. Mars strained, trying to remember the voice yet again, to place it. The magic surged in response, and the answer came to him with all the force of a gale wind.

Bekka.

Another fox of the Fortune's Den was here at the Assembly, and a member of the Fifth's guard, no less. Now *that* was an avenue worth exploring.

It was a simple thing for Mars to locate the guard called Braga. All he had to do was tell the first soldier he found after exiting the March that Fura Torvald wished to thank the quick-footed soldier who'd gone for help. He was directed to the mess hall, but once arriving, it had taken a fair amount of time to figure out which of the white-armored soldiers was her. He'd never realized what a difference hair color could make.

Safely hidden in an alcove, he searched every face. At first, his gaze passed over a woman with short black hair and a compass rose tattooed on her neck as just another nameless stranger. In fact, he only looked at her a second time because the tattoo reminded him of Fura's pendant. It was then that Mars realized it was Bekka sitting there, chatting with a fellow soldier. Once again, her voice was unmistakable.

Having located his quarry, Mars waited where he was until some ten minutes later when Bekka and the other soldier got up from the table and exited the hall. Mars followed at a distance. He needed to get her alone, although before long he started to doubt such an opportunity would present itself. She and the other guard seemed to be partners, the two of them reporting for duty outside a small meeting chamber where several members of the Helm had gathered for some preliminary meeting. Tomorrow, the Assembly would start in earnest, with a lengthy overview of all the bills being presented for approval.

Mars ducked into another alcove. Great, he'd be stuck here forever. After a half hour of waiting, he was about to give up and try again later when a messenger appeared, bearing a summons from the Fifth—for Braga.

Thanking his luck, Mars followed her. He took soft, careful steps, willing the magic still thrumming through him to silence any noise. At least long enough for him to draw up behind her without her noticing.

"I see you're making powerful friends, Bekka," Mars said.

She lurched sideways in surprise, then came back with a wild kick that was more instinct than intention. Mars caught her foot easily and used it to knock her back into the wall. Her head smacked the stone with a dull thump, and he let go.

Recovering quickly, Bekka glowered at him, hands balled into fists at her sides. "You're lucky I didn't kill you."

"What are you doing here?"

She rubbed the back of her head. "Working a job. Same as you."

"Yeah, what kind of job?" Mars folded his arms over his chest.

"Like I'd tell you." She rolled her eyes and resumed walking. "You seem to have forgotten the rules, Mars."

"I haven't forgotten." But he had hoped to catch her off guard with the question. Although it wasn't unexpected that there'd be more foxes at a place as rife with political intrigue as the Assembly, her presence here still unsettled him. Una did nothing carelessly or by accident. She'd chosen Bekka specifically for the job, knowing full well how he would feel about it—how he felt about Bekka.

"You need to work on your follow-through, then." Bekka rounded a corner, striding now as she hurried to answer the Fifth's summons. "Rafnar sends his best, by the way," she said, taunting him.

Seeing no point in playing games, Mars grabbed her arm and hauled her to a stop, forcing her to face him. He braced, expecting a violent reaction, but none came. "Did you set the salvo?"

Bekka stared at him a moment, her expression puzzled. Then a grin curled over her lips. "You sure are worked up about it. You sweet on that girl?"

Mars let go of her arm, uncertain if she meant Katrìn or Fura. "Don't be absurd. What I'm worked up about is the idea that you're trying to get in the way of me completing my job."

Bekka sighed like a weary teacher with a clueless student. "I don't know why you're here or what job you're working. Nor do I care."

Liar. Even an idiot could've deduced he was here in connection to Fura Torvald. From such an anonymous position as that of soldier, Bekka could've observed him with Fura easily without him knowing it. She also would've guessed that his purpose wasn't to assassinate Fura—the boyfriend charade was unnecessary for such a task. But he had no doubt that Bekka would seize any chance to make him fail.

"Believe it or not, Mars," Bekka said, resuming her walk, "the world doesn't revolve around you."

He fell into step beside her. "Not the whole world. Just yours."

Bekka snorted.

"What's with the tattoo, anyway?" he asked.

"Gellir's handiwork." She touched her neck, the gesture automatic, as if she were self-conscious about it.

Mars had suspected as much but was glad of the confirmation. So the tattoo was specific to the job. A compass rose. The connection to Fura bothered him, even though he knew Una did not accept contradictory contracts from clients. She'd built the Den's reputation by ensuring that once a job was taken, it would be fulfilled. So whatever Bekka was doing here, it wouldn't involve harming Fura.

The thought reminded him of another problem he needed to address. He pulled Bekka to a halt once more. "Let me have your extra weapon. Your hidden one." She was a part of the

Fifth's guard, the only people permitted to be armed in Hàr Halda.

She shrugged free of his grip. "Find your own."

Mars scowled, regretting his choice to put her on the defensive. He had planned to fashion a weapon out of whatever he could find, but hadn't had time to do so yet. He hadn't anticipated an attack on the very first day.

"Please, Bekka. I'll be in your debt."

With a sudden grin, she ran her tongue over her lips and reached into a hidden pocket in her tunic, pulling out a dagger. "I'll look forward to collecting." She handed it over, then rounded the corner, out of sight.

Mars turned the other way, hiding the dagger as he hurried off. Once he was a safe distance away, he slowed, taking a few breaths to gather his thoughts and figure out his next move. He replayed the events yet again, this time from his enemy's perspective. The mental exercise was easy—he had no doubt a mercenary had placed the salvo. The question, though, was how much foreknowledge the person had about the Bounding. A good merc would've done their research. They would've known that the staffs were handled by the servants first, not the kith heirs. But there were plenty of bad mercenaries for hire out there as well—any who didn't belong to the Den. Such a merc might've assumed that the kith heir would've been the person to handle the staffs.

Somehow, Mars needed to figure out which it was. If the latter, the person would surely make another careless attempt on Fura's life. If the former, that meant Katrìn had been the target all along. There was only one reason he could think of for attacking Katrìn, a mere servant and no one of consequence—except for how much she meant to Fura, who loved her like a sister. Extortion was the oldest trick in the book. Want to coerce someone? Threaten to harm someone they love. If so, then the attacker's next move would be to demand whatever it was they were after. But what?

Could be anything. Money, influence. Or maybe even—the Primer formula.

Abruptly, Mars turned and backtracked to the corridor he'd just passed, taking it with purposeful strides. He needed to get back to the Red Court and Fura's rooms. That was the most likely place for the attacker to leave a note with their demands, along with a meeting time and place for delivery, perhaps.

Mars was nearly running by the time he entered the Red Court and rounded a corner to see Fura and Askalon walking just ahead. *Damn*, he'd hoped they hadn't left the infirmary yet.

He called out to them. "How is Katrìn?"

Fura came to an abrupt halt, then faced him, displeasure clear on her face. "Still asleep. I would've stayed, but I must get changed for the welcome feast. My mother insisted."

Mars grimaced on her behalf, understanding her irritation. Elìn didn't care a single herring about the harm that had befallen Katrìn. He glanced down at his own state of dress, his grime-covered tunic, torn sleeves, and missing surcoat. "I suppose I should clean up as well." Mars waved at Askalon. "I can see Fura back to her quarters. I'm sure you have pressing duties to attend to."

Askalon flashed Mars a glare hot enough to melt snow

and folded his arms over his chest. "What did you discover on the March?"

"Nothing." Mars shrugged. "Not yet, at least." He held out his arm to Fura.

For once she took it with no hesitation. "Please check on Katrìn," she said, addressing Askalon, "if you can."

"Of course, lìtja, and I'll make sure there's a guard outside her door until she's cleared to leave."

"You lied to him," Fura said, once Askalon was out of sight. "You do know something more about the attack."

Mars frowned, wondering if he was really that easy to read. Lying was so second nature to him that she was either merely guessing or paying very close attention. The possibility that it was the latter sent a discomforting flush of heat curling up his neck.

He cleared his throat. "I have a theory, but nothing certain." Then he told her about salvos and their typical use in his profession. Fura listened raptly, her lips drawing into a thin hard line and staying there.

When he finished, Mars waited for her response, certain she would understand that the attacker had been trying to get to her, but she held silent.

When they arrived at the door to Fura's sitting room, Mars opened it for her, which meant he was the first to see the letter lying in the entryway, shoved under the door by a passerby.

Mars picked it up before Fura could react. The envelope was sealed with wax, but there was no stamp identifying its sender.

"Let me have it." Fura tried to pluck it from his fingers, but Mars ripped it out of reach.

"Remember what I said about anonymous packages?"

She relented, remembering it far too well in light of Katrin's injuries. "All right. What do we do about it, then?"

Turning away from her, Mars headed for the nearest lamp and held the letter up to the light. "We treat it with care." The light revealed nothing useful, not that it mattered. This was all for show. Mars already knew there was nothing dangerous in the letter—no poison or traps—the flow of magic still thrumming inside him had told him the truth the moment he had picked it up.

Still, he couldn't resist a good performance. Next, he asked Fura to fetch him a handkerchief, which he wrapped around his hand before breaking the seal. Then, with excruciating slowness, he pulled out the letter and unfolded it across the table.

Fura leaned over his shoulder to read it along with him, the scent of the lavender perfume she wore teasing his senses nearly as much as the heat of her body pressed so close to his. With an effort, he forced his gaze on the letters evenly printed across the page:

Deliver the Primer or worse will happen. Midnight, tomorrow night. Orrery Tower.

Mars's pulse leaped in his throat as he turned to Fura, taking in her expression. "What's this Primer?"

Fura's lips parted, then closed again. She took a step back from him. "I've . . . no idea."

Press carefully, he told himself, struggling to counteract the thrill building inside him.

"Are you sure?" He waited, breath held.

She didn't respond, her gaze focused on the letter. Several moments passed, the only sound the soft swish of the pendulum on the clock above the mantel.

"Whoever set that salvo is a professional, Fura," Mars said, gently pressing. "They will try again. We might not get so lucky next time."

Fura sucked in a breath, swaying on her feet for a second before reaching out to him. "Don't say that, Halfur. Please, promise me you'll keep Katrìn safe."

Mars pursed his lips, something inside him rebelling at the question. He shouldn't say yes. He was here to protect Fura, not Katrìn—and yet the idea of saying no wasn't an option. "Of course I will. I'll do whatever I can."

She squeezed his arm, her lips parting.

Before she could speak, he covered her hand with his. "But I will have an easier time if you tell me what this Primer is and why someone would go to such lengths to possess it."

Her lips closed, then opened, then closed again. She shook her head. "I . . . I honestly can't tell you."

Can't or won't? he thought but didn't say, knowing the answer already. Still, it was progress. Sooner or later, she would tell him. It was just a matter of time.

THIRTEEN

THE FOLLOWING DAY, the Assembly began in earnest with an opening debate scheduled in the afternoon. The sessions were closed affairs, Mars had learned during his stay with the Torvalds, with only members of the Helm and their aides permitted inside the chamber where new bills were discussed, amended, and voted into law—or rejected. The reason for the secrecy was to limit the kiths' influence in the Helm's decisions—an attempt so hilariously futile, Mars thought they might as well try teaching horses to fly.

No, the real politicking happened between the sessions, every spare moment an opportunity to influence their outcome. Mars experienced the intensity of it firsthand as he and Fura attended the first formal morning recess. It was held in an area in the Mid Court known as the Tiered Garden. Walking arm in arm, Mars and Fura descended the trellis-lined stairway covered in flowering vines that led to the garden. A sweet fragrance filled the tunnel, the air cool and welcoming.

Fura let her fingers idly trail over the flower petals as they walked along. She'd been more somber than usual this morning, which wasn't surprising with Katrìn still recovering in the infirmary.

"I must admit," Mars said, as they exited the stairs to arrive on the first terrace, a stone wall forming the outer edge with the other overlooking the next terrace below, like nestled tables, "this is beautiful."

"Isn't it?" Fura sighed, her gaze lingering over the view before them. Flowerbeds lined both sides of the path, with an occasional slender tree here and there, along with statues of nude figures in various states of repose.

An odd pattern carved into the edge of the flowerbeds caught his attention: rectangular breaks that looked oddly like drawers, evenly spread through the stones. Drawing near to one, Mars stopped to examine it more closely.

"Be careful." Fura reached for his hand, stopping him before he could touch the misshapen stone. "That's an Ice compartment."

Mars withdrew his hand and straightened up. "All of them?" He motioned to the dozens of such compartments lining the beds.

Fura nodded. "How else do you think this place could flower so remarkably? The roads here are only clear a few short weeks before the Assembly."

He'd known this, of course, but he hadn't really considered the time frame. Realizing it now, it made perfect sense. No one lived in Hàr Halda long enough to keep up this sort of maintenance. Still, the idea of how much Ice must've been transported here just for the purpose of the Assembly made his head spin. The kith had spent a fortune to make this place so decadent, and for what? Their own enjoyment? Then he remembered all the soliciting the Fifth had done to fund his trip here and wondered how much of that money went to pay for this sort of extravagance.

Now that he knew the truth, Mars couldn't help but see the indulgence of Ice at every turn as he and Fura continued on their way, soon arriving at the ground level. Here the flowerbeds, bushes, and fountains stretched out before them in a maze of greenery and color. And above them as well, the three terraces creating a wall of stone and flowers around the place. But Mars's appreciation of the view had soured somewhat now that he knew what was at its heart.

Crowds of people were scattered throughout the garden, groups of two and three and four. As had become his habit, Mars immediately searched out the Skorris, finding both Ulrik and Gregor standing in the shadow of a statue of the titan Salveig. Two helmsmen of the West Farthing were with them, the man and woman both listening intently to something Ulrik was saying—promises of wealth or retribution, no doubt, if they didn't vote the way he wished. The sight of it disgusted Mars. He'd known the truth of the political structure in Riven for years, but it was one thing to hear of the corruption and quite another to watch it playing out so casually before him. All the more reason to find his way free of this place.

To that end, he leaned close to Fura and whispered, "Be on your guard today. Any one of these people could have written that letter."

She stiffened at the reminder, and for a second her eyes

shifted to the right, in the direction of the Skorris. Seeing the tell, Mars wondered if the supposed retribution for an attack in the Ice mine had all been a lie. *Or maybe,* he considered, *the attack was related to the Primer formula somehow.* He couldn't shake the feeling his theory was true, especially when he considered the Wake's involvement and the subject at the heart of all the debate and conversation at the Assembly: the dangerous proliferation of the Ice mines, and bill fifty-one. The kith had built their empire through their absolute control of Ice, both its mining and its sale. Perhaps this formula affected the chemical composition of Ice, making it far easier and less costly to mine in larger volumes.

With these speculations continuing to unspool in his mind, they wandered farther into the garden, Fura choosing their pace and direction. Before long, he guessed her purpose as he spotted her mother engaged in conversation with two of the South Farthing helmsmen—Stefàn Jarlsvane and Egla Hildursdòttra.

Coming to a halt, Fura swore under her breath. "Does she never give it a rest?"

Mars didn't have to ask what she meant by that, even though the comment hadn't been directed at him. "The apple and the tree, Miss Torvald," he muttered back. Fura shot him a glare, but the heat in it didn't last long. Even Fura couldn't deny that she and her mother shared some similarities—especially when it came to their singlemindedness—and to getting what they wanted.

"I take it you're waiting for a chance to speak to the helmsmen as well?" Mars asked.

"I didn't come for the views."

Mars started to reply but broke off at the sound of people gasping in awe. Turning, he found the source of it, awe rising in him as well—along with a sudden rush that came from the feel of the Rift's power flowing near him. Two familiar figures, both with their hands clasped in hobbles, stood before a statue of the titaness Magda. Their attendants stood next to them, carrying the small daggers used to draw the adepts' blood. Magda had been rendered in her typical naked form, breasts and belly swollen with child. As the Torvald adepts stretched out their hands, blood dripping down, ivy sprouted from the ground beneath Magda, quickly growing upward and spreading out to form a robe around the titaness, flowers of pink, red, and white blossoming all around. The flowers' scent filled the air like freshly sprayed perfume.

As the adepts finished their work, the watching crowd applauded. Mars glanced at Elìn, noting the pleasure in her cheeks, even though she hadn't ceased her conversation with the helmsmen.

"What sort of shameless nonsense is this?" Mars said, forgetting himself.

A scowl appeared on Fura's face. "It's common practice at the Assembly to show off with one's adepts. This might be neutral ground, but the kith never stop competing with one another."

"That's . . ." He couldn't quite think of the right word to finish the sentence.

"Sickening," Fura finished for him. "I know."

Her response surprised him, until he remembered Henrik.

There was little chance she didn't know his secret. Mars considered her cloak, wondering if perhaps her father had crafted it—and what else he might've made for her. Mars examined her face, his eyes lingering on the tattoo on her forehead. Perhaps she had something hidden there, same as he did in his. Then the thought occurred to him that she could have the formula hidden anywhere on her person, but he pushed it away, feeling an uncomfortable warmth pooling in his belly at the notion of trying to uncover it.

Turning his attention outward, Mars once again scanned the crowd, this time looking for more adepts. He found one lingering not from the Skorris, a woman wrapped in a black cloak with bright, shiny hobbles around what remained of her hands—three fingers and a thumb on one, two fingers on the other. She was tall and thin as a reed, with skin so pale that purplish veins were visible at her temples and on her neck. Her lips looked blue, like those of a corpse. Unlike Una's Dùnn, this adept had retained her eyes, and she had them set on Gregor Skorri, palpable hatred glistening in them.

At a slight tug on his arm, Mars followed Fura as she approached the South Farthing helmsmen, now free of Elìn's hold on their attention. It seemed the dòttra had been pulled away by the Fifth; she and Patrek were deep in discussion about safety procedures, from what Mars could overhear.

"Hel Jarlsvane, Hel Hildursdòttra." Fura curtsied, a polite smile cresting her lips. "Might I have a few moments of your time? As you know, my proclamation as Torvald heir will be occurring in just a few days now."

"Ah yes, Fura Torvald." Stefàn bowed. "I'm so looking

forward to the ceremony. I must say, you've blossomed into quite a capable young woman. Your father would've been so proud. Please let me share my condolences at your loss."

"Thank you, hel." The polite warmth she'd shared in her greeting vanished like a shadow in a sun. "But with my new status, I hope to express my concerns about bill fifty-one."

Egla, who had yet to offer so much as a smile toward Fura, snorted. "You and everyone else."

A faint blush climbed Fura's neck, and Mars sensed the tension spreading through her body. He didn't blame her, not with these people talking to her as if she were a child. But Fura wasn't to be deterred so easily. She plowed ahead, her tone hard and unwavering. "Although I know my mother is in favor of one of the recent proposed amendments—expanding our trade agreement with Osway on the mainland in exchange for them sending Oswayan men and women to work the mines—I must express my opposition to the idea. Ice is Riven's problem and should be handled by Riveners."

Mars resisted the urge to shake his head at her audacity in making such a demand, not to mention the bleeding-heart naivete. From where he stood, bringing in foreigners to do the work sounded like an ideal option, when set against the idea of Riveners being forced to serve a second tithe.

Hel Stefàn folded his hands in front of him, his expression serious, but something about his tone was condescending. "And how would you propose we deal with this problem?"

"To begin with, we should outlaw the practice of proxy tithing."

A sigh slid through Mars as understanding clicked in

him. This was about Natasja—Fura's guilt over having another take her place.

A placating smile appeared on Stefàn's face, while next to him Egla suppressed a laugh. "I hardly see how requiring more of our own people to suffer is a better option than using conscripts," Stefàn said.

"Our people already suffer. We should do so equally. Rivna demands it."

Now Egla did laugh. "Oh, child, what a romantic notion. It's refreshing, at least."

Mars tensed, half expecting Fura to hit the woman.

"Excuse me," a newcomer said, joining them. He shuffled closer to the group, walking with a visible limp. He was a young man, nicely dressed in a navy frock coat trimmed in gray fur, but his white shirt beneath was linen instead of silk, and there was no kith mark on his forehead. "Miss Torvald makes a fair point. Eliminating the proxy system will not only help ensure that the burden is carried equally, thereby making for more efficient mining operations, but by keeping the problem solely within Riven, we can avoid making ourselves beholden to other countries."

The two helmsmen became openly hostile at the young man's arrival, but rather than addressing his point, they both made quick excuses and departed.

Sighing, the young man bowed his head toward Fura. "I apologize, Fura. I'd only meant to assist your cause, not chase them away."

"No matter. They're sheep and cowards both." Fura's scowl looked sharp enough to cut steel.

"But I'm being rude," the man said, extending his hand to Mars. "I haven't met your companion."

Mars clasped it at once. "Halfur Karlsvane."

"So I've heard. Nephew of the Torvald truss, returned at last from sea."

Mars disliked the familiarity in the man's tone, the way it sounded as if they were sharing some private secret.

"This is Ivar Patreksvane," Fura said, "Son of Patrek Arnasvane."

The Fifth's son? That explained the lack of expensive clothing and kith tattoo. Mars examined the youth more closely, noting the similarities to his father, as well as the evidence of Ice burns on his face, neck, and hands. Here was a person who evidently hadn't had the luxury of a proxy. Mars released Ivar's hand, his own fake enneagram brand feeling like a weight tied to his wrist.

Ivar returned his attention to Fura. "I was hoping you and I might find time to chat, privately, about this bill fifty-one, among other things."

Mars slid his arm around Fura, wishing to remind her of their agreement that she go nowhere without him. She opened her mouth to reply, but broke off at the sound of a raised voice. It was Gregor Skorri, calling for everyone's attention.

"My friends, I'm pleased to provide you all with some entertainment this fair morning—those of us interested in adventure, that is."

A murmur spread through the growing crowd, the smaller groups joining into one, surrounding Gregor. He stood at the edge of a series of paving stones laid out in a strange pattern, a complicated geometric shape involving a circle and several triangles. Gregor's father had disappeared somewhere, but the Skorris' adept remained with Gregor, along with the adept's handler. Gregor motioned to the adept, and the woman reluctantly came forward after a push from her handler.

"Give me the dagger," Gregor said to the handler, and the man obeyed at once. "Hold out her hand."

The handler grabbed the adept by the wrist and forced her arm out toward Gregor, the palm of her hobble turned up. The Skorri heir quickly unclasped the small lever over the palm, exposing the adept's skin. Then, with a look of sadistic pleasure, he rammed the dagger through the hole, deep into the adept's palm. The woman flinched but did not cry out, her hate-filled gaze locked on Gregor.

With blood now flowing freely over the adept's hobble, Gregor stepped back. "Raise the relic," he said to the handler, who tightened his grip on the woman's wrist, then forced her down to her knees, placing her palm against one of the stones. Mars caught a faint glimpse of a symbol etched into the stone before the woman's blood covered it.

The ground began to tremble, the sensation rippling up Mars's legs, and his skin tingled with the magic of the Rift. He and Fura, along with everyone else, took a step back as the stones began to rise from the ground. The magic flowing out of the adept into the relic was so strong, it made Mars dizzy, his senses going hazy. Whatever this object was rising from the ground, it was large—and powerful, hungry for the magic being fed into it.

"Look at the adept," Ivar shouted, and Mars forced his bleary gaze onto the woman. She'd gone from pale to a color so dim, it was almost translucent. Her life force, her kull, was draining out from her.

"Stop this, Gregor," Fura said, marching forward. "This much effort will kill her."

Gregor laughed. "Don't be absurd, Fura. The Skorri adepts can handle far more than this paltry relic."

Only, she couldn't. The threat was clear to everyone except Gregor, who simply stood with his head thrown back, watching the monstrous relic forming overhead, eager to see what it was.

Fura tried again, screaming at him, but he continued to ignore her, even as the adept started to plead for her life, begging her handler to free her from the stone.

With bile rising in his stomach, Mars watched the inevitable unfold—the adept soon collapsed, and the relic along with her.

As the dust settled, Fura pointed a finger at Gregor. "You could have killed her. This is all your fault."

Gregor, his face clouded in shock, shook his head. "Shut up, you judgmental cow. As if you have any—"

Whatever he intended to say, no one heard it, as Mars—his head at last cleared from the magic's assault—marched up to Gregor Skorri and punched him in the face.

Afterward, as Mars sat alone inside a locked room in the Mid Court, a pair of the Fifth's guards on the other side of the door, he had time to contemplate his rash decision. It had been foolish to strike a member of the kith, especially a Skorri, who knew him to be a Torvald. The Fifth's guards present in the Tiered Garden had rushed in at the first sign of violence, pulling Gregor away before he could retaliate. Not that he would've. Mars's punch had left the young man flat on his back, staring up dazedly at the sky. The guards had surrounded Mars and escorted him out of the garden and into this cell without so much as a word. Now here he sat, pondering his fate. Elìn could send him away for this. He'd lose all chance of finding the Primer. He would belong to Una forever. He would—

The sound of footsteps approaching halted the rough road of his thoughts.

"I'm here for Mr. Karlsvane," Fura said from the other side of the door. "He is to be released, and all concerns over this matter forgotten. By order of the Fifth."

There was some shuffling noise and, after a moment, the sound of a key being shoved in the lock.

Mars stood just as the door swung open and Fura appeared. She met his gaze, her expression blank. "Please come with me, Halfur. You're to be confined to the Torvald apartments until the next sunrise, and the dòttra is to write an apology to the Skorris for the insult you gave them this day."

Hiding a wince, Mars nodded, but he could think of nothing to say. Surely his true punishment would come when they reached the apartments.

Silently, he followed Fura from the room and out into the

corridor. She held her silence for the long walk back to the Red Court, leading him directly to the door to her apartments—not Elìn's.

She opened the door and ushered him inside. Wordlessly, Mars obeyed.

When she came in behind him, closing the door, he turned to face her, an apology already forming on his lips.

But then every thought fled his mind, as Fura raised her hands to his face, stood on her tiptoes, and kissed him. It was fierce and over in a second, Fura dropping her hands away and stepping back from him, her chest heaving.

"Now," she said, her voice as fierce as her kiss had been. "Tell me what it was like to hit that worthless bastard."

FOURTEEN

THAT NIGHT, MARS hid in the shadows of the Orrery Tower, counting each minute past midnight. He had plenty to occupy his thoughts. It seemed his rash assault of the Skorri heir had been viewed as the act of a young man defending his girlfriend against an insult, not an act of anger against such gross abuse of an adept—a human person. *Just as I am a person. That could've been me.*

The thought chilled him every time it slid through his mind. And yet remembering the quick kiss Fura had bestowed on him afterward drove it away, at least for a time. He knew the kiss meant nothing. And yet the memory of it lingered, that brief connection he'd shared with her in their mutual hatred of Gregor Skorri.

The sound of wind blowing outside the tower drew Mars's attention back to the present. The orrery was a good spot for this sort of business; whoever was making the demand knew what they were doing. The massive model of the solar system spread across the tower floor offered countless places to hide. Each star, crafted from some sleek metal, was as large as a boulder, the planets the size of tree stumps. Cylindrical rails connected the pieces, creating a miniature labyrinth across the floor. There were also six exits spaced evenly around the circular room, all of them in easy reach so long as you watched your step through the model.

Despite the tower's usefulness for conducting clandestine meetings, Mars found its existence puzzling. He knew the general purpose of an orrery, of course: to model the movements of the heavens. But this one seemed a chaotic mess. There were simply too many pieces crowded across the floor to get a good picture of the movement of the system's bodies. And although several observation terraces encircled the tower above, they seemed too high up to be of much use, either.

Or perhaps the darkness was the issue. He supposed viewing the orrery in daylight might help. And right now, that seemed like a distinct possibility. He'd been here forever, and so far, no sign of the party responsible for the attack on Katrìn.

Holding in a sigh, Mars crouched on the floor beside the model of the sun to wait. Not that he needed to be careful. After he'd convinced Fura to let him come alone, she had insisted he borrow her artifact cloak. Mars had Katrìn to thank for Fura agreeing so easily to stay behind. Although she was mending well, the attack had shaken her. She barely wanted to leave her room—and she didn't want Fura leaving if she didn't have to, either. Fura was content to agree to her injured friend's wishes for the moment.

Yawning, Mars rested his head against the sun behind him, resisting the urge to check his pocket watch. He knew from experience that checking wouldn't make the time pass any quicker. It was likely well past midnight now, but there was no telling when whoever sent the note—or more likely, a mercenary they'd hired—might show.

More time passed, until finally Mars gave in to temptation. It might be late enough to call the whole thing off. Even with his eyes adjusted to the dark, he couldn't see well enough to read the clockface. He needed to either abandon his position or risk using his magic long enough to check the time. He opted for the latter, knowing it would accomplish the task faster. Without thinking, he flicked his wrist across the blade in his cuff.

Magic surged into him, so powerful it stole his breath away, leaving him gasping for control. He silently cursed himself for forgetting. The past few times he'd used his magic, it had been like this, like a storm breaking. It didn't seem to matter how big the sacrifice, either. The magic simply came, eager as a hot horse in a too-soft bit. He wrested back control, extinguishing the light at once.

He took a breath, preparing to try again, but a faint glow across the room drew his attention. On instinct, he moved toward it, carefully threading his way through the model. He expected the glow to fade—it seemed as if it might be just his imagination or a lingering ember from an extinguished torch—but it remained.

Reaching it, he found the glow emanated from the wall itself, and it was in the shape of a symbol of some kind. A circle with two small half spheres drawn through its top and bottom, each facing the opposite direction of the other.

"What in the nine . . . ?" Mars reached out, meaning to touch it, but froze at a flicker of movement in his peripheral vision. He was no longer alone.

No sooner had the thought occurred to him than the stranger rushed forward. Mars spun at once, reaching for the dagger Bekka had given him. He raised it in time to deflect the assailant's blow with a weapon of a far cruder make. The metal scraped roughly against his blade, catching at it like sandpaper on skin.

His assailant used this to his advantage, shoving Mars backward into the wall he'd just been examining. Mars pushed himself upright with one hand, his palm grazing a rough edge in the stone. He gasped as something on the stone seemed to pull at him, drawing his hand down. His skin buzzed, and he felt the energy being drawn from his body like air into a bellows. Magic burned through his hand and up his arm. The thing felt *hungry*; it didn't want to let him go. The memory of the Skorri adept flashed through his mind, and he jerked his hand way.

The assailant came at him again, this time brandishing a chain whip. With a flick of his wrist, the chain came snapping at Mars's face. He was able to dodge out of the way, and the chain struck the wall instead. Mars barely heard the impact over the loud groaning sound filling the room. He blinked against the spreading light, aware that the orrery was coming to life, all the bits of the solar system spread across the floor starting to turn. The moving parts complicated matters. Mars tripped and nearly fell as he tried to dodge the chain whip again. It caught his arm, wrapping all the way around it, biting as it did. The assailant jerked it, pulling Mars off-balance. He tumbled, then rolled as the whip released him.

Spinning about, he regained his bearings quickly, dagger at the ready. The assailant stood across from him, a shiv in one hand and the chain whip in the other. A scorpion tail was visible on the man's forehead. Mars couldn't tell if the Skorri tattoo was a fake, but he doubted it. The man wasn't a professional mercenary, his movements rough and unrefined.

Mars pressed forward, eager to end this. Someone was sure to notice the disturbance. The model, once strewn carelessly across the floor, now filled the empty space above him in the tower. The planets and stars glowed, casting light throughout—pale yellow, soft whites, deep dark blues. It was as if the night sky had suddenly been transported inside the tower.

The Skorri shuffled to the left, trying to get the edge on Mars. Mars shifted as well, keeping him centered. Growing desperate, the man lashed out with the whip. Mars ducked it easily, but as he pivoted, his foot caught on one of the arms of the orrery. As he stumbled sideways, the Skorri took advantage, lashing out with the chain whip once more. It struck Mars across the chest, the metal slicing through his shirt.

Cursing, he lunged forward, then rolled underneath another piece of the orrery, using the metal to shield him from the Skorri's next blow. As Mars regained his footing once more, he reached for the magic. It surged into him, eager. Power spread through his body, strengthening his muscles, sharpening his senses. With new clarity, he wheeled toward the Skorri, the Rift magic allowing him to anticipate the orrery's movements, almost as if time itself had slowed down in answer to his need.

As Mars drew near, the Skorri lashed out with the chain whip again. This time, Mars didn't move to dodge it. Instead, he reached out with his free hand and grabbed it mid-strike. Pain lanced through him, but the magic kept it from registering in his mind, allowing him to maintain his grip on the metal. He yanked. Caught by surprise, the Skorri let go, surrendering the weapon. Mars wasted no time pressing the advantage, lashing the man across the chest.

The Skorri, recognizing that the scales had tipped, began to retreat. Mars moved to cut him off, but the man turned and grabbed hold of one of the planets as it moved by, riding it up and out of Mars's reach. Mars followed, dropping the chain whip as he grabbed the nearest moving object. But the one he selected soon spun in the opposite direction, giving the Skorri a chance to put distance between them. Mars didn't fret, his enhanced senses showing him the best path to intersect with the Skorri once again. He launched himself off the object and grabbed another one moving up. Then he quickly jumped to the next, gaining ground on the Skorri easily.

With the magic flowing through him like a rushing river, Mars became invincible. No jump was too high, no gap too big. In moments, he had tracked the man down, crashing into him with one last leap. They landed on the ring surrounding the moon. With the Skorri already on his back, Mars pinned him down with his knees and pressed the blade of his dagger against the man's throat.

"You're after the Primer formula."

The man thrust his head back, teeth gritted. "Go to hell."

"What do you want with it?"

"I won't tell you."

"Then you'll die."

"I don't fear death. Asvaldur waits for me."

Stupid fool. "Fine. Have it your way." Mars grabbed the end of the man's cloak and wrapped it around one of the gears driving the moon's movement. A creak went through the metal, and the Skorri let out a strangled cry as the fabric about his neck began to squeeze. Mars stood over him, watching the panic build. It was one thing to die a quick, honorable death in battle. Quite another to find it in the slow, steady churn of a machine.

"I will free you. Just tell me why you want the formula."

"You stupid Torvald. The formula is gone. We want the Primer itself."

Itself? "Why? What does it do?"

The Skorri let out a strangled laugh, his face beginning to redden. "Ask your girlfriend. She's the one who has it."

Fura has the Primer? The idea seemed impossible. "Tell me what it does." Mars kneeled over him once more, dagger at the ready. "This isn't the death you want."

The cloak squeezed tighter and tighter. The man yanked at the fabric, his nails peeling away the skin at his throat in his frantic attempt to free himself. But he was no match for the machine that held him.

He drew a ragged breath. "The Primer . . . is . . ."

That's when an arrow went through the man's throat, and he gasped as blood issued from the wound.

"Shit." Mars ducked, barely dodging a second arrow meant for him. Already summoning the Rift to protect him, he turned and scanned the alcoves for the attacker, but there was no sign of anyone, only the faint sound of irregular footsteps quickly retreating. Mars charged across the platform and leaped toward the nearest terrace, clearing it easily, only to stumble as he tripped over the bow the assassin must've dropped before fleeing. The fall slowed him down, the footsteps barely discernible now. Mars followed, struggling to hear over the sound of his own labored breathing.

He raced down the spiral staircase, and in moments charged from the tower onto the lawn outside, certain he would spy the assassin in the open grounds. But there was no sign of him. There was no sign of anyone. Not for the moment, but distantly Mars heard more footsteps, these far slower and even. The sound of a guard walking patrol.

"Shit," he swore again, then doubled back into the Orrery Tower. For a moment, he didn't know what to do. He hadn't thought this meeting would end with someone dead. But there was nothing for it now. He couldn't risk trying to dispose of the corpse, not this close to dawn and with guards on patrol. Besides, there was no telling if the killer would come back—or if there were others waiting out there.

For one thing was certainly clear—there were more people after the Primer.

Still, questions remained for Mars. Why did the second attacker kill the Skorri just when he was about to reveal his secrets? *He should've killed me first.*

Deciding it best to flee, Mars hurried to the glowing symbol on the wall and pressed his palm to it. As before, he felt the relic's hunger, its desire to be fed the magic that fueled it. Squeezing his eyes closed, he willed the magic back and the machine to stop.

Moments later, the machine finally returned to its resting state. Sweat dousing his skin from the effort, Mars turned, and taking cover beneath Fura's cloak, fled the tower.

He slept late the next day, rising shortly before noon to a servant knocking on his door with a summons from Fura. He dressed quickly, scarfed down a couple of biscuits from a tin on the desk, then ventured next door to find Fura standing atop a cushioned step stool in the middle of her sitting room, being fitted for a new dress.

"Where have you been?" Fura craned her neck to look at him over her shoulder, keeping her arms out to the sides while the seamstress pinned and adjusted the seams of an unfinished garment.

"I . . . ah . . . had a late night." Mars cast Fura a significant look, inclining his head toward the plump elderly woman with the pincushion.

"You may speak freely. Perla does not know our language." Fura indicated the woman, and Mars realized she had the distinctive look of someone from Vest.

With a shrug, he turned and sat on the sofa, wincing at the stab of pain that spasmed through his chest. Of the three hits he'd taken from the Skorri's chain whip, that one had proved the most damaging.

"Are you hurt?"

"Only a little." He placed a palm against the bruise on his chest. "The person who attacked me at this supposed 'meeting' had a chain whip. The first person, that is. The second wielded a weapon far deadlier."

Fura sucked in a breath. "There were two? What happened?"

"Someone arrived in the tower a little past midnight, and he attacked me without preamble. That one was a Skorri."

"You mean he was hired by the Skorri," Fura said.

"No, he was a Skorri. He bore a scorpion's tail." Mars motioned toward her forehead.

She made a face. "That means nothing, given the tattoo you wear."

He gritted his teeth, frustrated by her obstinance, her naive refusal to believe a kith would do such a thing as attack a man in the dark. "When I threatened his life, he said he welcomed death because Asvaldur waited for him. No hired assassin would accept death in that way."

With her lips pursed, Fura shook her head, but she conceded the argument in the only way she knew how—by changing the subject. "Where is the man now?"

"Dead, but not by my hand." Mars scratched at the skin beneath his braid, wishing he'd had time to shower before being summoned here. "The Skorri was killed by someone else, who then also tried to kill me."

"Who was it?" She rotated on the step stool to better see him, motioning to the seamstress her desire to change position.

"I didn't see. He hid in an alcove and attacked with a bow and arrow"—Mars snorted—"which is a surprisingly sophisticated weapon for a place that's supposedly banned them."

"It's not surprising at all." Fura shrugged at his puzzled glance. "The archery tournament is a tradition at the Assembly, but this year the Fifth brought all the equipment and ordered it kept under guard."

Mars had forgotten about the tournament, even as he was reminded that he was supposed to take part in it. "Do you know where it's being kept?"

Fura shook her head. "It's a secret. For obvious reasons."

"Yes, only someone figured it out." Mars considered this. Could the fact that the assailant had access to the equipment help him figure out who it was? He made a note to determine how difficult it was to uncover the location of the archery gear.

"I assume the killer got away?" Fura said.

"Unfortunately, yes. I didn't get so much as a glimpse." Mars sighed. "But one thing is certain—there's more than one party interested in the Primer, whatever it is."

Fura cleared her throat, a lie already in her gaze, but before she could speak it, the sound of a loud crash reached them.

They both turned toward the source of the disturbance— the closed door leading to Katrìn's room. Mars clambered to his feet, thoughts of an assassin waiting in ambush flashing through his mind.

But before he took a step, the door opened and Katrìn appeared, pushing her way through and quickly closing the door behind her. In that split moment, Mars caught a glimpse of the room beyond—one cluttered with odd objects, looking nothing like Mars's own bedchambers. In fact, it looked like Gellir's worktable back at the Den.

Or Henrik's secret laboratory.

At once the Skorri's claim that Fura already possessed the Primer came back to him. He hadn't given it much credence—

not when Una had sent him here after the formula, her information surely the better of the two. Only . . . something didn't add up here.

Unless both sources of information were true, at least in part.

The possibility made his heartbeat double, and it took Mars a second to realize Katrìn was talking to him, urging him to sit back down.

"I'm fine, Halfur," she said, "I just knocked over a table by accident. No harm done."

Mars nodded, allowing the lie to pass unchecked. His mind was too preoccupied with what he'd seen. Then the truth struck him like a wave breaking on the sand. Fura didn't already possess the Primer as the Skorri claimed—she was trying to make it. And the only way she could do that was with the formula. That explained all those late nights spent in Henrik's observatory. Fura wasn't pining for her father—she was trying to finish his work. By creating the Primer—and using it. But to do what? His ignorance on the matter frustrated him, and with his fingers clenched, he returned to the sofa he'd vacated a few moments before.

Fura returned to her place atop the stool, and the befuddled seamstress resumed her work. "Halfur was just telling me about what happened last night, Kat," Fura said. "He says the Skorris were behind it."

Katrìn made a disgusted noise. "Who else."

"Has there been any word about a dead man in the Orrery Tower?" Mars asked, glancing between them.

"Not a word," Fura said. "Not yet, anyway. If it was indeed

one of the Skorri, his people would've cleaned up the body before it was discovered. They would want to avoid the scandal."

Mars ran his tongue over his teeth, deciding this made sense. Another thrill of excitement went through him. The Skorri's desperation to possess the Primer, combined with the other assassin's willingness to eliminate the competition, only proved how valuable it must be. Invaluable, perhaps—and surely worth enough that Mars could use it to press his advantage with Una. It could be as simple as possessing the Primer himself, then ransoming it for his freedom. If so many kiths were after it . . .

At the thought, his gaze flicked to Katrìn's closed door, then to Fura, who stood watching him with a piercing look.

He smiled at her. "At least that works in our favor. The fewer who know of these disturbances, the better."

"Yes, but what about the other person, the one who killed the Skorri?" Fura said, watching him like a mouse might watch a cat.

Mars shrugged, doing his best to appear nonchalant. As if this were just another day, just another contract. "Whatever the man's intent in killing the Skorri, I doubt very much he's done. He's likely after this Primer as well, whatever it is. We will have to be vigilant. There are four weeks left in the Assembly, after all."

"You're right." Fura nodded, then paused. "I'm glad you are okay."

"That makes two of us." Mars stood and stretched, wincing at the pain that shot through his body. "If there's nothing else, I need to clean up after last night's excursions." He was anxious to get away, needing space to clear his head and determine his next steps. He had time—it didn't seem as if Fura had succeeded in making the Primer yet, not given the state of Katrìn's room—but he couldn't be certain how long it would be until she did, and there was no telling what she might do afterward.

"Don't wander far." Fura waved at him. "You'll need to be fitted as soon as the seamstress is done with me."

"What for?" Mars failed to keep a note of petulance from his voice. The last thing he wanted was to get poked and prodded. He'd had enough of that back in the Torvald estate when Elìn had had him fitted for his outfit for Fura's proclamation, set to take place only two days from now.

"The Quiescence. It starts next week with a costume ball." Fura indicated the dress, which Mars now realized wasn't much of a dress at all, more like an elaborate robe wrapped around her body in a circular pattern. "I am going as Lady Ingrid, and you will be the Hunter."

Mars blinked. "The Hunter?"

Fura scoffed. "Surely you must know the story."

"Indeed I do." It seemed an odd choice, though, a sappy, miserable tale of star-crossed lovers. They both died in the end—at each other's hands.

Then again, he realized, as he headed for the door, maybe it was a fitting choice. For if Fura knew the truth about him, both what he had done and what he planned to do—she would certainly want him dead. But now that he knew where to look, nothing would keep him from getting the Primer.

FIFTEEN

IN THE DAYS that followed, Mars regretted convincing Fura and Katrìn how critical it was that he always be with them when they went out. Their vigilance to the guidance made breaking into Katrìn's rooms to find the Primer formula impossible. And when they weren't out, Fura and Katrìn were in their rooms. To make things worse, his schedule at the Assembly was even more packed than his schedule at the Torvald estate. From dawn until well past dusk, every hour was filled with all sorts of engagements, from spectating at political meetings—none of which Fura was ever willing to miss—to attending the social recess events to participating in various sports outings designed to entertain the young people in attendance.

This last set of activities, Mars didn't mind so much, particularly the ongoing archery tournament, which he was sure to win. Falconry, too, proved useful, giving him an easy opportunity to send Feykir off to Una with an update on his progress. He detested the foxhunting outing, though, and not just because it required him to spend an exceedingly long time astride a horse. The death of the poor fox seemed needlessly malicious and drawn out. The animal stood little chance of escaping the pursuit of so many dogs, despite its frantic attempts. For a people so concerned with honorable death, it seemed a cruel irony. To make matters worse, those dogs had been trained not to kill the fox but to capture it, prolonging its suffering as it let out a volley of shrieks and yelps. The kill was reserved for Gregor Skorri, who had organized the hunt and brought the dogs. How proud he was to slit the poor struggling animal's throat, as if doing so were some sort of triumph.

"And you call *me* a monster," Mars had said while Fura's peers applauded Gregor.

She didn't applaud either. "Riven," was all she said.

The day of Fura's proclamation proved to be busier than all the days before. Mars rose early, as scheduled, to don the outfit Elin's adepts had crafted for him. He sensed the magic in the frock coat the moment he slid his arms into the sleeves. When he'd asked Elin what the magic was for, she'd explained that all the Torvalds' outfits were being crafted as part of a larger shield that would form when all the wearers were together, like individual scales in a suit of armor.

"As Fura's beau, you won't be able to protect her during the ceremony," Elin had explained. "You'll be expected to be in the audience, too far away to be of any help in the event of an attack."

"Do you anticipate an attack during the ceremony?"

"I always anticipate everything. It's why I'm still alive," she'd replied, without offering any clarifying statement. She hadn't needed to. It was why *she* was alive—her husband, however, had not anticipated such an attack.

Still, wearing the coat now, Mars was grateful for Elìn's foresight in keeping her daughter safe, giving him a chance to relax for once. The magic in the clothing was far more complicated than he could've imagined, but he knew it would work—he sensed the strength of it, made even more pronounced when he joined Fura and Katrìn in the sitting room, both wearing their magicked clothing as well. Once again, he wished for some excuse to skip the ceremony altogether and break into their rooms, but there was no excuse to be had. His absence would be noted by all.

"Are you nervous?" Mars asked Fura, noting the faint flush in her cheeks. She looked beautiful in her austere gown of black and gold with the Torvald eagle emblazoned on the front, like a soldier wearing a coat of arms into battle.

"A little, yes."

Her candor took him off guard. She seemed more willing to be honest with him lately. *About everything but the Primer, that is.* "Well, don't be. You were born for this."

She smiled then, but it faded quickly.

"Come on or we'll be late," Katrìn said, and they made for the door, soon joining Elìn, Askalon, and the rest of the high-ranking Torvalds in attendance.

Walking as a single unit, Mars and the others made their way to Yrsa Hall in the Mid Court, the largest gathering place in Hàr Halda, aside from the grand ballroom. By the number of people heading into the place when they arrived, Mars could see why it had been selected. It seemed as if everyone at the Assembly was attending the official proclamation of Fura as heir to the Torvald Kith.

"Where shall we sit, Halfur?" Katrìn asked as they left Fura and Elìn in the antechamber where they would wait to make their formal appearance during the ceremony.

Mars shrugged. "Wherever you like. Preferably away from anyone annoying."

Katrìn grinned. "So nowhere near Gregor Skorri."

"You know me so well."

"You and Fura both."

Mars tried to ask her what she could possibly mean by that, but she didn't give him a chance, instead marching down a nearby aisle, selecting a seat on the edge for herself. Mars took the one beside her.

"You would've given Fura the aisle seat," he muttered, sitting down.

Katrìn laughed, patting the top of his arm. "Like I said, so similar."

Mars scoffed. He and Fura were as unalike as two people could get. *Well, aside from our feelings about how awfully adepts are treated,* he realized. And their mutual love of coffee, which he'd only recently discovered since arriving here. *And our hatred of Gregor Skorri, and . . .* He stopped the train of his thoughts, distrusting the direction they were headed.

He forced his attention onto the room at large, grateful in that moment for Elìn's insistence on the magical shield he now found himself a part of. Without it, Fura would make an easy target for any would-be assassin in this place as she ascended the stage at the center of the hall. The tiered seats in which he and Katrìn sat gave way to a mezzanine level at the top of the building. The nearly solid balustrades surrounding it, interspersed with thick columns, provided ample hiding places. And while there were plenty of the Fifth's guards here on the bottom level, the top appeared deserted. If Mars had been tasked with eliminating Fura, that's how he would've done it, from that high vantage point with a pilfered bow and arrow. He'd spent much of the past two days uncovering the location of the weaponry wielded by the guards. The armory was surprisingly well hidden, in the kitchens of the Mid Court, of all places.

Despite the magical protection, the realization of how exposed this area was made him uneasy, and he crossed one leg over the other, resisting the urge to excuse himself and race up there to patrol the balustrade. Only the feel of the magic woven into his frock coat kept him from doing so.

Before long, the other seats began to fill, a familiar figure taking the one next to Mars.

"Good day, Mr. Karlsvane," Ivar Patreksvane said, extending his hand in greeting.

Mars shook it, his smile genuine at the realization that his seatmate would be the son of the Fifth and not one of the kith heirs. Ivar was vastly more tolerable.

"Is Fura excited for the ceremony?" Ivar asked.

"As excited as I am for it be over," Mars replied, honestly.

"Me as well." Ivar grimaced. "I grow tired of all the pomp. Given the choice, I'd much rather be outside, enjoying the sun and nice weather while it lasts."

"Really?" Mars cocked his head. "I haven't seen you at many of the outings." None at all since the Tiered Garden, he didn't think, save for the archery tournament.

Ivar sighed and thumped his right leg. "I'm afraid my leg prevents me from partaking in most of the activities."

Mars frowned, only now remembering the young man walked with a limp. "What happened, if you don't mind my asking?"

"It was an Ice blister that turned malignant," Ivar replied. "A parting gift from the Ice mines at the end of my tithing. The surgeon had to remove a good portion of the leg to save my life."

"I'm sorry. That sounds . . . dreadful."

Ivar shrugged. "Could've been worse. My older brother had a malignant blister as well. But his was in his lungs."

Mars shifted in his seat, a sick feeling rising in his stomach at this information, and he regretted having asked the question. "Is he . . ."

"Dead, yes." Ivar's tone was flat, as if they were merely discussing the weather. "Some people are more sensitive to Ice's toxicity than others. Did you know? It seems to run in families."

Mars didn't know. He'd never had reason to learn. He glanced at Ivar's enneagram brand, wondering just how old it might be. He couldn't be much older than Mars was himself.

"That is awful about your brother," said Katrìn. "You must be anxious about the outcome of bill fifty-one."

"More like terrified." Ivar made a face, downplaying his words, but Mars could see the truth beneath his expression, his fear like that of the fox during the frenzy of the hunt. "My father is waiting until after the Helm has made their decision to cast his vote."

"I don't understand." Mars glanced at Katrìn, then back at Ivar, aware that he was missing something in the exchange.

"It's a Ninth Year."

"A what?"

Ivar gave a polite cough. "My goodness, you really have been lost at sea."

Mars managed to keep a scowl from his face long enough for Katrìn to come to his rescue.

"Every ninth Assembly, the Fifth is granted a special privilege known as Reclamation," she said. "It allows the Fifth to enact or rescind any proposed law they choose as representative of the people, regardless of the way the Helm votes."

"Like the trump card in a hand of Nines," Mars said.

"Yes, only this is no game." Ivar clucked his tongue, the sound like the hammer being drawn on a pistol.

No, Mars supposed it wasn't. "How did this tradition come to be? The kith detest any power that isn't theirs."

Ivar's gaze flicked to Mars with noted intensity, and too late he realized it was a question that a member of a kith would hardly ask.

"The rule is intended to keep the kith's power in check," Ivar said after a moment. "It's been that way since the Cataclysm. There are those who believe that if we'd had such a check on the Consortium, the Cataclysm might not have happened."

Mars doubted it. Those in power always found a way to protect it, to give none of it up. He cleared his throat. "And you think your father will use this special privilege on bill fifty-one?"

"I don't know. I suppose it depends on what the Helm decides. But either way, he will reserve the right to enact until the very end of the session."

Seeing the wisdom in this, Mars nodded. He considered

the stakes at hand in the outcome of the bill, recalling Fura's questions to the South Farthing helmsmen. He knew without doubt that they wouldn't vote to outlaw the use of proxies— not when the kith made such liberal use of them—nor would they care about any proposal that would keep the Ice flowing, no matter how much the commoners suffered. But what if the Fifth used the Reclamation to do it? It seemed he might at least be considering the idea, given the sacrifices his own sons had made by their service to Riven.

In that moment, Mars wanted to be anywhere else than where he was. He considered excusing himself just to get some air, but it was too late as the ceremony had finally started.

A blast of trumpets filled the auditorium, the sound raining down from the mezzanine level, where the musicians now stood between the stone pillars. The procession started, first with four figures dressed as Rivna Knights marching down the center aisle to the foot of the steps. They lined up, two on each side, facing each other, their starsteel armor glistening in the light of Ice-fueled chandeliers hanging above.

The leaders of the kiths entered next, save for Elìn. Each vane or dòttra carried a small finger bowl cupped in the palms of their hands, carefully held as they ascended the steps and formed a large circle on the stage. The Fifth trailed the kith leaders by only a few strides; he too carried a bowl, although one of significantly larger size. He joined the others in the circle, leaving a gap for Elìn, who entered last.

Then, it was Fura's turn.

Although Mars had been with her just a few short moments ago, the sight of her marching down that aisle with her head lifted high, her arms rigid at her sides, and her determined look sharp enough to cut glass made his breath hitch as he drew it in. He'd called her princess more than once, and she'd never looked the part more. Her black dress trimmed in gold fanned out behind her like raven's wings as she walked. Her pale hair, tied in a multitude of braids, resembled a golden crown.

"Your mouth is open, Halfur," Katrìn said, slight mocking in her voice.

Mars closed his jaw so hard his teeth clacked together. She was mesmerizing—and he wasn't the only one to have fallen under that spell. Nearly everyone in attendance watched raptly as Fura gracefully ascended the stairs and walked past the kith leaders into the center of the circle.

Once there, she faced her mother, who had closed the circle behind her. Smiling genuinely for maybe the first time since Mars had met her, Elìn stepped forward and began to speak in a voice that rang nearly as loud as the trumpets had across the great expanse of the hall. "I, Elìn Erisdòttra, dòttra of the Torvald Kith, do declare my daughter, Fura Elìnsdòttra, as my sole heir and successor. There shall be no others, save through the will of the Titans and Asvaldur. By the name of Svölnir, I accept you." As Elìn spoke the titan's name, she dipped a finger into the bowl she held, then raised that finger—now covered in blood—to Fura's forehead, where she drew a red slash from her brow to her nose.

Fura bowed once to her mother, then turned left to face the next kith leader. "I, Liam Ornsvane, vane of the Jens Kith, do acknowledge Fura Elìnsdòttra as heir to the Torvald Kith.

By the name of Magda, I accept you." He too reached a finger into the bowl, then drew a red mark on Fura's forehead next to the one Elìn had placed there. Fura bowed once more, then turned left again, this time facing the leader of the Krog Kith.

Once again, the leader accepted her, this time in the name of Alanta. The ceremony repeated a total of nine times, until all nine of the kiths and all the Titans had been invoked, leaving only the Fifth remaining.

"Kneel, daughter of Riven," the Fifth said as Fura faced him. She obeyed, sinking to her knees with the same regal grace she'd possessed since first entering the hall. Once there, she tilted her head back, keeping her eyes locked on the Fifth. He raised his hands over Fura's head, the bowl balanced between his palms. "I, Patrek Arnasvane," he said, "the Fifth of Riven, chosen by its people and endowed by the Titans and Asvaldur to ensure peace, prosperity, and honor in our country, do acknowledge Fura Elìnsdòttra as heir to the Torvald Kith. By the blood of Jörn, I accept you."

He upended the bowl, sending a shower of blood spilling down over Fura's head, turning her pale hair into a red, wet crown.

With the blood now spilled, Fura rose from her kneeling position. She surveyed the assembled crowd, her face smeared with red streaks, her dress stained. She looked like a warrior returned from battle. "By the Titans and Asvaldur, I vow to honor my kith and my country. I will honor Riven and serve her with all my heart and will."

As she spoke, Mars felt a tremble slide through his body. He remembered that day in Festivale when she'd vowed she would change the world. He hadn't believed her then. But now, here, surrounded by all these politicians, the power plays and backstabbing, all in the halls once walked by the Consortium of old, he suddenly found he believed her. If only for a moment. He still didn't know what the Primer could do, but one thing was certain. If Fura Torvald ever got her hands on the power to change the world, she would do it.

SIXTEEN

THREE MORE DAYS passed before Mars finally got the chance to investigate Katrìn's room. Though it wasn't one he manufactured.

"What do you mean I'm not invited?" Mars asked, staring over his cup of coffee at Fura, who had finally joined him in the solarium, where he'd been waiting for her for nearly an hour this morning.

Although the solarium was central to the Torvald apartments, it was rarely occupied, having little inside it to lure would-be visitors. A single slender birch tree was the only green and growing thing inhabiting the area, the flowerbeds as empty as freshly dug graves. The only color came from the yellow cushions the Torvald servants had placed atop the stone sitting areas, and the only warmth from a thin swath of sunlight penetrating the birch's leaves.

Well, that and the warmth of the delicious coffee. Mars inhaled the revivifying smell as he waited for Fura to answer.

"It was Christel's idea. And probably Liv's as well. You know the two of them." Fura rolled her eyes as she bent toward the tray set next to Mars's chair and poured her own cup of coffee, topping it off with two sugars and a splash of cream.

Mars had no trouble imagining Liv, heir to the Jens Kith, and Christel, heir to Hadder, scheming this together. Those two were like squirrels fighting over the same nut.

"A women-only trip to the sacred springs, though?" Mars arched an eyebrow.

"Indeed." Fura took an unladylike slurp of her drink.

Mars hid a smile behind his own cup. He'd heard tales of the springs, the very place where the Titans once took their leisure. The water there sprung from the earth hot as a bath, pure and fresh. He understood the appeal but disparaged the design, the opportunity it might provide Fura's enemies. It had been quiet the past few days—too quiet.

"Is there no way to get out of it?"

Fura shook her head. "My mother is going. She believes it will be all right. The guards on duty at the springs are some of Riven's best. Apart from them, only the dòttras and their daughters will be there, as well as our lady's maids as servants. Ones with proven service."

"To ensure none of them is like me," Mars said, and Fura nodded.

He supposed that would make it reasonably safe, and it would give him the chance he needed to finally explore Katrìn's room. That made the risk worth it. Still, he knew better than to just accept the situation easily, lest he raise suspicions.

"I could always follow from a discreet distance, keep an eye on things."

Fura snorted, a hint of amusement in the sound. "Nice try. But you know perfectly well we're going there for *nude* bathing."

Mars grinned back at her. "All the more reason for me to follow." He was only teasing her, as he'd been doing more and more often the past few days, but her answering blush caught him off guard. Memories of the way it had felt to kiss her crept into his mind, but he shoved them away at once.

Clearing his throat, he stood. "Very well. But if I can't go, you should take this with you to be safe." He handed over Bekka's dagger. It was his only conventional weapon, but he would be fine without it. "I know you can handle yourself."

Fura accepted the dagger, her lips parted in thought. She didn't ask how he came to have it. Instead sliding it into a fold in her skirts, she only said, "Thank you." Her gaze lingered on his, the sudden silence like a heart beating between them.

Mars took a step toward her, uncertain of himself around this softer, warmer version of her that she'd been showing more often of late. "If you want, I could show you a few tricks. Some techniques your Rivna mentors likely didn't teach."

He expected her to say no, rejecting the offer to learn any form of fighting beyond the honorable practices of the Rivna Knights. Instead, she tilted her head and motioned to the solarium. "Will this place suffice?"

He glanced around. "Perfectly."

He stood, stretched, then stepped into the open center area of the solarium. "First," he said, as she joined him, "it's wise to know the basic ways to get free of any hold. I'll demonstrate. Here, grab my wrist." Mars held out his arm, and after a moment, she slid her fingers around the cuff, the leather pressing gently against his skin.

"Like this?" she said, still hesitant.

"Harder, like you mean to drag me all the way to hell."

"It's not easy with this cuff in the way." She stretched out her fingers, tightening her grip before loosening it again with an annoyed snort. "Why do you wear these, anyway? Are they for protection?"

Mars shook his head. Of course they *did* protect him, but not in the way she thought.

"Then why do you wear them? I've never seen you without."

"They are my tribute," Mars said, always ready to deflect such questions. "All foxes of the Den carry an accoutrement special to them. If we die in service to the Den, our tribute is placed on a shrine to Ragna in remembrance."

"Ragna? The hidden Titan?" Shock colored her voice.

"Indeed. Mistress of shadows and patron of mercenaries."

Fura shook her head, a look of bemusement on her face. "And to think of all those times you teased me for my devotion to Rivna." She laughed again. "Maybe we're not as different as I once thought."

He smiled, a hundred different arguments flitting through his mind, but he ignored them all. "Maybe not."

The next hour passed in a blur as Mars walked Fura through his best maneuvers for fending off an unanticipated attack from behind, from the sides, and even from above. Fura proved a quick and eager learner, her lithe body and agile mind well suited for the training.

"It's funny," Mars said, standing behind her with his arms wrapped around hers, pinning them to her sides, "but you would've made an impressive merc." His breath teased the hair by her ear as he spoke, and he felt a shiver slide through her body.

"I suppose I should take that as a compliment." She stepped closer to him, preparing for the move.

"You should." Mars tightened his grip around her, planting his feet to make the release a challenge. His thoughts drifted to the night of the Felling, and for a wild moment he considered spinning her in his arms and re-creating their kiss.

But in the next instant, Fura jerked both her arms upward, forcing his grip higher on her body. Then she stepped to the left, thrusting out with her hip to disrupt his balance as she moved her right leg behind his left, then grabbed his other leg and knocked them both to the floor. His grip broke as he fell, and she landed half on top of him. From there, she pivoted, using her knees and shoulder to pin him down in a hold he'd just taught her.

She leaned her face close to his. "Very well, then. I shall."

Instinct nudged at him to raise his head, take the chance, but before he could do so, the door to the solarium opened.

"What in the nine are you two doing?" Katrìn put her hands on her hips.

Fura scrambled off him, quickly rising to her feet. The flush in her cheeks had little to do with the exertion.

Mars, too, felt a flush spread through his body, the sensation an alien one. He climbed up and brushed the dirt from his clothes. "I was just showing her a few tricks for fending off an attack."

Katrìn folded her arms. "I see. It seems to be going well." Her lips twitched, but she managed not to smile. Or perhaps she was too weary to smile. Although she'd recovered from the salvo's injuries, her health seemed to be in decline these past few days, her skin pale and wan, and the reddish hue of her burn scars more prominent than usual. Bluish half-moons hung beneath her eyes. He supposed the stress of being here, combined with whatever work she and Fura were doing in her rooms, was the likely cause of it, and he hoped a long soak in the springs would help. Legend claimed the waters possessed healing qualities.

Fura clapped her hands, dislodging the grime from their grappling. "It was very useful, yes." She sounded breathless.

Mars forced his gaze onto Katrìn. "You both need to be careful and vigilant. Take nothing for granted."

"We won't," Fura said. "And same to you as well. I wouldn't put it past my enemies to regard you as a target even in my absence."

She had a point. The interested parties had shown little regard for collateral damage. Still, wanting to ease her fear, he placed a hand over his heart, affecting his most charming persona. "Your concern is touching. I will do my best not to get killed between now and this evening."

Fura cast him a playful scowl. "See that you do. I'd rather not have to feign sorrow at your unexpected demise."

Mars laughed, then shook his head. "All kidding aside. Don't linger overly long. If you're not back in time for dinner,

I'll come looking for you. Nude bathing or not." He winked, the gesture coaxing another blush from Fura.

Then, downing the last of his coffee, he excused himself and left the solarium, his pulse starting to quicken. Half a day to get into Katrìn's rooms. More than enough time.

By evening, the Primer formula would be his.

Mars wasted no time heading to Fura's apartments as soon as she and Katrìn had departed. He wore Fura's cloak to hide his movements, seeing no reason to waste his own energy if he didn't have to. The only true obstacle was the Fifth's guards standing at the door. They were there at Elìn's insistence. She feared an assailant might break in, lying in wait for Fura's return. Mars supposed the precaution was wise, except he knew it was possible Bekka wasn't the only false guard here.

Still, so far none of those who wished Fura harm had made it inside. With a bit of misdirection, courtesy of Rift magic, Mars lured the guards away long enough to slip inside undetected. Wasting no time, he headed for Katrìn's door, and was unsurprised to find it locked. He made short work of it and stepped inside, relocking it behind him as a precaution. Turning, he faced the room, excitement swelling in his chest at being so close to finally possessing the formula . . . only to deflate like a burst wineskin. The bedroom was in perfect order. There was no disarray, no sign at all of the equipment he'd spotted. In fact, it appeared so clean and perfect that it looked nearly unlived in. This couldn't be. He refused to accept the truth his eyes insisted on telling him.

Spying the wardrobe nearby, Mars threw the doors open, hoping to find the items in there, but only clothing awaited him. He checked the drawers, the corners, under the bed, everywhere in the room he could think of. Nothing.

Growing desperate now, he went next door to investigate Fura's room. It, too, was orderly and clean. He checked the wardrobe, beneath the bed, in every drawer. But again, there was nothing out of place, not so much as a scrap of paper with a scribbled note to read. Dismayed, Mars returned to Katrìn's room. Had he imagined it all? No, he'd seen what he'd seen, this room covered in objects. But they were gone now.

She knew, Mars realized. Of course she did. He retreated to the bed and sank down on it in defeat. Fura had suspected him and had moved whatever they'd been working on somewhere else. But where? There were no other rooms in these apartments, and he was with Fura and Katrìn all day long, picking them up here in the morning and leaving them here at night. The equipment must be here.

Mars stood, flicking his wrists to make the sacrifice as he willed the Rift to sharpen his senses and focus his mind, giving him the insight he needed to answer this puzzle. Holding his arms out at his sides, Mars slowly turned in a circle, allowing his eyes to roam over every surface. He examined the walls, the floor, the furniture, everything.

As he came full circle, his gaze finally landed on the mirror positioned directly across from the bed. Intricate lines ran through the gilded frame, a blur of curling, random shapes, organically flowing over the metal like vines. Only . . . they weren't all random. There in the right-hand corner was a shape he'd seen before—a circle with two small half spheres drawn through its top and bottom. Just like the one in the orrery.

Mars took a step back, wanting a better view of the mirror. It was so large that if it had been a window, he could've stepped through it. Uncertain of what sort of relic it might be, Mars lowered the hood of Fura's cloak, wanting to check his reflection in it. Although it was strange to see his bodiless head, nothing else seemed out of place. He approached the symbol, the magic already flowing through him growing stronger, as if it anticipated the relic waiting to be fueled by it.

Holding his breath, Mars placed his palm against the symbol. Darkness thick as curtains enveloped him, the magic tingling down his skin like soft caresses by a thousand tiny hands. For a moment, there was no one else in the world save him, no *thing* else. Then the darkness parted like a crashing wave, and he found himself in a narrow corridor that disappeared into reams of darkness.

Disoriented by the sudden change, he spun, then froze at the presence of a window, the same size and shape as the mirror, that looked into Katrìn's room. He approached the window, searching for the back side of the mirror, some sort of hole in the wall. But there wasn't any. The wall and window were solid, offering no way through. That is, until he spied the relic symbol in the window's right-hand corner. The relic must be a portal of some kind, working in the same fashion as Una's cloak, which allowed her to disappear and reappear somewhere else.

Mars frowned. What in the nine were those old adepts up to, building something like this? Although Hàr Halda had been the capital of Riven before the Cataclysm, the Consortium had built the city and been its caretakers. The only purpose this window could've served was to spy on the room's occupants.

He turned back, summoning fire into his palm to illuminate the area. To his surprise, a small worktable stood a few short strides down a hallway to the left, its surface laden with scientific tools and accoutrements. This must be where Fura and Katrìn were working, a table similar to Henrik's and Gellir's. Only he couldn't figure out how they'd gotten it in here.

The muffled sound of a door opening behind him made Mars jump. He spun toward the window, dousing the fire in his palm as he stared through it, horrorstruck to see Fura and Katrìn sweeping into the room beyond.

"I'll check the mirror," Katrìn said, heading straight for Mars. "You check the other rooms. But be careful. The intruder might still be here."

Resisting panic, Mars pulled the cloak over his head and stepped out of the way just as Katrìn pricked her finger with a sewing needle pulled from a hidden fold in her skirt and pressed her palm to the relic symbol.

A moment later, she arrived in the corridor. Mars held still, back pressed to the wall, trying not to breathe, even as shock tore through him, making his blood roar in his ears.

Katrìn was an adept.

She searched the area, nodding to herself as she examined the items on the table. Mars was suddenly glad he hadn't already investigated them himself, knowing how difficult it was to leave such a clutter undisturbed.

A moment later, Katrìn turned and exited through the

portal back into her rooms. Mars edged close enough to the window to watch what happened next. Although he wasn't entirely certain whether he could be seen in the mirror from this side, with the cloak on he wasn't worried.

Fura appeared in the doorway. "There's no sign of anyone being here."

Nodding, Katrìn motioned toward the mirror. "Everything is how we left it in there as well."

"Thank the nine for that." Fura said. "But I wish we could've gotten here sooner."

"You should be glad I was able to sense the alarm at all from so far away." Katrìn approached the door and leaned toward the lock. "But there's no doubt someone came through here and set off the sear." She withdrew a thin metal pin from where it was hidden inside the door beneath the lock.

Mars cringed at his mistake. Not that he would've had any reason to believe such a device was there. Sears were subtle magic, run on a tiny sliver of Ice, barely detectable. Only, as Katrìn reinserted the pin, Mars realized it must run on Rift magic instead. A sear run on Ice would've been useless after being triggered.

Katrin is an adept, he thought again. A secret one, just like him, only living as a lady's maid in a kith house. It was like being a mouse inside a lion's den, Mars knew. For he was certain that if she knew, Elìn would never allow Katrìn to go free, not when her powers could be so useful. The Torvalds had two adepts already, but Mars doubted that would matter. Elìn was like Una in that—some power was never enough when there was more to be had.

And not only was Katrìn a secret adept, but she knew how to make artifacts as well, Mars realized with a pang of jealousy. Her best friend and confidante was daughter to both a dòttra and a secret adept in Henrik. Fura would've had little trouble obtaining the knowledge for her friend. For a moment, the depth of their relationship overwhelmed him. She and Katrìn were as close as sisters, and Fura loved her even though she was an adept, the most hated beings in Riven. Fura must've been keeping Katrìn's secret for years, protecting her from the danger her presence among the kith put her in. And despite Katrìn's power, her freedom to go where she wanted, she stayed to be with her friend. Mars couldn't fathom it. For a moment, he pictured Orri's face, the hatred and betrayal there when he'd realized what Mars was. For Orri, hatred had been the only option. Mars had long thought it the only option for anyone.

"Do you think it was Halfur?" Katrìn peered around the room.

"Who else," Fura said darkly. "He's been chasing the Primer formula from the day he arrived."

Mars sucked in a breath at her words. She'd suspected him from the very beginning. Shame stole through him that he hadn't realized it sooner. That he'd underestimated her from the start, seeing only her naivete and ignoring her cleverness.

"What if it wasn't him, though?" Katrìn said. "An assailant might've been in here and planted something dangerous."

Good girl, Mars thought, feeling some small reprieve for his foolishness.

But Fura shook her head. "It was him. None of the assailants we've encountered so far could've broken in here so quickly and left not a trace behind. They've been blundering fools by comparison."

Mars didn't know whether to be proud or annoyed by her assertion, true as it was.

"Maybe so, but we should still tell him, in case it wasn't him. Just to be safe."

"No." Fura made a cutting gesture with her hand. "I don't want to put him on his guard. Getting past him when the time comes to leave will be hard enough as it is."

"You mean *if* the time comes." Katrìn turned and sank down onto the bed, like a weary traveler on a journey with a thousand miles yet to go. "I've been trying everything I can think of, and I'm still no closer to increasing the orb's strength."

Orb? What orb? Mars glanced over his shoulder at the worktable. The sight of a large glass ball, roughly the size of a toddler's head, jumped out at him at once. He couldn't believe he hadn't noticed the strange object at first look.

He turned back to the window in time to see Fura sit down beside Katrìn and wrap one arm around her, pulling her friend's head down to her shoulder. "Don't fret. We'll find a way there, somehow or another."

A way where? The question burned inside Mars's brain, making him crazed with the desire to leap into the room and demand an answer.

Katrìn sighed, leaning into Fura's shoulder as Fura rested her head atop Katrìn's. "I hope you're right. We're running out of time. The vote on bill fifty-one is only two weeks away. If it goes the wrong way—"

"I know. But even if we fail to get back in time, it won't change the final outcome. It'll just delay the inevitable for a while. So long as we succeed, that's all that matters."

Katrìn raised her head to look Fura in the face. "But every moment we delay, the danger you face here grows."

Fura shrugged. "That's what Halfur is for. He's already proven himself capable of the task."

A wry smile twisted Katrìn's mouth. "Thank the nine your mother's protectiveness proved helpful for once." She paused, her head tilting like a bird's. "It's a shame we can't hire him to help us directly. It would make everything easier."

"We can't trust him, not when we know he's after the formula." Fura shook her head. "We couldn't afford him, either."

Katrìn looked hesitant. "I'm not so sure. I don't think he's the heartless beast we first assumed him to be. His sense of morality is certainly skewed, I know, but it is there, nonetheless. You should've seen him with that orphan girl in Geldur Court. He might understand what we're trying to do enough to resist his baser instincts. He's not incapable of recognizing injustice. Like how he reacted when Gregor nearly killed his adept."

"Perhaps. It's almost as if . . ." She trailed off, suddenly lost in thought.

Mars stared at her, wondering what she had been about to say. He wished he could pry open her mind like a chest and rummage through her thoughts, uncover all her secrets. She seemed to have far more of those than he would've guessed, with all that talk about leaving and this orb.

With a quick glance at the mirror, Fura stood from the

bed. "Come on. If we hurry, we can still catch up to the caravan. A day at the springs will do us both some good."

Mars watched the two women leave, his mind racing with all he'd just learned and all he still didn't know.

Alone again, he summoned a light once more and approached the worktable. He examined the orb more closely, trying to make it reveal its secrets. It was magic, that was clear from a glance at the thin metallic-blue lines infused through its surface. And when he touched his hand to it, letting the Rift magic flow out from him, he felt it responding, coming to life. But he couldn't tell what it was doing. From where he stood, nothing happened except that the glass grew dark, as if it were suddenly filled with storm clouds. Was this the Primer? He couldn't be sure, or make sense of it at all, and, worried about alerting Katrìn to his presence once more, he gave up trying.

He moved on, examining the other objects on the table. Nothing jumped out at him as significant, until he found a notebook sitting beneath an empty wooden box. He skimmed the pages, finding two distinct sets of handwriting inside. The main text he recognized as Henrik Torvald's, but someone else had made notations in the margins. Mars searched for the Primer symbol, taking a moment to activate the artifact in his tattoo so that it was fresh in his mind. But he didn't find anything close to it anywhere. And no mention of it, either. Instead, the journal seemed primarily concerned with the Mistgrave. There were notes on the creatures said to be living in there, riftworms and draugrs, as well as long rambling sections about the corruption of Rift magic after the Cataclysm.

With his frustration growing, Mars put everything back the way he'd found it and contemplated his next move. He didn't know what to do, not about the Primer formula or this orb business. He didn't want to take anything that might not be what he needed—Fura and Katrìn would surely move everything if they found anything disturbed, and that could lose him any opportunity to get what was he after for certain. So instead, he focused on the only thing he could—finding a way out of here. He couldn't go through Katrìn's room, not with the sear back in place, so he chose the corridor on the right, hoping it would lead somewhere useful.

Before long, he came upon another window, this one looking into a sitting room much like Fura's, but with the seahorse crest of the Lux Kith hanging over the door. The Lux were housed in the White Court, a fair distance from Fura's rooms in the Red Court. Mars couldn't fathom how it was possible he'd traveled so far. Yet there was no denying it. He moved on, soon arriving at an intersecting hallway. He chose the left turn here, and after a while spotted another window, this one looking in on the barracks occupied by the Fifth's guard. That was in the Mid Court, an impossible distance away compared to what he'd actually traveled.

Mars carried on, realizing with growing certainty that this maze of hallways existed somewhere beyond the physical boundaries of the city. It was the only explanation that fit, despite how improbable it seemed. Then again, the adepts who had designed it were responsible for the Cataclysm. There was no telling what else they'd been capable of.

One thing he knew for certain, though, was that those old

adepts must've been a touch mad. The windows he came along followed no logic or reason, the portals appearing at random.

Some of the windows he encountered hung on the right side of the corridor, and some on the left. He even came across one set in the middle of the floor. Whatever room it led to was too dark for Mars to see, and he didn't dare step through it without knowing more. For all he knew, it might deposit him inside the Mistgrave. One window opened upon the great hall in the Mid Court, where the Fifth and his cabinet were taking lunch, Ivar among them. Another revealed the kitchens in the Red Court, and yet another the servants' common room. There were also a disturbing number of bedchambers and bathing houses.

Finally, Mars came upon a window into the great library of the Mid Court. With no one in view, he placed his hand against the relic symbol and stepped out through the mirror. Then he slowly made his way back to his rooms, his body tired from the adventure and all the magic, his mind weary from searching for the answer of what to do next. For despite the revelations, nothing had really changed. He still needed the Primer formula. It remained his sole chance to escape Una forever.

Only, he was lying to himself about not having the answer. He did have a solution; he just wasn't sure he could go through with it.

Katrìn. She was the key to Fura's secrets. Her love for her friend was the weak spot in her armor. All Mars had to do was apply the right pressure. Blackmail was the oldest trick in the book, after all, and he knew how to employ it well. Katrìn was a secret adept, and Fura would do anything to keep her safe. Even turn over the formula to keep him from revealing the truth about Katrìn to the kiths—who would enthrall her the moment they learned it.

Mars swallowed bile burning the back of his throat. He was thinking about doing to Katrìn the very thing Orri would've done to him.

He's not the heartless beast we first assumed him to be, Katrìn had said.

How wrong you are, Mars thought, picturing Orri. *How wrong you are.*

SEVENTEEN

ALTHOUGH MARS SAW the path before him clearly, he would not act. Not yet. There was still time, he told himself. If he played his hand too soon, he risked losing it all. He still had to keep Fura safe through the remainder of the Assembly, and doing that would be a lot easier if he wasn't also blackmailing her. Then again, he knew she was planning to go somewhere, leaving him behind. He had to be mindful of that as well, choosing the right moment to press his advantage before it was too late. But for now, he could relax, taking his ease. And the Quiescence ball would be just the thing, a night of dancing and feasting and pretending he was just a wealthy kith playboy and not a mercenary.

As he donned the Hunter's black mask, he couldn't help but once again see the irony in Fura's choice of costumes. In the story, the Hunter was a nobleman who was only pretending to be an outlaw, the hero disguised as a villain. Mars turned to the mirror. His reflection proved a pleasant surprise, as he ran his hands down the sides of the tunic. The seamstress had designed the clothes to complement his frame. With the fitted waist, emphasized by a leather belt, he made a dashing figure, the sight an unexpected boost to his confidence.

He supposed, given the quality of his own costume, he shouldn't have been surprised by Fura's—and yet when he first caught sight of her dressed as Lady Ingrid, he felt his jaw loosen and his breath grow shallow. The shimmery gown looked like woven moonlight delicately draped across her body. Without the rigid bodice and petticoats she normally wore, she seemed soft and fragile in the gown. All except for the lithe muscles of her arms, visible through the wide gaps in her sleeves from her shoulders to the gathering at her wrists. Mars opened his mouth to compliment her but found himself unable to speak.

If Fura noticed his silence, she made no comment as she held out her arm for him to take.

"I must say," Katrìn said, joining them in the sitting room, "you make an excellent Hunter, Halfur." She wore a dress fashioned to resemble a peacock, complete with a whimsical shawl made of real peacock feathers that framed her shoulders and head in a green-and-blue halo.

"And you make one alluring bird." Mars winked, provoking a twinkling laugh from her. For a moment, he couldn't help seeing Katrìn in a new light—a secret adept, maybe even a kindred spirit. He wondered what it would be like to confess his own powers to her, to discover if her experiences matched his—the thrill of Rift magic rushing through him, the terror of almost being discovered, and the ever-present need to wield the power. But no, she wasn't like him, he realized, glancing at Fura. Katrìn had shared her secret, her burden. He'd never told anyone—not on purpose. For a second, his heart ached for his lost friend, regret at what he'd done like a throbbing wound.

Locking the emotion away inside himself, Mars escorted Fura to the door. Together, the three of them made their way to the ball. If not for Katrìn and her habit of idle chatter, it would've been a silent affair. Fura seemed at once both strangely distant and far too close, like standing too near an open fire on a wintry day. He wanted to both lean into her and retreat at the same time.

The sounds of the soiree enveloped them long before they reached the grand hall of the Mid Court. The music pulsed like a heartbeat and the shouts of voices crackled like caged lightning as they stepped through the doors, held open for the evening. Mars had heard the Quiescence ball was the pinnacle event of the Assembly, and it was true. Hundreds of people thronged the chamber, spilling out of doorways and lining the stairs, while couples moved across the dance floor, keeping the crowd at bay with swirling skirts and stomping feet. Everyone in Hàr Halda was in attendance, from the kith to the politicians to the servants.

Suspended from the hall's vaulted ceiling were nine massive chandeliers crafted to look like the moon surrounded by seven glowing stars. The Ice fueling them cast a silvery light that slowly faded to blue, then to purple, then back to silver again. Even Mars, who rarely took the time to bother with such things, paused to admire the dazzling sight, at once mystical and romantic. Then, noticing Fura's bemused observation of him, he moved on, guiding them toward the least crowded area he could find.

In moments, a Torvald servant attended them, offering glasses of rosé, Fura's preferred wine. Mars took one for himself as well, downing nearly half of it in one go as he searched for a way to break the odd tension that still clung about them.

Fortunately, Ivar soon joined their party, providing a welcome distraction. He greeted Fura and Mars warmly enough, but the smile he offered Katrìn seemed to heat the room. She returned it willingly, a nervous fluttering about her mouth.

"I believe they're calling for a quadrille," Ivar said as the current song ended and another began. "Shall we?" He gestured first to Katrìn, then to Fura and Mars.

Katrìn placed her hand into Ivar's, her enthusiasm answering for all of them. Not that Mars minded. It was a ball, after all, and a group dance was better than the frenzy of the waltz or the intimacy of a sagnasar. In his current state of mind, he preferred not to dance so close to Fura if it could be avoided.

Moments into it, though, he began to relax and enjoy himself, the liveliness of the music and movements coaxing it out of him. Fura, too, seemed more at ease as the song ended, her cheeks pink from the revelry.

Feeling warm himself, Mars suggested another drink. He and Fura left the floor while Ivar pulled Katrìn willingly into the next dance.

"They make a handsome couple," Fura observed a few moments later, another glass of rosé in hand.

"I suppose so." Mars took a drink, then shrugged. "Although I imagine Katrìn would complement any partner. She has such a generous disposition." *Among her other charms,* Mars silently added, noting the many admirers Katrìn seemed to be garnering in her peacock dress. "By the nine, even Gregor seems to have noticed her." Mars inclined his chin toward the man, whose gaze at Katrìn bordered on lecherous. An uncomfortable image of Katrìn locked into a hobble flashed through his mind.

Fura scowled, crossing her arms over her chest. "Yes, but he'd never stoop so low as to dance with a lady's maid, even with the relaxed social rules of the Quiescence."

"Thank goodness for that. If he were to try, I'd happily offer to relocate his nose to some other part of his face."

Fura snorted. "I'd pay a thousand herrings to see it."

"That, I would do for free."

Fura laughed, but before she could comment further, Askalon appeared. He was dressed as the titan Salveig in a horned circlet and sleeveless leather jerkin.

"May I have this dance, lìtja?" Askalon held out his hand.

Fura glanced at Mars. "Think you can manage to stay out of trouble by yourself for a few moments?"

Mars feigned a wounded look. "I think I can manage an hour, at least."

Askalon shot Mars a scowl as he led Fura onto the floor.

Mars turned to find a suitable partner for himself, and a moment later, he joined the dance with a girl named Mikaela, the same girl who'd flirted so obviously with him the day of the Bounding. She made for an enthusiastic partner as Mars led her through a sagnasar, a traditional story dance of Riven. This one told the tale of two young lovers fleeing the persecution of the jealous titan Magda, who envied their innocence and unblemished beauty. It was supposed to be a tragic song and a tragic dance, but Mikaela giggled through the whole thing, taking advantage of every spare breath to talk to Mars. He smiled and nodded, hoping the dance would end soon.

Not that the end made any difference. Mikaela immediately claimed the next dance with him—and the next. Mars had begun to fear there would be no getting rid of her when finally Fura appeared beside them.

She held out a glass of wine to Mars. "So sorry to deprive you of such an affable partner, Mikaela, but I'm afraid Halfur suffers from weak ankles and is in need of a rest."

"I what?" Mars sputtered.

"Come now, there's no denying it. I saw you wobbling a moment ago." Fura pressed the wineglass toward him again, and he took it, uncertain if he wanted to smile at her for saving him from Mikaela or scowl at her for the rumor about his supposed weakness that would surely result. The kith heirs were sure to enjoy teasing him for it.

"Oh, I'm sorry to hear that." Mikaela faced him and curtsied. "Until next time, Mr. Karlsvane." She hurried away, off to claim her next victim.

"Thank you," Mars said, inclining his head to Fura.

"I know a cry for help when I see one." She turned, and together they made their way off the floor and to a set of chairs for a welcome rest.

"Is dear old Askalon off to bed already?" Mars said, scanning the room. "Must be exhausting trying to dance with a stick shoved up one's arse." His gaze landed on Bekka among a throng of dancers across the way, and stifling a scowl, he glanced back at Fura.

She made a face at him, doing her best not to be amused by his comment. "I think he wears it special for you." She sighed. "But don't take it personally. The only person he trusts with my safety is himself."

"And do you trust me?" Mars said, taken by surprise at his own question. He hadn't meant to ask it. It had simply slipped out of him like a spill of wine from a glass held in a shaky hand.

"I don't even know your real name." Fura shook her head, as if just now realizing this for the first time. The truth struck Mars like a whip, the sting made worse by the knowledge of his betrayal, both the one that had come before and the one that would soon follow—that is, if he failed to discover the Primer formula on his own. He supposed there was time to give it another try....

Aware of the silence growing around them like a cloying weed, Mars rose to his feet and stretched. "Are you hungry? I spotted some delicious offerings at the refreshment table."

Casting him a droll smile, Fura stood, just as another song ended and the first dulcet tones of the next began, the tune a famous one.

She cocked her head. "Oh, I believe that's 'Ingrid and the Hunter' they're playing now."

"Yes, it is." Several people were already watching them expectantly. Mars sighed. His feet were hurting, but he couldn't see a way out of it. "I suppose we shouldn't miss it."

He led Fura onto the dance floor, where he came to a stop and turned toward her, drawing her slowly around until her back faced him. Then he stepped toward her and to the side, his chest pressed to her shoulder blade as he placed one hand at her waist and held the other up to the side in the shadow position that would begin the dance. He leaned his head close to hers, and a slight shudder went through her as his breath touched her neck. Of all the sagnasars, this dance was the most challenging in the way it ranged from cool to heated, slow to quick to slow again, as it told the tragic story.

When the dance started, Mars urged Fura forward, her body willing to his lead. He followed, first pushing her away, then drawing her back again. Never in all their practices had they danced like this. Gone was the rigid tension Fura had always held toward him. Instead of steel, her arms were supple as willow branches. Instead of cold, she was caged heat, her eyes fixing on his every time they entered a promenade or completed a turn. He found himself searching for her eyes as well, hungry for her gaze. An invisible veil seemed to descend around them, the rest of the world falling away until there was nothing but the two of them and the dance.

As the music reached its sad crescendo, Mars dropped Fura into a dip. But he didn't arch his back away from her as the steps demanded to symbolize the final separation of the lovers in death. Instead, he leaned forward and kissed her as he'd wanted to do since the dance began, since he first saw her in the moonlight dress.

Or maybe since the night of the Felling.

At once, her mouth opened to his, her torso folding upward to meet his body. It wasn't like the last time, at the Felling, forced and insincere. This kiss was warm and intentional, building to a crescendo as Mars raised Fura back to her feet and pulled her forward until their bodies were joined chest to chest and hip to hip.

When the kiss finally ended, an uncertain amount of time later, Fura's cheeks were flushed and her gaze liquid, like melted emeralds. She opened her mouth as if to speak, but nothing came out. Mars didn't speak either, words failing him. His body felt on fire, his skin buzzing as thoughts whirled through his head. In a daze, they left the dance floor, in an unspoken agreement to find more to drink and to eat.

The rest of the night passed in a blur for Mars. He knew he conversed with people, Katrìn and Ivar for certain, but he could not remember afterward what they'd discussed. His mind was consumed with Fura, her nearness, and the hunger gnawing inside him to claim another kiss.

By and by, Mars suspected she might be caught up in the feelings as well. Her fingers kept grazing his as if by accident, her shoulder brushing his side. Her head seemed always inclined toward him, her lips in view, her gaze furtive yet lingering each time it crossed his. Soon Mars began to consider excuses for them to leave, to find some place they could be alone. He bolstered his courage with wine and smiles and casual touches, each one accepted without a flinch, her body reacting toward his instead of away.

"I'm ready to retire," Fura said sometime later, her voice soft, tentative. "That is, if you are."

Mars nodded, his throat tight as he searched for Katrìn. Protocol dictated that she go with them.

"Kat is still dancing," Fura said, anticipating his thought. "Let's leave her to it. No one will notice."

Mars glanced around, realizing it was true. A fervor clung about the crowd, the release of so many weeks of pent-up energy and tensions. Tonight, the rules did not apply.

They headed for the door, stealing through the crowd like thieves. They'd almost made it when Askalon appeared before them, blocking the way. Mars let out a curse, braced for an unwelcome escort.

But Askalon merely bowed his head politely toward Fura. "Forgive the intrusion, but I've a message from the dòttra." He turned to Mars. "For Halfur."

Frowning, Fura stepped aside, releasing her claim on his arm. A chill spread through Mars in the absence of her touch.

"What is it?" Mars said, impatient, as he and Askalon retreated a few steps. His attention remained on Fura, his thoughts distracted by the memory of their kiss and anticipation of the next one.

Askalon leaned over Mars, his voice a whisper but his words like the strike of hammer against anvil. "She can never be yours. Don't forget it." Then Askalon pulled back, bowed once more to Fura and disappeared into the crowd.

"What was that about?" Fura asked, twining her arm through his once more.

"Nothing."

"Come on, then. While we still can." She tugged him into a walk.

Mars went along, one foot following the other as the haze he'd been under slowly began to dissipate. For a moment, he felt outside himself, able to recall the dance, the kiss, and the strength of his desire, but without getting lost in it. Soon he could think clearly enough for the doubts to seep in. *What am I doing?* What was he allowing to happen here? He was no fool, not some naïve inexperienced boy. He'd been here before often enough to know where it led.

She can never be yours.

Oh, but she could be. For tonight, at least, or for as long as this lasted. This . . . *contract.*

A contract, a job, just like the one he had worked before, when he killed her father.

We are the weapon, not the will.

It didn't help. Mars pressed his eyes shut against the memory and the image that followed it of Katrìn locked in a hobble.

"Are you all right?" Fura touched his hand, drawing him back to the present. They'd reached her quarters, the guards standing wordlessly aside to allow them entry.

Mars nodded and reached for the door, opening it for her. She stepped inside and he followed, closing it behind them. The lights in the sitting room had been left on but turned low, casting deep shadows about the place. It was the perfect atmosphere for secret passions. Fura came to a stop in the middle of the room and faced him, her eyes at first fixed on a spot on the floor before slowly rising to his. He'd never seen her look so hesitant, so uncertain.

Mars swallowed the lump in his throat, waiting for her to make the next move. A part of him hoped she would not, but another part hoped she would. For a single moment, he let himself imagine a life with her in it, the two of them together. Close, connected.

Fura stepped toward him slowly, placing a hand on his arm. Her lips parted in a sigh—and before he knew what was happening, her fingers dug into the skin of his forearm as she yanked the cuff from his wrist.

Cursing, he jerked his arm away. "What are you doing?" But it was too late. Even in the dim light, she'd seen—because she'd known to look.

Breathless, incredulous, she spoke the truth out loud, each word landing like a thunderclap. "You *are* an adept."

EIGHTEEN

MARS TOOK A step back, his emotions whirling as he tried to make sense of what was happening. She'd brought him here, lured him here—to expose his secret.

"Don't be absurd," he said, quickly refastening his cuff. "I think you've let the wine go to your head."

"It all makes sense." Fura nodded to herself. "You were there. We saw the footprints."

He knew at once where she meant—beyond the mirror in Katrìn's room, down that ancient hidden hallway where no one had trekked for years. He drew a deep breath to slow his racing heart. *She knows, she knows, she knows.* The truth kept repeating inside his brain, threatening to shatter him from the inside out.

But the answer to this impossible situation was right before him. The card he'd been planning to play all along.

"You are mistaken, Miss Torvald," Mars said, his voice cold, the Shadow Fox on full display. "The only secret adept around here is Katrìn. You expose me, and I will expose what she is to every kith in Hàr Halda." He paused, allowing the threat to sink in. "Starting with your mother."

Fura blinked, confusion rising like a slow tide over her expression. Then the color drained from her face.

"You bastard." Her hands balled into fists. "You miserable bastard. How dare you threaten Katrìn!" She threw a punch at him, aiming for his face. But she'd had enough to drink to impair her skills as a Rivna Knight. Mars stepped back out of the way easily and caught her hand mid-motion, tightening his fingers around her wrist hard enough that she unclenched the fist.

"I suggest not making a scene." He indicated the door. "Unless you want to explain to the guards the source of your ire."

Fura gulped, seeing the trap. She pulled free of his grip and took a step back from him, cursing low under her breath. Every foul and vile word in existence came out of her mouth, directed at him. Mars held still, unflinching at her quiet tirade. He'd been called worse. And yet the insults stung; they burrowed beneath his skin, like bloodsucking insects. He wanted to defend himself, to argue back, but he did not. That wasn't the part he was here to play. The heartless beast must not care what anyone thought of him.

After a time, the tirade ended, leaving Fura red-faced and panting with outrage. "Every threat you make against Katrìn is the same one you face yourself," she said.

Mars held his breath, knowing she was right. It was just a matter of who could prove it, who would be believed. It was a game whose outcome he couldn't predict, couldn't cheat. More than anything, he didn't want to play, but there was no going back.

She knows what I am. The thought sent fear ripping through him.

At his continued silence, Fura turned away from him and crossed the room to a tray where a servant had left a decanter of the sherry she sometimes drank before bed to help her sleep. She pulled out the stopper and poured a glass. But she didn't drink, only held it in front of her like a shield as she faced him once more. "What do you want?" she asked.

"You already know what I want," Mars replied.

Fura narrowed her eyes. "Despite the rumors you've heard, the Primer formula does not exist. My father destroyed it before he died."

Mars tilted his head. "You can't really expect me to believe that. Not when you spent all those hours in your father's observatory trying to make it for yourself." He watched her, waiting for confirmation of this truth to dawn in her eyes. But all he saw was the anger there, the hatred.

Of him.

Steeling his gaze, Mars ran his tongue over his teeth. "I'm not unreasonable, Fura. If you give it to me, I will keep Katrìn's secret until the day I die."

"And who will keep yours?"

"You have no proof to substantiate your claims about me."

Fura laughed. "As if I would need proof. My word is enough, especially for my mother."

"Even if it means exposing Katrìn as well?" Mars clenched his fists. He pictured Orri then, and wondered if he could do it again. If he could kill Fura to save himself.

She stared at him, unblinking, her knuckles white around the glass as she held it before her, one arm crossed over her waist. Mars stared back, keeping his expression calm, border-ing on smug. *Yes, that's right. I will do what I threaten*, he let his eyes speak, even as his heart protested.

Fura bristled beneath that gaze. He had her now. Despite her bravado in threatening him, she would soon give in, turn over the formula. Then he could forget all this. Forget her.

But then a slow, certain smile slid across her lips, and she took a deep drink from the glass of sherry. "You know," she said, exhaling in satisfaction, "I think Katrìn is right about you after all."

Mars tensed, recalling that conversation all too easily. He didn't reply, afraid of giving away too much. Let doubt stumble her instead.

Only it didn't. She nodded to herself, her expression turn-ing haughty. "She says you're not the coldhearted mercenary you pretend to be"—she paused to cough—"that secretly you do care about things other than yourself, other than money."

"She is mistaken," Mars said coolly, even as his thoughts rebelled—bombarding his mind with images of Katrìn maimed and hobbled, living out the life he'd fought so hard to escape.

"Even if she is, you still won't do it. You wouldn't risk the danger to yourself. You're—" Fura started coughing again, louder this time, and with a sharp edge to it, as if she were breathing razor blades.

Something in the sound raised the hairs on his neck.

"Halfur," she said around coughs, and blood flew from her mouth, flecking her dress. That wet red looked obscene across the shimmery material.

Mars reached for her, his heart rising into his throat. He put his nose toward her mouth and breathed in. A smell like putrefying roses struck him, and he reeled backward in alarm, recognizing the telltale sign.

Hoar. The worst of all poisons. It killed in minutes—and there was no antidote.

Fura was dying.

For an impossible moment, time seemed to stand still. Thoughts raced through Mars's head as he scrambled for what to do next, coming up with nothing. None of the antidotes in his room would slow down the poison's relentless destruction. And even if he could find a nurse, they wouldn't be able to heal her in time. He didn't know if the poison could even be drawn out by Ice at all.

But he couldn't let her die—the thought of it unleashed a terror inside him like he'd never known before. *No, she will not die.* He would not let her.

The frozen moment seemed to retract back to the present like a released bowstring. Mars tightened his grip on Fura, catching her before she collapsed to the floor. Her breathing had worsened, the sound like a blacksmith drawing a rasp over a horse's hoof. But Mars welcomed it, glad that her lungs hadn't failed yet. He lowered her to the ground, panic gripping him, turning instinct into action.

Scraping both his wrists across the blades in his remaining cuff, he summoned the Rift. The magic surged into him at once, making his head spin. *Heal her,* he willed it, willed himself. At once he felt his senses being drawn into Fura, awareness of her body filling his mind—the flow of her veins beneath her skin, those tiny rivers of blood like the magic coursing through him. He traveled down her throat to her stomach, his senses splintering into a thousand different pathways as he searched for the poison.

There it was. He sensed it like an intruder, a devastating force chewing its way through her body. He willed it gone with the magic, imagined sifting it of her like through a sieve. The magic responded, drawing the poison out of her, but the paltry sacrifice of blood he'd offered wasn't enough. The wounds dried up, and the magic ceased.

"No!" Mars screamed, returning to himself long enough to register the pallid color of Fura's face, the stillness lying over her body like a death shroud. He reached for the dagger hidden beneath his tunic and pulled it free. Then he slashed it across his forearm, quick but deep, ensuring the flow wouldn't stop so easily.

Once again, the Rift answered, surging into him. He descended into the trance, seeing inside Fura, tracking down the poison like a hunter after a wolf. The magic proved an eager participant, filling him up, even as it began to siphon him away. Before he knew what was happening, the magic seized control. Instead of working for him, it worked through him. It became the puppeteer and he just the puppet, just the sacrifice. The blood flowed down his arm, a heated, sticky river, and it did not stop as the Rift continued to do what he had willed it to, searching out every remnant of the hoar inside Fura and destroying it.

Slowly, Mars felt the cold enter his body, spreading through him as his blood drained away, vanishing into the unquenchable thirst of the Rift. The world of his existence began to fade to a grim twilight, then to black. His consciousness slipped away, unraveling like a pulled thread. Just before the last of him came undone, he sensed Fura stirring on the floor, life coming back to her.

Even as the Rift pulled away the last of his, taking him under at last.

NINETEEN

THIS IS WHAT it feels like to die.

The furtive thought slid through Mars's mind as he came back to consciousness, going from an empty, black void to the brightness of life in an instant. He felt as if he'd been erased only to be redrawn. Opening his eyes, he drew a shallow breath that took a monumental amount of effort, like scaling a cliff made of sand.

He was lying in a bed in an unfamiliar room, shirtless, his arms bare. The absence of his cuffs sent a shock through him, and he sat up. His head lurched at the sudden movement, his vision blurring as an ache surged through his body. He collapsed back onto the pillows with a groan.

"I would advise not moving. You were basically dead a few hours ago."

Carefully Mars turned his head toward the speaker, his gaze falling on Katrìn seated in a chair in the corner of the room, an embroidery wheel in her lap. This was Katrìn's room, he realized, recognizing the mirror across the way.

Her gaze fixed on his, her expression inscrutable. "I don't

suppose anyone's ever told you it's unwise to give the Rift so much blood."

"Where is Fura?" All at once the memory had come to him—Fura, with blood on her lips and death in her eyes.

Katrìn's expression softened. "She's fine. Thanks to you."

Mars swallowed and shifted on the bed, turning his wrists down to hide the scars. But there was no hiding the truth. A thick bandage covered half his arm, the wounds beneath a dull throb. Any relief he felt at hearing that Fura had survived vanished at the realization that his secret was well and truly exposed. There was no lying his way out of it now.

"You, however," Katrìn continued, "are only fine because of me. That makes us even now. Two adepts, both with much to lose if anyone else discovers our secret."

Mars closed his eyes, an unfamiliar flush of shame washing over him. He would've betrayed her to save himself. And yet she had saved him.

He heard the sound of footsteps and opened his eyes to see that Katrìn had risen from her chair and crossed the room to the bed. She stood peering down at him with hands on hips. "Would you really have done it?"

Mars stared back at her, hearing all the unspoken questions that came with it—*How could you? You, who were also a hidden adept, who knew what it would mean, what it would cost?*

He answered as truthfully as he could. "I didn't want to. But you must understand that I have my reasons for wanting the formula—for *needing* it—and they have nothing to do with money."

"And what are those reasons?" Katrìn folded her arms, waiting for his explanation.

Mars turned his head, trying to avoid her gaze. He couldn't tell her. He didn't want to tell her. Not when doing so might require him to speak of Orri. Besides, his reasons no longer mattered, now that his secret had been exposed. There was no taking it back, not without killing both of them. The thought turned his stomach.

"Has Fura gone to tell her mother about me, then?" he said, barely able to get the words out.

"Not yet."

Mars considered this, wondering if maybe this wasn't the end. He still knew Katrìn's secret, after all. That was a currency that could be spent in this game. That is, if Elìn or one of the other kiths even believed him. He couldn't be certain anymore. It was one thing to be a mercenary, low in the social hierarchy, but quite another to be an adept, lowest of all—and yet most highly coveted as well.

Only, even as he thought it, he understood the truth. No one would believe him over Fura. If he played that card, the game was over.

Accepting defeat, Mars eased his way into a sitting position, managing to hold in a groan at the pain. He felt like one of Una's once dead ravens. "What's she waiting for, then?"

Katrìn dropped her arms to her sides, smoothing out her skirts. "That depends on you. Now, if you'll excuse me. Fura will want to know you're awake."

Mars sat motionless on the bed after she departed. His

instincts told him to flee. That was his only option. He could do it, too. He knew the way through the mirror. But even as he considered it, his stomach flipped over. He wasn't ready to channel more magic now, not even the trickle needed to pass through the portal. Even if he was willing to attempt it, he wasn't sure he could make it across the room under his own power. He truly had almost died. The magic had almost taken everything from him. For the first time in his life, he fully understood what was meant by lifeblood, by what was known as *kull*. The terror of it made his stomach churn. Yet it was nothing compared to the fear that had gone through him as he watched Fura slipping away.

Despite his perilous position, a swell of relief came over him when Fura appeared in the doorway. She looked pale, dulled around the edges, but alive. He wondered if she knew just how lucky she'd been to survive a hoar poisoning.

Fura stepped toward the bed, her cold expression sending gooseflesh prickling down his arms. She cleared her throat, the sound rough as a mill grinder. "Katrìn tells me you're lucky to have survived the magic you worked on me."

Mars cringed at the rasp in her voice, hoping it wouldn't be permanent. He nodded.

"Why did you do it?"

He considered his response carefully, wondering what she was after and what might give him the best advantage in whatever she was planning next. "The poison you were given is known as hoar. Have you ever heard of it?"

Fura raised a hand to her throat. "Yes."

"Then you know that it is completely merciless. It acts

quickly, and there is no antidote. The Rift was the only way to save you."

Fura lowered her head. "That is not an answer to my question. Why bother saving me at all?"

Resisting the urge to squirm beneath her gaze, Mars rolled his eyes. "Keeping you safe—and alive—is what I'm getting paid for."

"No, it's not." A glare heated Fura's gaze. "You made it perfectly clear that your true purpose in being here is the Primer. So why do it? Why risk your own life just to save mine?"

Mars searched for an answer that would satisfy her, but was unable to find one. An old Rivna proverb sounded in his mind: *The worst lies are the ones we tell ourselves.* His temper snapped at the impossible position he found himself in.

"I did it because I had to, all right? I . . . I couldn't let you die when I could stop it. I—" Mars broke off, sinking deeper into the pillows. In truth, he didn't know why he'd done it. He hadn't given it any thought. There'd been no hesitation. It was simply something he'd had to do.

Fura said nothing. She only stared down at him, as if she could see something she was choosing not to speak of.

Mars shifted once more on the bed, wishing he had the strength to stand. He didn't like facing her like this—weakened and on his back. "So," he said, unable to take her silence any longer. "What happens now? Do you turn me in to your mother?'

Fura folded her hands in front of her. "It's what I should do. What my instinct at first told me to do, but . . . you saved my life. And according to Rivna, a life saved is a life earned. I will not turn you in."

Mars hadn't realized he'd been holding his breath until the sweet burst of air suddenly filled his lungs at her words. Never before had he been so thankful for Rivna.

"But at the same turn, you must promise not to reveal the truth about Katrìn, either."

"I understand." Mars touched a hand to his wounded arm. Katrìn had saved his life. He wouldn't repay her with such a betrayal. "Well, what happens now?" He still needed the Primer, needed a way out. Nothing had changed that.

Fura knew it, too. "We are at an impasse there as well, I'm afraid. You still want the Primer formula, but I can't just give it to you."

Mars had expected no less. "Again, what happens now?"

"You could give up." She smiled as she said it, as if knowing the suggestion was absurd. "Except you're a mercenary and the code you follow means you must do what you're paid to do until the end."

Her words surprised him. Not because they were true, but because she seemed so accepting of them, accepting of him. *She knows what you are and yet here she is, treating you like a person, not some monster to run away from,* the old voice said.

"You're not wrong."

Fura cocked her head, her gaze penetrating once more, seeing deep inside him. "Katrìn told me you want the formula for something other than money."

Mars slowly nodded, but as with Katrìn, he couldn't bring himself to say more.

Fura reached out a hand to touch the bandages on his

arm, her fingers warm and gentle through the gauze. "Tell me why you need it so badly. Maybe I can help."

A bitter laugh escaped his throat. "You won't understand. It's dishonorable business, after all." A bitter memory of their first meeting rose in his mind, how she had regarded him as something less than human.

Frowning, Fura withdrew her hand. "That may be, but since meeting you, I've come to realize I can't just ignore such business, either. I must learn to face it, maybe even work within its rules."

His jaw slid open. "Never in a million years would I have thought you'd say such a thing."

"I know." She grimaced. "Only, it's not just about your life as a mercenary. I may not understand that very much, but I know what it's like to live as a secret adept. I've lived it with Katrìn. I've watched adepts beaten and tortured and treated like chattel. And I've known the fear of how just one mistake, one careless moment, would seal Katrìn's fate, too."

Maybe she would understand, Mars realized. He weighed his options, feeling something break apart inside him, like a wall standing on a compromised foundation. He still needed a way free from Una, but maybe there was more than one way to get there. Maybe there was some alternative to the formula. He would never know unless he was brave enough to try.

"Very well," he said, clearing his throat. "I need the formula because it is the only way I can get free of my employer."

"You no longer wish to be a mercenary?" Fura raised a hand to her mouth as if she found the notion incredulous.

"For some time now I've been trying to escape her, to

escape Riven. As you said, I live in constant fear of discovery. But getting free of a life like mine is not so easily done." Drawing a breath, he told Fura of the ten months he'd spent working the docks, only to have Una reel him back, forcing him into taking this contract.

"If it's just about the money," Fura said, "I can help with that. Once the Primer—"

"It's not just the money. If I try to leave, if I betray her in any way, she'll kill me. She has a vial of my blood stored in an ampoule made into an artifact. All she need do is break it, and that'll be the end of me."

Fura picked up the end of her braid and began fiddling with it, looking lost in thought. Mars left her to it, content to lie still and quiet. He felt as if he'd aged a hundred years in a single night.

Finally, she dropped the braid, coming back to the present from whatever path her thoughts had taken her down. "There might be a way we can help each other. Katrìn and I need to get to Skarfell."

Mars gaped. "Why would you ever want to go there?"

"Have you learned yet what the Primer does?"

"No." He leaned forward, tense at the possibility that he might finally learn that now.

Fura hesitated, still uncertain of him. But at the same time, he was fully in it, now that he knew the truth about Katrìn.

"The Primer destroys Ice."

Mars rolled his eyes at the preposterous notion. Ice couldn't be destroyed—it could only be used and used, the resource forever renewing. "There's no point in lying to me this deep into the game."

Fura placed her hands on her hips. "I'm not lying. It destroys Ice permanently. Used directly on a mine, it even keeps Ice from growing back."

He gaped at her again, making no effort to hide his disbelief.

"Do you recall the sabotage in the Skorris' Ice well my mother told you about?"

"Yes, of course." But even as he said it, he made the connection. "That was the Primer?"

Fura nodded. "Like any good scientist, my father needed to test his experiment. But he knew better than to try it on our mine, for fear of my mother finding out. Needless to say, she would not have approved of an invention capable of destroying Ice."

"No kidding." Despite how droll he sounded, Mars was reeling inside at this news. He'd known the Primer was valuable. But this? The kiths would do anything to possess such power—both to wield it themselves and to keep others from wielding it against them. There was no price too high to possess the Primer. And it wasn't just the kiths, either. Una, too, would do anything to have such a weapon. With it, she could control all the kiths—keeping their power in check with the knowledge that she alone could ruin them. For the first time, it occurred to Mars that maybe there wasn't a second client on this contract at all. Maybe it had been Una all along. If indeed she knew what it did.

His pulse quickened. Either way, it didn't matter. His freedom would be a small price for her to pay. He fixed his gaze on Fura, the one obstacle that remained in his way. "What does this have to do with going to Skarfell?"

"The Primer requires a final ingredient that can only be

found there. The version my father used in the Skorri mine was unstable. Dangerous. This ingredient should resolve that."

"Should?"

She shrugged. "There's always a measure of uncertainty in experimentation."

Mars shifted his weight on the bed, his neck starting to ache from the press of the pillows behind his head. "All right, but why do you need to make the Primer?"

Fura hesitated half a moment, her gaze flitting about the room. "I need to prove that it works. If I can convince the Helm that Ice can be eradicated completely—and safely—we can end the suffering of thousands."

Mars sighed, dismayed by her continued naivete. "They will never agree to it, Fura, no matter what you show them. The kiths fill the helmsmen's purses with money made from the very Ice you wish to destroy."

Her expression hardened, and she folded her arms over her chest. "I'm not interested in your political opinions, Halfur. Only in your magic."

Mars flinched, stung by her words. *I am only ever as good as what I can do*, he thought—then banished the notion. There was no time for self-pity. Not with so much on the line. "So what do you want from me, then?"

If she noticed the resentment in his tone, it didn't show on her face, which remained as hardened as before. "The Primer requires an ingredient that can only be found at Skarfell, as I said. My father had a secret laboratory there. It's where he did most of his work."

"How, though, when the way there is impassable?" Mars

said, even though he had already guessed the answer. But to admit it now would be to admit what he'd done and jeopardize his chances of getting the formula.

"Like you and Katrìn, my father was also a secret adept."

Mars closed his eyes, taking a moment to clear his head of the memories that had come rushing in at speaking of her father so openly. "Did your mother know?" he asked a moment later.

Fura surprised him with a nod. "She knew about his ability to channel Rift magic, a fact she used to her advantage for years. She had no knowledge of the Primer, though. By the time my father started working on that, their marriage had gone cold. To put it mildly. They loved each other, but neither could see past the other's politics."

Mars tried to wrap his mind around this, but failed. "How could your mother have married a secret adept and yet still keep enthralled adepts in her household?"

Fura sighed. "My mother is . . . a complicated woman. She has many flaws."

"That's an understatement. She keeps your house adepts addicted to dust. From where I stand, that makes her a power-hungry monster."

"Perhaps. But she was born into this way of life same as I was. Same as you were born into the life you lead." Fura uncrossed her arms, holding them rigid against her sides. "She has done terrible things, things I can never forgive. But I believe she can change. With the right motivation."

Mars opened his mouth to argue, then closed it again. What did he know of mothers, or the complicated love between them and their children? "Very well. You need to get to Skarfell. Where do I come in?"

"My father created an artifact designed to allow him to cross the Mistgrave unharmed. But it requires a constant sacrifice, and the journey is three days on foot. One adept cannot do it alone. We need two, minimum."

"How did your father manage it, then?" Mars paused, then sucked in a breath. "Did he know about Katrìn?"

"Yes, although she never went to Skarfell with him. He had two friends, colleagues, really, who often accompanied him."

Mars wondered where in the nine Henrik had found two other secret adepts, but he was too tired to ponder the question just now. "I see the dilemma, but what about your father's friends? Couldn't they have helped you?"

"They're dead. Same as him." A pained look crossed her face, as it always did when she spoke of her father's demise.

Mars's stomach twisted into a knot, and he drew a deep breath into his belly trying to get it to release. "Were they killed because of the formula?"

Fura nodded. "All of them. I'm sure."

Mars was, too. Again, the tremendous threat the Primer posed struck him. It wasn't just the kith and what they might lose, but all of Riven itself. Ice was everywhere, used in every machine and convenience, from the lights in the Den to the power that ran the trains. To destroy it all would cripple the nation.

"But why go after it, then? Why risk your life when so many others have already died? Why not give it to me? I'll make sure the threat against you vanishes."

"No." Fura planted her feet. "For as long as I can remember, my father wanted only one thing—to free Riven from the tyranny of Ice. It rules our lives, governs who has power and who does not. And those who do not will always suffer. He wanted to level the field and end that suffering."

"You mean suffering like Natasja's?"

Fura flinched at the name. "Yes, just like hers. It was my father's dream. And I mean to see it fulfilled."

Mars recognized that tone in her voice, the one that said she wouldn't back down from this, not for anything. He sighed. "All right, let's say we make it to Skarfell and you get this ingredient. What happens then?"

"I don't know. Not for sure." Fura sat down on the edge of the bed, as if she'd lost the strength to stand. "But I will make you a deal. If you help us cross the Mistgrave, if you help me make the Primer, I will pay you the full price of your employer's contract."

Mars opened his mouth to protest, but she cut him off with an upraised hand.

"And Katrìn and I will devote our full effort to finding a way to steal this blood ampoule and destroy it." Fura hesitated, biting her lip. "I can see your doubt, Halfur, but believe me when I say that Katrìn's knowledge of artifacts is vast. She was trained by my father, after all. If we can steal the blood ampoule, she can undo the magic. I'm certain of it."

Holding his breath, Mars let the possibility roll through his mind, testing it for all the weaknesses and risks. There were many. But . . . it didn't matter, not now, at least. She was offering him a deal, yes, but that didn't mean he had to honor it. He wasn't bound by the laws of Rivna. But if he agreed to help her now, he would surely earn her trust. The formula would be within his reach.

Or he could honor the deal and take his chances that he might win himself free another way.

"What say you, Halfur? Do we have a deal?" Fura held out her hand to him.

Mars stared at her, a strange feeling spreading through his limbs. Something like elation or dread. Maybe both. But whatever it was, he welcomed it. No matter what he ultimately decided, there was no changing the fact that Fura knew the truth about him, as did Katrìn, and yet neither had treated him like something evil, something to be feared. They'd treated him much the same as they always had, as a hired mercenary, albeit one with greater usefulness than before.

Mars accepted her proffered hand, a thrill shooting through him. "Yes, we do." He hesitated, his stomach fluttering with nerves at this unknown position he found himself in, his deepest secret willingly laid bare for the very first time. Remembering their conversation from the night before, which seemed nearly a lifetime ago, he added, "Only, if we're going to be in business together, I suppose it's time you call me by my real name."

"Really? And what is that?"

"Mars Darksvane."

"Mars." She said his name slowly, as if it were a nibble of food she wanted to taste before taking a true bite. "It's nice to meet you at last."

TWENTY

IT TOOK TWO days for Mars to recover enough to travel. And even then, he still felt sluggish, as if he were living in an alternate time from everyone else, a few seconds behind.

"Honestly, you're lucky to have recovered as much as you have," Katrìn said. "It must be our close proximity to the Heart here at Hàr Halda."

"The heart of what?" Mars looked up from the knapsack he was loading with food and supplies for their journey across the Mistgrave. They would leave tonight, after the Fifth's Feast, a ceremonial dinner that marked the end of the Quiescence. They planned to slip away before the feast ended, when the guard on the March was likely to be light.

"The *Heart* of the Rift," she said. "The source of it, the place where Jörn fell after the Titans slew him. It's located at Skarfell, and the Rift's magic is strongest there."

Mars considered this, wondering if that were the reason behind the strangeness he had felt when he first arrived here, that awful plucked feeling that only channeling his magic could banish. He adjusted his cuffs, comforted to have them back in place, and shook his head. "I thought the Rift was a vast underground lake beneath Riven."

Katrìn's brow furrowed. "If there is a lake, its source is at Skarfell, with the magic branching out everywhere else like tributaries. That's why the Consortium chose it as their stronghold."

"The White Keep," Mars said, having learned the day before that this was their true destination, the place where Henrik had conducted his secret experiments. Once it had been where the Consortium trained their adepts and performed their most powerful magic and experiments—including the one that had caused the Cataclysm.

"Correct." Katrìn beamed at him as if she were a teacher and he a student.

Mars shook his head. "How do you know so much about all this?" He suppressed a small shudder at speaking so openly about the Rift and magic after a lifetime of avoiding it.

"Henrik's research. He delved deep into the Consortium's history. He was obsessed with it. Speaking of which"—Katrìn put her hands on her hips—"did you read the journal I gave you?"

"Sure I did."

"Really?"

He scowled at her skeptical look. "I skimmed."

Katrìn snorted. "Your skills in deception seem to be deteriorating, Mars. Not that I mind. Mars," she said again. "I like that, too."

Warmth rose up his neck, an uncomfortable swell of affection spreading through him for her. It was true. He was slipping, but he found he didn't mind. Not with Katrìn—and maybe not so much with Fura, either, although he found the former easier to be around, his emotions more manageable. Whereas with Fura, they were like a tidal wave, constantly threatening to drag him under. Their alliance was uneasy at best.

"You really ought to read it, though," Katrìn scolded. "It's important, even if it doesn't make for pleasant reading."

"That's an understatement." Henrik's journal detailed all the horrors of the Mistgrave in vivid detail. Reading it, Mars soon discovered he'd rather not know just how many hooks each riftworm was said to have lining its body—one thousand forty-two, each one sharp as a razor blade. Or that the draugrs craved the taste of human flesh and would do anything to consume a person who disturbed their rest.

"Do you think we have enough water?" Katrìn said, distracting him.

Mars eyed the bladders they'd filled earlier, two for each of them, sitting on the nightstand next to Katrìn's bed. "We'll need to ration it on the journey, but so long as there's drinkable water at Skarfell we'll be fine."

"Oh, there's plenty of water. Food might be another matter."

"Maybe we'll find riftworm meat tasty." He'd only been joking, but Katrìn looked at him, aghast.

"You'd better hope we don't have reason to find out. They're no small task to kill. Some can be as big as a train car." Katrìn shook her head, pressing her palm to her face, hiding her scars in an unconscious gesture he'd seen her do often before. "You really should've done more than skim the journal."

Deciding it was time to change the subject, Mars said, "I've been wanting to ask, how did you get those burn scars?" He had no idea what lent him the courage to ask such a personal question, other than it seemed now that he knew of their shared magical secret, he wanted to know more about her and her life, which was so very different from his own and yet fundamentally the same.

Katrìn blinked, surprised by the question. "To be honest, I don't remember. But Henrik told me it happened in the fire that killed my parents."

"You don't remember it?"

"Not a bit." She grimaced. "And Henrik refused to tell me more about it. I never even learned their names."

Mars wondered why Henrik would keep something so important secret, but before he could ask the question, the door to the sitting room opened and Fura came in. She cast him a tentative smile.

"Are we all set?" She surveyed the pack items spread across the bed.

"As much as we can be." Katrìn made a face.

"It'll have to do. We need to leave for the feast." Fura was already dressed for it in a pair of fitted pants beneath an open-front skirt that fanned out at her sides like a pair of wings. It was a cunning outfit; in a matter of moments, she could be ready for their long hike to Skarfell.

"I'm ready," Mars said, picking up his frock coat from where he'd hung it across a chair. In his mind, he did a final inventory of his packed items. He'd sent Feykir off this morning with another update to Una, telling her he was close to finding the formula. It was true, after all, and it would serve to keep her satisfied in case word got back to her of his departure from the Assembly.

He and Fura bid farewell to Katrìn, who would meet them on the March at the agreed-upon hour, then departed for the Mid Court.

"Do you remember the plan?" Fura asked as they walked along. It was a pointless question, designed to fill the silence, but he humored her all the same.

"We will stay through the main course," Mars rattled off, "but before dessert is served, you will complain to your mother of a stomachache and ask permission to be escorted back to your rooms. I will attend you, of course."

"Of course."

"And we'll have to hope Askalon doesn't volunteer to join us," Mars added, the worry having occurred to him previously.

"He won't," Fura insisted, same as she had the first time he'd mentioned it. "The Fifth's Feast is the unofficial restart of the Assembly. Moving forward, the Helm will convene in private. This is the last chance for my mother to make her wishes known. She will expect Askalon to participate."

"Sounds delightful." Mars laid a palm against his chest. "So sorry we'll be missing it."

Fura snorted. "You might find yourself yearning for political intrigue once we're in the Mistgrave."

Picturing the riftworms again, with all one thousand forty-two of their hooks, he supposed she might have a point. He opened his mouth to make another joke, but held back at the nervous way Fura was clasping the compass rose pendant at her chest. She rarely showed such trepidation, especially around him.

They arrived at the Mid Court to a crush of people on the lawn making their way into Hroth Hall, which occupied the entire southern side. Hroth was nearly as large as Yrsa, but instead of a stadium design, it was long and sprawling, large enough to allow everyone of note at the Assembly to sit at one of the fifty ten-person dining tables spread throughout it. No one table stood out, ensuring that all who feasted here feasted as equals—as the Fifth intended.

Although this was the Fifth's event, the scenery remained as decadent as at every other social event Mars had attended. A giant mesh ball, plated in gold, hung from the ceiling in the middle of the room. Slowly revolving inside of it was a grand piano set on a narrow platform, the pianist playing a lively tune that carried throughout the hall as easily as if there were twenty instruments playing instead of one. Large swans made of blown glass perched atop the tables, each one with glistening, glowing eyes formed of Ice. As Mars and Fura sat down at their assigned table, he realized the glass swans were singing an accompaniment to the piano.

Fura had expected to be seated with her mother, but instead the seats surrounding them began to be taken by other sons and daughters of the kith, along with their respective dates. To Mars's relief, Gregor was not among them. Those who were—the Aster twins, Christel Hadder, and Liam Belen—were far more tolerable. As was Ivar, who joined them last of all. He looked harried as he took his seat.

"Something wrong, Ivar?" Fura asked.

He grimaced. "It's nothing. Just an argument with my father." As he spoke, his gaze darted to the other side of the room, where the Fifth had just taken his seat. A pair of guards stood just behind him with several more not far away, close to the exits. In fact, there were guards posted everywhere about the room's perimeter, Mars noted. Although having so many of the available guards here at the feast worked in their favor, it seemed excessive, almost as if the guards were there to keep people in instead of keeping assailants out.

Mars shook his head, trying to dislodge the paranoia. It didn't help when he returned his gaze to the Fifth and realized Bekka was one of the two guards nearest him.

"Say no more." Fura picked up her water glass in a mock toast before taking a tentative sip. Mars had advised the precaution. Poisons were far easier to detect in water than in other beverages, especially hoar, which would turn liquid white. "There's no one worse to argue with than one's parent," she added.

Ivar picked up his wineglass. "Cheers to that."

Mars didn't join the toast. He couldn't relate, after all.

With the anticipation of their departure, the dinner passed slowly. Surrounded as they were by Fura's peers and such vapid conversations as whether there should be sumptuary laws preventing commoners from wearing leopard fur or if Oswayan chocolate should be exempt from tariffs, Mars found himself wishing for the political intrigue he and Fura had joked about earlier. The sort taking place three tables over where Elìn and Askalon sat with two of the four helmsmen of the South Farthing.

Finally, the main course was served, and despite his growing tension at their clandestine escape, Mars forced himself to eat his fill and then some, doing it as quickly as he could without drawing attention. There was no telling how long it would be before he again ate a true meal once they descended into the Mistgrave.

Right on cue, five minutes after the hour struck eight, Fura set down her fork with a loud clank and ran a hand over her stomach.

"You'll have to excuse me, friends," she said to the table at large. "I'm not feeling well."

A look of alarm flashed across Ivar's face. "Was there something wrong with the food?" He stared down at the venison glazed with honey sauce they'd all been served, then glanced over at his father, seated some four or five tables away. The source of his fear occurred to Mars at once as he remembered all that business with the Ninth Year and the Reclamation. A valid concern for more reasons than one, Mars realized, making note of Bekka once more. He ought to warn Ivar about her, but he couldn't think of how to do that without revealing more about himself than he wished to. Perhaps if he told Fura . . .

"No, Ivar," Fura said, rising from the table. "I'm certain this is just me. My stomach has been uneven of late."

Mars stood beside her, offering his arm. "Would you like me to escort you back to your apartments?"

Fura nodded. "But let me tell my mother first."

With their charade almost complete, Mars led Fura through the tables, avoiding the servants clearing dishes, toward Elìn's table. The dòttra hadn't noticed their approach. Fura started to speak her name, but trailed off as the glass swan on the table began to sing louder than before. The sound was sweet at first, almost mesmerizing, but it soon turned into a screech that seemed to lance Mars's eardrums and set his heart to racing.

Danger, the sound said to him, whispering a hundred different memories of jobs he'd worked before. Something wasn't right here. Something—

The swan before them exploded. Mars lunged toward Fura, shielding her on instinct as screams erupted all around them, punctuated by the sounds of more swans exploding. Shards of glass bit his cheeks, throat, and hands, anywhere his skin was exposed, and while they made him flinch, he knew at once that they were minor irritations. Nothing that would kill or permanently maim. Not that it mattered. His only thought was of getting Fura out of there.

Wrapping his arms around her, he started hauling her toward the exit, even before Elìn shouted, "Get Fura back to her rooms!"

"Leave off." Fura dislodged his grip on her easily. "I can walk on my own. I can—" She broke off, her gaze drifting upward.

Mars looked up as well, his gaze drawn to a shimmering, golden-red light, rising from the shattered remains of the glass swans like liquid fire. The light swirled violently before coalescing into the form of a raven—the very image of Jörn, the World Raven. Glancing around, Mars saw there were fifty such ravens floating in the air above the tables now—and they were starting to speak in eerie unison.

End the Tyranny of Ice, they chanted, their voices growing louder and higher pitched with each phrase. *End the Tyranny of Ice. End the Tyranny of Ice. End*—Mars covered his ears as the shouts grew unbearable. In the next moment, all the glass in the room shattered—everything from the water goblets to the portal mirror hung on the wall.

A deathly silence fell, no one speaking or moving or even daring to breathe, it seemed.

But then another cry rose in the room, this one human and frantic. "The Fifth! He's dead!"

Pandemonium descended once more, everyone moving at once—most to flee. All save Ivar, who Mars spotted racing across the room to where his father had been seated. The man now lay on the ground several feet from the table, blood pooling around his head from a gash in his throat.

Bekka, Mars realized. She had done this; she had killed the Fifth. He didn't know what part she had played in the swans and ravens, but it didn't matter. She had used the chaos as the perfect chance to kill Patrek Arnasvane.

And to vanish.

For try as he may to find her, there was no sign of Bekka anywhere. Of course not. Her work here was done.

Or so Mars hoped.

TWENTY-ONE

"COME ON," MARS said, grabbing Fura's hand. "We need to get out of here."

"Go with them, Askalon," Elìn said. "Make sure my daughter stays safe."

Mars bit back a curse, despising these complications. Fura said nothing, merely hurried along beside him, her eyes downcast. When they arrived at her quarters, Mars went in first, checking it was safe. Then he motioned for Fura to enter. When Askalon tried to come with her, Mars held up his hand.

"I've got this. She will be safe. You should see to the dòttra. There's no telling who the killer will target next."

A torn look crossed the man's face, and for a moment, Mars worried he would stay. But concern for Elìn won out, and Askalon turned on his heel, heading into the hallway. "Lock the door until I return," he said, before disappearing around a corner.

Mars did as the truss bid, taking his time in the effort, trying to clear his thoughts. But they remained clouded as he turned and faced Fura.

She had sat down on the settee next to the fireplace, her

face buried in her hands. "I can't believe he's dead. I can't—" She choked on a breath that might've been a sob.

Crossing the room, Mars kneeled before her, taking hold of her wrists and gently pulling her hands away so he could look into her eyes, which were clouded with tears. "It's not your fault. You didn't do this."

But I know who did, he silently added, aware that if he'd only given warning, this might not have happened. Only, that wasn't his place. It wasn't who he was, no matter if it might've spared Fura this pain. Spared Ivar as well.

Fura shook her head. "You've no idea. That message . . . those ravens . . . it was for me."

End the Tyranny of Ice, the birds had chanted. "The Primer," Mars said, making the connection.

"Yes."

"But who would want the Ice destroyed?" Mars said, then stopped himself as his mind made another connection, recalling the attack back at the Torvald estate. "The Wake."

"Yes," she said again.

He frowned, dismayed to realize there was a lot more to this story than he'd been told. Letting go of her wrists, he stood. "What aren't you telling me, Fura?"

"It's nothing," she said at once, panic creeping into her voice. She stood as well, forcing him to retreat a step. "There's no time. We need to go. It's more important than ever that we make it to Skarfell."

"No." Mars blocked her path, arms crossed and feet planted. "I'm not going anywhere until you tell me what's going on."

The debate raged in her expression, but only for a moment. He knew she needed him and his magic more than ever now. "My father . . . he was a part of the Wake. They helped fund some of his research. And those adepts that traveled with him to Skarfell were members as well."

Given the rest of Henrik Torvald's secrets, this one wasn't as surprising as it might have been, considering that the Wake sought to destroy the kiths, including the one his wife headed. Then again, maybe that was the reason he had worked with them.

"But the closer my father got to completing the formula," Fura continued, "the more he began to distrust some of the Wake's members. He feared if given the formula, they would not use it to begin dismantling the ice mines, but rather to extort the kiths for all their wealth. He knew he couldn't trust them with it. And once he realized his life was in danger, he destroyed all his research and sent the only copy of the formula to me."

"And now they want it back." Mars recalled the unknown assailants that night in the orrery and wondered if they had been members of the Wake.

"Yes."

End the Tryanny of Ice, the ravens had chanted. "But I don't understand. Do you believe killing the Fifth was part of the warning?"

Fura bit her lip. "Maybe. I don't know. But we must get moving, Mars. Katrìn is out there alone, waiting for us on the March."

She had a point. "Let's leave through the mirror," Mars

said, heading for Katrìn's room. "I know a shortcut to the stables." They needed to be seen heading there to help solidify
the tale. If the dòttra did come after them, she would look in the
wrong direction.

Taking Fura's hand, Mars opened the portal, and the two
of them stepped into the corridors beyond. They brought a
torch with them to spare Mars from wielding any more magic
than he had to before entering the Mistgrave.

They emerged from a mirror in an abandoned sublevel
of the Mid Court, but as they stepped onto the lawn, they
heard distant shouts and the noise of conflict. There was
no telling what ripple effect Patrek's murder would have, although secretly Mars hoped some of the noise was the sound
of the Fifth's guards catching Bekka.

They made their way down to the stables quickly, making no effort to hide their furtive movements. To their relief,
the place was quiet. Mars headed for the tack room, where
he'd previously noted a relic mirror, only to stop dead in his
tracks at the sound of a familiar voice calling out to them
from behind.

"Where are you going?"

Silently cursing, Mars turned to face Askalon, Fura doing
the same beside him.

"Askalon?" Fura said on a gasp. "What are you doing
here?"

"I asked you first, lìtja." He answered with a dark look, as if
he knew perfectly well what was happening.

Fura threw back her shoulders, her manner suddenly

haughty. "I'm going home. I've left my mother a note. I've had enough of the Assembly."

Askalon's expression softened. "I understand, but you cannot travel alone with only him to protect you." He pointed a finger at Mars.

Fura took Mars's hand in hers. "There is no one I'm safer with than him."

Mars blinked, surprised by how convincing she sounded, as if she really meant it. Only, it didn't matter to Askalon.

"If you insist on leaving now, I will go with you," Askalon said. "That way we can both keep you safe." He shot Mars a murderous look as if he were to blame for all of this.

Drawing a deep breath, Fura let it out in an audible sigh. "Very well. Go and pack for the journey. We will wait for you here."

"I will let your mother know as well."

Fura nodded, and a moment later, Askalon left the stables.

"Well done," Mars said, impressed yet again by her ability to deceive.

"Hurry, let's get out of here before he gets back." She motioned to the mirror.

Mars wasted no time, grasping her hand as they reached the mirror and pulling them into the labyrinth. He hurried down the corridor, unsettled by the brush with Askalon. How had he known they were heading for the stables? Was it mere chance? He didn't think so.

A short time later, they exited a window into the great library of the Mid Court. Same as the stables, the place was deserted. That was good. From here on out, they needed to not be seen. Fortunately, the continued commotion of the Fifth's death played in their favor, and the March was quiet as a graveyard as they ascended the stairs.

Reaching the top, they hurried toward the light of a torch in the distance, where Katrìn was waiting for them at the entrance to a hidden stairway leading down to the Mistgrave.

The closer they came to the light, the more Mars felt his pulse increase. Something was wrong. There were two people ahead, not one.

Mars called out to Fura to slow down. "We've got trouble."

Fura didn't question him, slowing her pace. Drawing nearer, Mars saw Katrìn frozen in place, pinioned to the chest of a man standing behind her with a knife pressed to her throat—Ivar Patreksvane.

"Ivar? What are you doing?" Fura came to a halt, her mouth making an *O* of surprise.

"It's your fault he's dead," Ivar spat, his bloodshot eyes fixed on Fura. "If you'd just given us the formula, none of this would've happened."

Fura flinched at his words, which so closely echoed her own earlier in the evening.

Mars stepped forward, aware of the shaky way Ivar held the knife, how one mistake would cost Katrìn her life. "Let her go, Ivar. We both know you don't want to hurt her."

"My father is dead." Ivar's hand grew steady, his eyes narrowed. "But it will not be in vain. Give me the Primer, Fura, or I will kill her."

He meant it; Mars was certain. He'd seen enough killers to

recognize one. The pain and grief of his father's death might've pushed Ivar to the edge, but this young man had walked there before. Wanting to stall long enough to find a way out of this, Mars said, "You're part of the Wake, aren't you?"

Ivar's eyes flashed to Mars. "And you're a paid mercenary." He turned back to Fura. "The Primer. Now."

"I don't have the formula, Ivar, but I know where it is." Fura took another step forward, reaching out a hand toward him. "We're on our way to get it now. If you'll just let Katrìn go, I promise I will give it to you."

"Your promises are as worthless as your father's." Ivar eased the knife a little closer to Katrìn's throat. For the first time, fear flickered across her face. "If you're on your way to get it, then you will take me with you."

Mars had heard enough. They needed to be on their way before someone spotted them. He took a careful step forward, being sure to keep his hands at his sides, unthreatening.

As Fura continued pleading with Ivar, Mars edged closer, waiting for a chance to strike. When the moment came, Ivar's attention fixed on Fura, Mars seized him by the wrist with one hand and shoved Katrìn free with the other.

As Katrìn stumbled out of the way, Mars moved in, reaching for Ivar's other hand as he pressed his fingers into the man's wrist, trying to force the knife free. But Ivar didn't drop it. He barely seemed to feel the pressure. Before Mars could capture Ivar's other hand, he pulled out a second knife. Mars saw the attack coming, but was too slow to block it, the other man quick as a cat. Mars could only jump back, avoiding the worst of it, the tip of the blade just catching him in the side.

Hissing at the sting, Mars shoved Ivar and let go. Ivar lurched backward but recovered at once and charged Mars again, both blades flashing with an unnatural light that Mars immediately recognized—the knives were infused with Ice. Mars shuffled backward, aware of the burn in his side, the itch of corruptive magic. He flicked his wrist, summoning the Rift with one hand while reaching for his own knife with the other. He was done with this.

"Don't kill him!" Fura shouted, even as Ivar made another vicious swipe at Mars, nearly taking his head off.

Mars ducked the blow. "No problem. Shall I just stand here and let him skewer me like a fish?" The magic was flowing into him now, but it was sluggish, slowed by the weakness lingering in his body.

Ivar attacked with the ferocity of a wounded animal, his swings wild and all the more dangerous for it. Mars could barely follow them, barely stay ahead. He willed the magic for help, but it didn't answer. It wouldn't obey such a paltry sacrifice. Growing desperate, Mars raised the dagger, prepared to deliver a killing blow.

But before he could deliver it, Ivar suddenly rose into the air like a straw man on a hoist. Then he dropped, hitting the stone floor hard enough that both knives fell from his hands. Ivar tried to reach for them, but an invisible force held him back. With a jerk, it pulled his arms to his sides, holding them firmly in place. With a quick glance over his shoulder, Mars understood—Katrin was standing there, both hands held in front of her as she channeled Rift magic.

He turned back to Ivar's peals of wild laughter, the sound of someone on the verge of breaking.

"So," Ivar said around his cackles, "that's how you've managed all this time—with a secret adept at your disposal."

"Shut him up." Fura waved at Katrìn. "Before he draws the guards."

Ivar's mouth closed with a loud *clack* as Katrìn forced it shut with her magic.

"What do we do now?" Katrìn said, biting her lip in concentration.

The answer was simple, of course—kill him—but one glance at Fura's torn expression told Mars that she would never allow it. Mars even found that he was reluctant to take that option. Ivar had been a friendly port-of-call in the hostile sea of the Assembly. And his father had just been murdered in front of him.

Letting out another curse, Mars met Fura's eyes. "We take him with us. If we let him go now, there's no telling who he might tell."

Fura nodded, then faced Ivar. "Do you understand? If you want the secrets of the Primer, you must do everything I tell you to from here until we return."

"And if you attempt to betray us, I will kill you, Ivar," Mars added. "Do not doubt it."

Ivar tried to respond but failed, until Katrìn released her hold on his mouth—though she didn't release the rest of him. "I will do as you say until we return."

"Very well." Fura motioned to Mars. "The notch to reveal the ladder is just there, if you would."

Turning, Mars spotted the familiar relic symbol carved into the wall. Making a fresh sacrifice, he pressed his palm to it, the magic soon revealing a crudely made ladder that led straight down the wall into the mist.

"I'll go first." Fura stepped toward the ladder, only to freeze at the sound of Askalon calling out to them.

"*Wait!*"

Mars swore again, louder this time. Could nothing go right this night?

Reaching them, Askalon stumbled to a halt as his gaze took in the impossible scene of Katrìn standing there, holding a man prisoner with magic.

No one spoke. Fura stared at Askalon, speechless. Mars felt the same, wondering how in the nine the truss had found them again.

Askalon came out of his stupor first. "What are you doing?"

"Something I have to do," Fura said. "You wouldn't understand. But I'm begging you to leave, and let us go in peace."

"I can't do that, Fura. You know I can't." Askalon shook his head, as if he truly regretted it. "I must look out for you. And this"—he motioned to the exposed ladder, the undeniable truth of their destination—"is madness."

"I'm leaving, and nothing will stop me." Fura took a defiant step toward the ladder.

Askalon made to stop her, but Mars stepped in front of him, knife at the ready. "You will not beat me, Askalon. I promise." Even wounded as he was, Mars was certain of it.

The truss halted, wise enough not to try. He turned a

pleading gaze onto Fura. "Then let me go with you. All I want is to make sure you are safe."

"Not this time. You are my mother's truss. Not mine."

"Then I pledge my loyalty to you, Fura." Askalon placed a palm over his heart. "I give you my bond."

Mars held back another curse as he saw Fura's resolve soften. He felt the trap closing in around him. If they were going to Skarfell, it had to be now, and the only way for their plan to move forward was for Askalon to come with them. But if Mars allowed it, there would be no hiding his secret, and Askalon would certainly use the knowledge against him the first chance he had. But it was too late to stop it now.

"Very well." Fura held out her hand. "I accept your bond."

Askalon reached into his pocket, but Mars waved him off. "We don't have time for this. If you're going, then let's go. Before someone else sees."

"I go first." Katrìn patted the knapsack at her side, the orb safely stowed inside.

Ivar followed next, then Fura, and then Askalon. Mars climbed over last. For a moment, he thought he saw a shadow moving through the mist in the distance. With any luck, maybe that riftworm would get the two interlopers in their group. Mars doubted it, though. Considering how things had been going for him of late, the riftworms were more likely to get him. Exhaling a resigned sigh, he climbed down into the darkness below.

TWENTY-TWO

THE DESCENT INTO the Mistgrave took an age, a lifetime.

With each rung on the ladder, Mars felt the weight of it pressing down on him. The thick air clawed his throat as he breathed in and out. It burned his eyes and made his skin crawl. The wound in his side pulsed, and he wondered if it spelled his doom—the Ice's poison intensified by the Mistgrave's. He hurried as quickly as he could without falling, eager to reach the ground.

Somewhere below him, he sensed magic beginning to flow as Katrìn activated the orb. The area seemed to grow brighter, beckoning him toward it. He knew the moment he entered the orb's area of influence, a faint warmth sliding over his skin, enough to banish the chill that had sunk deep into his bones during the long climb down. For the first time in too long, he was able to draw a full breath.

The others were waiting for him, standing in an uneasy circle around Katrìn. She held the orb clutched between both hands, a dim glow emanating from it. Without a word, she turned and started walking, taking the lead. *Following the orb,*

Katrìn had explained to him earlier. The device showed the way to Skarfell. It was the only compass they had in this formless wasteland.

Mars looked right and left as they walked along, trying to get the lay of the land. But there was nothing. No features, no hills or ditches, nothing but hard, flat ground. A tremor went through him at the unnatural feel of the place. It was as if he'd left Riven altogether and emerged in an alien world, one he had no hope of escaping. He took a deep breath, fighting off momentary panic.

After a while, Askalon finally broke the eerie silence, asking where they were going. Mars listened closely to the explanation Fura gave him—about her desire to finish her father's secret work—aware that Ivar was doing the same. There would be no keeping secrets from the two men now that they were here.

When Fura finished explaining, she stopped and faced Askalon. "Now it's your turn to explain how you found us on the March. And you'd best not say it was mere luck."

Askalon took a long time before answering. "I used this." He reached into his pocket and withdrew a pendant that even in the poor light Mars could see was exactly like the one Fura wore.

She snatched it out of his hand. "This was my father's." Her fingers closed around it, and the look of fury she turned on Askalon could melt steel. "How did you get this? It was buried with him."

Askalon shook his head, not meeting her eyes. "The one

buried with your father was a replica. Your mother claimed it was too valuable an artifact to give up." He held up a hand before Fura could castigate him. "I didn't know what she'd done. Not until we arrived at Hàr Halda and she gave me the real one. Your mother wanted to make sure you were safe in every way possible."

Mars gritted his teeth, annoyed at this revelation. Elìn should've given it to him. It seemed the two pendants were connected somehow, allowing Askalon to track Fura's movements, not unlike how Una's ravens tracked him. Only, Mars knew who Una was from the start, whereas Fura had trusted Askalon. This was a betrayal. He waited for Fura to tear into Askalon, but her anger seemed beyond words. She merely slid the pendant into her pocket and continued walking.

The eerie silence returned and remained their companion through the long night. There was no sound at all in the mist—no groan of wind or shifting of rock; even their footfalls were strangely muffled. Mars tried to find comfort in the knowledge that silence meant they were passing unnoticed by the creatures that inhabited this place. And there *were* creatures out there. When a mound of strange, pale rocks appeared in their path, Katrìn led them far around it, warning them not to disturb a single stone of the cairn. One of the draugr rested there, she explained. They were said to be the once dead victims of the Cataclysm's initial explosion of corrupted magic, the one that had leveled the ground they walked on here. The entire Mistgrave was nothing more than a massive burial pit.

Hours later—how long Mars couldn't tell, as his pocket

watch had ceased working—they stopped for a rest. He guessed it must be close to dawn, but there was no way to be certain. The only light came from the orb, the mist surrounding them an endless, shifting gray. They ate and drank sparingly, Fura sharing some of her provisions with Ivar. He didn't take much. He seemed unnaturally quiet, lost in the chasms of his thoughts and despair as he sat on the ground, hands resting on his bent knees.

Mars consumed more food and water than he'd planned, worried about his strength and the nagging ache in his side. Fura caught him cupping the area with a hand and demanded to see the wound. Too tired to argue, Mars let her, sucking in a breath as her cold fingers touched the clammy heat of his skin.

"What did you do to that knife?" Fura said, turning a glare on Ivar.

He smirked back at her. "He'll be fine. The body can handle a lot more Ice than what he got."

Mars didn't doubt it, but still, the thought made his stomach churn. He wasn't keen on Ice poisoning, even if it wouldn't kill him on its own. Making no reply, Fura searched in Katrìn's knapsack for the bottle of surgical spirits they'd packed. Mars gritted his teeth as she pressed an alcohol-drenched cloth over the cut.

"I hope you enjoyed that," he muttered as she finished.

"Immensely." She smiled at him, her hand lingering on his side for a moment.

Once he finished eating, Mars took the orb from Katrìn. It was his turn to power it so that she could recover. He flicked his wrist to draw the needed blood. The moment his fingers pressed against the glass, he felt its power rush into him—and out, drawing the magic as it went. A haze came over his vision, but rather than dull his sight, it enhanced it, allowing him to see through the mist. As he'd expected, there wasn't anything to see, just empty tundra spotted with draugr cairns. That is, until he turned and spotted a single mountain in the distance, its shape outlined in a corona of light as if from the sun setting behind it. Skarfell.

"You're an adept, too?" Askalon's harsh, accusing voice drew Mars's attention back to their lonely camp.

"What of it?" Mars glared back him.

"I guess that explains your reputation. It's all a cheat." Askalon spat on the ground.

"Leave him alone, Askalon," Fura said. "Mars works for me now, and he is under my protection."

"Besides," Katrìn added, "you can't blame a person for using all the advantages given them at birth. And without him, we'd never make it to Skarfell."

"Not to mention getting out again," Mars muttered under his breath. It rankled his nerves that Askalon now knew his secret. Even worse was knowing that killing the truss wouldn't be an option if Fura had any say in it.

Once Katrìn finished her own hasty meal, they started off again, traveling as long and far as their legs would carry them. But when Katrìn stumbled and nearly fell, Fura called a halt once more. Although Mars had never been so tired in his life, he too insisted she rest first while he maintained the safety provided by the orb. After a few weak protests, she gave up and stretched out on the ground, her head cradled on her knapsack. The others soon joined her, everyone drifting off to sleep nearly at once. All save Ivar. He shifted and turned and shifted again, as if his body were incapable of staying still for more than a minute or two. Mars watched him from where he sat atop his own knapsack, guilt gnawing at him as the memory of the Fifth's assassination returned to him, reminding him of the chance he'd had to change the outcome.

Too tired to grapple with that now, he stood and began walking in a circle around the party to stay awake. That is, until he noticed Fura stirring. He stopped as she rose to her feet and approached him.

"How are you feeling?" She pressed a gentle hand to his side.

Mars hid a wince. "Better."

"Liar," she teased. "But come, sit down. You must be nearly ready to pass out."

With a sigh of agreement, Mars sat, setting the orb in the cradle of his crossed legs. So long as he kept one hand pressed to it, the flow of magic remained. Relief spread through his arms to no longer be holding its weight.

"Thank you, by the way," he said, glancing at Fura as she settled in next to him. "For defending me to Askalon."

She made a sound like a growl. "I still can't believe that he, of all people, would deceive me like that."

"Well, it wasn't only him."

Fura tensed, and he braced for an angry defense of her mother, but then the fight went out of her. "You're right. But my mother deceiving me is something I'm used to by now."

Mars coughed, unused to the awkwardness that had descended over him. He didn't often talk to anyone about such personal things, and yet he didn't want the conversation to end. "I take it the pendant is important to you?"

Nodding, she slid her hand into her pocket and withdrew the pendant she'd taken from Askalon. "My father made them both." She held the compass rose in her hand next to the one around her neck. They were identical in every way, including the needle that didn't quite point north.

"May I see it?" Mars held out his hand, and Fura placed the pendant in his palm. He sensed the magic imbued in its structure, subtle, but there, contained somehow. He felt a gentle tug from it in his mind, pulling him toward the other pendant as if the two were connected by a piece of wire. "It's an artifact?" He handed it back, and she returned it to her pocket.

"Yes. He used them for all sorts of things when I was growing up. Games, mostly. One of my favorites was sending secret messages to one another." She raised the pendant at her neck to her mouth and pressed her lips against it, speaking some phrase too muffled for Mars to hear. Then she turned the pendant sideways, gripping the top of the needle. She gave it a twist, and it came off in her hand, revealing a small cavity. Hidden inside was a miniature scroll of onionskin paper, which she pulled free. "This is the last thing he sent me."

Mars tensed, remembering another piece of onionskin paper. "What is it?"

"The Primer formula," she whispered, as if afraid Ivar might overhear her. She was right to be afraid, but not only of him. She handed Mars the scroll.

With trembling fingers, he unfurled it. He recognized the Primer symbol at once. Here it was. The thing he'd been looking for for so long. Even if he'd searched a hundred years, he might never have found it; it was so well hidden, protected by a magic that only responded to Fura's words.

And yet she'd handed it to him willingly, trusting him with her father's legacy, the prize Henrik had died for and she'd fought so hard to claim. The enormity of her trust stole his breath away. With an effort, he forced air into his lungs and handed her the scroll. But he wouldn't forget where it was.

"He knew he was going to die," Fura said, carefully returning the onionskin roll to its hiding place. "The formula arrived with his body." She paused. "It arrived *on* his body. Inside that pendant." She patted her pocket where she'd placed the pendant her mother had stolen and entrusted to Askalon.

"I'm sorry," he said, cringing at the inadequacy of the words, at the lie that stood between them like a vast ocean, one that could never be crossed. *If she knew . . .*

No, she would never know. And yet, that fact offered him no relief.

"Thank you," she said, not meeting his gaze. "But now I think you really must rest."

And with that she stood and roused Katrìn from her sleep. Mars handed over the orb, then settled down on his knapsack. He was asleep a moment later, but nightmares plagued his dreams.

TWENTY-THREE

MARS WOKE TO the ground shaking beneath his body.

"What in the nine?" He lurched up, stumbling to his feet. For a moment, he was certain he was still dreaming.

He wasn't. All around him the others were struggling to stay upright as the earth quaked.

"What is it?" Fura said, staring at Katrìn, who stood with the orb above her head, trying to cast its light farther into the darkness.

"A riftworm."

Mars cursed, wishing they'd taken the time to raid the guard barracks for weapons before leaving Hàr Halda. He raised his arms, prepared to summon the Rift, but Fura placed a hand on his shoulder, stopping him.

"Wait. The orb should protect us." She stared toward the direction from which the vibrations seemed to be emanating.

With an effort, Mars obeyed, lowering his hands once more. "You've a lot of faith in your father."

"He knew what he was doing." Fura pursed her lips. "We'll be all right."

Mars still wasn't convinced, but neither did he have any

idea how to defend against a riftworm, if they were indeed as big and fierce as the stories claimed. Surely they must be, he realized, as the ground quaked again.

A moment later, his eyes confirmed what his senses had been telling him. Something dark and massive appeared beyond the border of the orb's circle of light. At first Mars couldn't make out much, but as the thing drew closer, the whiplike appendages sticking out from its sides came into view. *Its hooks*, he remembered from Henrik's journal. There were dozens of them, each longer than a spear with a tip that ended in sharp pincers, large enough to cut a man's body in half with a single snip. They flared out from the creature's lower half, which slithered across the ground in search of prey.

Mars held his breath as the creature reached the edge of the orb's power. Several of its hooks spread toward them, then stopped, as if blocked by the magic. A sound like a thousand voices shrieking in unison suddenly filled the air. Choking on a gasp, Mars covered his ears with his hands as pain lanced through him. He hunched over, struggling to remain upright as the sound seemed to rip into him. His vision blurred, then his eyes started to move of their own volition, turning left, then right, then left, over and over again in a pattern that made his head throb and his body lose all sense of which way was up and which was down. He fell, powerless to stay standing with the world spinning around him.

He didn't know how long the vertigo lasted, but when it finally passed, he emptied the contents of his stomach. Sitting up, he peered around at the others. They were all suffering the same as he, but at least Katrìn still held the orb—and the rift-worm had moved on.

Praise be to the nine.

"Is everyone okay?" Fura asked. Slowly, they all answered, but more than an hour passed before they were recovered enough to resume the journey.

Katrìn led the way most of the day—or night—or what-ever time it was. Mars didn't know, and the inability to track the time grated on his nerves. Not to mention the fear of attracting another riftworm. Hours later his vision still hadn't returned to normal.

He caught himself staring at the mist swirling by, his imagination conjuring shapes that weren't there. He wished he were strong enough to handle the orb for the entire journey. At least with the orb he could see Skarfell and maintain some sense of progress. Anything was better than this feeling of aimless wandering.

"It can't be much longer now," Askalon said when they stopped for another rest. "We've been out here two days, at least."

"How can you be sure?" It was the first time Fura had spo-ken to him since he'd returned her father's pendant.

Askalon cast her a hesitant look. "Just a guess, but I've al-ways been good about such things."

Mars scoffed. Askalon was no more certain of the time than the rest of them. But he kept the observation to himself. Everything about the Mistgrave discouraged conversation, any unnecessary noise a threat to the hypnotic silence. Mars raised a water bladder to his lips and took a drink. It was run-ning low. They needed to get to Skarfell soon. He glanced at Katrìn, still holding the orb, and hoped that when he held it next, the mountain would be close at last.

A strange movement drew his eye to where Ivar sat at the very edge of the orb's sphere of light. Same as each time before, he'd drunk and eaten little. He'd wrapped his cloak over his front, and the fabric trembled around him from the violent shivers running through his body.

For a moment, Mars feared he was ill, but then the truth dawned on him. Wordlessly, he fetched the bottle of surgical spirits from Katrìn's bag. He sat down next to Ivar and held it out to him. "It'll taste like shit, but it might take the edge off."

Ivar stared at the bottle a moment, his expression dazed. Then, accepting it, he raised the bottle to his lips. He sipped and coughed as he finished. Wiping the spittle away with his shirtsleeve, he arched an eyebrow at Mars. "How did you know?"

Mars shrugged. "I've seen withdrawal enough to recognize the symptoms." He hesitated a couple of beats, the only sound the distant rumble of a riftworm passing. "What's your poison?" It was a deeply private question, Mars knew, but at the same turn, this man knew his deepest secret as well.

"Dust."

Mars closed his eyes, wearied by the response. "Don't you want to destroy the Ice? Isn't that why you're after the Primer?"

"I want that more than anything."

"Even though it'll destroy you?" Mars knew the stories. Once started, no one overcame a dust addiction. Although he had to admit that Ivar had been good at hiding it.

"It'll be a small price to pay." Ivar shrugged. "Besides, once I've fulfilled my purpose, I won't need the dust anymore." He paused, reaching down to pat his leg. "I use it for the pain, you know. It's the only thing that helps."

Mars recalled his story about an Ice blister that had turned malignant. The same affliction that had killed his older brother. *And now his father is dead, too.* Mars wondered which was worse—to have never known your family at all, or to lose them all one by one. He didn't think he wanted to know.

"I understand." Mars swallowed the painful lump rising in his throat, as he understood what Ivar meant by not needing the dust anymore. The man was prepared to die. Maybe he was even eager for it.

He cleared his throat. "I'm sorry about your father."

Ivar stiffened but said nothing.

Reaching a hand to his braid, Mars carefully removed the bond Patrek had given him. He held it out to Ivar. "Your father gave me this. I don't believe in Rivna or the giving of bonds, but if I can, I'll make sure your father didn't die in vain." It was little consolation for the part he'd played in the Fifth's assassination.

Ivar stared at the proffered bead, and for a moment, Mars thought he would refuse, but in the next, the Fifth's son took the bead and threaded it into his hair.

Fura approached them then. Mars guessed she'd been listening, not that she could help it, given the small space. She stopped beside Ivar and held out her hand, a bead sitting in the cup of her palm. "I do believe in Rivna, and I give you my bond that we will rid Riven of Ice once and forever."

Ivar looked away from her. "Your bond means nothing, same as your father's."

Mars fisted his hands, angry on her behalf, knowing how much Ivar's words must've hurt.

But Fura showed no reaction as she lowered her hand to her side. "My father always did what was best for Riven, no matter how hard. There was a reason he gave the formula to me and not to the Wake."

"Your father was a coward. He always was."

Mars held up a hand toward Ivar. "There's no call for that and no ground for it, either. Henrik Torvald tested the Primer on a vein in the Skorri mine. No coward could've done that."

Ivar pointed a finger at Mars, then at Fura. "Henrik could've ended all this twenty years ago, but just like with the Primer, he chose not to."

"What are you talking about?" Fura said, her hands going to her hips.

"I'm saying that I might know more about your father than you do," Ivar seemed to snarl up at her. "Enough to know that I won't believe a word you say until I see it done."

And with that Ivar stood and walked away, as far as the orb's light would let him go. When Fura moved to pursue him, Mars grabbed her hand. "Let him be for now. He's been through enough."

She simply nodded. She understood as well as he did that the only way to help Ivar was to make good on their promises.

The group soon resumed their journey, another round of walking, resting, and walking again. Despite the alcohol, Ivar's condition worsened. He lagged behind the rest of them, barely staying within the orb's protective circle. He had also started muttering to himself.

"Should we be worried he'll draw unwanted attention?" Mars asked Katrìn as they trudged along.

She shook her head. "So long as he stays inside the circle, we should be fine."

"*Should be?*" Mars didn't like the sound of that. But there was nothing to do about it. None of them had any way to help Ivar.

The next time Mars carried the orb, Skarfell appeared close at last. His spirits rose at its looming height ahead, and he longed to quicken his pace, but he couldn't muster the strength. He doubted Katrìn could, either. The orb had taken its toll on them both. Even so, when Fura called for another rest, Mars made to argue that they were so close they should carry on.

But Katrìn shushed him. "Fura's right," she said. "Even if we reach the mountain, there's another long climb to safety."

Mars sighed and gave in, sitting down with the orb resting in his lap. In moments, the rest of them had eaten and were lying down to sleep. Even Ivar laid down, and for the first time he was still and silent. Mars didn't speculate on what that might mean. He merely embraced the relief it brought him.

Too much relief, as it turned out. Before he knew what was happening, he'd drifted off to sleep.

The scream woke him.

Mars snapped back to consciousness at once, lurching to his feet. The world had gone black as pitch around him, as if there were no world anymore at all, just darkness.

"What's happening?" someone shouted from far off. Katrìn, he thought, although he couldn't be certain. The awful weight of the Mistgrave was pressing down on him, dulling his senses. He fought against it as he fell to his knees, searching for the orb. There was no telling how far it might've rolled. He scrambled in the dirt, the rough ground biting his skin. Another scream echoed all around, this one different from the first. Piercing and unnatural.

Inhuman.

Every hair on Mars's body stood on end as a smell like foul water and putrid flesh reached him. Frantic now, he widened his search for the orb, finding it at last. The moment he touched it, its light burst forth anew, peeling back the darkness. He spotted Fura, Katrìn, and Askalon at once, but there was no sign of Ivar.

The scream echoed again. Mars turned toward the sound, hurrying forward with the orb as the others followed close behind him. A few strides later, the orb's light revealed Ivar, lying next to a broken pile of stones.

A creature was kneeling over him.

It had once been a man. That much was clear from its shape. Dark gray skin covered its skeletal form, and when it looked up at their approach, its eyes glowed like lit lamps. It held Ivar pinned to the ground with bony knees as it grasped his mangled forearm between its clawed hands. Baring sawlike teeth, it bit down on Ivar's arm and resumed its eating.

Ivar screamed again, trying weakly to free himself. Mars swallowed the bile climbing his throat. He could sense the creature's hunger, could almost feel it echoing inside himself, stirring an unnatural hunger in him as well. Despair wrapped around him at the sensation. It felt as if he would never be warm again.

"Kill it!" Fura screamed, and the sound ripped Mars out of the momentary stupor he'd fallen into.

Askalon charged forward and sank a knife into the creature's chest, then yanked it free again. The creature didn't react or move at all. It was as if the blade had passed right through it, as if the creature were nothing more than mist. Yet the blood flowing from its mouth and the flesh torn away from Ivar's arm was all too real.

"Draugr can't be killed," Katrìn said. "Not with weapons."

"How, then?" Mars said, reaching for his own knife.

The moment the blade was free, Fura pulled it out of his hand and charged the creature, slashing across its throat. It made no move to defend itself. As with Askalon's blade, Fura's attack seemed to pass right through the draugr. Unprepared for the lack of resistance, Fura knocked herself off-balance with the swing. She fell against the creature, hitting it with a shoulder. She didn't pass through it like the blade had; the weight of her body knocked the draugr back, off Ivar.

"Take this." Mars shoved the orb toward Katrìn, then dove toward Fura and the creature, already drawing his wrists across the blades in his cuffs in a fresh sacrifice. The magic answered, his weariness chased away by the fearful energy surging through him.

Askalon reached them first, grabbing the draugr by the arms just as it lurched toward Fura, who had regained her feet and was trying to drag Ivar to safety. The draugr hissed, spinning toward Askalon, teeth snapping. It grazed his throat, leaving behind a smear of blood. Askalon's grip weakened at the assault, and the creature broke free.

Mars charged in, channeling raw magic through his hands, willing it to strengthen him and do what damage it could. He slammed his palms into the creature's chest, the blow knocking it backward and away from Askalon. But the draugr recovered at once, unharmed.

Moving toward Mars, the creature returned the blow, mirroring Mars's actions, palms to chest, but the force was doubled by whatever power gave the draugr its unnatural life. The strength of it lifted Mars off his feet and flung him several yards as if he weighed no more than a rag doll. He landed on his back atop a scattering of rocks, the wind knocked from his lungs. For a second, he couldn't move, couldn't breathe, even as he heard the creature hiss again, teeth gnashing.

Willing his body to obey, Mars rolled over, and let out a yelp of terror as he nearly tumbled into the deep pit that must've been beneath the cairn Ivar had disturbed. For a second, Mars's body teetered on the edge, like a spinning top that has started to wobble. He caught himself at the last moment, his head and half his torso dangling for a second, one made to seem thrice as long by the yawning depth of the pit below. It was an impossible way down, with something like a black river waiting at its bottom. It shone with a sickly light, like the glare of sunlight on a slick of oil.

Mars scrambled back from the pit. Clambering to his feet, he saw Fura and Askalon grappling with the draugr. Since it couldn't be killed, they were trying to subdue it. But the creature was too powerful—and growing stronger. No, not just stronger. It was growing in size. Already it was taller and heavier than before, towering over Askalon and Fura as it broke free of their feeble hold.

"Katrìn, what do we do?" Mars searched for her, finding her across the way, trying to help Ivar and keep hold of the orb at the same time.

"Send it back where it came from."

The pit. Mars glanced over his shoulder at it, shuddering. It would've been simple, if only the draugr weren't imbued with all the strength of the Titans combined. Nevertheless, he charged forward, joining Fura and Askalon as they renewed their attempts to subdue it. Summoning fresh magic, Mars grabbed one of the thing's arms, while Askalon grabbed the other and Fura jumped on its back.

The draugr leaned its head toward Mars, teeth bared. It bit at his chest, ripping through his tunic. Mars shrieked and leaped back as the creature spit out the fabric and made another grab for his exposed skin. That sense of unquenchable hunger struck Mars again, making him dizzy.

With Mars out of immediate reach, the draugr turned toward Askalon, seizing the man's wrist with its mouth. Askalon choked out a scream and tried to pull free but couldn't. Desperately, Fura pounded on the creature's face, trying to break its hold on Askalon by mere force. It worked after a moment, but the draugr reached up and grabbed Fura by the neck, pulling her off its back as easily as if she were a kitten.

Mars leaped toward it before it could close its mouth around her throat. He knocked it back, shoving Fura out of the way as he did. At once the creature bit at Mars again. Its hunger was all it knew, all that mattered.

"We need to bait it," Mars said, thinking aloud as he jumped back, out of the creature's reach. But how? The only foodstuffs they had were hardtack and salt pork. The draugr craved blood and flesh.

It lunged at Mars again, faster this time, managing to grab his shoulder with one of its clawed hands. But before it could drag him forward to its waiting mouth, Ivar appeared, shoving his bloodied arm under the creature's nose.

The draugr let out an eager hiss as it willingly accepted the offering, its teeth sinking in. Ivar gasped but didn't pull way.

"Do it now," he said, panting.

Mars didn't question it, tamping down the horror he felt at what was happening. He grabbed the distracted draugr and started hauling it toward the pit. Askalon joined him, their combined strength enough to move both the draugr and its prey forward. In a moment, they'd reached the pit.

Mars reached for the creature, trying to wrench its jaws open where it held Ivar by the crease of his arm—what was left of it. Bits of flesh and sinew hung from bare bone like shredded cloth. The sight sent bile up Mars's throat, and he swallowed it down. Even if they could get Ivar free, he was dead already.

Ivar seemed to know it, too. "Push us in," he said.

"No!" Fura screamed. "Don't do this."

"Do what you promised." Ivar turned a heated glare on her. "Destroy the Ice. Set Riven free."

With a strength that defied his injuries, Ivar curled his body into a ball and lengthened again with a sudden force strong enough that it knocked the draugr off-balance. Both man and monster fell over the pit's edge, disappearing from sight. From the very world itself.

PART THREE

ADEPT

TWENTY-FOUR

THEY MADE IT to the mountain a few hours later, bruised and bloodied but alive.

Most of us, at least, Mars thought as they started the long climb upward.

Unlike their descent from the March, their journey up to the White Keep atop Skarfell involved an actual staircase, one crafted by the adepts of old into the side of the mountain itself. There were even the remains of an iron railing, although time and the elements had rendered it untrustworthy.

Despite his weariness, Mars couldn't keep his mind from racing with thoughts of Ivar—the way he'd looked at the end, and how he'd sacrificed himself to save them. Mars couldn't fathom it, the truth like a weight pressing against his chest. One made worse by the knowledge that it was his fault Ivar had stumbled onto that draugr cairn. If he hadn't drifted off to sleep, none of this would've happened. He tried to console himself that at least Ivar's suffering was over, but it was no comfort. *You owe him a life,* that voice whispered in his head. The old Rivna ideal had always seemed absurd to him—he'd never owed anyone anything, any more than he'd been owed. But now . . .

Destroy the Ice, Ivar had said, his last thoughts still on the purpose he served.

Then Mars recalled another life owed, a life taken, Orri's face forever imprinted on his mind.

When they finally climbed out of the mist, Mars had to shield his eyes against the light of the setting sun. After days in the thick gray of the Mistgrave, even that weak light burned. His legs ached from the climb, his arms heavy from hours of holding the orb and making the sacrifice to the Rift. All he wanted was to lie down and sleep.

The staircase terminated in front of the wide area before the White Keep, an imposing square structure with a severe facade constructed of pale limestone. Everything about it seemed designed to turn away trespassers; they were not welcome here. Where Hàr Halda boasted grand architecture replete with ornate designs, the White Keep looked like a prison. Mars shivered at the sight of it. Even the door, he noticed, had no handle or knob.

Nevertheless, Katrìn approached it confidently, laying her palm against its center. As the magic flowed out from her hand and the small sacrifice she'd made in her palm with her sewing needle, thin lines of blue light spread across the door like vines.

"Did the Consortium do nothing without magic?" Mars said, exhausted by the mere thought.

Katrìn shrugged as the door slowly opened on its own. "I doubt it. Why would they?"

"Because it's tiresome to shed blood all day long?" He peered at the darkness beyond the door, breathing in the smells of ancient dust and stale air.

"Magic didn't require a blood sacrifice when they built these relics." Katrìn stepped aside, allowing Fura to enter first.

"What?" Mars stumbled over the slight rise in the threshold as he followed the two women, Askalon coming last with wearied steps.

"It's true," Katrìn continued. "Before the Cataclysm, adepts were able to tap into Rift magic at will, like turning on a faucet. It did require energy to work, but no different than, say, climbing a flight of stairs."

"That's the very reason we're here." Fura gestured around them. "It was because the magic had *stopped* flowing so freely that they made their fateful attempt to fix the Rift."

"And broke it instead," Mars said as they passed through a large doorway. No one had to say the word: *Cataclysm*. He swallowed, remembering the Ice mine in Valdri. All those people paying the price. The same one Ivar had paid. "So what now?"

They were standing now in what must've been the keep's dining hall, the area crowded with long wooden tables and benches. A massive fireplace rested along the far wall, framed by a pair of unraveling tapestries that depicted the Titans' defeat of the World Raven and the founding of Riven. A doorway to the right led to what appeared to be the kitchens, while one on the left revealed a spiraling staircase to the upper levels. A third doorway across the room opened onto a hallway.

"Now, we rest," Fura said, "and see to our wounds." She glanced at Askalon and the bloodstained rag wrapped around his wrist, covering the bite the draugr had given him. "There are dormitories on the fourth floor. We can each claim a room."

The bedrooms looked more like prison cells, each one

smaller than Mars's rooftop hideout in Jakulvik, furnished with only a narrow bed and a cramped writing desk and chair. Still, compared to sleeping in the Mistgrave, Mars's room felt like a palace. He collapsed onto the bed and closed his eyes.

But sleep refused to come. Thoughts of Ivar filled his head at first, the way the man had died to save them. These slowly shifted to thoughts of Orri. Two men, both dead because of Mars. The separate memories seemed to combine into one as sleep teased Mars with its nearness, only to flit away whenever he drew close to it.

With a groan, he finally gave up trying and left the room in search of a wine cellar. Surely there had to be one in this place. He didn't know much about the Cataclysm, but he doubted any of the adepts who'd survived it had bothered packing before they fled.

He headed back to the ground floor and into the kitchens, relieved to find the pantries well stocked with dry goods. Most of it didn't even appear very old—Henrik and his friends must've brought supplies with them on their journeys here. These included, it seemed, a couple of bottles of bourbon, which Mars found tucked on a bottom shelf. He swiped one and made his way back to the dining hall.

The quiet here was nothing like that of the Mistgrave, yet the place felt oppressive in its dead stillness, the air stale like the inside of an abandoned cellar. He debated going back outside for whatever fresh air could be found, but he didn't feel like using magic on the door.

Instead he opted for the hallway leading deeper into the keep. Closed doors lined both sides, and he opened the first one

he came to on the left. The room beyond contained woodworking tools—a large, hand-cranked lathe, a bow saw, a planer,
and various clamps and chisels. Ancient, musty sawdust lined
the floor, a cloud of it swirling in the wake of the door opening.
Coughing, Mars backed away and shut it. He moved on.

Behind the next door was an armory, filled with weapons and suits of armor forged from starsteel. There were even
several pairs of hobbles. The crystalline metal glinted in the
weak light, despite the dust coating it. There was enough in
here to outfit an entire troop of Rivna Knights. Marveling, Mars
stepped inside and picked up one of a dozen swords hanging
from a rack. The starsteel felt warm in his palm, the grip well
fitted to his hand. Its weight and purpose felt something like a
relief in this place, and he selected a sheath for the blade and
belted it to his side.

Closing the door behind him, he continued on, this time
choosing the door at the end on the right. It led outside, into
the largest and strangest courtyard he'd ever seen. Easily the
size of a city square, the four wings of the White Keep framed
it on all sides. In the center of the courtyard, occupying most of
the space, was a vast pool ringed by curved white pillars. Each
pillar stretched several stories high and canopied over the
pool like fingers, not quite touching. Tufts of withered, dead
weeds had disturbed most of the cobblestones surrounding
the perimeter, making the place feel feral, and weary.

Mars approached the pool, drawn by the shimmer of the
dark water in the moonlight. Only, as he reached it, he realized
it wasn't water at all, but the same substance he'd seen in that
moment when he'd dangled over the edge of the draugr pit.

The liquid was black as pitch, and yet somehow glowed with a dark light, hints of color swirling about in it. Despite the stillness of the night air, the liquid seemed to be moving, flowing like a river. One that came from nowhere and went nowhere. It simply was.

"I wouldn't suggest going for a swim."

The voice made Mars jump. He spun around and glared at Fura, though he was more frustrated with himself for being snuck up on than he was with her. "Why aren't you asleep?" he asked.

"Why aren't you?" She folded her arms over her chest.

Mars turned back to the pool, mesmerized by the rippling surface. "I couldn't."

Fura stepped up beside him. She ran her gaze over the wide expanse of the pool. "It's beautiful. I didn't expect that."

"What is it?" Mars couldn't pull his gaze away from the mesmerizing view.

"The Heart of the Rift."

He inhaled, the truth falling on him like a gentle rain. The Rift. Somehow, he'd known it all along. He'd sensed it, hadn't he? He thought it might've been the reason he'd come this way in the first place. The magic here calling to the magic that flowed inside his veins. His kull. His lifeblood.

Fura took the bourbon bottle from his hands and sat down on the edge of the pool, close to one of the curved pillars. "That black shimmery stuff? The Consortium called it marrow. It's one of the ingredients needed to make the Primer."

His brow furrowed. "Is it not the key ingredient? The one we came all this way for?"

"No." She pulled out the stopper and took a long swallow of bourbon, then held the bottle out to him.

Mars frowned down at her, wondering at her terse answer and what other secrets she might be harboring. Accepting the bottle, he sat down next to her and took a drink. For a second, it tasted like Fura, the way he remembered from the kisses they'd shared.

"Did it always look like this?" He peered into that shimmering blackness, some deep part of him uneasy at the sight, like watching distant thunder clouds rolling in.

"No. My father said that before the Cataclysm it was like a lake of liquid crystals in every color." She reached out her fingers to touch the curved pillar next to her. The material, he could see from this close, was pitted, porous.

"Did he read that in one of his books?"

"I suppose so. But I never thought to ask." She dropped her hand back into her lap.

Mars offered her the bottle once more, aware of the longing in her voice and wishing he could silence it.

Waving it off, Fura tilted her head toward the night sky. "I know it's childish, but I wish he were here now. That none of this had ever happened."

Regret made Mars's throat clench as he once again felt the full weight of the part he'd played in these events. If he hadn't killed Henrik . . . Fura wouldn't feel this way, Orri and Ivar would still be alive, and Mars's secret would still be safe.

"I sometimes think of him in Asvaldur, happy and at peace, spending his days blissfully drunk on berry wine," Fura said.

Mars managed a smile, even as her words made his stomach twist harder. "Perhaps he is." He took another drink, long and deep.

"Ivar's death is not your fault, you know."

Her words struck him like a slap, a blow delivered to an already tender place. He wondered how she'd known what he was thinking and feeling. Or more precisely, what he was trying not to think and feel.

"Yeah, I know. Bad luck." He tried and failed to keep the sarcasm from his voice.

Fura placed her hand on his forearm, her touch light as a breeze but comforting. "I mean it. You were exhausted. We all were. And Ivar chose to sacrifice himself for us. There is no more honorable death than that."

Mars tensed. Rivna again. Always Rivna. It offered him no comfort. Only a debt he couldn't pay. A debt he hated feeling responsible for.

But you are responsible, even before now.

Bekka, he remembered. If he'd simply warned Ivar about her, the Fifth wouldn't have been killed, and Ivar wouldn't have tracked them to the March and insisted on coming with them.

What is wrong with me? Mars thought, placing his palms to his temples. *Why do I even care?*

He didn't know. Somewhere along the way, something inside him had started to shift and change without him even being aware of it. He glanced at Fura, wondering if this was her fault, if she had rubbed off on him, infected him with her foolish ideals.

But no. It wasn't Fura. She was only the lens, and the sight she revealed was Orri. The guilt over his death, the growing certainty Mars had been feeling that if he'd only given Orri a chance to understand, maybe he would have. Maybe Orri could've understood, been a friend to him, keeping his secret, like Fura was to Katrìn. *Like she's been with me.* Only, Mars never gave him the chance.

His anger eased at the thought, the guilt returning. He faced Fura, clearing his throat as he summoned the will to speak. "The mercenary who killed Ivar's father. I know her. And I knew she was at the Assembly before it happened."

Fura went still, like a stunned animal. Then slowly she withdrew her touch from him. "Did you know she was there to kill the Fifth?"

"No." Mars closed his eyes. "And I couldn't have. Our employer forbids us from discussing our assignments with one another."

"Your employer is a monster," Fura said.

"We are the weapon, not the will."

Fura drew a breath. "I've heard you say that before. What does it mean?"

"It's a creed we use at the Den. An . . . excuse, I suppose. Our clients are the will behind the death and mayhem we deliver. We are just the tool in their hands."

"It's not who you are, Mars," Fura said. "It's only what you do."

He shrugged. "Same difference."

"No, it's not. It's a choice. You could choose to do something else. The choices you make determine who you are."

"I tried that, remember? Ten months I tried living a different life, only to get forced back into this." He gestured at the Heart. "That's how life in Riven works."

Fura drew an uneven breath. "Then let's change it." She shifted her body, angling toward him. She reached for him, taking his hands in hers. "We have a chance to do it, Mars. From right here. We can end it all."

Momentarily distracted by her touch, Mars lifted his eyes to her face. "What are you saying, Fura?"

"I'm saying that I wasn't entirely . . . honest about my reasons for coming here." She took a deep breath and went on. "The Primer does require the marrow, as I said. But the reason we're here is not just to collect the marrow—it's because this is the only place to access the Heart."

"Why does that matter?" Mars asked.

"This is where the Cataclysm originated—it's the wound. Ice is like an infection in the blood—in that way, the two are connected, like the veins in a body are connected to the heart. If we use the Primer here, it will destroy the Ice in every mine. All at once." She hesitated. "At least that's what my father claimed in his final message to me."

Mars stared at her, words failing him in the shock of her revelation. He'd assumed that like any other bomb, the Primer would have to be delivered to each Ice mine, deployed at the source of each growth the way Henrik had tested it on the Skorri mine. He supposed that would be true if Ice were mere infrastructure, like a bridge or a storehouse held by an enemy, but Ice was more, wasn't it? It was something . . . alive, as the Rift was alive, flowing beneath all of Riven like a vast ocean. No, like rivers all connected to a single lake—the Heart, lying before him. The Ice was connected to it, too, but only as an infection, as Fura had put it. It was a truth he'd sensed all his life, even if his thoughts had never given light to it before now.

Pulling free of her grip, Mars stood. "Why are you telling me this, Fura?" His gaze flicked to the compass rose around her neck.

Seeing his eyes shift to it, Fura raised a hand to the pendant, hiding it beneath her palm. She stood, retreating a step from him, as if she didn't trust what he might do. She was wise not to trust, Mars thought. He could overpower her in moments, steal the compass—and then what? He was trapped here, same as Fura and Katrìn and Askalon would be without him.

"I'm not stupid, Mars," Fura said. "I know you still hoped to steal the Primer from me, even as you agreed to come here. But I thought after all we've been through, with Ivar, that maybe you'd changed your mind. To fight for everyone's freedom, even if it meant risking your own. I believed . . . I *believe* in you."

Her words struck that tender, wounded place inside him again.

"And no matter what, I still meant what I said." Fura stuck her chin out, defiant. "I will honor my promise to help you find the blood ampoule and destroy it. But I need to know you won't try to stop me from using the Primer. That you won't get in the way."

That tender place started to throb, the sensation spreading over him, making his legs feel unsteady, his eyes stinging.

Fura was starting to babble now. "I don't know how I can trust you, or what I can do to stop you if you try, but I swear to the nine and all things else—" She broke off as he took a sudden step toward her.

He raised a hand to her head, doing it slowly, making sure she wouldn't flinch away in fear. He ran his fingers over her braid, until he felt the gentle nub of her bond, the one she'd offered Ivar. With a quick, practiced hand, he unwound it from her hair, then brought it to his own braid and secured it there. All the while, she watched him, unspeaking.

Fura's bond now rested next to the one Una had given him. But of the two, Mars had no doubt which he believed, which he could trust. It wasn't the woman who'd owned his every move since he was a boy, who'd sent him to kill and steal and harm. No, it was the one standing before him now. The one who believed in him enough to trust him with this, her greatest secret, even knowing what he was. Both mercenary—and adept.

Besides, Ivar had saved his life. All their lives. It was a debt owed—and it was in his power to help repay it.

"I won't stop you," he said, the words feeling as if they weighed a thousand pounds in his mouth. And yet as soon as he'd released them, he felt lighter. "And I'll do what I can to help."

Something lit Fura's face. For a moment she was transformed into that young girl in pigtails from Henrik's portraits. She stepped forward, throwing her arms around him. "Thank you, Mars. Thank you."

Overcoming his momentary surprise at her sudden affection, his arms closed around her. He savored the feel of her body against his, the smell of her hair, the warmth of her skin. For a moment he wished they never had to leave this place at all. He could stay here like this forever and never want for more.

TWENTY-FIVE

"WHAT HAPPENS TOMORROW?" Mars said as they walked back to the keep, hand in hand. "Do we just make the thing and . . . set it off?" He didn't know the right words to describe how the Primer worked, having never seen it before, and could only rely on his experiences with conventional weapons.

"No," Fura sighed as they mounted the steps. "I must find my father's instructions first. He promised they would be here, though hidden, of course, in case someone else intercepted his message."

"Like your mother?"

"It was a possibility, I'm sure. But I got to it first." Fura's fingers tensed around his as she spoke, and he guessed the memory a sore subject.

"So we find the instructions and then execute. Simple." Mars nodded to himself, trying to convince his restless mind that for once, this would be true.

They'd just arrived at the hallway on the fourth floor, the doors to Katrìn's and Askalon's rooms still shut, the two presumably asleep. Mars's gaze lingered on the latter door as they passed by. "What about Askalon?"

"What about him?" Fura said, her voice dropping to a whisper.

"I doubt he'll stand idly by while we destroy his dòttra's legacy."

Fura darted a look at him. "I'm his dòttra now. He gave me his bond."

Too tired to argue, Mars nodded. "If you say so."

Arriving at the doors to their respective rooms, Fura came to a halt and faced him. "I don't intend to tell Askalon any more of what we're doing here than I have to." A smile flashed across her face. "Besides, if he does attempt to betray me, I assume you would be keen on putting him in his place."

Mars grinned back at her. "That I would."

She leaned forward and planted a quick kiss on his cheek. "Off to sleep, then. We're going to need it."

Yes, we will, Mars thought as he closed the door to his room and climbed once more into the bed. Although their task here should be easy, it wouldn't be, Mars knew as he drifted off to sleep, ill at ease with the notion. Whether Askalon or something else, there would be a catch. There always was.

Despite Fura's desire to find her father's instructions, the first orders of business the following day were food and a bath. Thankfully, the White Keep could offer both. Katrìn, who'd woken first, had made a large pot of oatmeal seasoned with cinnamon and dried pieces of apple. After days of hardtack, it was a kingly meal.

The bath, though, was fit for the Titans. Like nearly everything else in the White Keep, the bathing chamber ran on magic. All Mars had to do was offer a small sacrifice—much easier after finally getting a few hours of real sleep—and the chamber answered with hot running water and scented soap as soft as melted chocolate from the mouths of the porcelain fishes arrayed around the massive tub. Why the bathing chamber was the only place to have such ornamentation in the keep, he couldn't guess. The adepts of old must have taken their bathing very seriously.

Mars emerged nearly an hour later feeling and smelling like a new person. He had to admit, these relics were handy, and he found himself wondering what it had been like to live in Riven before the Cataclysm, when magic didn't involve a sacrifice of blood. It must've been a paradise. To think, if he'd merely been born at the right time, he could've lived like a king, even if he was born on the streets.

He joined Fura and Katrìn in the kitchen once more, Askalon having returned to bed for more sleep. The wound the draugr had inflicted on him was taking a toll. Mars and the two women made their way to Henrik's laboratory on the third floor. As with the observatory on the Torvald estate, it was crammed full of books and beakers and dozens of other pieces of scientific equipment whose purposes Mars couldn't guess. He whistled at the sight of such a mess.

"It'll take us forever to find Henrik's message in here," Katrìn said, grimacing.

"We'll manage," Fura said, her dauntless attitude in full measure this morning, renewed by a meal and a bath.

They split the room into thirds, each of them taking a section to search. Fura's included the writing desk, and she started her efforts there. Mars began with the wall-length bookshelf in his section. He was unsure what exactly he was looking for—whether Henrik's message might be hidden in an artifact or something else—and so he began by examining the books. He touched the spine of each one, feeling for some hint of magic marking the book as an artifact. He read the titles as well—those that bore one, such as the collected volumes of Riven history. Those without titles, he pulled off the shelf and leafed through, more out of curiosity than anything else. Most of these turned out to be personal diaries of Consortium adepts or ledgers from when Skarfell was in operation, filled with accountings of supplies like lumber, cotton, and steel.

He soon came across a book with a familiar symbol on the cover: the bisected circle with two half spheres. Mars opened it and began to read. It concerned the making of artifacts—or *vessels*, as the Consortium had called them. The first part of the book seemed concerned with theory—where the magic used to fill the vessels came from, how it worked, and even speculations on why the magic behaved the way it did in different vessels. This part, Mars skipped entirely, uninterested, especially as magic hadn't worked the same since the Cataclysm.

The second part contained instructions for making vessels. To his dismay, the construction seemed to have as much to do with math and science as magic. There was an entire section devoted to geometry and the relative power and weaknesses of various shapes. Triangles, for instance, were the strongest shape, resilient to external forces, both physical and magical. The circle, prone to breaking and bending, was weakest but also the most versatile in its uses. Other shapes, such as the pentagon and the octagon, had various uses—the more edges it had, the more complicated the magic it could hold.

Another section of the book discussed the unique attributes of the various materials used to create vessels—the pliability of wood, the enhancing properties of silver, the shielding quality of iron. It seemed that to excel as an adept, a student had to be as skilled at woodworking and metallurgy as they were at tapping into Rift magic. Perhaps that explained the woodshop he had discovered the night before.

"Find something interesting?" Katrìn asked, hiding a yawn behind her hand. Mars was tired already as well, and it wasn't yet noon.

"Yes, but not about the Primer." He showed her the cover.

She nodded. "I've read that one."

Remembering that Katrìn knew how to construct artifacts, a thought occurred to him. "Is this similar to how artifacts are made these days?"

"It's more than similar. The books used nowadays are mostly copies of the practical applications in that one. Most adepts aren't allowed to read them, of course, but the architects are, so they can learn to create the physical aspects of the artifacts they then have the adepts empower."

Like Gellir, Mars thought, picturing the odious little man crafting his objects for Una.

"The new books include additional steps for determining the ratio of the required magical inertia to the force level of the sacrifice offered," Katrìn added.

"Oh sure, sounds easy." Mars rolled his eyes.

Katrìn frowned. "You've never made an artifact, have you?"

He shook his head. "There aren't books like these available on the streets." Whatever book Una had supplied to Gellir must've cost her a fortune on the black market. Mars wondered which had cost more—the book or the adept? It was a peculiar, disheartening thought.

"I'm sorry," Katrìn said, looking embarrassed. "I forget sometimes how lucky I've been to grow up with Henrik. But it's never too late to learn. Here." She took the book from him and headed for the nearby desk to retrieve an ink pen. Mars followed, looking over her shoulder as she scribbled something in the book—a mathematical formula of some kind. He knew his sums, of course, thanks to Una, but this formula contained strange symbols he'd never seen before.

Katrìn handed the book back to him. "Keep the book—and actually read it, don't skim. But you'll need this formula to go with it." She grinned. "I think you'll find there's nothing quite so satisfying as creating an artifact."

"What does this mean?" He pointed at the flamelike symbol in the formula.

"That stands for kull."

"Are you serious?" Mars knew what kull was supposed to be—the lifeblood inside each person born in Riven, which was much more voluminous and concentrated in adepts, giving them their power—but he'd never before thought of it as something quantifiable, measurable like liquid in a beaker.

She squeezed his arm. "Don't fret. It simply means the amount of magic the adept creating the artifact is capable of channeling. We're all a little bit different. If you don't know your kull level, there's an easy way to figure it out. I'll help you when we've got some spare time."

"Okay. Thanks." Mars rubbed his forehead, unsure if the pursuit was worth it. If everything worked out, maybe, but if not . . . well . . . there was no scenario in which Mars would be practicing magic freely like Katrìn apparently had with Henrik. Fortunately, she didn't detect his doubt, offering him an encouraging smile as she returned to her search.

Mars returned to his as well, but his mind began to wander into speculations about shapes and objects and what sort of magical properties might be applied to them. He considered the complicated shape of the compass rose pendants Henrik had made. Mars guessed Henrik must've been quite gifted at both magic as well as physical craftsmanship. Realizing this, Mars guessed he was wasting his time look through books. Henrik would've used something more powerful for his message. With this in mind, he surveyed the room anew, and a nearby workbench soon caught his attention.

Dozens of objects of various shapes covered its surface, a gyroscope, a sextant, and a set of balance scales among them. Mars had dismissed these as tools, but now he saw them in a whole new light—tools, certainly, but also potential vessels. He walked over to the bench and picked up each object in turn, trying to examine them with his internal senses, the ones connected to the Rift. But no object felt like anything more than it seemed.

Still, he was certain he was on the right path. His gaze fell on a clock sitting on the bookshelf directly across from the desk where Fura currently sat, rummaging through a few of her father's old journals. The clock bore an elaborate face, one with a brass plate at its center shaped like a nine-pointed star—an enneagram, same as the false brand atop his hand, symbol of service done in the Ice mine.

It was also a complicated geometric shape. One capable of holding complex, sophisticated magic.

Mars knew his hunch was correct the moment he pulled the clock off the shelf and sensed the faint pulse of magic in it. He examined it carefully, certain it was an artifact, but he had no idea how to access it. The magic was there, but trapped, like water flowing beneath a crust of ice on a river.

He carried the clock back to the desk and set it before Fura. "The pendant your father made for you. Does it open only for you?" He pictured the way she'd pressed the pendant to her mouth and spoken some word to it before showing him the Primer formula.

Fura looked up from the journal. "Yes. We have a secret word, one only I know."

Complicated magic indeed. That explained Henrik's use of the compass rose for the pendant. "I think there's something in here. For you." Mars tapped the top of the clock with his finger. "It's an artifact, but I can't reach the magic inside."

From across the room, Katrìn drew an audible breath and swept toward them. "Let me see it. If it's what I think it is . . ." She trailed off as she picked up the clock, examining its shape. With a soft gasp, she set it down again a moment later. "Oh, Fura. It's an Echo."

"A what?" Mars cocked his head, looking at the clock for something he'd missed.

Katrìn turned to Mars. "It's powerful magic. And very . . . special." She took a step back from the table, waving at Mars to follow her. "We should leave Fura alone for this."

"Why?" Mars looked at Fura to find she had gone completely still, as if time had frozen around her.

"I'll tell you outside." Katrìn shooed him, but Mars held his ground.

"Not until we know that thing is safe."

"It won't hurt me," Fura said in a breathless voice. Her skin, pale with shock, turned her eyes a brilliant shade of green as she pulled her gaze off the clock at last. "It's the message from my father."

Katrìn smirked. "That's like calling the sea a pool of water." She glared at Mars, hands on hips. "An Echo allows a person to trap a bit of themselves in an object. When Fura opens it, it'll be like her father is in this room with us."

Mars swallowed. The last time he saw Henrik Torvald, the life was slipping out of the man's eyes. He turned for the door. "I'll wait outside, then."

Fura spoke softly. "No, Mars. It's all right. Please stay."

"Are you sure?" he said.

"Yes." Fura met his gaze. "There have been enough secrets between us already. Let there be no more."

Then, without giving him a chance to respond, she placed her hands on the clock and pulled it toward her, whispering that secret word low on her breath. At once the brass plate on the clock's face began to move, twisting to the right as if by an unseen gear—a gear formed and fueled by the magic contained inside it. Mars felt the stirring of it in the air, coaxing gooseflesh down his arms and setting his palms itching with the need to touch the Rift and draw its power forth.

A substance like smoke or vapor began to pour out of the clockface. It rose into the air, swirling about with purpose, like something alive. All three of them took a step back, giving it room. The smoke coalesced in the area in front of the desk, taking the shape of a man. It was a slow process, like watching an artist shading in a sketch. But once done, Henrik Torvald was standing in the room with them. Or some ghost or shadow of him was, at least. Although the surcoat he wore was brown, the color was dull, almost translucent. So were his skin and hair. Everything except for his eyes. Those were exactly as Mars had remembered them in the moments before the man died, both weary and penetrating.

Aware of his beating heart, Mars took another step back, wishing he could flee.

Henrik's shadow faced Fura, the magic drawing them together. The way the man's eyes fixed on his daughter's sent an eerie shiver down Mars's spine, a fear that this same gaze would fix on Mars with recognition of a different nature.

"Fura, my dearheart, my darling. If you're hearing this, then I am gone. And I'm so sorry to have left you behind, and with so little in the way of guidance. And yet here you are." The voice of this shadow Henrik was much like its form, faded and distant. Still, the words held weight and substance, drawing tears to Fura's eyes at once. Mars glanced at her, then looked away just as quickly, unable to bear the raw sorrow in her expression.

We are the weapon, not the will.

The refrain didn't help this time.

Henrik's Echo was moving on. "I can only hope you have kept the Primer formula safe and yourself as well, and Katrìn, too. My dear, sweet Katrìn." The shadow seemed to shudder at her name. Mars glanced at Katrìn, noting how pale she'd gone. "I'm so sorry. Both for what I've done and what I'm about to do."

Henrik's shadow went still for a moment, and Mars felt the air in the room grow tense in anticipation. *Nothing good can come from this,* he thought. But there was nothing he could do to stop it.

"I brought you here under false pretenses," Henrik's Echo continued. "I promised you a better way to use the Primer to destroy all the country's Ice at once, and while I can give you that, it comes with a terrible price. If you wish to walk away from this now, I understand." The Echo paused, as if to give Fura the chance to do just that. But anyone who knew her would know that that would never happen. A moment later, the Echo went on. "You know from my use of the Primer in the Skorri mine that it triggers a deadly reaction when it comes in contact with Ice. The amount we used there was minuscule, a few drops, and yet hundreds of miners died in the resulting explosion. So many innocent lives lost." The shadow paused again, another shudder passing through it. "The weight of my reckless decision to test it there haunts me. I should've known better, done better, only . . ." He trailed off for a moment, lost in thought.

When he resumed, he seemed harder somehow, more resolved. "What I learned in that failure is that using the Primer in that manner had been folly from the start. If the Helm, the kith, the very people of Riven had all been willing to eradicate the Ice together, it might've worked. We could've emptied the mines, made sure people were at a safe distance before deploying it, but I'm afraid Riven is incapable of such unity."

Mars silently agreed. Their small group struggled to share a unified vision—how could they expect anything else from the entire country?

"I was unwilling to do what needed to be done to destroy the Ice in that manner," the Echo continued, "and this caused the Wake to turn on me. They had no such compunctions. They would've used it without care or thought, deploying dozens of fighters across all nine mines of Riven in a preemptive strike. One that would've left Riven and its people devastated. I know, Fura, that you will be unwilling to sacrifice so many innocents to our cause."

He knew his daughter well, Mars thought, glancing at Fura. Unbidden, the face of the little thief he'd schooled in Geldur Court appeared in his mind. Then he saw Natasja's mother, then Natasja herself. Giving faces to those thousands of lives made Henrik's warning all the more disturbing.

"There is an alternative," Henrik's shadow said, "one that requires the sacrifice of only one innocent life to save thousands. But the decision won't be easy. It may, in fact, be impossible." The Echo paused, the intervening silence heavy as a stone. "Katrìn. She is the key, the final ingredient that will allow us to end the tyranny of Ice forever. Not by destroying it, but by healing the Rift."

Katrìn? Mars turned his head toward her, fear already taking hold of him. He knew her well enough to know that she would certainly be willing to give anything to this cause, same as Fura. But healing the Rift? Dozens of questions flooded Mars's mind, but he had no one to ask.

Fortunately, Henrik was far from finished with his explanation. "In order for you to understand, I must go back to the beginning. The true beginning of my quest to create the Primer, which started long before you were born, Fura. Before you were even a thought in my mind.

"The year I married your mother, she brought me with her to the Assembly for the first time. With my elevated status, I was allowed to visit the Archives, a place restricted to all but the kith. Even the Helm are not permitted to read the books kept there. In them, I found personal accounts of the Consortium adepts—both before the Cataclysm and after. I learned the Consortium had been trying to heal the Rift, but their attempt backfired and gave rise to the Ice. I soon began to wonder if the process could be reversed somehow—if the Rift could be brought back to the state it had been in before the Cataclysm. In my youth and arrogance, I believed myself capable of doing it. And so I dedicated all my life and energy to the pursuit.

"The answer to healing the Rift, I discovered, lay in the very nature of its creation—ages ago—the death of the World Raven. Here at Skarfell it died, its rib bones forming the very pillars surrounding the Heart. However, the Rift's creation was not just by the animal's physical death, but the sacrifice of its kull, its lifeblood. If I could re-create an infusion of kull of equal measure to Jörn's, then that lifeblood could be used to restore the Rift. To that end, I began to experiment on creating such a being . . . using human children. And starting before they were born."

A chill slid down Mars's spine at the implication in the man's words. Next to him, Fura raised a hand to her mouth.

"I'm not proud of it," Henrik's shadow said, "and my shame of those early days has only grown in the years since. Back then, I wasn't concerned with the sanctity of human life, not as I am now. My pursuit was purely scientific, I'd convinced myself—attempting to create a vessel, an artifact, out of a human body. The most complicated shape of all. To do that, I began recruiting secret adepts or rescuing them from the black markets when I could. All came to my cause willingly, and some of the women volunteered to give birth to the vessel children, as I came to call them.

"As with all experiments, there were failures . . . many of them. Most of the fetuses died in the womb. And at first, those successfully born didn't live longer than a few days. That is, until Katrìn."

At the mention of her name, shock prickled down Mars's arms. She had been an experiment? Henrik Torvald had bred her like a prized hunting dog? He thought he might be sick. Katrìn, too, looked unwell, her skin sallow and her expression grim.

"Katrìn was born healthy. I had succeeded." Henrik's shadow flashed a sad, bitter grin. "You might be wondering why I didn't go through with it. Why I didn't sacrifice this baby to the Rift as I intended. There are two reasons. You were born a mere seven days after Katrìn. The first time I held you in my arms, I loved you. And yet you were the same as the vessel child. Small, helpless, innocent. I knew then that I could never go through with it. I couldn't kill a child. I couldn't be that monster, despite the monstrous things I'd already done. And when another vessel child was successfully delivered a week later, I knew I had to change my strategy entirely.

"But any possibility of that ended entirely when a fire erupted at the secret compound where I had performed all my experiments, a warehouse in Jakulvik. Katrìn and her mother were still living there when it broke out. Katrìn nearly perished in the fire. To my great sorrow, her mother was not so lucky. Like her daughter, Lena Helgadòttra was fiercely noble and brave. When the fire started, she saved Katrìn first, then returned to the warehouse to save the other vessel child and that child's mother. But none of them made it back out."

Katrìn drew an audible breath, the sound rife with tears. Mars resisted looking at her, unwilling to witness the pain she must be feeling.

"After that tragedy, I adopted Katrìn, bringing her to live with us as a playmate for you, Fura. And I loved and raised her as one of my own. And yet my desire to end the world's dependance on Ice was far from defeated. I turned instead from trying to heal the Rift to trying to destroy the Ice itself—and the Primer, with all its flaws and risks, was the end result. And yet my success with the vessel child remained. Even now, Katrìn has it within her to heal the Rift and end the Ice. But she must make the sacrifice willingly, giving the Rift all her kull, same as the World Raven once did."

Fura gasped. She ripped her gaze from her father's shadow and turned it to Katrìn. "Absolutely not. I won't allow it. I won't—"

"Fura," Henrik's shadow said, and for a moment his voice was so lifelike, it was as if he were actually in the room with them, "I know what you must be feeling and thinking. For I have felt the same as well. It's an impossible choice. And it's also not one either of us can make. The choice must be Katrìn's. She and she alone can do this.

"And yet even as I tell you these things, my heart hopes that there may yet be another option. Katrìn is clever, the smartest pupil I have ever trained. She has a scientific mind and insight. Given enough time, she might find a way to refine the Primer formula so that she may combine its power with her kull in such a way as to heal the Rift without losing her life. That is my greatest hope in bringing you here."

Now Henrik's shadow rotated, turning toward the place where the clock had resided on the shelf. He held out his hand, and Mars felt the magic respond. A hidden panel in the shelf slid aside, revealing a small compartment built into the wall. A journal lay inside it. "All of my research, concerning both the vessel child and the Primer, resides in that journal. Guard it with your life, Fura. No one else must know what Katrìn is."

Henrik's shadow turned back to Fura, flickering in and out with the movement. Mars sensed the magic weakening. The artifact's power was like a candle that had nearly been spent—one that would never be lit again.

"I must leave you now, Fura, at least until we meet again in Asvaldur. But first, I beg your forgiveness, daughter, for all the things I once did and for the terrible burden I leave for you now. I love you, Fura, and Katrìn as well. Always."

Henrik blew Fura a kiss and bowed, a sad gesture to replace the embrace he wasn't capable of giving in this form. Then the magic went out of the room, and the Echo of Henrik Torvald faded away into nothingness.

TWENTY-SIX

NO ONE SPOKE afterward. Or moved. They hardly dared to breathe.

For his part, Mars felt as if he were caught in a dream or a story, a scenario so horrid and incredible it was nearly impossible to believe.

Katrìn was the first to break the spell gripping them. She marched toward the secret compartment and pulled Henrik's journal from its hiding place.

"What are you doing?" Fura said.

Ignoring her, Katrìn set the journal on a nearby workbench, then began shuffling the beakers and other equipment out of the way.

"Katrìn," Fura said, "what are you doing?"

Again, Katrìn ignored her as she flipped the journal open.

Quickly reaching the end of her patience, Fura marched over to her friend and placed a hand on her shoulder. "Katrìn?"

"What?" Katrìn jerked her head over her shoulder, casting Fura an incredulous look, as if she found the interruption inconceivable. "You heard the man. I've work to do."

Fura bit her lip, tears brimming in her eyes. Mars understood, feeling the same pluck of despair in his chest at the pain in Katrìn's voice, barely hidden beneath her false determination.

"Yes, I heard what he said. All of it. About you and your mother and . . ." Fura drew a deep breath. "I need to know you're going to be all right. And most of all, that you're not going to do anything stupid."

Katrìn faced Fura, arms crossed over her chest like a shield. "Like what? Slash my wrists and hurl myself into the Heart?"

Fura flinched, crossing her arms as well, the two braced for battle. "Yes, exactly that. I know you. I know that's what you're secretly telling yourself, that it's an option."

"It *is* an option." Katrìn stuck out her chin. "How could it not be? I care about our people same as you. Maybe even more so, if only because of how much it means to you, Fura. I love you . . . I owe all my happiness and every good thing in my life to you. I would do anything to see your dream fulfilled. . . ." The tears she'd been trying so desperately to hold back began to fall in earnest.

"Oh, Katrìn." Fura started to cry as well. She unfolded her arms and pulled Katrìn into a hug. Katrìn resisted at first, head down and arms tight around her chest, but moment by moment her resistance drained away, until at last she returned Fura's embrace, her head resting on Fura's shoulder.

A painful lump rose in Mars's throat, and he swallowed it down as he looked away from the two friends. He felt undone by their emotions, shamed by their love, one he didn't understand, couldn't understand, because he'd never experienced the same himself. Not even with Orri. But then, Orri never really knew who he was, did he? The lump rose again in his throat at the thought, as tears leaked from his eyes and stole down his cheeks. He wiped them away quickly, hoping no one would see.

"I'm so sorry," Fura said, stroking Katrìn's back. "I don't deserve you. Especially now, knowing what my father did to you."

Katrìn nodded. "I can't believe it." She pulled back from the embrace, meeting Fura's eyes. "And yet, does it really matter, after all that he did for me later? He took me in, Fura. He made me your sister. Surely that makes up for it."

"Does it?" A muscle ticked in Fura's jaw, punctuated by the sound of her teeth grinding. She motioned to the clock. "He still brought us here with the hope that you would go through with it. That you would do what he made you to do."

Katrìn stood up straighter, chin raised at a haughty angle. "He did not make me. I am the sum of my choices. *My* choice, Fura. No one else's."

"To hell with that. I won't allow you to—"

Katrìn silenced her with an upraised hand. "I'm not going to sacrifice myself to the Rift. There has to be another way. There always is. And I will find it. I promise. You just need to give me time."

Fura gave a grudging nod. "All right. Time. That I can give you. As long as it takes."

Watching this exchange from a few a feet away, little more than an outsider looking in, Mars shook his head; neither woman saw. He did it just once, sad and resigned to a truth Fura and Katrìn didn't yet realize. Time was not on their side.

Sooner or later, someone would come looking for them. This was a race, and coming in second place would mean death.

While Katrìn was getting started, Fura and Mars debated what to tell Askalon. It was a stroke of good fortune that he hadn't been present for the discovery of Henrik's Echo. He also hadn't yet pressed much about the Primer or what Fura intended to do, but Mars suspected the truss would start to once he was feeling better. In the meantime, they agreed to stick to the original story—that they were here to make the Primer—but with the added embellishment that it would be more complicated than they'd anticipated.

To help ensure Askalon didn't accidentally uncover the truth, Katrìn converted Henrik's secret shelf behind the clock into a true artifact, one only the three of them could open. Whenever she wasn't using Henrik's journal, she would stow it safely away.

Once these decisions were made, Katrìn demanded that Fura and Mars leave her alone so she could read the journal. Fura agreed, but only, Mars suspected, because she desired some time to herself. Henrik's revelations had struck them both hard, if in different ways. Katrìn would process her emotions through the work, Mars guessed. He wasn't sure about Fura.

And he wasn't sure about himself, either. He didn't fully become aware of his own emotional turmoil until he found himself alone, with nothing to do but think. Memories of Orri pressed in, bringing with them all the doubt and pain he'd been trying so long to ignore. Henrik's death haunted him, too—the cold, unrelenting memory of how he had killed the man, and the certain knowledge that Fura would never forgive him for it if she found out. He tried to tell himself it didn't matter. He didn't need her forgiveness. He didn't need anything from her, aside from the help she'd promised him. Either that, or the Primer formula, which for now remained as valuable as ever. And would continue to, so long as Katrìn didn't succeed in her attempt to modify it and heal the Rift.

But it did matter. For reasons he refused to give voice to, even inside his own head. The ache he felt, the longing, for a connection with someone else like Fura shared with Katrìn, silently ate away at him.

Before long, he decided to address it in the way he knew how—by burying himself deep in a bottle of bourbon.

Sometime later, with night slowly descending, Mars wandered through the keep in a daze, his thoughts and feelings deadened by the alcohol but still there, like the dull throb of pain from a fingernail cut to the quick.

The hallways he traversed were lined with busts of dead Consortium adepts, their eerie stone eyes seeming to follow him as he passed, watching him, judging him. He'd been gone for hours now, randomly walking here and there, climbing stairs, rummaging through rooms, avoiding areas strewn with rubble. All in a sorry attempt to distract his mind from the awful truths that kept cycling through it in a relentless wave. He pressed his fingers to his eyes, wishing he could pluck the memories out and cast them away.

He stumbled onward, determined to wander until his legs fell off. But then the sound of something being smashed reached him. Frowning, he headed toward it, half hoping a dangerous creature from the Mistgrave had made its way into the keep. A good fight would lighten his mood considerably.

A set of double doors stood open ahead, and more noises of commotion issued from the doorway—heavy breathing and the distinctive sound of a blade being swung through air. Mars set the bourbon bottle on the ground and pulled the sword he'd purloined free of the sheath at his hip. He stepped toward the doors and peered inside, cautiously.

It was Fura, practicing her swordplay with a starsteel blade she must've found in the armory. She hadn't bothered to don any armor.

Unready to face her, Mars tried backing away unnoticed, but she spun toward him, her sword hissing through the air. She froze, and for a second, they stared at each other like enemies across a battlefield. Mars lowered his sword first, and Fura followed a moment later.

"I heard a noise." Stepping inside the room, he could see now it was a Rivna temple, albeit one vastly different from the one on the Torvald estate. That temple had been austere and solemn as a tomb; this space was almost cheerful, the walls hung with brightly colored tapestries that depicted stories of Riven's ancient past, tales so famous that even Mars was familiar with them. Human-size statues of the Titans stood at even intervals about the round room. The one of Vigny was missing its head—a loss that had occurred recently, Mars wryly surmised, given the fresh cloud of dust surrounding it.

Fura shrugged, stiffly. "I wanted something more than air to practice on."

"You? Desecrate a statue in a Rivna temple?" Mars snorted, as he sheathed his sword. "I don't believe it."

Turning away from him, she swung at Vigny once more, this time taking off the arm that held the titaness's famous cauldron.

Mars grinned, fully appreciating Fura's coping mechanisms. "Do you want to talk about it?" He didn't know what possessed him to ask such a question, which thankfully didn't come out as sarcastically as he'd feared.

Fura rolled her eyes. "No." She wielded the blade again, prepared to strike the statue, but then lowered the sword as if finding its weight too much to bear. "I thought I knew him."

"Your father?" Mars guessed, knowing there wasn't anyone else it could be.

"He murdered babies."

Mars frowned at her choice of words. Was it murder? The intent wasn't for the babies to die, after all. It seemed Fura was seeing the world as she always did—as a binary thing, black and white, good and evil—and disregarding the complexities that lay in between and all around.

"That's a bit harsh, don't you think? The adepts volunteered for the experiments, and your father didn't intend those deaths any more than a general intends for his soldiers to die on the battlefield. They were consequences of a cause he thought worth the risk."

Fura scowled. "That argument is a slippery slope. By such logic, any cause is worth any consequence so long as its ends are met."

Mars couldn't argue with that, having seen the truth of it

many times before. Every patron of the Fortune's Den told the same lie to themselves as they sought to dampen their suffering with drink and dust and sex, anything that worked, no matter the cost to themselves or others.

"At least your father did the right thing in the end," Mars said. Katrìn was still alive and with them, after all, and Henrik had devoted his remaining years to the Primer.

"Yes, I suppose he did."

"Because he loved you," Mars gently pressed, remembering what Henrik's Echo had said—becoming a father had changed him.

Fura sheathed her sword, purposefully not meeting his gaze. "So he claimed."

Mars sighed. "Well, at the very least he stuck around. That's more than some can say." He turned back to the doorway to retrieve the bourbon bottle and raised it to his lips for another drink.

"I suppose you've got a point." Fura held out her hand for the bottle, pulling it from his fingers. "It still seems a twisted sort of love, though." She sat down, laying her sword on the ground next to her and keeping one hand on the bottle. "I used to think that love could transcend any challenge. Now I wonder if it's just a curse. It seems easier not to feel anything at all."

"I'm sure you're not the first to think that," Mars said, sitting down next to her. Silently, he hoped she would never manage to cast off the depth of her feelings. She wouldn't be Fura any longer if she stopped feeling, if she became a heartless beast. *Same as me.*

"That only proves my point." Fura tapped a fingernail

against the bottle. "Look where my father's love has taken us." She gestured to the room, as if the desecrated statue of Vigny represented all her sins. "I risked our lives crossing the Mistgrave, got Ivar killed, and for what? The off chance Katrìn succeeds?"

"You don't think she will?" For some reason, Fura's doubt made Mars uneasy, like watching thunderclouds form on the horizon. Belief and conviction came so easily to her. Her doubt made him feel as if a stranger wore her face.

"How can she? My father was brilliant, with years of experience, and he failed to do it."

"Well, yes, but did he even try?" Mars shifted his weight from one hip to the other, vaguely recalling that he'd bumped into a table earlier in his mindless wanderings. "The way it sounded to me is that he only recently considered the possibility of modifying the Primer. And I might not know much about scientific experiments, but surely he would need samples of Katrìn's blood to test anything."

Fura opened her mouth to protest, then hesitated. "I suppose you might have a point." She drew her knees to her chest. "Very well. Maybe there is a small chance."

Relieved at this small concession, Mars patted her arm. "There now. That's the spirit."

Fura nodded, but she didn't smile at his patronizing joke. "What about your stake in this? If Katrìn fails, there's still the Primer itself. It hasn't lost its value." As if to emphasize the point, she picked up the compass rose pendant at her neck and began to turn it round in her fingers.

"That's true." Mars contemplated taking it once more, but

only for a fleeting second. As before, he stood no chance of escaping this place without Katrìn. Only, it was more than that. So much more. That longing for connection struck him again. "But I think I'd rather take my chances with you and Katrìn."

Fura's fingers stilled around the pendant. "Do you really mean that?"

He shrugged, trying to downplay his feelings before they got the best of him. His throat felt wrapped in twine. "Unlike my employer, you mean what you say and do what you promise. That's pretty special."

A sigh escaped Fura's lips, and she reached out and took his hand in hers. "That means a lot." She stroked the top of his hand with her thumb. "I'm sorry I misjudged you so badly when we first met, simply for being a mercenary. You're a good man underneath."

The apology caught him by surprise, robbing him of thought for a moment. It would've been so easy to simply accept it. To forget the things he'd done and carry on, Fura none the wiser. Only, he couldn't. Something deep inside him refused to let him do so. "No, I'm not. I've never been good. You've no idea the things I've done."

Fura twined her fingers through his. "You're right. I don't know. But you're no different from my father. You can be good through the things you're trying to do now no matter what you once did."

Mars pulled away from her, standing up. For a moment, all he could see was Henrik standing there—with Orri waiting just behind. He remembered them playing at the Den, each game a race to see who was fastest, strongest, most agile. So many times Mars had let the other boy win, resisting the temptation to use his magic to his advantage, if only to see the grin on Orri's face when he succeeded.

"It's not so simple. It's—" Mars broke off, words failing him.

"What is it, Mars?" Fura rose as well, standing close to him. She touched his arm gently, as if he were a statue made of sand. "You can tell me."

He opened his mouth, the truth pressing against his teeth, longing to be spoken, to be set free. He forced his lips together, refusing.

"Please, Mars. You can trust me with anything."

Not this. Fear wouldn't let him, fear of breaking her, of breaking this relationship he had with her and Katrìn, whatever it was. They would both turn him away. See him as a monster. Just like Orri had, even if for different reasons.

You are a monster.

"I killed . . . my best friend." They weren't the words he'd intended to say, but they were nevertheless a truth he'd never shared with anyone. He felt something crack open inside him, a release so powerful, he had to swallow a gasp.

"What?" Fura stilled, but didn't retreat from him. "What happened?"

"His name was Orri. We were working a contract together. He was supposed to be my lookout, while I . . . while I finished the job. Only, things went wrong. I had to use my magic, and Orri saw."

"Oh, Mars," Fura said, beginning to understand.

Mars nodded, feeling his eyes starting to burn. "I was afraid he would expose the truth about me. He looked at me with such hate . . . so I . . . stopped him. I killed him to save myself."

Fura said nothing, but she didn't retreat, either.

With the confession now made, Mars felt bitterness stinging the back of his throat. "And for the longest time, I thought I was justified in killing him. That I'd done what I'd had to do. But then I met you and Katrìn. You've always been her friend, despite what she is. Maybe . . . maybe Orri would've been, too. If I'd given him a chance."

Again, Fura said nothing, and her silence felt like a vise closing around him.

He forced a laugh. "So you see. Not a good man. Not at all."

Finally, the terrible stillness that had fallen over Fura broke as she shook her head. "You're wrong. The fact that you can regret and question what you did is proof." Then she surprised him by taking a step toward him, eliminating the space between them. She wrapped her arms around his sides, pulling him into an embrace. His arms closed around her in answer.

"You did what you had to in the moment. It's not your fault. Our world is broken, Mars. It makes us all broken people."

Although he didn't believe her, couldn't believe her, some of the weight on his shoulders drifted away at her acceptance.

Fura held him tighter. "And I swear to protect you, Mars, just as I protect Katrìn. No matter what happens. We'll find a way to keep your secret safe, and to get you free from your employer. If I can't save Riven, saving you and Katrìn will be enough."

Again, Mars didn't fully believe her, but it didn't matter. Just her wanting to was enough for him. Unable to speak, he drew her into a kiss instead. She melted into it. It was unlike either of their two kisses before. Not feigned like at the Felling, nor reckless like at the ball. This was deeper somehow, truer. It touched some deep part of him beyond his physical body. He clung to her like a man hanging from a precipice, her mouth on his the only thing keeping him from plummeting.

This was what he wished could last forever. For a moment, all the ugly truths he'd grappled with were gone. Henrik, Orri, Una's control over him, the Primer, everything they promised, or threatened. None of it mattered.

But like all moments, it passed. Far, far too soon.

The sound of a throat clearing broke them apart. They both looked toward the doorway, where Askalon stood watching them with a hooded gaze, his arms folded stiffly over his chest.

"What is it, Askalon?" Fura said, her voice breathless. Crimson climbed her neck into her cheeks.

"Katrìn is asking for you."

"Oh, of course. Thanks for telling me." Fura stepped away from Mars, heading for the door.

"Not you, Fura. Him." Askalon pointed at Mars.

"Me?" He couldn't imagine what Katrìn could possibly want from him.

But as he left the temple and made his way back to the laboratory, he found out quickly enough. It was something he'd been asked to give only once before in his life, by Una.

A vial of his blood.

TWENTY-SEVEN

DESPITE LIVING IN an abandoned old castle with little in the way of distractions, the next week passed quickly for Mars. After his conversation with Fura that day they discovered the Echo, he'd become invested in Katrìn's success, which brought with it a tangled mess of hope and worries. He soon found himself taking up her coping mechanism of choice—staying busy.

He spent his mornings working in the laboratory with Katrìn, which mostly involved providing her with samples of his blood once or twice a day for her experiments so she could compare the kull in his blood with her own to isolate the variables. As she explained, there must be some difference in her blood compared to that of any other adept because of Henrik's experiments, and if she could figure out that difference, it might be what they needed to solve this puzzle.

The rest of the time, he either spent leafing through the old Consortium books, picking out useful tips and tricks about magic, or trying to master the craft of making artifacts. Katrìn had willingly taken the time to show him how to determine his kull level, since she needed the information for her own experiments.

"Huh," she said when she had finished the calculations. "Well, it's not the kull level that marks the results of Henrick's experiments. Ours is practically the same."

"Does that matter?"

She shrugged. "If anything, it makes my job easier. Since we're equal in power I won't have to adjust for any differences."

"Equal in power? I thought your kull was special."

Katrìn made a face. "Don't get too excited. Power is only one small piece of a person's kull. Many adepts share the same level. There's even an average."

"Surely we're above average, right?" He winked.

She smiled. "Yes, but only slightly. So don't let it go to your head."

"Me?" He placed a hand on his chest. "I wouldn't dream of it. I'm the humblest person I know."

"Right," Katrìn snorted.

"But what makes your kull so special, then?" He stared at the paper on which she'd written the sum.

Katrìn shook her head. "No idea. That's what we're here to find out."

With his kull level defined, he'd been able to craft a couple of basic artifacts, the kind he had read that all first-year Consortium adepts attempted. He'd made a keyless lockbox that would only open at his touch, a palm-size fabric ball that generated more and more heat the longer it was held, and a whistle that was supposed to be heard only by adepts. Mars didn't quite succeed with the last one—it was so loud in his own mind when he first blew it that it had rendered him unconscious. Katrìn and Askalon had found him lying on his back with a trickle of blood coming out his nose.

"Don't take it too hard," Katrìn said as Askalon helped Mars to his feet. "You're not the first adept to fail at that one. It's more complicated magic than it looks on paper. It was exceedingly loud, though."

"You heard it?"

She nodded. "I almost fell myself."

"Did he?" Mars thumbed a finger at Askalon, who looked thoroughly amused by the situation.

Katrìn shook her head. "It's silent to non-adepts, at any rate."

Mars vowed to be careful when testing his artifacts from there on out.

The afternoons, Mars spent with Fura, the two of them practicing swordplay in the Rivna temple. It had started off as a way to pass time while Katrìn fretted over her most recent failure to find a solution to the Primer problem. But it had grown into something more, almost like lessons where they were both teacher and student. Fura taught him a little of the Rivna fighting styles, and he in turn showed her more of the combat techniques he'd honed in the shadows.

A week into their stay at Skarfell, Mars joined Katrìn in the laboratory one morning with an offer to help. At the moment, there weren't any other artifacts in the textbooks he felt like tackling.

"If you really want to help me," she said, making no effort to hide her annoyance at being interrupted, "you should go back in time and bring Henrik here to help me figure this stuff out."

Mars gritted his teeth in frustration. Partly because he knew he could be of more use to her if she just gave him some direction, and partly because of his complete lack of understanding about what she was doing. Feeling ignorant and useless was not something he was used to.

"I'll just sit here and say nothing, then." He pulled out a chair, scraping the legs against the floor. "Think I can manage that."

Katrìn arched an eyebrow. "Are you sure? Because I'm having my doubts."

Mars rolled his eyes at her, then winked—and was pleased to see a smile curl across her face. In his experience, she was liable to accomplish more if she relaxed a bit. He eyed Henrik's journal lying on the desk, curiosity getting the best of him. He'd avoided the journal, having no interest in touching anything of Henrik's, but now he felt up to the task.

Sitting down at the desk, Mars opened the journal to the first page. As expected, it primarily concerned Katrìn's conception, the experiments she'd endured while still in the womb, as well as her eventual birth. Having little else to do, Mars sat back and began to read. To his surprise, he soon found himself engrossed in the story.

Katrìn's mother had been an adept belonging to the Lux kith. The Luxes had managed to secure Lena Helgadòttra at the age of nine, and by all accounts she'd been a willing adept, thereby avoiding the maiming and hobbling most coerced adepts endured. By the time she turned nineteen, Lena had apparently earned her masters' trust, and was seemingly adored for her sweet nature.

Mars found it difficult to hide his disgust at the way Lena had been regarded by the people who had kept her in thrall. He had to wonder how much of this "likability" the Luxes saw in her was an act she put on for her own survival and protection. Rebellion came in many forms, after all.

When Lena was twenty, the Lux vane had hosted a party of wealthy foreigners from Osway for several weeks at the kith's estate. Among these Oswayans was a young man by the name of Tanix Reinhold. Who he was exactly, whether wellborn or servant, the journal didn't record. All that was said about him was that he and Lena shared a love affair that ended with her pregnant and him sailing back to Osway. Mars suspected that learning their adept was pregnant hadn't gone over well with the Luxes. The consequences for Lena had been dire enough that she had used her magic to flee to Jakulvik, finding haven with Henrik and his people.

Mars wondered how much convincing it had taken for Henrik to get Lena to volunteer for his vessel experiments. Had Lena seen the potential in what he was trying to accomplish? Or did she see Henrik as nothing more than another rich person looking to take advantage of her magic? Mars suspected there was no way to know. He looked up at Katrìn, buried in some experiment. She had surely read these pages; he couldn't guess how she must be feeling, no matter how committed she was to the cause Henrik had worked for.

From across the room, Katrìn growled again in frustration. Deciding he'd read enough, Mars stood from the desk and approached the table where she was working, then stood hovering over her. Eventually, she decided she had no choice but to look up at him. A scowl marred her pretty face. Eyeing her burn scars, Mars wondered what she thought about them, now that she knew the full story of where they'd come from—her mother saving her from that fire. *Just as Katrìn saved me,* he reminded himself, recalling the night of the Quiescence ball.

"This is impossible. It makes no sense." She slapped the table, causing a pair of glass test tubes to rattle in their wooden holder.

"So you keep saying. But what exactly doesn't make sense?" Mars motioned to the table, crowded with her notes and various empty vials that had previously held his blood and hers.

Katrìn rolled her eyes. "It's complicated. You wouldn't understand. Not without a solid background in chemistry."

"Try me."

She made a face.

Mars put his hands on his hips. "Even if I don't understand the science of it, I might make a connection you haven't. Or the act of telling me might trigger an idea for you."

"Oh, all right." She huffed once and waved at the mess across the table. "I guess I don't need to go into detail. The problem is actually very simple. I'm trying to isolate the variable in my kull that makes me a vessel by comparing it to yours. The reactions should be different, but no matter what I do, I keep getting the same results."

Narrowing his gaze, Mars tried his best to look as if he

understood perfectly. "Is that why these two look the same?" He indicated the test tubes, both containing a liquid that wasn't quite red and wasn't quite purple, but some nameless shade in between.

"Precisely." Katrìn thumped the table again. "This one held your blood and this one mine." She indicated each test tube in turn. "If I'd gotten the formula right, the two should've reacted differently when I added a few drops of the Primer to it." She indicated a vial full of a golden mixture so bright, it looked like liquid sunshine. She'd made several vials of the Primer that first day and had nearly spent them all in her experiments. Only this one and another, stowed in the secret compartment, remained.

"I see." Mars rubbed his chin thoughtfully.

"No, you don't. You're just saying that. But our blood reacting the same means my theory is off, and I need to start again from the beginning." She suddenly sank back into her chair, crushed by defeat. "I can't make any progress until I can figure out exactly what changes Henrik's experiments produced in me."

Mars stared down at her, uncertain what to do or say, how to comfort her. He cleared his throat and placed a hand on her shoulder. "You're being too hard on yourself. Maybe you should take a break, give your mind time to rest."

Katrìn grunted. "Henrik wouldn't have taken a break."

"Henrik spent his whole life coming up with this stuff. You've been at it a week. Give yourself some grace." Mars reached into his pocket and withdrew a palm-size ball he'd found in his room, left there by an adept long ago. "Here. It'll take your mind off things. Maybe shake something loose." He took a few steps back and tossed it to her.

She rolled her eyes. "What's this made of?" She squeezed the ball, marveling at its soft texture as Mars had done when he discovered it.

"No idea. Come on, throw it here." He held out his hands. Reluctantly, Katrìn stood and tossed it to him. He caught it easily, then volleyed it back to her.

In moments, they were enveloped in the game. There was something satisfying about it, not just the simple skill it took to catch it, but something about the ball itself, the gentle way it struck the palm, as if it longed to be held and let go again.

"Fura and I used to play like this all the time when we were little," Katrìn said as she made a tricky catch—Mars having lobbed the ball a little too high for her.

Mars grinned back at her, although he couldn't help the tug of envy that went through him. Even when he and Orri had played together, it had never been so simple, and never just for fun—they made games out of practicing their knife skills, a useful supplement to their training. There was an innocence to this game, though, one that made Mars feel like a kid again. Or more like the kid he might've been if he'd been born under different circumstances.

He was just starting to sense that Katrìn was beginning to relax when the door swung open and Fura rushed in.

She raked her gaze over the two of them, the whites of her eyes flashing. "Someone's coming."

"What?" Mars snatched the ball from the air. "Across the Mistgrave? How?"

"Come on." Fura raced from the room, heading for the stairs.

In a frenzy of pounding footsteps, the three of them hurried to the top of the White Keep, stepping out onto the southern tower. A warm breeze whipped across Mars's face as his eyes fell on Askalon, standing on the edge of the tower wall with a spyglass raised before him.

Mars joined him, glancing down at the Mistgrave. As always, the mist was impenetrable, a wall of gray so solid, the sunlight seemed to bounce off it.

But Askalon wasn't peering down with the spyglass, but across, at the horizon, tracking something in the distance.

"Are they still there?" Fura said, coming to stand between Askalon and Mars.

Nodding, Askalon handed her the spyglass. She raised it to her eye and a moment later made a strangled noise.

"What are you seeing?" Mars squinted against the light, detecting a faint blur in the distance, some isolated storm cloud.

"Look for yourself." Fura shoved the spyglass into his hand.

Raising it to his eye, Mars aimed at the dark spot, only to take a step back in alarm.

A small ship was sailing right for them. No, not sailing—*flying.* Hovering low above the Mistgrave. The skiff had no sails and no oars, no visible means of movement, save for a distinctive glow around the gunwale where the deck met the hull.

Ice. The thing was fueled by Ice.

As far as he knew no one had ever attempted something

like this. If the magic failed, or if they couldn't land before the Ice ran out, it would mean death. He tried to make out the figures sitting in the skiff, but it was too far out. For now.

"Who would be crazy enough to use Ice to make a ship *fly*?" Mars lowered the spyglass in shock.

"My mother," Fura said. "Who else?"

Katrìn bumped up next to him. "What do we do?"

"There's no telling how many people they have on that boat...." Mars said.

"Do you think we can fight them off?" Fura laid her hand on his arm. "Or perhaps ambush them somehow?"

"Killing them would be a whole lot easier." Mars could think of a dozen ways of knocking that skiff down well before it reached them. If the fall alone didn't do the trick, the draugrs and riftworms waiting in the Mistgrave below would.

Fura grabbed his arm. "It's my mother, Mars."

"We might be able to capture them," said Katrìn. "A magic trap of some kind. But where to set it?" She looked behind and around them, casting about for an idea.

"They'll have to land down there." Fura motioned over the edge. "We could try and fortify the door. This is a fortress, one that was protected by magic. Surely there are mechanisms to prevent invasion."

Mars frowned. "That might work. They can't get through the door unless—"

"They brought an adept with them." Katrìn shook her head. "Which they surely did. A few, I'd wager, to keep that ship flying."

Mars started to respond but broke off as something

caught his eye. He raised the spyglass again and swore. "There's a second one."

"Another skiff?" Fura shielded her eyes.

Mars nodded. He shifted to the right, trying to get a better view with the spyglass. He scanned as far and wide as he could, but didn't see any others. Even so, two ships' worth of Elìn's people would surely be more than they could handle. "How did she know we were here? Could she have known more about Henrik's work than she let on?"

"No way to know." Katrìn widened her stance, as if bracing for a fight. "I think our best bet is to lure them into the dorms, then barricade the doors. I can craft a seal to keep them from breaking out."

"Oh, they'll definitely walk right into the dorms looking for us," Mars said sarcastically. He ran a hand over his hair, his rough skin catching on Una's bond, tied to his braid next to Fura's. "Maybe we can leave a trail of cookies from the door to the dorms to lure them in."

Fura glared at him. "Okay, then, you're the mercenary. What do we do?"

Mars sighed, dread churning in his stomach. Once again, he couldn't see a way out of this. The best he could do was damage control. Fura would be fine; Elìn was her mother, after all, and Fura could handle herself. As for him, he couldn't let his magic be discovered. If he could help Katrìn avoid the same fate, he would, but if his secret was exposed . . . Elìn would surely be furious to find them here, but that fate was nothing compared to what would happen if he was discovered as an adept.

Fura was right. It was time to rely on his abilities as an assassin.

He turned away from the tower's edge, a deep calm settling over him, as if the Shadow Fox were a costume he kept tucked inside himself, to slip on whenever the need called for it. It was time to do what he did best.

The first order of business was Askalon. "What's your story?" Mars gestured to the man. "Are you with us on this?"

Askalon stared back at him, his expression stony. "I'll do whatever is necessary to keep Fura safe. I gave her my bond."

Mars didn't like the practiced nature of his answer, but Fura didn't give him time to probe further.

"Tell us what to do, Mars," she said.

He nodded. "We'll need to time this perfectly to pull it off." Quickly, succinctly, Mars detailed the plan. His mind raced as he spoke, playing out scenarios and possibilities, everything that could go wrong and how to make it go right. It was a simple plan. Fura would lure their enemies into the keep and through the door into the dining hall, where Mars and Katrìn would be waiting to spring a magical trap, one designed to render anyone who passed through the door unconscious. Mars would first deploy a smoke bomb, to hide the magic involved. He could build one quickly enough, thanks to the piles of resources he'd discovered in his wanderings, left behind by the Consortium. Once the assailants were asleep, Mars and the others would bind them, taking control of the situation.

"Is everyone clear on what to do?" Mars said when he had finished, running his gaze over his companions, a niggle of doubt reaching him. He wasn't used to relying so much on others. The last time he'd relied on anyone like this had been with Orri.

"Let's go, then." Fura clapped her hands, then spun and headed for the stairs. Mars and Katrìn followed, Askalon staying behind to keep watch as Fura bade him. They needed an accurate count of the people on those skiffs, and assurance that they were going to land on the lawn. If they didn't, Mars would have to improvise, fast.

Mars gathered the ingredients for the smoke bomb first, and with Katrìn's help, soon had it ready. Then they converged in the dining hall. Mars motioned to the large entryway. It was arched at the top and framed with wood, the shape making it both versatile and pliable for the magic they needed to work.

"Do you see?" Mars said, glancing at Katrìn.

She eyed the shape, nodding. "We'll have to be careful. Circles are fragile. One mistake, and it'll fail."

"Can you do it, though?" Mars might finally understand how to make artifacts, but his skill in doing so were nothing compared to hers.

"Yes, but you'll have to follow my lead."

"All right." Again, a moment of doubt struck him. Maybe he should help Fura lure the intruders through the doorway. He'd never done this exact type of magic before. He'd rendered people unconscious, as many as three at once. But there would be many more than that here soon, and he'd never tried channeling the Rift through an object, anchoring it to a particular space like hanging a curtain from a rod. If it worked, the intruders would make it several steps into the room before collapsing. Then it would be up to Katrìn to keep them under while

Mars, Fura, and Askalon bound them. Mars just hoped they would have enough restraints. Fura was already gathering what she could, ripping off strips of the nearest tapestry and cutting down the cords.

Leaving her to it, Mars and Katrìn took up positions on either side of the door. Then they began to work the magic, summoning the Rift and channeling its power through the doorframe as if they were creating an artifact. The blood flowed quick and warm from his wrists; as always, that sense of coming fully alive swept over him, a sensation he now understood was his kull, his lifeblood. He'd always seen his magic as dangerous, whether to himself or to others. Here it felt like a part of him in a way it never had before.

Don't get used to it, that voice warned him. *There's no one to protect you if you're discovered.*

Mars banished the thought, eyes focused on the faint lines of blue spreading through the wooden frame. He felt the moment his magic met Katrìn's, an intimate sensation like brushing her fingers with his, spirit to spirit. He nearly pulled away, the shared power unsettling in its intimacy, but hearing a loud noise outside, he surged forward, sealing the power into the doorframe.

They were ready. They just needed to keep the magic flowing long enough.

The sound of footsteps pulled Mars's attention to the staircase and Askalon's arrival.

Fura said, "Is it indeed my mother?"

Askalon turned his gaze to her, a strange expression on his face. He nodded.

Fura swore, her face growing pale for a moment. Then color surged back into her cheeks as she clenched her hands into fists.

"How many?" Mars asked.

"I'm afraid it doesn't matter," Askalon said, and the words, spoken so softly, so regretfully, were slow to register in Mars's mind.

By the time they did, it was already too late.

Mars turned his head just as Askalon raised the whistle to his lips—the failed artifact that Mars had made. Like a fool, he'd left it in the lab, a weapon to be used against him by his enemy.

There was no sound. No warning at all. Just a pressure inside Mars's head for a single, aching second. Then his vision blurred and went out as he slumped to the ground, Katrìn falling next to him.

TWENTY-EIGHT

MARS WOKE IN hobbles.

The cold metal seemed to weigh a thousand pounds, pinning him to the ground, as effective as any cage. Glistening like scales on a fish, the starsteel encased his fingers and palms, blocking his magic. For several long moments, the hobbles were all he saw, all that existed in the world. His ultimate nightmare made real. He could feel the Rift there, but beyond his reach, like a friend that had turned its back on him. Cut off from that life-giving source, he'd never felt more alone, more lost, and the feeling terrified him.

Slowly, Mars became aware of the scene around him. He was lying on the floor of the dining hall, Katrìn was next to him, still unconscious, with blood trickling down her nose. She'd been hobbled, too. Outrage and horror fought for control of his emotions, but Mars shoved them back, willing his mind to cool, to think.

He rolled over, hearing footsteps.

"Stay down." A man stood stood next to Mars, aiming a pistol at his head. A talon framed the man's eyebrow, marking him a Torvald.

Mars had no idea how the truss had done it, but Askalon must have been the one who led Elìn and her crew there. He cursed himself for not keeping a better eye on the man, for being foolish enough to believe he might honor the bond he'd given Fura.

Fura. Where was she? Mars peered about the room, but she wasn't there. There was no way to tell how long he'd been out. Fura wouldn't have been affected by the whistle as he and Katrìn had been. Which meant Askalon would've had to subdue her. He knew that must have been easier said than done.

Arching his head up, Mars spotted Askalon lying at the foot of the stairs, unmoving. Whether dead or unconscious, Mars couldn't tell. It didn't matter. Elìn Torvald kneeled beside her truss, a hand pressed to his forehead. A grim satisfaction at knowing Fura had bested Askalon spread through him.

But where was she now? Mars hoped she'd gotten away, disappeared somewhere into the keep. The week they'd spent here learning its secrets would give her an advantage when it came to hiding from their attackers. For a time, anyway.

Several figures came down the staircase into the dining room, and Mars's hopes were dashed as he spotted Fura among them, captive. For a moment, she was all Mars saw—the murderous look on her face, the splotch of red across her left cheek that would soon darken into a bruise, the way she struggled to free herself from the hands of the guard holding her arms, how her head was canted back from the yanking grip one of the assailants had on her hair. Tears filled her eyes but hadn't yet fallen.

Tension spread through Mars's body as he fought the instinct to leap up and fight. He couldn't, not with the hobbles. He was powerless. *For now, but—*

The thought broke off, his mind paralyzed by shock as he realized the guard gripping Fura's hair was Bekka Darksdòttra.

She still wore the false tattoo and the white armor of the Fifth's guard. Next to Bekka, holding Fura's arms, was Rafnar Magnùsvane. Two of Una's mercenaries were here, including her executioner, the man who ensured anything owed to Una was given to her. Their presence here could only mean one thing.

Una was here, too.

And now she knows. Mars's heart thudded against his breastbone. Despite all he'd done, killing Orri, trying to escape her, she had found him out. Hobbled him. Mars turned his head far to the right, his eyes finding Una at last. She stood in the doorway to the dining hall, surveying the scene with the solemn surety of a woman who knew her power over her world and those who inhabited it. Feykir perched on her shoulder— the foul thing letting out a *kack* as it noticed Mars looking at it. At the sight of his blood ampoule hanging from Una's neck like a grotesque necklace, Mars felt a crushing weight, even heavier than the hobbles, pressing down on him.

Askalon had betrayed them, but he wasn't the one who had led them here. This was Mars's fault. His own blood had led Una here. They had never stood a chance.

"Where did you find her?" Elìn said, rising from Askalon's side. She was addressing the third assailant holding Fura prisoner, this one a Torvald guard.

"Third floor. She was throwing some papers on the fire," the man replied. "Seemed in a hurry to get rid of it."

Hearing this, Mars understood at once what had happened, and why Fura hadn't managed to escape. Instead of hiding, she'd done what she could to keep Katrìn safe by burning Henrik's journal and all of Katrìn's notes, which they'd carelessly left out on the table. *Good girl*, Mars thought, feeling a twinge of relief in his chest. They'd discovered Mars's and Katrìn's power, but neither Elìn nor Una could learn the real threat Katrìn posed. Life as an enthralled adept would be the worst sort of misery, but still, there would be hope, a chance to escape as Katrìn's mother had done.

If they knew the truth, Katrìn would be good as dead.

Elìn's gaze narrowed on her daughter's face. "What was it?"

When Fura refused to answer, Bekka shrugged. "Looked like some books and notes and such. Nothing salvageable."

Elìn's nostrils flared slightly, the only sign of her anger. Like Una, she was a woman well aware of the power she held in the world. "Restrain my daughter in a chair. Gently, please."

"Let me go." Fura kicked and struggled, fighting with all her strength. But it wasn't enough to overcome three trained guards. Few could best Bekka in combat—even fewer could take on Rafnar. Mars held his breath, worried what the Reaper might do, the pleasure he would take in hurting Fura. The man could easily snap her neck with his bare hands if he so chose.

But Rafnar seemed to be on his best behavior today, helping the others place Fura in the chair with a disturbingly calm demeanor. With his thick beard full of jangling tokens, it was impossible to read the man's expression, his dark eyes like pieces of flint, sharp and cold.

The Torvald guard standing over him watched, too. Taking advantage of the man's distraction, Mars slowly sat up, each movement an agony as the hobbles tugged at him.

Once they had managed to secure Fura, Elìn approached her daughter. Una drew close as well, but remained a respectful distance away. Deferential, one might think, if they didn't know her better. Her hands were folded in front of her, her head slightly bowed toward the dòttra, but Mars didn't buy the act for an instant. He was certain she was still after the Primer, and she would stop at nothing to have it.

"Fura, my darling," Elìn began. "I know you're angry, but I also know that you will come to see reason in time."

Fura screamed and kicked out, nearly catching Elìn in the knee. But the dòttra didn't flinch. She merely stood there and waited for the storm to pass. When it did, she offered her daughter a satisfied nod. "That's better. Now, why don't you tell me what was in those documents you burned."

Fura stared back at her, saying nothing. A muscle ticked in her jaw, tension threaded through her whole body like coiled wire.

"Was it the Primer formula? Another message from your father?" A smile that might've been mistaken as kind spread over Elìn's face.

Mars gaped, confounded by her knowledge. When had she found out about the Primer? Perhaps she'd learned about it from one of the other kiths during the Assembly. But then he remembered who else was here—*Una*—and for the first time, it occurred to him to wonder how Una had learned of it. The real answer struck him, the shock of it falling on him like a boulder.

"It was you," he said, fixing his gaze on Elìn. "You hired me to steal the formula from your own daughter." He shifted his gaze to his employer, searching for confirmation and finding it there in the subtle glint in her eyes.

"Of course it was me." Elìn's smile turned into a snarl. "And if you'd simply proven yourself as good as you claim, we wouldn't be in this mess now."

"Mother, how could you?" Fura's lips trembled as if she might cry.

"Don't act so surprised." Elìn turned back to her daughter. "We both know you would never have given it to me if I'd asked for it. You're too much like your father. An idealistic fool."

Fura flinched as if struck. Mars did, too, regretting every time he'd thought the same about Fura.

Fura's expression hardened. "The Primer formula is gone. I destroyed all record of it forever."

The lie sounded convincing, even to Mars's ears, but he knew at once from the skeptical look on Elìn's face it wasn't going to work. A shudder lanced down his spine as he realized that even with Henrik's journal gone, the threat of the Primer remained. He glanced at Fura's neck and saw no sign of the compass rose pendant. What had she done with it? She hadn't thrown it in the fire—the metal wouldn't burn. No, she must have hidden it in the secret compartment.

"I know when you're lying, Fura." Elìn sighed, hands on hips. "But no matter. Askalon will recover it soon enough."

At the defiant look on Fura's face, Mars lowered his head to hide the relief he felt that at least they'd managed to keep the truth from Askalon. Doubt crept in, though. Had they really kept the truth from Askalon? Mars hadn't watched the man every moment, after all. Cursing himself for letting his guard down, Mars squeezed his fingers, trying to make a fist, but the starsteel held him fast.

Soon he would become an enthralled adept. The horrible realization piled on top of all the rest. Una knew the truth about him. His fate would be the same as Dùnn's—hobbled, mutilated. His life no longer his own.

It never was, the voice reminded him as his gaze flicked to the blood ampoule around Una's neck. But the knowledge didn't lessen the pain.

Mars turned his gaze to Askalon, who had started to rouse. With a groan, the man sat up, a hand against his forehead.

A victorious smile spread over Elìn's face as she beckoned to her truss. "Help Askalon to his feet."

The Torvald guard did so, although Askalon brushed him off as soon as he was upright. He approached his dòttra on his own power and bowed.

"You've done well." Elìn touched his shoulder. "Fura and these adepts might've succeeded in fortifying the White Keep against us if not for you."

"Thank you, my dòttra." Askalon bowed his head, his eyes not straying from Elìn, not even to glance in Fura's direction.

"My daughter says she destroyed the Primer formula as we arrived. Is that true?" Elìn demanded.

Again, Askalon did not look at Fura. He didn't have to. Everyone in the room could feel her hatred for him like the burning sizzle in the air after a lightning strike.

"I'm afraid it must be," Askalon said after a moment. "She got away from me. If she made it to the lab, that would doubtless have been her only goal."

Elìn let out a curse, but Mars felt as if his heart might leap from his chest. So the man hadn't discovered the truth.

"Why would she destroy it, though?" Elìn said. "It makes no sense."

Askalon nodded. "She did it to keep anyone else from using it, I'm sure. That's why she came here. Henrik wanted her to be the one to use the Primer. He claimed that, in the wrong hands, it could've been turned into a terrible weapon."

"The wrong hands being yours, *Mother*," Fura spat, lunging against the cords binding her to the chair.

Elìn ignored her. "Very well, then. I suppose it is for the best that the threat the Primer posed is no more. But at least this hasn't been a total loss." Without warning, the dòttra turned her gaze on Mars, then Katrìn. "Two secret adepts. Now *that's* a valuable discovery."

Mars glared, his hands flexing against the hobbles. He'd thought Una would be his problem now, same as she'd always been, but he'd forgotten the law—the one that said adepts could only be owned by the kith. Elìn could claim him as her property and there would be nothing Una could do to stop it.

Mars glanced at Una, wondering how she would react. If she would just let him go to the Torvalds without an argument. But she wasn't looking at him, almost as if she hadn't heard. Her gaze was fixed on Fura and no one else.

That is, until Elìn turned to her. "Well now, Madam Una, it seems my contracts are complete. Come, let us find a place to adjourn in quiet. We will need to discuss a revised payment, given the failure of your mercenary to retrieve the Primer formula. Perhaps you should've put this one to the task instead." Elìn motioned to Bekka, who took a ridiculously ostentatious bow. "She handled the execution of the Fifth with admirable elegance."

Mars thought he might be sick. Elìn had ordered the execution of the Fifth as well? What was she after? Did she mean to make herself queen of Riven? He shook his head, unable to fathom her motives.

"I will take that into consideration next time." Una inclined her head in something that wasn't quite a nod. "And we have plenty of time to discuss things. I recommend we stay the night. It's too dangerous to risk crossing the Mistgrave after dark."

Elìn narrowed her eyes, clearly unsettled by the possibility. "Very well. Let's settle in, and plan to leave in the morning.

"As you wish." Una bowed toward the dòttra, but her gaze flicked to Mars, sending him a silent message.

But it was unnecessary. He'd understood what Una was doing the moment she had touched her hand to her artifact ring while listening to Fura's claim about destroying the Primer.

Una knew Fura had lied. And she now had her own agenda.

TWENTY-NINE

THEY LOCKED FURA, Katrìn, and Mars in separate dorms, sealing them the old-fashioned way, with wood and iron. Mars listened to the hammering as he sat on the cot, his hands resting heavy in his lap, weighed down by the hobbles. His thoughts churned like the sea, tossing him this way and that. He knew he should be planning his escape, contemplating ways out of this room, how to get to Katrìn and Fura. But he couldn't.

His mind kept turning back to the hard truth of his situation. His worst fear, the nightmare that had kept him company so many times through the years, had finally come true. He was a prisoner, a thrall. A commodity to be bought and sold. It was even worse than he imagined. Not the humiliation of it—but being cut off from the Rift. Nothing had prepared him for how it would feel. It was as if he'd been torn in two. There was Mars, the Shadow Fox, master of himself and of magic. And then there was the Mars he was now. *Nothing. No one.*

With the weight of this truth tugging at him, he lay down on the bed and closed his eyes. Sleep refused to come. The thoughts refused to quiet. He let them have full rein, giving in to them, letting them carry him away.

They soon led him down even darker paths. He saw Katrìn hobbled beside him, her fate the same as his. He saw Fura, tied to that chair, her face bruised and eyes red from tears she refused to shed. Then he saw her father, the way Henrik had looked before he'd died. A man dedicated to changing the world. One willing to die for what he dreamed could be possible. A world without Ice and all the suffering it had wrought.

And Mars had killed him.

We are the weapon, not the will.

The hardest truth of all hit him now, stealing away his breath. Una's maxim, the one he'd always used to justify his actions, was a lie. It always had been. At any moment he could've chosen differently. He could've stayed his hand. He could've chosen not to do so.

And now he had no choice at all.

Just as those people in the mines have no choice.

His fingers drew together in a half fist, the best he could manage with the hobbles encasing him. This was what it really meant to be a weapon, a tool. To be the power in someone else's hands. He pictured Natasja then, her raw skin, her dull, dead eyes.

Regret flooded him, until he was drowning in it. He didn't know how to navigate these waters, and so he sank further into them, drifting away into nothingness.

Sometime later, after darkness had completely fallen, the door to his room opened, letting in a shock of lamplight. Mars recoiled, coming to full consciousness at once. For a long while, he'd been drifting in and out of sleep, of dreams and nightmares.

Bekka stepped inside, shutting the door behind her. Mars was mildly surprised to see her. He'd been expecting Una to come to him first.

Setting the lamp on the small table beside the bed, Bekka stared down at him, a sneer twisting her features into something grotesque in the uneven light. "So. The Shadow Fox turns out to be a secret adept. I always knew you were a liar and a cheat. And you betrayed Una, too, coming here. Trying to help that silly girl build her father's weapon."

Mars stared back at her. "What do you want, Bekka?" He sat up on the bed, refusing to appear cowed before her. His gaze drifted to the room's small, high window and the black curtain of night shading it.

"Honest answer?" She turned and retrieved the room's only chair from its corner, turning it around and sitting astride it, her arms resting on the back and her weapons in easy reach at her sides. "Just a few moments to gloat." She grinned so broadly, it seemed to split her face in half. Then she laughed. "I didn't realize just how good this would feel. To be here to see you fail. To take the place you once held by Una's side."

"Congratulations." He couldn't keep the image of Ivar's face from rising in his mind, the despair he'd felt at his father's death. A death Mars could've stopped, but hadn't. Bekka could've chosen differently as well. They were each accountable.

"Thank you." Bekka bobbed her head, the triumph on her face sickening to behold.

Mars closed his eyes.

"I think I've finally decided what my title will be at the Den," Bekka went on, reveling in his discomfort. "The Platinum Fox, maybe."

Opening his eyes, Mars laughed, the sound bitter, jagged. "You're welcome to it." Una was a viper, and those she kept close were just mice she planned to devour the moment it suited her.

There was a faint knock on the door. Bekka opened it, then stepped aside to allow Una entry.

"Keep watch outside," Una said to Bekka, who nodded and complied at once, leaving Mars alone with the mistress of the Fortune's Den.

He regarded the woman coldly, his hatred for her enough to push aside his despair. For a moment he considered attacking her—his magic might be hobbled, but the metal encasing his hands made them highly effective blunt weapons. But then what? He couldn't overcome Bekka, much less the rest of Una's and Elin's guards.

Turning the chair around to face him, Una sat down, folding her hands in her lap. She wore gray pants beneath a split black overskirt and a bodice trimmed in silver piping. Diamonds sparkled at her ears—perhaps the most ostentatious part of her appearance, unless you counted his blood ampoule hanging around her neck. At least she hadn't brought the stupid undead bird with her.

"I'm sorry to see you like this, Mars," she said. "I was hoping it would never come to this."

The words took him by surprise, especially how sincere she sounded. It made him doubt her, doubt everything. He said nothing.

"Come now, darling, there's no reason to act so hostile." Her eyes glistened in the lamplight, a hint of mirth in them. "I've known the truth for quite some time, my secret adept."

His world seemed to tilt, the seams of reality coming undone. "You knew?" It came out an accusation, as if she were to blame for what he was.

"Of course," Una tsked. "I've suspected from the beginning, but it wasn't until the Eldur diamond that I became certain."

A flush rose in his cheeks. It was the job that had made him, earned him the title of Shadow Fox. He'd worked the job with a young initiate still in training by the name of Sigmund. Sigmund's only purpose on the mission was to set up the zip line Mars needed to make his escape from the roof of one building to a window in the building next to it, but Sigmund had forgotten the grappling hook required to secure the cable. When Mars arrived on the roof, guards trailing him, he'd had no choice but to make the jump without the line—using the Rift to aid him. Sigmund had arrived a moment after Mars tumbled through the window, the Eldur diamond in his possession.

"How did you do that?" Sigmund had asked, sputtering in disbelief.

Mars had groaned, the landing harder than he'd anticipated. "All guts, no brains."

Sigmund had not only bought the lie, he'd spread the tale to everyone at the Den, including its mistress, it seemed.

Now Mars swallowed, the cords in his throat tight. "I don't believe you. If you knew, why didn't you enthrall me? Or turn me over to a kith for a not-so-small fortune? Why did you wait so long to do this?" he asked, jerking his hands upward, the metal clacking.

"You were happy to use your powers in my service. Why mess with a good thing?" She sighed. "Besides, I hoped one day you might confide in me yourself."

Mars scowled. "Why would I ever do that? All you've ever done is use me, and the moment I tried to leave, you stole my money and reeled me back in like a hooked fish."

Her withering look made him feel small. "If you had truly wanted to leave, you would've done so long ago. With your abilities, you could've gotten the money you needed easily and managed to get free of this." She held up the blood ampoule for a moment. "All that working for the fishmongers was just an excuse to delay."

"That's absurd." Only, as soon as he said it, doubt crept in, that old voice, so condescending and sure. *Una is right. You were never going to leave, for one reason and one reason alone.*

Mars turned his gaze down to his hands, flinching at the ugly sight of the hobbles. His magic. Was that why he'd never left Riven? Because he couldn't bear the idea of losing his connection to the Rift? He turned the theory over in his mind, testing his intentions, his heart. An ache answered him, the desperate longing to touch the Rift stronger than it had ever been, now that he was cut off from it.

Una sighed again, the sound far too knowing, as if she'd listened in on his thoughts. "Believe it or not, I've been looking after you all your life. In fact, you owe your whole life to me."

"I always suspected you were delusional." Mars drew his legs to his chest, letting his arms rest on his knees.

"Or perhaps I am just very good at manipulating the world around me without anyone becoming the wiser." Una tilted her head.

"Funny," Mars said. "But I don't recall you being around until I was recruited to the Den. Before that, I was the only one looking out for me."

"Indeed." Una pursed her lips. "You did quite well, considering you had no memory of your parents, or how you ended up on those streets."

He opened his mouth only to discover he had no response. It was true. He had no idea where he came from or how he'd survived before his first memories of the streets. And those were vague at best—nights spent sleeping on dusty floors or in damp alleys, his belly pinched with hunger and an ever-present fear of any adult he saw.

Growing impatient with her false magnanimity, Mars scowled. "Just tell me what you want."

Una shifted her weight on the chair, allowing the silence to stretch around them like a web meant to catch him. Mars knew better than to break it. Finally, she said, "You owe your life to me because I'm the one who rescued you and gave you a place to live after your parents were killed."

Mars snorted, not buying this tale for an instant. Una despised children, and she never saved anyone without being paid up front first. Unless, perhaps, his parents had worked for her. The idea that his mother or father might've been a fox of the Fortune's Den intrigued him more than he cared to admit. "Why would someone like you bother saving an infant?"

Una's brows slanted over her eyes. "I didn't plan on saving you. It happened by accident. Rafnar is to blame. Or thank, rather. He took a contract to destroy the building where you and your parents were living. But in a rare moment of compassion, he stole you out of your crib before lighting the fuse on the bomb."

Mars ran his tongue over his lips, turning this news over in his head. He'd had a family. And Una and Rafnar had known it all along. Except— "Compassion? Rafnar? Really?"

"I know it's hard to believe," Una said with a dry laugh. "Imagine how I felt when he showed up at the Den with a squalling bundle of dirty rags in his arms and asked if he could keep you."

"What?" Mars sputtered.

Una laughed again. "He'd gotten it into his head that he could raise you himself, like a son. But the moment I pointed out that you were more likely to regard him as a rival than a father, he changed his mind. Instead, I had him watch you from afar, ensuring your basic needs were met while you were still an infant, keeping you safe, but never allowing you to remain in one place long enough to get attached to whichever woman was caring for you from one week to the next."

It seemed implausible, although nothing in Mars's memory could deny the claim. "Okay, let's say I believe you," Mars reluctantly admitted. "Why did you raise an orphan? Why not dump me in the nearest alley as rat food?"

"You do know me so well, Mars." Una let out a breath, the sound more resolved than regretful. "And I would've, if not for the reasons behind the contract that thrust you into my path in the first place. You see, the building where Rafnar found you was being used as a laboratory by Henrik Torvald. A person rumored to be trying to find a way to manipulate the Ice. It seemed odd to me that a child would be living in such a place, but when Rafnar described the way you'd been kept—in a room surrounded by scientific equipment and charts and all manner of strange things—it provoked my curiosity as to why. There was no way of knowing, of course, not with the building destroyed, but I decided to keep you alive, to watch and see what you became. And I wasn't disappointed when you turned out to be an adept."

Shock crackled inside Mars. He'd been a part of Henrik's experiments?

"You see, I never destroy a thing until I know exactly what it is first." Una leaned forward in the chair, the ancient wood groaning at the motion. "That's the reason I assigned you to assassinate Henrik Torvald, the very man who had done such odd things to you before you were even born."

Hearing this, Mars felt his heart stutter in his chest, the memory of Henrik's journal entry on the fire coming back to him, how Katrìn's mother would've lived if she hadn't gone back to the compound to save the other child.

A child, a baby boy.

A second vessel.

Throwing his legs over the side of the bed, Mars stood, too overcome with shock to remain sitting. Was it possible? Had he too been part of the experiment? The thought made his stomach twist. It soon became a wrench as his mind made another connection—Katrìn's experiments. She'd been using his blood as a control, but the results had turned out the same as hers.

Because he was a vessel, too.

Swaying on his feet, Mars retreated, leaning against the wall to steady himself. Dozens of other questions flooded his mind—about his parents, who they'd been, why they'd helped—but it was all too much to process.

"There, now." Una stood as well. "I see you're finally a believer. That's good. It will make everything easier between us moving forward."

The pleasure in her face liquefied his insides. How wrong he'd been to think the hobbles were the worst of it. Una wasn't done using him. She never would be.

"Now," Una said, casually twisting the artifact ring around her finger. "It's time for you to tell me where the Primer is and what exactly Fura and that other adept were trying to accomplish here."

THIRTY

HE COULDN'T LIE. She would know. The magic would tell her.

Stall, then, he thought. *Misdirect. Buy time.* Knowledge was currency, the only kind that truly counted with Una. She must not learn that Katrìn was a vessel, capable of healing the Rift. *That I am a vessel.*

The thought sent a shudder through him, and he forced his thoughts onto the Primer. *Only the Primer. That's all she knows about, all she can ask about.*

Mars folded his arms over his chest, doing his best to summon the Shadow Fox, but only a ghost of him came, enough to turn his voice steady, if nothing else inside him. "I don't know what she did with the formula, but it doesn't matter. There's a bottle of the Primer, already made, in a secret compartment, which is all you need to make more of the stuff. But the compartment is sealed by magic. Only an adept or Fura can open it, and I doubt she'll do it willingly."

Una arched a brow. "Oh, I'm certain she won't. But what about you?"

"That depends on how much it's worth to you." He spoke

with more confidence than he truly felt. Although his secret was no more, he still had plenty to lose.

And people he could possibly save.

"There's my boy." Una grinned, the expression ghoulish on her thin, elegant face. "As I'm sure you've guessed, the Primer is invaluable. Worth practically anything."

"Is it worth letting me go free?" He lifted his hands, the light catching on the hobbles. He knew he ought not to come out so strong, playing all his cards at once. But he only really had one to play.

"Perhaps." She spoke like a woman musing to herself, but Mars knew better. She was playing the game. She lived for it. A pleasant rosy color filled her cheeks, making her seem both younger and more alive somehow. She was a force of nature, like a snowstorm, one that couldn't be escaped.

"Don't take me for a fool, Una. With the Primer in your arsenal, you'll have every kith in your pocket. You'll be the veritable queen of Riven."

Una snorted. "That is Elìn's dream. Not mine."

Mars wondered what Una's dream was, for a moment, until he decided he didn't care.

"But you're not wrong," she continued. "The kith would be mine to control."

He felt hope rekindling inside him at her excitement. She'd been hunting this quarry a long time, and now she was close. But only he could give it to her. Fura never would. Neither would Katrìn.

"If I deliver the Primer to you, will you consider the contract fulfilled?" He paused, making sure she was listening. "Will you honor your bond to me?"

Her gaze drifted up to his hair, the red bead visible in the braid. "That bond was for the money I took from you. Money isn't going to change the fact that you are now a known adept."

Mars scowled, his hatred for her like a wind tearing through his body. "That money was meant for my freedom. Freedom from you."

"Freedom is a lie, Mars," Una said. "You, me, none of us are truly free. We are all players in the same game, one with rules that cannot be broken, consequences that cannot be escaped. No matter how far you go or how much you pretend, you will always be who and what you are. There will always be something chasing you. The best we can hope for is to keep playing the game."

He didn't argue. There was no point.

"However," Una went on, her expression turning solemn, "I am willing to give you back your life. In fact, it's the very thing I wish to happen. I hate seeing you like this." Her gaze drifted to the metal encasing his hands. "So cruel and barbaric. I've always believed you were meant for so much more."

An absurd urge to laugh struck Mars. This was the same woman who had no qualms about removing a girl's nose for disobeying her, who kept a blind, maimed adept imprisoned in her Lair. "Oh sure, you prefer your thralls to wear invisible chains instead. Threats of what will happen to them if they disobey." He gestured to the blood ampoule around her neck.

"Not true. I prefer their willing service, just as I've always preferred yours." Una took a step closer to him, her gaze imperious. "But by revealing your power to others, you've made that impossible. You heard Elìn Torvald. I've no doubt she plans to keep you for herself, and the law will surely support her if I try to fight it."

Mars shrugged. "One master is the same as another."

"Does that mean you would prefer Elìn?"

He swallowed, acid bubbling in his stomach at the idea. Although there were many similarities between the two women, Una was the enemy he knew. He understood her, the way her mind worked. And if what she said was indeed true, that she had overseen his upbringing, then that meant he was an investment for her. He mattered to her in a way he never would to Elìn. With Una, he perhaps held some leverage.

"No," he said, clearing his throat.

"I didn't think so." Una clasped her hands in front of her. "But the problem remains. Now that you've been found out, there's no going back. That is, unless we do something to make sure the secret stays between us."

There was only one way to do that. "Are you suggesting we kill the dòttra?"

A wicked smile flashed over Una's face. "It's only fitting. We can't very well let her continue on in this idiotic quest to rule Riven. Can you imagine? No, the Torvalds have made an unprecedented play for power in killing the Fifth, and must be brought to heel, same as the rest."

"And with the Primer, you will hold power over them," Mars said, her plan coming into focus. With Una, everything came down to power. She would be able to manipulate the kith directly now. No longer be forced to rely on contracts and secrets.

"Someone has to maintain the true order of things," Una said, solemnly. "And with you at my side—a willing adept, undamaged, unbroken, a partner, as far as anyone knows—there are few that could stand against me."

Undamaged. Unbroken. He pictured Orri and Henrik. How very wrong she was.

His thoughts at once turned to Fura. She was Elìn's heir. She wouldn't just bow to Una if Elìn were killed and leadership fell to her. His body tensed as his mind played out the inevitable. "What about Fura? She knows what I am as well."

"She must go the way of her mother, of course. Same as the other members of the Torvald kith the dòttra brought with her. But I'll keep the adept girl. Dùnn is getting old, after all." Una paused, touching a hand to her chin in thought. "We might be able to sabotage the airship on the way back. Make it look like an accident." She nodded to herself. "We will be on one airship, and Elìn and her daughter on the other."

"No." Mars folded his arms over his chest. The trembling, nervous energy fled his body as a calm, cold certainty took its place.

"No?" Una gaped in genuine shock. "I take it you object to killing Fura Torvald?"

"Yes, and I won't stand for Katrìn to be enthralled." He widened his stance, his heart pounding with his certainty. "Whatever services you hope to get out of me, I will never comply if you harm either of them."

Una wrapped her fingers around the artifact ring, but there was no lie in his words. "I can barely believe it. You're in love with Fura, aren't you?" Una laughed. "Let's be sure not to tell her about those you grow close to, eh? Lest she end up like Orri?"

Shame flooded Mars at her words, a flush rising to his face. He hadn't loved Orri. Not truly. The possibility had always been there, but it had been a seed planted in rocky soil. One not strong enough to survive the circumstances of the life he'd been living. He'd always done what he had to in order to survive. First on the streets, where the rules were be strong and clever or die, and then in the Den, when he had to separate himself from the task at hand when he had to inflict pain and suffering on people he didn't know, who might not have deserved it. When he thought the only person capable of loving him as he was was himself. But he knew better. He'd learned better. There were people out there who could accept him for what he was, without wanting to exploit him. Fura and Katrìn had shown him that.

Una raked her eyes over him, the amusement on her face clear as glass. "Does Fura know it was by your hand that her father was killed?"

Mars froze. Once again, he couldn't lie. "No."

"Wise choice." Una bowed her head. "But sadly, we can't afford such loose ends. Fura and her companion would pose too great a risk, knowing what they do about you."

"Will you kill Bekka and Rafnar, too, then?"

"They will do what I say when it comes to keeping your secret." Una's gaze sharpened. "They know the consequences of disobedience. As do you."

Mars couldn't argue with that. All she had to do was crush that blood ampoule between her fingers, and the magic in the artifact encasing it would do the rest.

But Mars refused to concede. Una would have to kill him first. He held her gaze, his heart still pounding with the truth inside him. He did love Fura. And Katrìn, too. They were the weak link in his armor, but he didn't care.

"Fura is reasonable," Mars said. "If we allow her to keep Katrìn with her, and keep Katrìn's secret safe, she won't reveal mine."

Una stared back at him, not yet convinced.

Mars went on. "She has spent all her life keeping the truth about Katrìn safe from the kith, from her own mother. She will do anything to make sure Katrìn doesn't have to live her life in these." He raised his hands, purposely clacking the hobbles together. "Fura will keep my secret. I'm certain of it."

"Even after we kill her mother?"

Mars flinched, the question like a knife prick. Despite their differences, Fura loved her mother. And she was the only parent Fura had left.

She will never forgive you, that voice whispered in his mind. *She will hate you forever.*

She already should, Mars answered, picturing Henrik's face as he died.

Resolving himself to the inevitability of Fura's hatred, Mars said, "Yes, she will. So long as the threat of exposing Katrìn exists, Fura will comply with your demands."

"Very well," Una said, her voice cutting. "I will consider your terms if they will agree to the secret, as you claim. But you must agree to mine as well."

Mars stood straight, squaring his shoulders. "And what are they, exactly?"

"First, you must hand over the Primer."

He nodded—that was a given.

A pleased smile rose to Una's lips. "And second, you must agree to remain in my service for as long as you live."

Even though he'd expected it, anger snapped inside him. He wanted to take her by the throat and squeeze, fury like a swarm of bees threatening to burst from his chest. Holding back, his voice became a snarl. "As if I've ever had any choice about that."

Una's expression softened. She walked toward him, stretching out her hand to cup his face like a mother would a child. With the wall behind him, he couldn't pull away.

"All I want is your willing service, Mars," Una said, her voice crooning. "I want you to set aside this silly dream of leaving Riven and instead truly embrace what you are. I will give you full rein over your powers. You can make any artifact you want, go and do as you wish, within reason. You can pick the contracts you want, rejecting any that don't appeal to you. You will live like a prince. A prince of the Fortune's Den."

Mars swallowed, his emotions churning as a vision unfolded in his mind. He saw himself back at the Den, welcomed there, welcomed home. He would be safe forever. He would belong as he never had before. And he would never be severed from the Rift again. Una had the power to make it happen. It was more than an adept could ever hope for. All he had to do was serve.

Could he live with that? Could he compromise one dream for another?

Yes, he realized, his thoughts turning to Fura once more. He could do anything, if it meant keeping her safe.

Mars met Una's gaze, staring into her eyes as if he could examine her soul through them. "Will you give me your word that Fura and Katrìn will be safe?"

Una held his gaze, staring into him in return. "You have my bond."

That was it. The guarantee of Fura's life. Once given, Una would not go back on it. And there were no strings attached, either. No little escape loops for her to slip through. A weary sort of relief began to seep into him. "Then you have mine as well."

Una dropped her hand away from his face, her expression cold once more. "Oh, I have one final condition."

Mars braced, dread pounding a fist against his breastbone. "What is it?"

"You must prove your loyalty to me. Your willingness to serve." She folded her arms over her chest.

"I give you my word, Una. That should be enough."

She tsked. "It would've been, if you hadn't tried to betray me when I arrived with Elìn." She raised a hand to silence any protest he might offer, her ring an inarguable point on the subject. "No, you must show me that I can put my trust in you. Once and for all."

Sensing there was no way out this time, Mars lowered his gaze to the ground and braced for the worst. "How?"

Una took her time answering, as if she enjoyed watching him squirm. "You will be the one to execute Fura's mother, just as you did her father. And you will do it with her watching. That way there can be no doubt—between us or in the young woman soon to be the new Torvald dòttra—as to whom you serve."

THIRTY-ONE

UNA'S WORDS ECHOED in Mars's mind long after she departed, leaving him trapped inside the room while she made her plans to ambush the Torvalds with the two foxes whose loyalty she didn't doubt.

He was to kill Elìn Torvald while Fura watched.

Mars couldn't say he was surprised. Not only was it an effective test of his loyalty, but it would also send a message to Fura of the danger Una posed, were Fura to cross her. And whether she intended it or not, it would mean that Mars's relationship with Fura would be all but dead, ensuring that his loyalties would not be divided.

But to know what it would do to Fura to watch, the disappointment and grief in her eyes . . .

Mars held back his tears. He must not let Una see them. He must not appear weak. *Fura will live.* He clung to this truth like a man tossed overboard would cling to a piece of driftwood. Elìn would die, but Fura would live. So would Katrìn. It had to be. It was the only way.

Forcing his mind to still, Mars lay on the cot and waited for the hours to pass and the moment of his reckoning to come.

With excruciating slowness, the darkness retreated from the window, soft streams of sunlight breaking through. Soon the sound of a commotion reached him through the sealed door—the clang of steel on steel, a pistol firing. It was the sounds of Una taking control, preparing the way for him, killing the Torvalds who would try to protect the life of their dòttra.

All too soon the noises ceased, and Bekka appeared at his door.

"We're ready for you." She gestured with the pistol gripped in her hand, a splatter of blood marring her sleeve.

He followed her into the hallway, where Rafnar's looming frame was waiting. He eyed Mars up and down, his expression inscrutable as always.

"You're to fetch the Primer for Una first," Rafnar said in his gruff voice.

Mars held out his hands. "I'll need my magic to get to it."

Bekka pulled a key from her pocket and dangled it before him. "We're only letting you have a finger, nothing more. And if you try anything, I'll put a bullet in your head faster than you can blink."

"Do that, and Una will put you down like a rabid dog," Mars said, with enough conviction to coax an uncertain look onto Bekka's face.

Without waiting for their permission, Mars turned and headed for the stairs. Arriving on the third floor, he found Henrik's laboratory in shambles, as if a windstorm had blown through it. Few books were left on the shelves, the rest strewn about the floor, and Mars guessed Una had felt the need to search for the Primer, just in case—it would only give her more leverage over him. Faint embers still glowed in the fireplace, yet a chill hung in the room. Mars shivered as he crossed the floor to the secret compartment. Once there, he held out his right hand, waiting for Bekka to release him.

As promised, she used the small key to release only his index finger from the starsteel encasing it. Once done, she stepped back from him quickly, raising her pistol. Mars would've laughed at her fear if not for his own, crouched inside him like a cat ready to pounce.

"I need to make a sacrifice." He pulled back his sleeve, exposing his wrist, covered in a multitude of scars. He felt naked without his cuffs, but Una had taken them when she placed him in the hobbles.

Bekka screwed up her nose in disgust. "Can't you bite your tongue or something?"

Mars rolled his eyes, holding out his arm. "No." In truth, he could make the sacrifice that way, and had done so in the past, but it hurt far more than was necessary and required more willpower than he could muster right now.

At the sound of a blade being drawn, Mars turned to see Rafnar raise his dagger and swipe at him, slicing a long cut over his forearm. Mars hissed at the flare of pain, the cut far deeper than it needed to be for such a small sacrifice as the sealed compartment required. A second later, the pain disappeared with the sudden influx of Rift magic. It swept through him, filling his body with warmth and making him feel airy and light, as if his insides had been replaced with sunshine.

"Get on with it, then," Bekka said.

Mars blinked, coming back to his senses. With a resigned

sigh, he turned to the compartment and pressed his finger to the hidden notch. The magic responded to his touch, and the door slid open, revealing the last bottle of the Primer that Katrìn had made. As he'd guessed, Fura had placed the compass rose pendant beside it. He brushed his hand against the cool metal of the pendant as he reached in and picked up the bottle. And although he felt he could break into the pendant now that he knew how artifacts were constructed, he decided he'd rather leave it alone. Leave it to Fura.

"Be careful with that, old man," Mars said as he handed the bottle to Rafnar. "That's all there is."

Rafnar slid the Primer bottle into his coat pocket. Then he raised his fist and punched Mars in the face. Mars's head snapped back, and he stumbled. The tangy taste of blood flooded his mouth from where his lip met teeth.

"Don't call me old."

Scraping the back of his arm across the wound, Mars stared back at Rafnar, pleased to see the sparkle of anger in the man's flinty eyes. "Whatever you say, old man."

Rafnar made to strike him again, but Bekka stepped between them.

"Leave off, Reaper," she said. "Una likes his face the way it is. Besides, don't forget what he is—blood is his weapon, and his finger is still free."

Rafnar took a step toward Mars, and he braced for another strike. But with surprising quickness for a man of his size, Rafnar grabbed Mars by the wrist and slid the hobble back into place over his finger.

The shock of losing his connection to the Rift hurt

worse than any punch. Mars sagged against the weight of it, a hollow feeling expanding in his chest. *Just get through this,* he thought. One more kill, and he would never have to feel like this again.

"Move along, pretty boy." Bekka winked at him. Now that he was hobbled once more, her fear had evidently retreated.

Mars turned on his heel and marched toward the door.

Rafnar roughly directed him down the staircase to the dining hall. Carnage awaited them there: two bodies sprawled across the floor, each in its own pool of crimson. They were the Torvald guards Elìn had brought with her. Broken chairs and dishes added to the mess, signs of the struggle that Mars had heard.

A third body sat propped on the edge of the fireplace across the way. Askalon's eyes remained opened, but they no longer saw. A hole gaped in his chest, gore spilling out, as if some alien creature had escaped from within. Vomit burned the back of Mars's throat at the sight. Flies were already starting to swarm around him. At least Askalon had died fighting. That much was clear by the sight of the sword lying at his feet. It was a fairer chance than Elìn would get.

Mars swallowed and carried on, following Bekka as she threaded her way through the destruction toward the far hallway. He kept his gaze fixed on her back, having no desire to see any more carnage.

They arrived in the central courtyard a moment later, Mars blinking away the stars in his vision from the sudden plunge into bright sunlight. The Heart looked different in the light of day, the glow of the black, shimmery liquid subdued

and yet more ominous somehow. It was like a gelatinous creature lying in wait to devour him if he strayed too close.

By contrast, the curved pillars framing the pool seemed
brighter in the sunlight, and now he could see that the pillars
truly were made of bone. It was just as Henrik's Echo had
claimed. They were the rib cage of Jörn, the World Raven. *Here
is where he fell* read the inscription on the pool's side. Mars
hadn't truly believed the story when he first heard it, but it was
easier to now. This was a place made of death.

Una waited by the pool, watching their approach, while
Feykir sat perched on the tip of a rib above her, silent and still.
Elìn sat before another rib, bound to it by rope wrapped around
her torso. Somehow the dòttra managed to retain her air of su-
periority, her head titled back and her gaze sharp. On either
side of her, Fura and Katrìn were also each bound to a rib, both
sagging from pain and exhaustion. A bruise on the left side of
Fura's face painted her skin a purplish black from temple to
chin. Katrìn's face was red and blotchy from crying, and she still
wore her hobbles, but she appeared otherwise unharmed.

"Welcome," Una called at their approach. "I'm so pleased
you could join us, Mars."

He ignored her, his gaze fixed on Fura. How he wished
she could read his thoughts. He wanted to warn her what was
coming—and why it had to be. And more than anything, he
wanted to beg her forgiveness—for what he'd done, and what
he was about to do. Both of her parents, dead at his hands.

Rafnar approached Una, bumping Mars aside as he
passed. Pulling the bottle from his pocket, he handed it to her.
"This was in the secret compartment."

The sight of the vial seemed to rouse Fura; she shot up and turned the knives of her gaze on Mars. "You traitor," she screamed at him, lunging against the ropes binding her.

Mars kept his expression neutral, trying to keep his emotions buried deep.

Ignoring Fura's outburst, Una turned and placed the bottle on the edge of the pool, then faced Mars, hands clasped in front of her. "Well done. You have delivered on your first promise. Now for the second."

Una approached Fura, staring down at her as imperiously as a queen on her throne. Even so, Fura remained haughty and unafraid as she gazed back at her, a muscle jumping in her jaw from her clenched fury.

"As part of his decision to return to my service, Mars had a single request—that you and your companion remain safe." Una gestured to Katrìn. "I have agreed—only because he assures me that you will be willing to keep his status as an adept secret, so long as we keep her status secret as well."

"Never," Elìn broke in, her shrill voice seeming to split the air. "You'll not give any sort of orders to my daughter, and you'll never be allowed to keep that adept. Kill me if you want, but Fura will make sure you never get away with this."

"I've already told you to be quiet." Without looking, Una crooked a finger behind her, and Rafnar swept forward to answer her beckon.

He came at the dòttra swinging, the blow landing square on the woman's nose. The crunch made Mars cringe and Fura cry out. Elìn whimpered, her head sagging against her shoulder, and said no more.

Una cleared her throat, calling Fura's attention back to her. "Let me make my requirements for your life clear. You have my word that you both will remain safe and under my protection for as long as you keep the secret about Mars. Understood?"

Katrìn nodded, but Fura only continued to glare up at Una. "What about my mother?"

Una shook her head. "I'm afraid I am unable to extend the same agreement to her." Turning away from the captives, she faced Mars, hands at her sides. "Choose your instrument." Her eyes flicked to the left.

Following the glance, Mars noticed a pile of weapons nearby, all of them blades. He approached the pile slowly, willing his limbs not to tremble. Although he couldn't reach the Rift, his senses felt heightened, the breeze flowing through the courtyard like fingernails scraping his face, the stench of blood and fear in the air strong enough to make him gag, and the sound of Fura's breathing like a drum beating inside his ears. He felt her gaze on him, her hope and fear bound together in a hopeless knot.

Mars examined the weapons. They were either covered in blood or broken—all save one. The sight froze Mars in place: Fura's starsteel blade, the one she'd used in their daily sparring matches.

With his heart beating in his throat, he picked it up, clumsily holding it in his hobbled hands. The smooth, polished blade would give Elìn a quick, merciful death.

Gripping the blade tight, Mars faced Una once more. Stepping aside, she waved him toward Elìn.

"No," Fura whispered as Mars took a step toward her

mother, the blade held in both hands now, the only way he could keep his arm from trembling with the agony of what awaited him. He didn't look at Fura, his gaze fixed on Elìn.

Fear clung to the woman like a shroud, her mouth open, her brows raised. She shrunk away from him, as far as her bounds would allow. She no longer resembled the fierce dòttra, mistress of all she surveyed. Blood spilled from her nose, over her mouth, and down the front of her bodice, staining the golden fabric a hideous brown. Her hair hung limply around her head from the force of Rafnar's blow.

"No, Mars," Fura said, her voice louder now. "You can't do this. You can't."

He closed his eyes, trying to silence her voice in his head. When he opened them and looked at Una, she only stared back at him, expectant. Fura's anguish was to be part of his punishment, his restitution.

Elìn drew a ragged breath, drawing his attention back to her. "Let me go," she said. "Free me and I will give you everything you dream of."

Bekka snorted. "Yes, and he'll be dead before he can turn around." She cocked the hammer on her pistol.

Mars took another step closer, near enough that his shadow fell across the once proud dòttra, turning her face ashen. He tried to raise his arms, but he couldn't do it. The sword was too heavy, the sound of Fura's tears too loud in his ears.

Slowly, he turned to Una. "May I let her stand? Everyone deserves a chance to die on their feet."

Una tilted her chin, considering the request. Then she shook her head. "Just get it over with, already. No need for such ceremony. Honestly, Mars, you're acting like you've never executed someone before."

He winced, hating the truth of who he was as the faces of all his victims flashed in his mind. His final kills—Henrik and Orri—lingered. They'd become one in his mind, people he'd killed not because he was charged with doing it, but because he was more concerned with his own survival than anything else.

"Please don't do this, Mars," Fura said, her voice thick with tears. "There has to be some other way."

He lowered the sword by a degree, a tremble sliding through his body.

The sound of footsteps drew his attention to Una, who was walking over to Fura, squatting down beside her as if to share a confidence. But when she spoke, it was loudly enough for all to hear. "Did you know that Mars is the best assassin I have ever employed? No matter how challenging the target, he has never once failed."

Fura stared blankly back at her. But Mars knew what she would say next.

"Una, don't—"

But she continued, as if he wasn't even there.

"Not even when I sent him to kill your father."

Fura's quick indrawn breath seemed to cut the air, the sound slicing Mars across the heart. All the color drained from her face then, her eyes growing wide in shock even as they turned on him. In that moment, she looked like the little girl in the portraits hanging in Henrik's laboratory. In the next, she looked broken, her despair like a shroud hanging over her.

He should've told her himself. Another choice that had

been his, and he had failed to make it when he could. He was a coward, just as he had always been. Regret flooded him, drowning him, but there was no changing the past. The mistakes he'd made would be his forever.

"I'm sorry, Fura," he said, unable to stop himself. "I didn't know—"

Fura turned her head away from him, her chest heaving.

Satisfied with the damage she'd wrought, Una stood up and took a step nearer to Mars. "Finish the job."

Finish it and Fura will be free, spoke the voice in his mind.

"Go on, Mars," Una said, her voice a little softer than before. She took another step toward him. "You are the weapon, not the will."

He closed his eyes, the familiar words like a brand seared against his heart.

"No," he whispered, low on his breath. He opened his eyes and the sunlight was bright once again. Mars saw himself as he truly was, as he'd always been. He could've stopped all this. He could've chosen differently at every turn. It was all on him—then and now. His choice, no one else's.

"I am the will, *and* the weapon," he said, the word ringing true.

Then he raised the sword and swung his whole body to the side, thrusting the starsteel blade straight through Una's heart.

THIRTY-TWO

THE SOUND OF a gun firing split the air. But Bekka was half a moment too late, caught off guard by Mars's sudden pivot toward her mistress. The bullet grazed his shoulder, then lodged in one of the pillars, the bone splintering in a cloud of white dust.

Mars wrenched the sword free of Una's body as she crumpled in a boneless heap on the ground. Then he spun toward Bekka and Rafnar. Blood rushed in his ears, drowning out all thoughts. Instinct took over, the will to survive stronger than any other he possessed. Above them, Feykir kacked.

Bekka came at Mars first, tossing her pistol aside now that it was spent. She drew the sword at her waist and slashed at him. Outrage blazed in her eyes, turning her face red. Mars welcomed the sight, knowing her emotional reaction would leave her open. He deflected her blade with a flick of his own, then returned with a counterattack that she only barely managed to catch. His blade slid down hers, all the way to the cross guard, where the two joined together. For a second Bekka tried to hold him back on sheer strength alone, but she was no match for his superior size. She lunged sideways, out of the hold.

With some of the emotion retreating from her face, she advanced again, smarter this time, more graceful. Mars parried the thrust, sidestepping to launch his answering blow. The blade nicked her arm before she managed to dodge. Mars continued turning, hoping to push her off-balance.

"Behind you!" Katrìn screamed.

He spun to see Rafnar moving in. The Reaper jabbed at Mars with his sword, his long reach covering the distance easily. Mars sucked back, lowering his blade to parry, but he didn't get clear of the blow, and Rafnar's sword caught him in the thigh. Pain lit through him, and he stumbled back in a daze.

Bekka came at him now, her swipe nearly catching him across the chest, but at the last moment, he tripped and fell backward, landing on the pile of broken swords and daggers. As he rolled to get out of the way of Bekka's next lunge, he grabbed one of the daggers with his free hand and tossed it toward Fura. He didn't get a chance to see if she caught it as he jumped to his feet in time to deflect Bekka's strike. Then he spun to meet Rafnar's.

The Reaper's blow felt like being hit with a hammer, leaving Mars certain that any sword not made of starsteel would've shattered. As it was, he almost lost his grip on the hilt, his shoulders nearly wrenched from their sockets. Frantically, he retreated, taking huge, desperate leaps over the uneven ground.

Bekka and Rafnar came at him together now. Mars shifted his stance, sword held in both hands. The grip felt weak with the hobbles encasing his palms and fingers, the Rift's absence making him an ordinary fighter, little match for these two opponents. It didn't help that the hobbles impaired his grip on the hilt as well. But at least he would die fighting. He just needed to live long enough for Fura to free herself and Katrìn. He risked a quick glance that way to see her stretching out her leg, trying to hook the broken dagger with her boot.

The next second, it was all he could do to defend himself from his two assailants. His primary strategy remained retreat—trying not to be there when each blow arrived. But with two of them, he barely managed to escape one before running into the other. Sweat streamed down his face, blurring his vision. His heart was making its best attempt to escape his rib cage. His feet kept catching on the weeds and rutted grass, but fortunately the rough landscape affected his opponents as well, neither of them quick enough to get around behind him.

But if he could get behind one of *them* . . .

It was risky, the cut on his leg making his steps sluggish. But if he didn't end this soon, exhaustion would claim him. Deciding Rafnar was the biggest threat, Mars focused on circling the opposite way, as if he were trying to get the best of Bekka. He leaped sideways once, twice. On the third hop, the edge of his boot caught on a tuft of wild grass, the force of the graze like hitting a wall. Losing his balance, he tumbled to the side, his elbow striking a broken piece of cobblestone as he landed. The sword shot from his hand at the impact, sending shocks of pain up and down his arm.

Bekka came for him, her sword pointed down to deliver a killing blow. Mars scrambled to the side, using the full weight of his body to sweep her legs out from under her with his own as she stepped into range. With a yelp, she fell next to him, dropping her sword. She quickly drew a dagger from her side and rolled toward him. At the same time, Mars rolled toward her, fist clenched as he threw a wild punch.

He struck her hard in the temple, the weight of the hobble augmenting the blow. A stunned look crossed her face for a split second, then she slumped to the ground, unconscious.

Momentary relief flooded Mars, only to vanish as a shadow passed in front of his eyes. Rafnar loomed over him like a mountain, his naked blade held prone. He was too close, too fast. There was no escaping. Mars went still as stone, waiting for the end to come.

Rafnar raised the sword high above his head, then stiffened as a jagged blade appeared at his neck, held in slender fingers. With one quick motion, Fura jerked the blade across his throat, cutting deep. Blood surged from the gash left behind like water spilling over a dam. The sword in Rafnar's hands fell first, and his large body followed soon after.

Mars remained still, disbelieving. Fura had killed the man. She'd done it the way he'd taught her to, coming at her opponent from behind, taking him by surprise. Pride mixed with relief—then anguish washed it all away. Fura was staring down at him, as cold as she had ever been. But she made no move to attack him as she had Rafnar, even though he deserved it.

"Fura!" Elìn shouted. "Release me!" But Fura ignored her mother, her gaze remaining fixed on Mars.

"This one isn't dead," Katrìn said, coming up beside Fura. She motioned to Bekka, who was starting to stir.

"Bind her," Fura replied. "There's been enough killing for one day."

Again Elìn shouted, demanding to be set free, but still Fura ignored her.

As Katrìn walked away in search of restraints, Fura fixed her gaze on Mars, her expression masked in frost. "Is it true?"

Slowly he got to his feet, his heart in his throat. "You know it is." She sunk away from him, and he resisted the urge to follow. "I'm sorry. I tried to tell you, but I was afraid . . . I've never regretted anything more." The confession came out of Mars like water from a faucet. He let it flow. "Your father fought bravely. He almost defeated me. His death was honorable, I swear it." *Asvaldur, if it was real, had surely taken him,* Mars thought.

Fura closed her eyes, tears escaping from between her lids. Mars fell silent, words failing him. He longed to hold her, but although she stood a mere few feet from him, she might as well have been miles away. Her silence told him all he needed to know.

Katrìn returned, rope in hand. Fura bent to help her bind and gag Bekka. As they worked, Mars retrieved the hobble keys from Bekka's pocket. When Katrìn finished, he released her from her own hobbles and she in turn did the same for him. The Rift flowed into him, banishing the pain and despair in one single, blessed moment.

Then it all returned, somehow even worse than before.

Fura watched them, still not speaking. Still a thousand miles away from him.

Katrìn rubbed her naked palms on her skirts, as if to remove the hobbles' taint on her skin. Then she turned to Fura. "What now?" Her gaze shifted to Mars, her look uncertain.

Neither he nor Fura replied.

Mars walked over to Una's body and carefully removed the blood ampoule from around her neck. He held it in his hands, the glass warm against his skin, the magic woven through it even warmer. With all he'd learned about artifacts since coming here, he easily saw the way it had been constructed— and how to undo it. With his blood already flowing from the wounds of the fight, Mars made the sacrifice—and dissolved the glass in his hands. His old blood, given so foolishly all those years ago, splattered to the ground and disappeared between the stones.

Mars stood, his head spinning from the sense of release. He was free at last. He was a fox of the Fortune's Den no longer. He had no profession, no home, nothing.

"We could resume our work on the Primer," Katrìn said into the continued silence. "It'll be hard without Henrik's notes, but I can try to carry on. We have enough food to last a little while longer, and I suppose we can keep the prisoners locked up for now." She broke off, doubt creeping into her expression. "If we can just heal the Rift, we can change the world."

"Fura!" Elìn cried, her shouting loud enough to raise the dead, from where she sat, still tethered to the pillar.

With an irritated sigh, Fura turned toward her mother at last. She slowly approached her, a weary grimace on her face.

"What took you so long?" Elìn said. "Release me so we can figure out what to do next."

Fura stared down at her, unspeaking. Except for her

eyes—those seemed to shout, the emotion standing clear and bright in them. She slowly shook her head. "I can't trust you, Mother. You've done so much wrong. You killed the Fifth. You would see Katrìn enthralled. Rivna means nothing to you. It never has."

Elìn's face began to turn red, and she spoke, trying to reason away all her unspeakable acts. A heated argument unfolded, the cadence of it all too familiar to Mars as Elìn tried again and again to manipulate, to push her will upon her daughter. She was used to wielding her power, addicted to it same as Una had been. Elìn would never change. The kiths would never change like Fura hoped. They wouldn't willingly cede power.

The only solution was to take it from them. *If we can just heal the Rift, we can change the world,* Katrìn had said. Change the world, just like Henrik had wanted. Just as Fura was striving to do even now, in this pointless argument with her mother.

The truth resounded inside Mars, drowning out all sounds. Drowning out everything except the beat of his heart in his chest. Slow and steady and certain. He looked down at his hands, savoring the flow of the Rift through him. Its yearning to use him and to be used, as the blood continued to seep from his many wounds.

He was the answer. He had been made for this.

I am the will.

I am the vessel.

Slowly, Mars approached the edge of the Heart. *Isn't this just running away?* that voice of doubt spoke in his head. *Like when you tried to leave Riven?*

Mars considered the question, testing his motives, probing his heart. He pictured Henrik in the moments before his death. The way the man had fought until the very end, how he had foreseen his demise and sent the formula to his daughter, how he'd left the Echo here for her to find. He'd been prepared to die for what he he knew was right, was necessary. Henrik had chosen his death with purpose. There was honor in that. Rivna.

And now Mars would see the man's purpose fulfilled.

"I am the will," he whispered, taking another step toward the edge.

"Mars! What are you doing?" Katrìn shouted.

He turned to look at her, then to Fura, who was watching him like a deer caught by surprise. "My parents must have believed in Henrik's vision," Mars said. The truth felt strange on his tongue, like someone else's words in his mouth. "Because of where Una's man found me when I was just a baby. The same baby your mother died trying to save, Katrìn."

"Oh," Katrìn gasped, raising a hand to her mouth, understanding.

Mars nodded. He felt the Heart calling to him, pulling him toward it, as if it, too, understood what he was—and longed for him. A strange lightness began to spread through him, like the way he'd felt when he first reunited with the Rift after wearing the hobbles for so long. With it came a sudden surge of strength. His head spun, dazzled by the feeling. He felt he could tear down mountains, to drain seas.

The human body, the human mind and spirit, the most complicated shape of all. Powerful enough to contain the magic needed to heal the Rift.

"Mars!" a voice shouted again. Fura this time.

With his heart and mind still soaring, Mars smiled at her for a brief moment. "It will be all right," he said. "It's a debt I need to pay, Fura."

"Get down from there," Katrìn protested, her hands clenched in front of her. "You'll die. We can find another way. We just need time."

"It's too late for that." Mars shook his head, touched by her concern, the tears in her eyes. He shifted his gaze to Fura, who looked torn between fear and outrage. "You don't need me to get safely back to Hàr Halda anymore. The airships will work."

"You don't have to do this," Fura said, her voice breaking.

"I want to." He smiled, hoping she could tell that he meant it. "I want to do it for you and for Katrìn and Natasja and all the rest." He paused. "I want to do it for your father. For the parents I never knew but who believed in this dream, too."

With that, Mars turned toward the pool. The Heart swirled before him, the multitude of subdued colors in it suddenly dazzling. Then, without another thought, Mars stepped off the edge and into the pool.

The Rift opened its Heart and welcomed him in.

THIRTY-THREE

THE LIQUID WASN'T liquid, but something closer to light. Or perhaps air—condensed enough to have physical substance. It wrapped around his body like a cocoon. Here was life, the Heart of Riven itself. He was a part of it, the same fibers woven through his being, binding him to the island.

For an unknowable time, Mars simply stayed there, content to drift and to be held. He was nothing and no one. He was a part of the Rift, unable to tell where he ended and it began.

Then slowly, his sense of his body crept back into his mind. Here were his legs, his arms, torso, chest. Here were his eyes, seeing and not seeing at the same time. He felt as if he'd been removed from himself, the shell of his body cast aside, leaving only his spirit behind. He was truly free—and yet he was dying. He could feel the drain on his energy, his kull slipping away from him.

At last, he remembered his purpose in coming here. *Heal the Rift.* Only, the wound those ancient adepts had made didn't reside here. It was deeper, farther down, farther in.

Concentrating his will, Mars searched for the source of the sickness. He followed it like a hunter after a deer. At once his movement felt like both swimming and flying. The world around him was nothing but dark light filled with color. He traveled forever and yet seemed to go nowhere, the landscape unchanging.

Then, finally, he found it: a swath of darkness like a hole riven through the Rift. He approached it, this place of death and decay and atrophy. It ran deep, a splinter through the very heart of the world. Terror filled him at the sight, and for a second, he almost turned away, but the kull streaming out from him wouldn't let him. He was caught by it, drawn further and further into the insatiable hunger of that open maw.

Mars resisted, concentrating his thoughts and energy on his purpose here.

Heal, he thought.

The magic stirred inside him, answering, but quickly fizzled out. He moved closer to the darkness, fighting against his fear and the instinct to flee.

Heal, he thought again, harder.

Again, the magic stirred, and again, it slid away.

His thoughts weren't enough this time. It had to be his will, his heart, his soul. Everything he possessed and was. Mars reached out to the darkness in the Rift, touching it. It seemed to come alive, surging toward him, enveloping him. For a moment, Mars nearly gave into its hunger for him, its primordial need. He resisted, reaching deep inside himself, to his very core. He made a channel of his strength and courage and fear and love, all that made him who and what he was. Then he poured it out as an offering to the Rift. His purpose of will became clear and absolute. He had been made for this.

Heal, he commanded, sending the force of it out, flinging it wide and true. *Take all of me. Heal this world. Save it. Make it new. Gives them a chance to start over again. To be free as they've never been before.*

This time, the magic surged into him like a lightning strike. It set every fiber of his being ablaze, as if he were made of nothing but light. Then, just as quickly, the magic sped out from him toward the darkness. Lines of metallic blue began to thread through the black. The Rift claimed him and did not let go. It would do as he commanded, and it would not stop. Not until the deed was done—the Ice no more—and its price paid. The sacrifice made and claimed.

Mars felt the loss at once, the way his kull drained out from him like heat being sapped by the cold. It couldn't stay. Nothing could stay in the force of such an onslaught. His life slipped away, his thoughts becoming a haze, his senses failing. And yet, even still, he could sense the magic working, the way the Rift was strengthening around him, like a creature rousing from a deep sleep. He felt it healing.

Peace came over him as he began to drift away. The flow of Ice would cease and no longer would countless others die to it. In the end, he realized he was the weapon and the will no longer.

He was the cure.

The end came, the last of his life unraveling like the last bit of thread coming loose from a spool. Mars sensed it, and waited, ready. Perhaps Asvaldur would accept him after all.

But the end did not come.

Suddenly, he was no longer alone in the Rift. A hand gripped his. With it came new power, surging inside him. Katrìn's magic joined his as it had once before, the two of them becoming one flow inside the Rift.

Then someone else took his other hand. Fura. Her kull—smaller, less powerful, but still there, as it was in all those born of Riven—seeped into him, replenishing what was lost, sharing her strength, the fierceness of her will. A triangle was made between them as the three held hands, forming the strongest shape. They hung there, suspended for an age, as around them the Rift continued to heal, becoming whole again.

Until at last, Mars felt the Rift's hold on him ease, the up-ending of his life and magic finally ceasing. The hunger was satiated. The old made new.

Wordlessly, Mars pulled Katrìn and Fura closer to him, and together they moved upward toward the world they had come from, where they belonged.

THIRTY-FOUR

THEY EMERGED FROM the pool dry and whole. The gash on Mars's leg had healed. The bruises on Fura's face were no more.

"Something is different," Katrìn said, and she leaned her head back to draw in a huge gasp of air.

Mars sensed it, too. The air tasted sweeter, the sun brighter, the courtyard awash with color. He turned to look at the Heart. The color of the Rift had changed from black laced with subdued colors to a crystalline white, as if all those separate colors had blended together into one unified whole.

Without a word, he crossed the courtyard to the keep, marching straight through the dining hall and out the main entrance. He staggered to a halt at the sight before him.

"I don't believe it," Fura said, stopping beside him, Katrìn following right behind her.

The Mistgrave was gone. The flat, desolate surface stretching from Skarfell to Hàr Halda lay before them like exposed bone. More draugr cairns than Mars could count dotted the landscape. In the distance lay the giant shape of a riftworm, massive and still, frightening even in death.

Yet as the three of them approached the edge of Skarfell,

they saw the riftworm carcasses shrivel, then crumble back to the earth, leaving behind rich, dark soil. Already there were tiny sprouts here and there breaking through the barrenness, the promise of green and growing things. Life restored. Mars thought of Jakulvik, crowded with too many people and too little space, and wondered, *For how much longer?*

What about the Ice? He closed his eyes, picturing the mine in Valdri. A vision flashed inside his head of the waves of crystal Ice like a vast ocean slowly starting to melt, to liquefy into that same crystalline fluid that filled the Heart now, the magic in it no longer poisonous, but safe. Life-giving. Mars opened his eyes again, the vision fading, but not the hope he felt that it was true. Only, it was more than hope. It was a certainty. The truth echoed deep in his soul, his kull singing.

"When I said let's change the world," Katrìn said in a voice breathless with awe, "I didn't think it would be quiet so . . . fast."

Mars laughed. "But we sure changed it, all right."

"Yes," Fura said, her hand sliding into his. "*We* did."

Her touch was so unexpected that Mars clamped his fingers around hers. He turned toward her, barely daring to breathe, incredulous at the notion that she would willingly touch him after knowing what he'd done. "I don't understand. How—"

"The debt is paid," she said, nodding once. "All of them."

"I don't believe it," Katrìn said, gasping. "Watch this." She stretched out her hand to one of Una's airships lying on the lawn nearby. With a groan of wood and metal, it rose into the air on invisible strings, on the power of the Rift alone.

"No sacrifice needed," Mars said, astonished.

Katrìn nodded. "And it's more powerful, too. I feel like I could do practically anything."

Mars searched inside himself, testing his connection to the Rift as well, and found the same. He was strong in a way he'd never been before. It frightened him for a moment, but then he turned his thoughts to the feel of Fura's hand in his, the press of her shoulder beside him, finding comfort there.

"I feel different, too," Fura said, biting her lip. Then she raised her hand as Katrìn had done, and another of the airships rose into the air on invisible strings.

"You're an adept?" Katrìn said, gaping.

"I think we all are now," Fura said, glancing at Mars. They couldn't be sure of that—not yet, but Mars felt it to be true. He remembered his sacrifice to the Heart, his willingness to die for his world and the people in it. To truly save them, to make them free. And so it gave all the people of Riven access to the magic of the Rift.

For a while, they stood there in silence, watching the new world dawning. For a while, life was simple and perfect.

"What do we do now, though?" Katrìn said, breaking their peace with the harsh truth that this wasn't over. It wasn't the end. Not by a mile, or a thousand. But at least it was a new beginning.

Fura tilted her head, contemplating the question. "I don't know. I expected we'd have to fly back to Hàr Halda in one of those airships, but that no longer seems necessary."

No, it didn't. They could take a leisurely stroll across the Mistgrave back to Hàr Halda. Or they could go around the city entirely, disappearing into the lowlands. Mars turned his head first to the east, then to the west. In truth, they could go anywhere.

"Yes, but I meant after that." Katrìn waved, her brow furrowing. "What do we do about your mother and all the rest of it?"

"She's right." Mars sighed. "There's a whole lot of mess waiting for us." There would be consequences for everything they'd done here. There would be chaos among the kiths, all of them frantic to discover how bad the damage was and what they must do about it. And Elìn still had power among the Torvalds. They would free her and place her back in charge the moment they found her.

And place the rest of us in chains.

Only, it wouldn't be so simple for them, Mars realized, not with the Rift within such easy reach, the power free and limitless and available to everyone. He wondered if there were others discovering their powers even now. He wondered what they might do. Some would do evil. That was a given. But others would do good. That was a given, too.

Fura's fingers flexed inside his grip. "We could leave. Find a ship to take us to Vest."

"Or Osway." Katrìn sounded strange as she said it, and Mars wondered if she was thinking about her father and her chances of finding him.

The yearning to leave, to find a new adventure, stretched wide over Mars. They had done what they set out to do, after all. They'd changed the world. They could leave it up to others to set it to rights.

Mars imagined the chaos that would be tearing through

the kiths, and the fighting that would ensue among the mercenaries at the Fortune's Den once they learned of Una's death. There would be panic and fear and suffering. Innocents would die in the tide of violence that would soon spread over the island.

They had wrought these changes, both the good and the bad. They were responsible for them. He remembered the Consortium adepts and their motto, *Service over self.* In the beginning, their intent had been true. *And we're all adepts now.*

Maybe, he speculated, just maybe, they could stop the corruption and decay that had led the Consortium down the path to the Cataclysm from happening again. Maybe they could get it right this time—Rivna not as an ideal, but as a reality.

"I vote we stay," Mars said, his voice firm despite the uncertainty he felt. "What we've done here will have consequences. People will be scrambling for power. We need to make sure the right sort of people get that power. Good people, with good hearts." He faced Fura, staring into her eyes. "People like you."

A blush painted her cheeks, her green eyes bright as she stared back at him. "I will need a lot of help."

He nodded. "Yes, you will. It'll be dangerous and difficult, and we might not make it out alive. But I'm willing to stay by your side, if you'll have me." He raised his hand to his hair, feeling Una's bond still clinging there. He pulled it free and held it in his palm. With a single thought, he willed the color to change, the red giving way to white. He left the fox, though, a reminder of who he was, where he'd come from.

Then he held the bead out to Fura. "I give you my bond."

Fura took the bead from his hand, clutching it tight in her

fingers. "I accept," she said, then threaded the bead through her hair, a piece of him to carry with her always.

They stepped into each other's arms, sealing the pact with a kiss.

After a while, Katrìn made a disgusted noise. Mars and Fura pulled apart in time to see her roll her eyes, but then she grinned at them. But they remained in each other's arms, bodies pressed together. For the first time, he realized this was what love really was: choosing to serve someone else over yourself.

Mars turned his head and stared out at the valley before them, his heart light in his chest, his spirit easy for the first time in his life.

"We changed the world," he said. "Now let's make it better."

"Yes," Fura replied. "Together."

THE END